Castle of Midnights

by

Katherine Highland

© Katherine Highland 2025
Cover design and images © Katherine Highland 2025

You may quote or reproduce content, but the source should be acknowledged. If quoting from any sources linked to in this book, please seek the relevant permissions from those sources.

No real solicitors, estate agents or surveyors are represented in this story, individually or corporately. All properties viewed by Susannah and the streets on which they are located are fictitious. The towns of Kirkbrigg and Inverbrudock and all locations therein are entirely my own invention; Susannah and Freya's workplace and its processes are not representative of any real company. Some brand and artist names are fictitious. Other locations used are real with the exception of the bookshop chain and the holiday apartment in Nairn.

This story includes occasional swearing and discusses instances of bullying at work, coercive behaviour, use of what is now rightly discredited terminology about dyspraxia, and harmful attitudes to neurodivergence including towards children.

ISBN: 9798296954022

Profits from the sale of this book in printed and electronic form go to Autism Initiatives (Scotland) to support their one stop shops for autistic adults.

Diamonds of lamplight dance
between dark margins of Tay.
Caught future glimpsed new-bright
crests upon a turning page.
Next season waits in gold,
penned in winter dusk, at bay.
Home, and what that means, stirs;
realigns. Fresh hopes engage.

Leaving strains a heart held
in a still tender remake.
The station cradles; knows;
right here in its oldest space,
gathers my journey's thread
in the Highland Chieftain's wake.
Bound, unfrayed, unafraid;
at last, woven into place.

The train draws memories
towards Inverness; onboard
convivial; a chain
of moments joyous, replete.
Colours reach back through Perth
in waves from a soul restored;
Lit windows pass at speed
the end of a quiet street.

With so much love and thanks to Thorntons Solicitors, Perth; Simple Approach Estate and Letting Agents, Perth; LNER's Inverness-based catering teams on the Highland Chieftain train service; the staff at Autism Initiatives Tayside one stop shop. All of whom shared the joy of my own eventual successful viewing trip about which this poem was written.

Contents

1: Grounds For Gratitude
2: Dunblair Road
3: Birthday
4: Foundations
5: Shifting Grounds
6: Protective Sister
7: Edie
8: Crieff Gardens
9: Energy
10: Adil's Wisdom
11: Building Hopes
12: Lorna's Light
13: Conduits
14: Mary
15: Chance Meeting
16: Jealousy
17: Trouble At Work
18: Julian Remembers
19: Curve Ball
20: She's Purring
21: Nairn
22: The Graveyard
23: Hiatus Weekend
24: Fair Maid's Mews
25: Conveyance
26: Affirming
27: Networking
28: Completion
29: Moving Day
30: Summer Solstice
Author's Notes

1

Grounds For Gratitude

Warm sweet cinnamon wafted upwards on an ethereal spiral of steam as the wooden spoon stirred against the glass wall of the cafetière, pinpricks of scent lending a sparkle to the humid air which fondly anticipated its distant first freshening of autumn. Susannah Silverdale quickly turned aside to sneeze, glad of the cool water flowing over her wrists as she washed her hands in the close heat of her small kitchen. Rinsing off the spoon and poising the plunger over the fresh coffee, she called to her best friend who was adjusting immaculately straightened hair in front of the living room mirror that she would be through in a moment.

Freya Lingard looked as Scandinavian as her name sounded with her pale blonde hair and blue eyes. Despite having walked through muggy streets for their routine Sunday coffee time, she exuded a crisp neatness which always made Susannah feel somewhat unready. Her dark brown hair fell below her shoulders in what she supposed would be called beach waves, if the beach in question were the sort with unruly baked-Alaska dunes and holes where half built sandcastles had collapsed as other activities distracted their architects.

Studiously avoiding Freya's tidily placed ankle boots in the hallway, Susannah stood with one hand on the doorframe as she declared that the coffee would be brewed in a couple of minutes. Freya smiled as she switched her phone to silent, the action reminding Susannah to do the same before switching on the colour changing mood light in the corner. On an overcast day like today, even in June, little daylight found its way through the sash window tucked in an inside corner of the building above the dejected huddle of bins.

Their Sunday late morning routine had grown from the Swedish concept of fika; getting together for coffee, infused as a ritual with the feelgood cosiness of Scandi culture as the memes would have it. However authentic a representation those may or may not be, it resonated with Susannah's affinity for the Northern countries. A particularly stressful period at their workplace with a bullying supervisor had drawn her and Freya together; relegated to the limbo land of the outsider by the arcane rules and structure of office social politics. Both Susannah's dyspraxia and Freya's defensive social anxiety activated the in crowd's 'Different' warning system; the dull heartbeat of distancing punctuated by irregular spikes of outright hostility. Somehow it shocked people when this exacerbated the traits which bothered them so much in the first place. Anxiety and coordination worsening in an unsafe, unaccepting setting; who would have thought it? Casting about for strategies to deal with the creeping slide into the downward half of the weekend, Susannah had designated her first cup of coffee on a Sunday as 'Grounds for Gratitude' time. Reflecting exclusively on reasons to be thankful during that half hour; however small, however repetitive, helped. While she would never minimise another person's experiences by advising them to be more grateful, she had shared it with Freya as something which had genuinely made her feel better and it had naturally evolved into their own version of fika.

Pouring the aromatic coffee into her favourite wide-based mugs, Susannah attentively carried them through from the kitchen and set them on the coasters which she always kept well back from the edges of the coffee table. More tense than usual with the news she was holding back until after their thankfulness session, she prayed that her occasional stress-related hand twitch would not betray her.

"First thing to be thankful for this week: I finally resolved the Fulton case!"; Freya enthusiastically opened with reference to a complex and long-running complaint in the customer service department of the national utility company where they worked. Modern billing technology being pushed onto customers while real world snagging issues were cropping up frequently in the early days of rolling it out meant that their department was always busy as problems arose more quickly than their technicians could solve them. Some of their more vulnerable customers, especially elderly people, were often deep into months of high bills and inaccurate records by the time they got to the complaint stage. John and Winnie Fulton had endured months of worry before their correct usage and payments were finally worked out, generating a rebate and compensation credit to their account. Freya's eyes shone as she recalled giving the elderly couple the good news. "I persuaded Valerie to authorise a pet shop gift voucher for Barney too; they'll be able to get him a better heat pad."

"That's lovely; well done, what a kind thought!"; Susannah smiled fondly. Freya's heart truly was huge behind its defences which were too easily read as entitlement. The Fultons' arthritic dog had been prioritised over their own needs throughout the long and stressful saga.

"Max thought so too"; Freya's glossed lips curved into a familiar smile as Susannah's heart sank. This was not the day to have to nudge Freya back on topic, nor to have *that* conversation again. "Anyway, sorry Suze; it's your turn."

"OK; I am thankful that I was up early enough on Tuesday to catch a Maeshowe moment! The sunrise on that sliver of wall was so bright it woke the cats; that inevitably led to me being woken up too."

Kirkbrigg was not a pretty town. It was the architectural equivalent of everyone's most no-nonsense relative or teacher; that efficient, sensible person who gets things done without any dramas but has no time for sentiment or frills. Susannah's building was a prime example; neat and low maintenance but not designed with the benefits of natural light in mind. Reading about the ancient site of Maeshowe in Orkney, where the sun shines briefly onto the back wall of the entrance passage once a year around the winter solstice, had led her to give its name to the opposite season's rare occasions on which a good dose of sunlight found its way to the dingy corner in which her living room window was located. Catching the kind of sunrise which turned the stonework a deep salmon pink at this time of year when it rose around 4am was a notable blessing.

"Yes; I saw your photos. I loved the black and white one; very urban noir! The one with the shadow too; was it Morgan, in the strip of sun on the wall where you could make out her whiskers?"

"Annika. Yes, I was especially pleased with that one."

Susannah's dark tortoiseshell cat padded into the room at the sound of her name. She stretched and yawned before jumping up into her human's lap with a squeaky miaow; her inquisitive nose stretching towards Susannah's coffee mug.

"Annika Strandhed Silverdale, you know better than that!" Susannah laughed as she gently guided the cat to settle into a purring ball. "I take it your daughter's still asleep then?"

Getting another cat had been a huge leap of faith; those final trips to the vet with Mulder and Scully three months apart had almost destroyed her. When the attractive little tortie with her blue-cream marbled kitten had become available at the shelter around the time the first new detective series to begin to fill the gap left for her by 'The X-Files' aired, the alignment had given her the encouragement she needed to open her heart to that emotional journey once more. Smiling down at the contented mother cat, she stroked her silky head before leaning cautiously over to sip her coffee.

"My turn now"; Freya was saying. "Apart from the Fultons, it's been a bit of a slow week for gratitude. The supermarket had everything on my list. That counts, I think?"

"Absolutely! Well, I found the perfect sibling card for London's birthday. Abstract art with shimmery details; they're going to love it."

"Fabulous! Ah yes; I just remembered now. I had my favourite dress out on the washing line yesterday and when I went to bring it in, there was an enormous bird deposit on the grass; right beside where it was hanging, but had missed it completely."

"You just remembered? That's a Grounds for Gratitude headliner!"; they both laughed heartily. "Actually, you know; for my turn, I am thankful that you saw the harmless bird splat. We often tend to be skewed towards noticing when the bad luck happens; we talk about it then. I mean people in general, not you and me. We start to look out for it and end up missing the balance a lot of the time."

"That's true. Ah! My mum and I had a surprisingly pleasant chat through the week, about the apple tree in the garden! She was remembering when it was planted, a few months before I went to university, and that she was looking out of the window at the sapling when the postie brought my exam results. I was bracing myself for her to turn wistful about my not being a CEO yet after the hopes she had for me, but for once she didn't go there; it was a feelgood conversation about a tree, end of."

Empathy tightened Susannah's throat as she watched Freya's thoughts turn inward. Frieda Lingard had been callously left behind by an upwardly mobile husband; the inevitable change to her energy levels and crisp corporate wife image after she became a mother had not fit in with his life plan. The long legs, flat stomach and ready availability of his equally ambitious secretary had proven too tempting. Her feelings reverting to unrequited before their marriage was old enough to fully lose its idealised shimmer had ensured that no subsequent prospect ever came close to replacing him. Freya remained an only child, raised to fight off shortcomings and shine brightly enough never to have to repeat her mother's self-perceived failure; Frieda's strictness driven by the fear of her daughter suffering as she had.

"Oh, Frey. I'm glad it stayed a happy conversation. You deserve to feel successful. Look at what you did for the Fultons. That's more important than climbing the corporate ladder. That is real achievement. People in situations like theirs need good folk doing jobs at our level. Fast tracks and bonuses mean nothing to them. Being heard, acknowledged and helped in a real way; that's what matters and what stays with people."

"Yes; you're right. I wish Mum could find comfort in that."

"Me too"; Susannah took another sip of coffee. "So what else am I thankful for this week? Morgan's little chirps when she wakes up, then the way the big yawn she does invariably dissolves into blissed-out purring."

"You definitely needed to be a cat mama again, Suze"; Freya's face relaxed into a lighter expression as she sipped her own coffee and settled back into the comfortable sage-green fabric of the chair. "I'm thankful for our garden"; Freya glanced over to the window before catching herself and turning to look at Annika instead. The dubious tact hung in the stuffy air.

"It's OK"; Susannah smiled wryly as she contemplated the dull rectangle of weary brickwork and drain pipe which constituted her living room view. "I'm thankful for your garden too." She raised her coffee cup in mock salute, downing the remaining contents like a shot of tequila and coughing as the few stray cinnamon-dashed grounds which inevitably got through the filter caught her throat. Her watering eyes met Freya's and they dissolved into laughter.

Annika, disturbed by the commotion, looked up and settled back down with a frisson of graceful feline indulgence, which set them both off laughing again.

"Really though, you need to be living somewhere that gives you a better view of the sky. I always enjoy your photos of cloud formations and the way you describe them. You deserve to be seeing them every day from your own place. Have you thought any more about moving now that you can buy somewhere?"

There could hardly be a better opportunity to face up to telling her best friend about her plans. An inheritance from Susannah's bachelor uncle had allowed her parents to offer her and her siblings a vital boost to their long term security; Freya knew this, but nothing had yet been said about quite how much change was coming to their established routine.

"I have; in fact, I've thought about it a lot, and the truth is, I do plan to buy, but not in Kirkbrigg. I want to move to Perth."

Freya's expression began a shift which visibly stuck on pause as she processed the implications; Susannah could practically see the spinning circle of buffering.

"Perth? But... that's, what, an hour away? You'd be adding a big commute onto your working day."

"Yes; it can be nearly an hour on the bus at busy times. The thing is, Freya; this is hard for me to tell you and I know it will be hard for you to hear, but I need to move on. I'm looking at options to change my job as well as where I live. I promise I will not abandon our friendship; I know how isolated you feel at our work and I will always hold space for you, I swear. I'd get both of us out of there if I could, and I will support you with anything you want to do to make your own new..."

"You're... leaving?"

"Nothing's decided yet, but yes, I'm looking to leave. Kirkbrigg and my job, not you. I may not be leaving our company altogether; there are jobs I could potentially do from home, travelling in maybe twice a week. It's feasible."

"You've been planning this for a while, then?"; Freya's voice hardened, brittle with pain as her steady support system teetered on the edge of uncertainty.

"Researching, yes, and I admit I've been cowardly about telling you and giving you time to take it in. I should have let you know before now."

"No; it's your life, Susannah. You don't owe me any explanation. I guess Perth isn't that far. I'd struggle to get a bus through on Sunday mornings for this, though!"

"I know, and believe me, this is something I've agonised over. We could do Grounds for Gratitude over video calling or chat, but I get that it won't be the same. I hope we can work together to find a way to continue it that suits us both. I need to do this, though; to make a life for myself somewhere that calls to me, as opposed to where I happen to have grown up and come back to because I never managed to put down firm enough roots anywhere else."

"Right. I know you need me to be excited and supportive, but it's a bolt from the blue and I need a bit of time to adjust."

"Of course; I get that. I've had time to think about all of this; you haven't, and I understand that it's a big change for you too. You're right; I need my forever home to be somewhere I can see the sky properly. Somewhere I can watch the seasons turn and the light change, year after year, properly; where I can fully experience these light midsummer nights where the sun never dips far enough below the horizon to be gone completely. Every year has a handful of nights where it's clear enough to track its journey from west to east; to watch it set in the feelgood fuzz of the last drink of the evening. Then in chosen company or with a timely burst of energy, to be rising with it hours later on a wave of freshly brewed coffee. I need to live somewhere I can see to stand on the bridge of those magical hours in between, Frey; I can't tell you how much I crave those nights when it's dark and yet it's all the colours, radiating from the promise of that sun at its peak marginally out of sight. I need my castle of opal midnights; my base for feeling alive. And yes, I'm sure there are houses here where I would have a better view of all that than I do in this forsaken corner, but everything in me is telling me that I need to branch out; to find that enduring light in a city that feels fresh and exciting, but peaceful. I feel that every time I go to Perth, and it's where I want to be."

"I want you to be happy. I just… How soon do you think all of this will be happening?"

"I honestly don't know, but I promise not to drop things on you like this again; I will keep you in the loop."

"Thank you"; Freya drank the last of her coffee, setting her cup neatly on its coaster. "I've enjoyed this, as always; I need time to take in your news so I'm going to head off now but I'll see you at work."

The flat door closed behind Freya; Susannah carried the cups through to the kitchen, placing Freya's in the sink and pouring the last of the coffee into her own. She glanced into her bedroom off the hallway as she passed. Morgan sat upright on the bed, staring at the window which afforded a better view than the living room did; the junction where the uninspiring driveway of the flats met the more attractive street which was the start of the nicer parts of Kirkbrigg, where Freya lived. The streetlamp at the end of that road marked the boundary; the first to match the height and shape of the estate lights, in contrast to the aloof march of the double posts overseeing the main road a little way beyond the junction. Morgan had a watchful air about her, as though some secret vibration were brushing against the sensitive tips of her whiskers before retreating to the undisturbed realm at the ceiling.

2

Dunblair Road

Number 15 Dunblair Road's weathered blue front door swung open revealing painted wooden stairs leading steeply upwards before banking sharply to the right. A faded mauve runner drew Susannah's focus towards the unseen front door of the upstairs flat as she gripped the chunky handrail, its painted surface smooth under her left hand. Fighting to keep her mind as blank a canvas as the pale grey walls of the stairwell, she mentally diverted Honor's sales pitch to flow alongside the crucial task of navigating the unfamiliar staircase; noticing the height of the risers, allowing her muscle memory to begin to record the ascent. Relieved to see a small, well-lit landing as she rounded the turn, she watched the estate agent turn the key and open the entrance door. A shade darker than the street door, its contrasting brass number 15A glinted in the hallway light as Honor flicked the switch.

"So this is your living room through here; watch yourself on the edge of those boxes there"; Susannah's stomach constricted as the chance to reassure herself that she would have successfully avoided the hazard without being prompted slipped away. She discreetly touched the doorframe as the inside view of that bay window which had drawn her to the listing showed majestically ahead of her. A cushioned ledge ran around the inside of the alcove; it looked wide enough to sit on, with a book or simply to watch the sky. Excited in the moment, rushing to the window her hypervigilance dipped briefly; the side of a drop-leaf table brushed lightly against her hip, the whisper of her loose linen trousers against the wood betraying the close call. Honor hadn't heard it; she was already enthusing about the view and the light as Susannah's mind reeled with imagined stacks of heavy books or fine china cascading from the almost-bumped table. *"That didn't happen"*, she silently and firmly told herself. *"Learn from it for once in your life; move on, and for heaven's sake,* focus, *you twit"*.

"The section of garden on the right is yours"; Honor gestured to where a narrow fence bisected the neat green expanse of lawn. "You access that from the path around the side of the building; your bins are around there too."

Biting back the urge to ask her not to refer to any part of the property as 'yours', Susannah reminded herself that she would have been told to; it was as much the estate agent's job to persuade her to think that way as it was her responsibility not to let herself become prematurely attached. The same, she reluctantly admitted, went for warning her about every conceivable hazard irrespective of how visibly cautious she strove to be. Turning reluctantly from the appealing view as Honor directed her to see the main bedroom, she smiled wryly at the sight of the current owner's vacuum cleaner near the door, its broad loop of hose resting on the sage-green carpet.

"I see someone's been cleaning up for us coming"; she said brightly, gesturing to acknowledge that she had seen the hose and wasn't going to trip over it.

"Indeed. Mind you don't catch your feet in that hose."

She wondered why she'd bothered.

The bedroom window was plain, lacking the feature appeal of the bay window, but it let in ample light. Reluctant to take photos when this was someone else's home, she picked her way over to stand beside Honor and look out over the garden; respectfully resisting her usual grounding touch as she passed the foot of the owner's bed, she allowed the restful spread of the lawn to calm her vibrating nerves.

"It feels good, Honor; I love what I've seen so far. The other bedroom faces the gardens too, I think?"

"It does. It's the kitchen and bathroom that are on the street side. Your guests will have the garden view too."

"Actually, the other bedroom would be more for storage and a proper play area for my cats; they're kept indoors but it would be lovely for them to be able to watch the birds from a big multi-level cat tree"; despite her resolve, Susannah found herself visualising Annika and Morgan comfortably ensconced in the complex of snug refuges, scratching poles, walkways and hanging toys which Julian had promised to help her build.

It's the first place you've viewed; the first listing you've been seriously interested in. Do not get carried away.

She turned her thoughts to more practical matters; noting how many sockets there were, how accessible the light fittings appeared for when bulbs needed changing, how much worktop space the kitchen afforded. The shower had an ominously smooth floor; she could stand on a flannel or use a non-slip mat for that. The home report was reassuringly straightforward; some repair work was recommended on the guttering and a few roof tiles needed to be replaced, but there was little else to take on over and above the purchase. Of course, the down side of that was how much more attractive it made the property to others as well as herself. Gazumping was rare in Scotland; unlike in England, if a seller accepted a higher offer from someone else before contracts could be exchanged then their solicitor would often decline to act for them, leaving them with the expense and hassle of finding a new one. With missives being signed earlier in the process and sealing buyer and seller into a contract more quickly, there was much less scope for gazumping north of the Border. For a property like this she would nonetheless need to act quickly to avoid missing out. She didn't see much point in asking Honor how much interest there was in this property; she would be bound to talk up the urgency. Susannah would make herself appear naïve by asking.

"I guess it helps that I have no need of a parking space"; she mused out loud as a compromise to the curiosity she couldn't resist. "The stairs might also be a tad steep for the liking of anyone with young children or elderly relatives who would be visiting."

"Absolutely", Honor nodded eagerly; her phone buzzed with a reminder alert and she apologised that they would need to bring the viewing to a close as she needed to get to her next client. Susannah acceded, thanking her for her time and double-checking that she had everything she had brought with her.

She would be here as an elderly person herself if she succeeded in buying this place; as they descended the stairs, a nebulous fear of future difficulties blurred the edges of her anticipation. The stairway was classed as a communal area since the entrance to the ground floor flat was off the hallway at the bottom; perhaps she ought to check whether she would be allowed to have a stair lift installed should it be needed in her much later years. It would need not to obstruct the door of the lower property and the handrail would need to remain for other people to use when accessing her flat. *The* flat, not *her* flat!

Waving Honor off, she took a deep breath and stood until her racing mind could be trusted to stay in the present and keep her safely alert in public. The bus journey back to Kirkbrigg was filled with distracted imaginings despite her determination; her feedback email to the estate agents already drafted in her mind and offer figures dancing behind her eyes.

3

Birthday

"Thanks for staying to cover the phones, you two: especially today"; Valerie Corbett put a small gift box of chocolates each on Susannah and Freya's desks. She gave a small shake of her head as she watched the rest of Freya's team disappear towards the exit, the excitement of a long-planned gig swirling around their hurried steps and hovering over heads leaning together in school's-out camaraderie. The frisson of other people's plans hung ghostly in the lingering perfume spritzed impatiently as the final minutes counted down; the scented air awkwardly out of place once left behind in the continuing sobriety of work. Local band Neptune's Hogmanay had been around on the rock music scene for long enough to appeal to the entire age range of the office; Donna and Lisa's mellow conspiratorial laughter blended with Lexy and Chanelle's squeals as they waved to Ranjit and Agata who were staying until six for the phones on Susannah's team. With Gregor off sick, Freya had been facing the dreaded Friday cover on her own until Susannah stepped up with the blessing of her own line manager; Morven had been happy to agree it, especially since it was Freya's birthday.

"They're all going to Giuseppe's for a meal first too; I'm so jealous!"; Candice whose desk was next to Susannah's had gushed as she got ready for her own rapid exit. She had cast a loaded glance sideways at Susannah as she mentioned the classy Italian restaurant near the stadium. "*You*'d have to be very *careful* eating there; all that rich sauce, and those tablecloths must cost a fortune! Meals out aren't really your thing anyway though, are they? You like your *quiet* weekends."

"I'm sure they'll all have a lovely time", Susannah had replied evenly; for some reason, Candice, Tanya and Maya had all found this amusing. Gritting her teeth, she had picked up her next call, tuning out the ever-present subsonic pulse of disdain which rattled her at a molecular level for all it eluded any useful description. Heaving the niggle to the growing dump at the back of her mind, she focused on thanking Valerie for the kind gesture of including her in the gifting of chocolates. Max Griffiths, the office manager, smiled as he walked through from his small private room.

"It's our pleasure, Susannah, and happy birthday, Freya. We all appreciate you staying today of all days to allow your colleagues to go to the gig. This is the kind of teamwork we like to see; encouraging social bonding as well as getting the job done."

"They're going to Giuseppe's."

Max and Valerie looked slightly taken aback at Freya's clipped delivery. Susannah flinched on her friend's behalf; she knew that Freya would not have intended to sound as though she were correcting him.

"I mean, before the gig"; Freya's cheeks blushed red, a belated echo of the signal she so often passed at danger in the complex network of workplace interaction. Susannah could practically hear the screech of the wheels braking to an emergency stop as she adjusted her tone, softening it to an apologetic fade.

"Ah; they're making an occasion of it then!"; Max smoothed over the moment, his broad shoulders relaxing. "Robin and I have enjoyed a few meals with our friends over the years there." His face softened further at the mention of his boyfriend. Freya seemed abruptly small and ill at ease in the pale pink and green sophistication of her new blouse; she looked at the phones as though willing one to ring. She didn't have to wait long, the brittle brightness of her voice cutting the air as she answered the call. Max and Valerie exchanged a brief quizzical look; Susannah busied herself arranging her own headphones and for the next hour, the customers took priority.

"There might be some noctilucent clouds tonight"; Susannah looked up at the wisps of cloud high in the softening evening sky as they walked the half-hour distance to the Lingard home. "I love seeing those. I always think they look like a portal in time; the ghost of a night long ago superimposed on the present one."

Freya shot her a grateful look; the unease of her interaction in the office evidently bothering her, relieved to be let off the hook with harmless and interesting talk instead of the kind of lecture for which she was permanently braced.

"Those clouds up there now; that's cirrus, isn't it?"

"Yes; the cirrus clouds are the high-up ones."

"What's the next level down again?"

"Alto. I like cirrus the best though."

"So is a mackerel sky cirrus or alto?"

"It can be either. Cirrocumulus or altocumulus. It's the shape and extent of the spread of those clouds that gets them that name."

"I should take more notice of the clouds when they're pretty and interesting like that. It feels as though we don't get the variety we did when we were children; there's much more uniform overcast, or that weird glaring greyish-white sky that makes my eyes water as much as bright sunshine."

"I know what you mean. When I first got interested in them, there did seem to be more variety to the shapes and patterns. I'm so glad we still get nacreous clouds every so often in the winter. That's the rare iridescent ones for which it needs clear, cold days, when there are ice crystals in the high atmosphere. Mother-of-pearl clouds."

"Yes, I know *those*"; Freya's sharp intake of breath betrayed her worry that she had sounded curt again, though it was less pronounced than it had been with Max. "From your wonderful photos. I hope you do get that flat where you can see much more of the sky. You have such a talent for sharing the beauty of it."

"Thank you; I hope so too. I'm afraid to get my hopes up too much until I know more about future-proofing for the stairs, but I know I'm going to have to be brave and make an offer soon."

The solar lights along the garden path were sure to be getting a full charge; Susannah almost wished it could get dark earlier so that she could see them on. Mrs Lingard, her cropped and layered blonde hair and fine bone structure adding to her glamorous appearance, exuded a guarded sophistication in her white summer dress with its bold pattern of red poppies. She stood up from her seat at the white-painted metal outdoor table on which a tapas style birthday tea had been laid out; net cloches covered the dishes and a large citronella candle burned in the middle to deter insects. A bottle of Prosecco stood in a silver-coloured bucket, kept cool in a gel sleeve.

"Hello, my beautiful birthday girl! And Susannah, thank you so much for coming, dear; let's sit... Ooh!"

The "Ooh" was the inevitable response to the spatial misjudgement which Susannah, so determined to avoid, had nevertheless managed to make as her knee caught the underside of the table. The plain but thin-stemmed wine glasses teetered precariously; the world stopped until they were safely stilled.

"Oh, no. I'm so sorry, Frieda; I did look, but my coordination is off. I don't know if Freya has told you, but I'm dyspraxic. I promise I will move more slowly in future, especially since I'm not here often enough to be familiar with the space."

"That's all right, dear. It must be difficult for you, I imagine, having to be extra vigilant. Forgive me for asking; is that a similar thing to Clumsy Child Syndrome?"

"*Mum!* You can't say that nowadays!", gasped Freya.

"That's OK; I don't mind genuine questions, though Freya is correct; that label is no longer considered acceptable. Dyspraxia is the neurodivergence which people used to call by that term. It's also becoming more widely known as Developmental Coordination Disorder, or Developmental Motor Coordination Disorder, but many dyspraxic people are uncomfortable with it being referred to as a disorder. It is a disability nonetheless, in that it requires reasonable adjustments. The old, colloquial name implied that the child was being reckless and not trying; selfishly not bothering to avoid causing chaos, embarrassing their parents and disappointing their siblings when outings keep getting cut short for or replaced by hospital trips. I was fortunate in that I had very few instances of injury, but other dyspraxic people do, and it is never a question of not trying. Believe me, the child, and the adult they become, is trying. Every day. People imagine that our lives are one long slapstick comedy act; the reality is, we may develop strategies and learn to reduce accidents but that in itself takes its toll on our energy levels and as we all know, tired people make more mistakes and have more accidents regardless of neurotype. So adding that to the dyspraxia, we're between a rock and a hard place, and constantly bruised from bumping against both! There's a lot more to dyspraxia than tripping up and bumping things, too; the same way there's much more to Tourette's Syndrome than swearing. That is *one* type of vocal tic, and those are *one* of the traits of Tourette's Syndrome. With dyspraxia, there can be difficulties with working memory and concentration; planning and organising tasks, following multi-step instructions, giving directions, to name a few examples. It can affect speech; getting the correct words, saying them correctly and in the right order. I personally have a frustrating glitch of saying the opposite of what I intend to, for instance 'I'll need my fleece; it's always warm in that building' when I mean 'cold'. The sentence is correct in my mind, yet somehow the wrong word comes out. Or being unable to decide between two words and ending up with a hybrid; 'maistly' instead of 'mainly' or 'mostly'. Though I got away with that particular one as I was talking to someone in Glasgow and it fit with the dialect! And yes; the more generally known aspects, the tripping up and bumping; they're not the full story or always as frequent and overt as people think, but they're not a myth. The upset and embarrassment constantly accumulates. There are things we can do to adapt"; Susannah gestured to the three-quarter sleeve of her royal blue top, trying not to notice that one metallic thread was working loose against her arm. "I never buy a top with loose sleeves because I can guarantee they'll catch on door handles. I spend more than I need to on shopping because I don't use loyalty cards; using cash less often helped to mitigate having heavy purses full of change because I would hand over a banknote rather than try to get hold of the exact coins, but having an additional card to scan is a hassle in itself. Then I keep having to explain that at the till once I'm known as a regular customer, and they put pressure on me to change my mind because it would save money so I give in but then the fumbling and dropping, taking ages to find the millimetre-precise positioning necessary for the reader and the glaring and tutting and the cashier apologising to the next customer for me holding them up get too much and I stop using them again. That's the kind of added cost people don't see when they hate on disabled people for claiming anything; both in work and out of work benefits. There's so much we can't predict at all. We live every day never knowing when we will next get caught out, and it's often in situations like this when it's most distressing for all involved. I can't speak for all dyspraxic people of course, but I do, and I'm sure most of us do, care about and respect other people's property. I don't want to be turning Freya's birthday into an infodumping session about my neurodivergence! I would love to be in the worldwide club of people who have full membership access to navigating the space around them; proprioception and all that jazz. I see the effort you've put into preparing this beautiful table and food for my lovely friend's birthday, and the last thing I want to do is spoil any aspect of it."

"Of course, I understand that, and thank you for speaking so honestly. Would you… I really don't want to get this wrong and insult or hurt you, but I want you to feel comfortable here as our guest. Would you feel happier with a different type of glass?" Frieda's hand unconsciously, protectively, curled around the stem of the wine glass beside her plate.

"Thank you for being thoughtful, Frieda. To be honest, I need to be able to manage these things like any other adult. I know that's probably internalised ableism, but to me, it's also realism. I have to live in the same world as everybody else. I'd feel every bit as bad sitting here drinking Prosecco out of something obviously not intended for it while you both drank out of 'proper' glasses. No; I'll do as I said I would, remember to move more slowly, and I'll keep everything within my reach well away from the edge."

"As you wish, then. It sounds as though you've done a good job of adapting. I'm sure it wasn't easy for you as a little girl, and I am sorry for the outdated language which I will not use again. It must have brought back some painful memories."

"Those are never far away. We had one neighbour, Mrs Hume; this was when we first lived here in Kirkbrigg, before we moved nearer to Glasgow. She had a prized collection of garden gnomes. One day I heard her saying to her husband and my mother, 'It's not Julian's football I worry about so much as CC's clodhopping feet!' Julian is my big brother, you see; he and his friends would often have a kickabout with a lightweight ball which did end up in her garden from time to time."

"CC?"; both Freya and her mother's eyes widened as the penny dropped.

"Yep: Clumsy Child, as in syndrome. That was what she called me."

"Goodness me, how crass. She said that in front of your *mother*?"

"She did. My mother, as she explained years later, didn't catch on at the time. She was trying to think which of Julian's friends Mrs Hume meant, going through all their names in her mind; there was a Craig and a Cameron, but neither of their surnames began with C. Then I piped up from behind the fence with all the fervent assurance of a people-pleasing child about how I swore I would keep well away from her ornaments. The Humes laughed and laughed, like it was the funniest thing ever that I had such a track record for clumsiness as to know fine well she meant me. The thing was, my auditory processing had let me down too; I'd thought she said 'Susie'. My mother thought the joke was about me jumping to the conclusion it was aimed at me, and how earnest I was being, so she started laughing too. It probably wasn't as loud as it is in my memory and it would have been more of an uncertain, nervous laugh on my mother's part, but I had no idea why they were all laughing at me. It was Julian who put the pieces together for me, a few months later when she said 'CC' again and he yelled 'Don't call my sister that; she's a person, not a syndrome!' He wasn't allowed out to play football with his friends for a month, for 'being rude'! Though I found out afterwards that once my parents realised she nicknamed me that and why, they did have a quiet word."

"Is that why you ask people never to call you 'Susie'?"; Freya's voice quivered, her eyes glistening in the late sunlight.

"Yes; people rarely call me that more than once! 'Susannah or Suze; nothing in between', that's what I tell them!"; Susannah determinedly injected some jollity into her voice, keen to bring the mood back up for Freya's birthday. "Only Edie, the librarian here when I was a child, got away with calling me 'Susie'. I'm not sure why, but somehow it never bothered me hearing it from her. She was so kind; the one adult who never judged me, told me off or expected the worst from me because of my poor coordination. It always felt as though letting myself be 'Susie' to her was something to do with repaying that kindness, though she was also the one adult I'd have known for sure would respect my boundaries if I'd ever asked her to call me anything else."

"Well, I am glad that you had people like Edie and your brother Julian to advocate for you when you were a child. Your parents too, of course"; Frieda looked across at her daughter, a shadow of guardedness descending over her expression. "There is a lot more understanding these days, of course, and from what Freya tells me, you're doing well in your job. It is good to see you beginning to make more friends at work, Freya; it is important that you keep on broadening your social circle. You know I never want you to be lonely."

Susannah held her peace; this was a moment for mother and daughter and she was a guest in their home. Not that this prevented the pain from lancing through her at what she read between the lines. *Don't settle here; don't get lumbered with being the Different one's sidekick and protector. Make sure you keep in with the abled ones too.* She got it about Frieda's worries that Freya would end up lonely. Of course she was going to prioritise her only child's emotional wellbeing. Frieda's elegant fingers caressed that fragile wine glass once more as she spoke; Susannah did a rapid audit of precisely where her own hands were in relation to anything breakable or spillable.

"...birthday, you and Susannah should be out having fun with a whole *group* of friends your own ages. Especially on a Friday night!", the motherly counsel was continuing.

"Mum, it's my day and honestly, this is way better than having to shout to have a conversation; queuing for ages to get served or go to the toilet and then again for taxis home; spending a fortune; having to constantly watch your drink for spiking; risking getting in the way of people fighting and being sick all over the place, and somebody guaranteed to end up crying or having to be helped home at the end of the night! OK, I'm not saying every night out is like that, but it's glorified far too much as the 'proper' or 'only' way to celebrate. It's becoming less expected these days as a way to establish yourself at work too."

"Freya's right. In Sweden, they have a tradition called Fredagsmys; it's all about winding down at the end of the working week, getting together in the cosy, relaxed and safe environment of home, catching up with friends and family in a low key, undemanding way with drinks and snacks and blankets, comfortable clothes, soft lighting and a gentle volume of TV or music in the background. I think a lot of people have always preferred that kind of socialising, at least some of the time, and been afraid to admit it to themselves let alone anyone else!"

"Ah yes; Freya told me you have an interest in these Scandinavian traditions. Is that the Swedish equivalent of the Danish hygge?"

"It's similar in spirit; I would say they coexist, rather than one being the equivalent of the other. The Norwegians have koselig, which is about the reward of indoor comforts after outdoor activities. Hygge is more nebulous. It's a feeling, rather than a particular ritual or occasion."

"And these traditions, when non-Scandinavian people adopt them; isn't that… what's the expression again? Cultural appropriation?"

"That's a tricky one. I'm not Scandinavian so I don't get to decide if it is or isn't; I do feel that something positive and universally practicable shouldn't be the exclusive property of those already privileged enough to be from a beautiful place and not in an oppressed minority. Nobody could reasonably claim that simply organising a relaxed get-together at home at the end of a working week is cultural appropriation! OK, perhaps there's an argument there against *calling* a gathering 'Fredagsmys' when nobody present has any connection with Sweden, but to acknowledge that it's along the same lines and pick up on its benefits as a routine shouldn't be a problem. Something as intangible as hygge, though, I can't see how that would ever have been intended to exist exclusively in Denmark or for Danish people. The Danes came up with a word for something that already exists everywhere if you know what to look for, and they gave a troubled world a valuable gift in guiding people to appreciate it, for which we do all owe them gratitude. I understand people not wanting their own national cultural identity to be diluted, but in my opinion, for a prosperous white-majority culture to call it 'appropriation' is appropriation in itself, of the issues faced by oppressed groups. In general, I think the main reason it could be seen as problematic is when a tradition is commercialised outside of its origin, as hygge has become in some quarters. When it gets twisted to make people think that the way to achieve it, or the best version of it, is to buy particular products and that the more expensive the product, the better and more authentic the hygge experience. *That* is wrong; it's taking away the spirit of the original. Hygge is not something that can be bought. By all means, buy the fluffy socks or the artisan hot chocolate if you want them in the first place, but hygge is the feeling you get from enjoying them, not the product you're buying. Hygge can come from whatever gives you that cosy feeling. It could be the smell of woodsmoke, or that first time you feel the change of the air at the start of your favourite season. It could be the first time after the summer that you're out when the streetlights are coming on. It could be the days when the temperature in the house is suitable for wearing your favourite nightclothes or casual clothes after it's been too warm or too cold for months. It could be when you've finally used up the body lotion you were a bit disappointed by but didn't want to be wasteful and throw it away, and you open the new bottle of your favourite one. It's elusive because it's so broad in scope and yet so personal, so to me it's hard to align that with the idea of it being cultural appropriation."

"That's an insightful analysis, and beautifully described, Susannah; thank you for sharing it."

"Absolutely", put in Freya; "and could you imagine trying to have such a profound conversation in a pub in Kirkbrigg on a Friday night?"

"Touché!"; Frieda was sporting enough to laugh as she topped up the Prosecco in their glasses and gestured to them to help themselves to food.

Susannah ate sparingly, concentrating on each well-controlled bite. Much as she appreciated the privilege of being able to share and promote better understanding in a comparatively safe setting, eating in front of other people after talking about dyspraxia unavoidably upped the ante. She winced as despite her best efforts, she bit the inside of her cheek; right where a blood blister had recently healed from the last instance. Surely she couldn't be accused of internalised ableism for finding this so frustrating. How was it possible to have clumsy *teeth*? How many times had she almost gotten rid of a painful mouth ulcer at the hinge of her jaw and then the clench of one sneeze caught the vulnerable spot again and put her back to square one? The pain and extra load on her immune system further depleted the resources she needed to cope with the neurodivergent life soundtrack; being pebble-dashed by tuts, sighs, 'Ooh!'s and 'You OK?'s. Sure, some of the latter were genuinely well-intentioned, but letting the glitches pass without comment and unobtrusively allowing her that bit of time and space was her ideal vision of inclusion and belonging.

"Are you OK there, dear?"

She hadn't gotten away with it unnoticed then, and now she had food turning to rock in her increasingly tense mouth. The last thing she needed was for it to catch her throat. She nodded, raising her free hand in a 'par for the course' gesture.

"Ah; did you bite your tongue? Is that a dyspraxia thing too?"

Because bombarding her with questions, putting pressure on her to either talk before her mouth was completely clear or gulp food down quickly, was so helpful; not. How could she possibly answer without seeming rude? Washing down the last of her mini quiche with Prosecco was unlikely to end well either.

"Mum! I know you mean well but it makes things worse if Susannah feels that she's being scrutinised when she's eating. Suze, I'm answering for you because you're being polite and not talking with your mouth full; I don't mean to talk over you." Freya might be aloof and a closed book at times, but she had some gold star ally credentials.

"Thank you both. Yes; I do have a tendency to bite my tongue or the inside of my mouth. It's something I have to live with, and it took me a long time to connect it to my dyspraxia. That's another reason why the 'CC' label is so harmful; besides the stigma of it, the focus on the stereotypical aspects of any condition prevents people with a different profile of traits from getting the information, support, solidarity and understanding that comes with recognition of it by themselves and others. Look, I'm always willing to talk about these things to help increase understanding for people like me, but I truly don't want it to take over Freya's birthday. You have a beautiful garden, Frieda; what are those purple flowers in the bed on the rockery?"

Mercifully accepting the abrupt change of subject with an acknowledging nod, Frieda talked about the various flowers she tended with pride as the three of them ate and drank without further incident. Freya visibly livened as she recalled helping in the garden as a child; laughing at memories of water fights and smiling gently over being rewarded with ice cream after putting her brightly patterned little gardening gloves away tidily and thoroughly washing her hands.

The sky deepened, the long day gracefully aging with a silvery-white growth of cirrus cloudlets; the sun yawned a stretch of shadows as it sank drowsily towards the horizon. Susannah insisted on helping to clear the table, accepting the obvious allocation of the smallest and cleanest dishes to carry with a mixture of resignation and relief.

"Message me when you're safely home", urged Freya; Susannah promised to do so, thanking them both once again for a lovely evening. The walk from Freya's home to her own hardly took ten minutes; it wouldn't be last orders time yet for the Friday night pub crowd.

The streetlight on the corner; the one she could see from her bedroom, was on although it wasn't dark enough and none of the others were. Shaking her head at the waste of electricity, she looked up fondly at its light peachy glow, smiling to herself at the coincidence after having mentioned the hygge feeling it gave her the first time of being out when the streetlights were on after the months of long Scottish summer daylight. As she passed the lamp post, the light flickered oddly to a greenish blue before reverting to its normal colour.

She hurried the rest of the way into the flats, slowing down again to climb the stairs before letting herself in and messaging Freya as promised once she had locked the door. She checked the cats' water bowl and the automatic feeder she had set to ensure they got some kibble before her later than usual arrival home; Morgan immediately ran to meet her, clamouring for attention. Laughing as she scooped up the purring cat, she glanced into her bedroom, confirming that Annika was peacefully sleeping on the bed. Through the window, nothing broke the monotony of the unlit streets; the light on the corner had switched off again.

4

Foundations

The list was beginning to take shape. With so many unknowns and not having put in an offer on the flat yet due to waiting for advice about the stairs, Susannah was focusing on building a framework of what would need to be budgeted for. It fit neatly into breaks from the more physical task of decluttering her current home, to streamline the packing and unpacking as much as possible when the time came.

"Legal fees; packing materials; removal firm fees; deep clean for here and possibly for the new place depending on its condition"; she counted off the obvious items before thinking more deeply about some of the less immediately visible expenses. "Perhaps a few days in a cattery for you two over the time of the actual move, when the doors will be propped open on the day and everything will be chaotic and unfamiliar anyway." She stroked Morgan who purred on the arm of the chair beside her. "Redirection of my mail; that needs to go in. Allow extra for a few meals out or takeaways around the time when everything is packed. Any additions, repairs or upgrades I want which are best done before all my stuff is in. Decorating. There are bound to be some new things I need for a different space. Taxi fares to charity shops or uplift fees for bulky items if I end up with a lot that won't fit in. There might be admin fees to do with the change of address. Dual council tax while I own the new place but am staying here while I get it ready and serve my notice period. The ongoing extras too, which will start immediately; I should list those separately. Insurance is going to cost way more; the policy will need to be for building as well as contents in my own place. Servicing costs for the boiler and central heating. Window cleaning. Potentially garden maintenance. Gutter cleaning and getting the roof checked periodically. Contributions to a maintenance fund if I end up in a tenement. I'm beginning to appreciate my landlord a lot more!"

Susannah went to the unit where she kept her stationery, cursing as she scraped her knuckles over the door handle. She would have to be prepared for more of that sort of thing than usual when she was more preoccupied and again as she adjusted to a new living space, unless she could somehow find the extra gear which people so often seemed to when life called for it. She took out her packet of highlighters and set about colour coding the budgeting items according to which were one-offs for the move itself and which would need to be accounted for on an ongoing basis.

Her entryphone buzzed.

How had it gotten to that time?

"Freya, I'm so sorry; the coffee isn't ready yet. I woke up early and started doing my list of expenses; the time completely got away from me."

"Well, I guess you're going to have a lot on your mind for a while. Could I have a glass of water for the time being, please? My mouth is a bit dry."

"Of course!"; Susannah guiltily fussed around in the kitchen pouring them each a glass before getting the coffee together. She quickly wiped a few stray grounds off the worktop and went to join her friend in the living room. Freya crouched stroking Annika, who was curled contentedly on the large cat bed. "…going to miss you both when your mummy moves away", she cooed as Susannah walked in.

"You'll keep seeing us all, Frey. I know I let the preparations distract me this morning but I promise I'm not going to drift out of your life. Coffee will be ready in a couple of minutes."

"It's fine. Before we start being grateful, Suze, I'm dreading going into work tomorrow. I tried again to connect with the young team on Friday after you left. Chanelle had changed into a new top for going out; it was lovely, it genuinely suited her. I said so and asked if that was the one she'd been talking about going out at lunchtime to pick up as her click and collect notification had come through. She looked at me as though I'd teleported in from outer space"; Freya imitated Chanelle's higher pitched voice; "Er, yeah?" Twisting her facial features to illustrate puzzled contempt, she mimicked a nonplussed gesture. "Then she and Lexy looked at each other and went off into giggles. They went out in their usual huddle like a couple of schoolgirls and when I left a few minutes later, I popped in to use the toilet and they were in there doing their make-up. They looked at each other and did that meaningful throat clearing thing, then went off into peals of mirth again. I wanted to make a catty comment along the lines of watching what they were doing with all that powder because that top must be dry clean only, but I knew it would make things worse so I ignored them and went straight into the nearest cubicle. Then I felt ridiculous for not having a comeback; not having the upper hand here when I'm almost twenty years older than them. And, well, nothing was *happening*, if you know what I mean. My body wouldn't do what I'd gone into the cubicle for. I was too tense for it to release, and as the time dragged out, I felt as though they must have noticed the lack of relevant sound coming from behind the door, for all my bladder function was logically of no interest whatsoever to them and they would have been focused on their going-out excitement. It got to the stage where I was in a complete panic, knowing fine well I'd been in there for way too long and wasn't going to get away with waiting until they left. They'd gone quiet and I could make out suppressed laughter. So I got the emergency sanitary towel out of my bag and deliberately made a racket pulling the backing off and crumpling it up, put it in place though I didn't need it, then made a performance out of yanking sheets of toilet paper out of the dispenser and flushed it away, so that it all sounded as if I'd come on and hoped they'd think the pause was down to cramps. I mean, how ridiculous is that? I walked home still needing the toilet, and I had to make sure the disposal bag was well hidden in the outside bin so my mum wouldn't see it as she'd know from using the bathroom bin that I'm in between that time of the month."

"Freya, I'm so sorry that happened to you. Those nasty little girls. Who do they think they are? You were wise not to risk inflaming the situation. It's bullying, but they're so savvy about it; they know what they can get away with. I hope you can see that you're massively the bigger person, because you handled it sensibly and resourcefully, and while reliving it to me with so much pain you can say with such sincerity that Chanelle looked good in her new top." Susannah swallowed a sudden lump in her throat. "That coffee will definitely be ready now; you get yourself comfortable and I'll bring it through."

Walnut essence, maple and nutmeg soothed the lingering sadness from the enclosed air of the living room as the friends began their Grounds for Gratitude reflections.

"I'm thankful that I've gotten that off my chest about what happened on Friday. It always helps talking these things through."

"Of course; any time. For my part, this week I want to start off by being thankful for Edie, the librarian here when I was a child. I hadn't thought about her so much lately, until the subject came up on your birthday; since then she's been on my mind a lot. She'll be long since retired, but I would have looked for her if I wasn't moving away. It doesn't seem fair to turn up in an elderly person's life after a long time, however positively, visit for a few months and then disappear again. Perhaps if I could see her one time to acknowledge and thank her, shortly before I go."

"Hmm, yes"; a sliver of an edge crept into Freya's voice. "It's always hard when someone close moves away, especially if you don't have many people in your life as it is." She set down her cup, her hand jerking in fright before steadying it quickly as it hit the coaster harder than she had intended. "Mum remembered more about Edie. She was known for always picking up on anyone being left out and helping them."

"Yes; I loved my visits to the library. Julian used to take me on a Saturday morning, before I was old enough to go on my own. I was already known for having clumsy accidents and so scared all the time; more of getting into trouble than getting hurt. I'm not blaming my parents and teachers; people didn't know about proprioception and vestibular perception and how the neurodivergent brain can get information so wrong. They genuinely believed it was all a matter of focus and concentration. I came to loathe those words! I took in more than my parents knew; they were afraid that Julian or London would end up as my carer one day if I didn't buck up my ideas and grow out of it. Then when Selina came along, the pressure increased all the more; I wasn't the baby of the family now and I had to *choose* to grow up, act my age and be more responsible so that I could pitch in and be helpful instead of taking all this extra attention! Which of course didn't happen at the rate and to the extent they wanted it to. Sure, I developed strategies and learned lessons as everyone does. Some of those strategies I use to this day. Touching the edges of furniture as I walk past, or doorframes as I walk through. People pick up on it and ask me things I don't want to disclose to strangers, or touch me without asking. No; I'm not partially sighted, and regardless, it's not OK to grab without asking! I tell people it's a grounding ritual. As a child, though, I didn't have the answers I do now. I resented

Selina for adding to the pressure on me, which was so wrong, and I hated myself for not being able to enjoy having a new baby sister. Naturally I wasn't trusted to hold her. We've become close in adulthood, but I can never get those years back. The trips to the library were a high point of my week; I knew even at that age that somehow Edie *got* me. As we'd say now, she had my back. There was one time when I'd tripped over my own feet and knocked over a stack of books. I was mortified and crying because I thought surely she would be angry about that. Instead, she picked up what I'm pretty sure was a completely random book and said that was lucky as she'd been looking everywhere for it, and then she crouched down beside me and said that she knew I was sad that it happened and that I hadn't wanted it to, but that her finding this book showed that sometimes things work out in ways we don't expect. She said that she knew I wasn't being careless; that sometimes how the world sees things can be like a photograph that's been put in a particular type of frame because somebody's misinterpreted the picture or seen what they wanted to see in it. She told me her mother had a photo of her taken on holiday with a group of her friends where she was wearing a white dress, and although Edie wasn't married, her mother displayed that photo in a fancy white frame as though it were a wedding album photo and although she'd reluctantly correct them, she liked it when people thought it was. 'You will grow into the power to choose your own frame, Susie'; I'll never forget her saying that. The whole memory stands out because she talked to me in a normal voice and because she didn't try to tell me it was OK. She knew that for me, it wasn't OK and nothing could change that. And I believe she also knew that we were both fully aware we lived in a society where it definitively wasn't OK. Julian and I helped her pick up the rest of the books, she made us laugh talking about a funny film she'd watched with her boyfriend, and then we carried on with our day. I loved watching her work;

her auburn hair swishing around was mesmerising and she wore such sophisticated-looking, fashionable glasses. She was kind, gentle and professional, but she'd have wiped the floor with Mrs Hume if she'd heard about the 'CC' business, or about her frequent malicious use of London's birth name. I'm not talking about forgetting or force of habit; she would deliberately deadname them in front of other people. It's one of the main reasons they hardly ever visit here and refuse to bring any of their friends, who don't know what their original name was. Fran knows what it was but London is too uncomfortable with the idea of their partner hearing it used, and thanks to Mrs Hume keeping it in everyone's mind, far too many people here are likely to use it."

"Wow, that's so out of order. It's a form of violation. It's a blessing that people like Edie balance that out. I second that gratitude, and I am thankful for Valerie. She circulated that email through the week about anti-bullying schemes, and after the nightmare we went through when Rafe was our line manager I remind myself how fortunate we are now. Despite being put on different teams when they reorganised after he left, we're better off now; Valerie and Morven are both so fair-minded and approachable."

"I agree, and yes, for my turn I am thankful for having Morven Jamieson as my line manager. You're right; it's important and also refreshing to be reminded not to take them for granted."

"I am thankful that Gregor is back at work and feeling better."

"Ah, yes; I saw him. I'm glad about that too. I am thankful that the weather has been less humid this week."

"I am thankful for the happy singing I heard in the stair on my way up to your door. It sounded like a little girl, though I didn't see her."

"That's interesting; I don't know of any young children in these six flats, but I guess it could have been someone visiting. I am thankful for a bit of professional support with my house hunting and sorting out what I'll need to do and in what order; I'm hoping to have a meeting with Adil at one of the local law firms. I get overwhelmed too easily trying to look everything up; too many options, too many complicated jargon-filled websites. I vaguely know him already; he was in Selina's year at school, and he's in conveyancing now."

"That will be useful. Someone physically in the room with you to talk through complicated things can help"; Freya drank the last of her coffee and set the cup neatly down beside her.

In the quiet of her flat long after her friend left, Susannah wondered again about the little girl Freya had mentioned. It was difficult to picture children in these dark, poky homes, though there must have been some in the two bedroom properties over the years and she knew of a couple of families with toddlers in the next block. She suspected that a lot of her neighbours used their smaller second bedrooms for storage, as she did; the flats had little cupboard space. She certainly struggled to imagine a child running about happily singing in her own flat.

She thought back to when she viewed it over two years ago. The lack of storage space, being made up for by the extra bedroom, had not been a major concern for her; it had been a sunny day so the extent to which she would be deprived of natural light had not been quite so apparent in the empty rooms with their bare windows. She had not fallen in love with the flat by any stretch of the imagination, yet she had felt strongly that it was the place for her at this point in her life; not forever, but that it was somewhere she was destined to stay for a time. The reasonable rent and proximity to her new job had sealed her decision, along with a few useful pieces of furniture having been left behind including a dressing table in the main bedroom which must have been there from when the very first people moved in around seventy years before. Julian had helped her to move it into the second bedroom; she rather liked its old-fashioned curves and dark wood with a memory of a sheen from coats of scuffed and faded varnish, but it wasn't what she wanted to see dominating the fairly compact primary bedroom every time she went to sleep and woke up. It seemed more at home in the smaller room; in space which was visited rather than lived in, where it could more tangibly hold its past time among her personal items in its many compartments.

Before too long it would be time once again to open the drawers in which she kept her thicker winter socks and tights and her thermal vests. Although she opened them periodically through the lighter months to air them out, those spaces smelled to her of the first Sunday evenings after the clocks went back; those oppressive hours when tea time was over, the Top 40 countdown had finished on the radio and all that remained was homework and the dark rise of school. It was the one time she wished it could be light all year round, much as she appreciated the timely return of cooler nights, the freezeframe glitter of the streetlamps and all the cosiness of autumn.

Susannah shivered in a sudden draught as she went into her bedroom to check that she had organised everything she needed to wear for the working week, her thoughts of the dressing table having reminded her. Morgan stirred on the bed and miaowed.

5

Shifting Grounds

"It's OK, Honor; I understand. Somebody got in quicker; I always knew that could happen while I was researching the future-proofing I needed to think about. I won't pretend I'm not gutted, but I appreciate you letting me know promptly so that I can start looking again. Yes; you too. Thanks again. Bye then."

Susannah sighed and slumped back in the chair, setting her phone down on the coffee table. Disappointment deflated its way through every nerve and muscle as she took in the transition from half-daring to imagine her forever home in the flat with the bay window to realising that she would never see it again.

Of course she had known from the beginning that it was unlikely for most people to get the first property they wanted, but no amount of managing expectations could have prepared her for quite how disorientating this would feel. The new chapter ahead of her had abruptly lost its structure; its tentative framework collapsing back into a featureless void, leaving her with all the work to do again from scratch just to get back onto that first step.

She needed it to be permissible for her to feel her emotions; to admit that knowing this was meant to be in order to lead her to something better didn't help now. It was too soon.

Tears blurred her vision as she turned away from the dingy wall view which jarred extra unwelcome in her line of sight. She swore under her breath; a shaky laugh bubbled up as Annika lifted her head to regard her human with typical cat disapproval from the bed in the corner. "How do you know which combinations of human speech sounds are swear words?"; she shook her head in amusement. "If you'd seen the room you've lost out on, believe me, you'd be yowling some expletives of your own." A rush of sorrow overwhelmed her at the irrational yet powerful sense that she had let her cats down by not acting quickly enough; she took a shaky breath as she wiped her eyes.

She wouldn't tell anyone yet. Only her siblings and Freya knew about the flat anyway, and she wasn't ready to convincingly reassure them that she'd be OK; she needed time to process and regroup. On which note, she had better start getting ready to head for the local pub where she was due to meet Freya for a drink.

Applying a slick of lip gloss and fluffing out her hair, Susannah reminded herself to pay attention to everything she was feeling; not merely the disappointment. If Perth was indeed the place for her, this was an opportunity to reinforce it; if it wasn't, there would be an element of relief. If she was better off staying in Kirkbrigg, she would feel a renewed sense of home as she walked through familiar streets to the Positive Return, the local pub which a national chain had bought when the building's previous owners, a brokerage firm, had closed their local branch. If her future lay somewhere else altogether, that would take longer to come through but the ongoing displacement would be eloquent in itself.

One of the chain's smaller venues, the Positive Return had the feel of a complacent local pub with little competition. A world-weary fawn carpet bore the booths and tables alongside the high windows and around the corner to what most patrons saw as the consolation prize of seating; where the marginally reduced noise level was offset by the regular flapping of the kitchen door. Freya had managed to grab a booth somewhere on the border. Susannah gratefully joined her, gallingly catching her foot on the step which she usually remembered; luckily, Freya already had their drinks in place so the lapse went unnoticed.

By their second round, the conversation had inevitably turned to work.

"I am not looking forward to appraisals. Even with the case you know about"; Freya prudently avoided saying customers' names in the moderately busy pub; "you know that it's as much an assessment of whose faces fit socially. I'm bracing myself for the usual slew of 'team player' comments."

"Yeah, me too, and it's more important than ever to get a good write-up this time when I'm going to be looking to transfer"; as Susannah said it, she knew in her bones that it remained her priority. Anticipation began to glow once more. "It's going to be interesting sussing out which pub in Perth is going to become my local. Though of course there doesn't have to be only one…"

Too late, she noticed the change in Freya's expression.

"Yes, well, we're certainly not spoilt for choice here. Perhaps I'll get to visit now and again."

"Of course you'll be visiting, and I'll come through here to see you. It's not that long a bus journey."

"I know you'll intend to. The important thing is that you get to live your best life. I will just have to figure out how to get on with the others. It's not as though I don't try already."

"I know you do, and I've seen how unfair they can be to you. I heard you ask Donna how her wee boy was when he'd been ill shortly before your birthday and she said something about you listening in to her private conversations, when she'd been talking about it at her desk where anyone passing would overhear."

"Exactly. I need to aim higher. Maybe this will spur me on to do enough to make Max see me differently."

"Freya, you know that's a dangerous road to go down. He's in a monogamous relationship."

"Yes, with Robin, but you remember when we had that diversity event and he told us he's bisexual?"

"For mercy's sake, keep your voice down! That was shared within the bounds of confidentiality at the event! Even if it were common knowledge, this is so wrong. I'm sorry, Freya; I truly don't want to hurt you, and I'm not judging you for how you *feel*; it's natural to be attracted to a charismatic authority figure. I wish you didn't have to cope with this pain. I saw the rush of hope it gave you when he said that and when we realised Robin is a man, and I didn't want to come across as judging you…"

"Yet here we are. Maybe not having you there to cushion the isolation is the push I need to focus on being good enough to complete the picture for him."

"What… Complete the picture? Are you saying that if I leave, you'll start actively pursuing Max and it will be because of me? Freya, please don't lay that at my door! He's our *boss*. Have you any idea how much trouble you could bring upon yourself? How much ammunition you would be giving the popular crowd if you ended up with a harassment complaint, not to mention the impact on your career and your relationship with your mum! Please don't get yourself into trouble with Max! There has to be a more constructive focus for you than this!"

"My mum would be delighted if I could be good enough to get someone like Max! If only to satisfy his bisexuality!"

"Freya, no. That's… I know you're hurting, but that's completely wrong. It's perpetuating a negative stereotype about bisexuality; that bisexual people cannot commit to one partner if that is their choice. It feeds into the myths about them inevitably being promiscuous, unable to decide, wanting the best of both worlds, or essentially straight and curious. Bisexual means that a person is attracted to two or more genders. It doesn't define what they do with that attraction. In the same way as someone who is attracted to one gender can experience attraction to people of that gender but not act on it because they're spoken for, a bisexual can choose not to act on any other attraction as part of their promise to a partner. Max isn't up for grabs to women by way of being bisexual and with a man."

"Susannah, could you just for once put a friend in pain before your righteous sexuality politics? It's all very well for you; this sort of thing doesn't touch you, with your laid back comfortable routine of having your own space and being happy with your life as it is, and now a golden chance to make it more fulfilling and contented without that involving any need of a partner. You've no idea how this feels, otherwise you wouldn't be lecturing me on top of leaving me!"

"I'm not putting my principles before you; I'm worried about the pain and actual danger you're setting yourself up for if you overstep with Max! You would destroy all trace of the cordial relationship you have with him as a valued employee. I am sorry for coming across as lecturing you. I'm honestly terrified for you, and trying to stop you from doing something destructive from which there would be no way back."

"Well, it won't be your problem soon enough; you'll be living it up in the Fair City, in your ideal flat with the big bay window."

"Oh, will I now? That might be a tad difficult, since I took a call from the estate agent before coming to meet you, letting me know that someone else has put in an offer and the seller has accepted!"

The words were already regretted before they had finished spraying out. How had she allowed herself to be provoked into striking such a low blow? Freya was out of order, but Susannah was one of the few people to see through to the real her; the damaged layers of unmet needs laid bare in the frozen mortification of the stricken face across the table from her.

"And you're telling me this *now*, to shame me right when everything's too much? You certainly did a good job of keeping that one up your sleeve. Now I'm a shitty person because I didn't know something you chose not to tell me, and I'm supposed to grovel and choke on humble pie."

"No, no, I shouldn't have thrown that in your face in anger. That was my misjudgement. I kept it to myself because I needed time to take it in and process my feelings; I had no intention of telling anyone this soon. I am sorry I blurted that out and made you feel ambushed. I stand by what I said about Max, though. For *your* sake; for your safety and welfare."

Freya pressed her fingers to her temples, her eyes squeezed shut. "Look, I can't; I simply can't deal with this here and now. With you sitting there so poised and perfect and holier than thou with right on your side while I fall apart. Everything's too much; I don't know if it's because of yet another birthday with nothing changing. I can't stay around being in the wrong yet again when I don't know how to put the brakes on. I need some air; I guess I need to relearn how to be on my own."

Freya scooped up her jacket, bag and phone and rushed out of the pub, not registering the tuts as she almost collided with a couple coming in. Susannah took a few minutes to gather her wits, finishing her drink and typing out a short message urging Freya to let her know when she was safely indoors and pledging to give her space once they each knew the other had made it back to their homes. Remembering the step this time, she thanked the bar staff as she returned the empty glasses then walked out into the growing twilight.

The streetlights were on; the first time this late summer. A lump rose in her throat as she remembered the conversation about hygge on Freya's birthday. Each opaque gem punctuated a passing moment in the gentle order of the walk home; a return of circadian lucidity after the prolonged sensory blurt of the endless summer daylight. Susannah let its structure take the weight of her churning thoughts, soothing her with the visual heartbeat of pale pinkish light. She smiled as she came to the last one before the pathway to the flats, noting its steady glow matching its neighbours.

"Hold that thought!"; she broke her stride with a half shocked, half amused double take as she passed the light and it turned the same shade of greenish blue she had seen on that Friday night. She stood looking up at the impassive lighted glass, the inexplicable hue within glowing as brightly as its usual shade before switching back to normal as her footsteps receded and the quiet night ticked by.

6

Protective Sister

"She actually said she was going to make a move on your boss and blamed it on you for *leaving* her?"

"Well, I don't think she means to make a move on him as such. More like step up her attempts to impress him. She's not a bad person, Selina. Yes, I admit she's being manipulative, but it's not really me or Max she's trying to control. It's the level of loss and isolation in her own life. I'm not saying that makes the actions acceptable, but demonising her isn't the answer. She's not some power-hungry narcissist. She's a classic example of ingrowing unmet needs."

"I hear you, Suze, but that's not your fault and you're not responsible for those needs. I'm not demonising Freya, but you're my sister and my concern is for you first and foremost."

"Yes, and who does Freya have to care about *her* like that? I've got you and Jules and London. She has no siblings and a mother who needs her life, and her, to be perfect to make up for her shiftless father running off with his secretary when parenthood got real. Which it doesn't take a psychologist to figure out makes her vulnerable to idealising someone like Max, and to feeling that the only way to attain a fulfilling life she can hold on to is to be on the winning side of some sort of competition for a partner who can afford to be choosy."

"I get that, and like you I'm not judging her for whatever she feels for this guy Max. Her private thoughts are her own business. My problem is with her putting this responsibility onto you and making you feel guilty for planning to move."

"To be honest, Sel, I'm not sure it is a case of her thinking I'm responsible for her needs. I think it's the opposite; she knows full well that I'm not and that is what terrifies her and makes her lash out like a cornered animal. She's not simply reacting to me moving away, she's primarily reacting to *not having right on her side in struggling* with me moving away. We really need to destigmatise people finding things hard when those things are not in themselves negative, like someone moving away or choosing someone else as a partner. We need to normalise being able to say 'This is a very positive thing for this person in my life but I need a bit of help and support with the ramifications for me', without it being seen as jealousy, selfishness or begrudging. So much ingrained anguish comes about because of valid emotions being forced underground and silenced. Freya has that in HD surround sound. She's learned from childhood that her mother's all-consuming pain exists because Frieda didn't manage to stay ideal enough to avoid losing her great love. She has seen that pain every day from far too young an age to understand and process what she was absorbing. I don't care what inspirational memes say about leaving childhood behind; there are some traumas which become ingrained too early to be fully disentangled from the adult that child becomes. I'm *not* claiming that everybody who behaves in a coercive and controlling way is a basically good person in pain. There *are* people who are wilfully toxic abusers. I am not an apologist for them. I'm saying that Freya isn't one of those people."

"Maybe not, *but she could become one*. Most are unhappy and behave as they do from a background of insecurity, repeating destructive patterns and so on as opposed to being plain evil and doing it for thrills. They believe that they're doing the sole thing they can to survive. The cycle can only be broken if Freya realises, and faces up to, the way she's headed and is willing to put the brakes on that. Which I don't doubt will be phenomenally hard and scary for her. It means committing to two things; accountability and healing, which she has this lifelong conditioning to see as mutually exclusive. All that on top of holding down a job where she's not supported and is socially isolated despite making an effort, which reinforces her insecurities and her conviction that she cannot be both fallible, and safe and loved. It's a desperately sad situation for both her and Frieda; I'd say they both need help. I didn't realise the extent of all this, and when you reframe it that Freya's struggle over you moving away is with the perception of being in the wrong for finding the adjustment hard, it aligns with how you describe her in general. How she means well but gets read the wrong way because she's got this invisible barbed wire around her."

"Absolutely. At work, we take our breaks together; it's an unspoken agreement that we have each other's backs that way because neither of us needs the added pressure of the in crowd gloating over a rift between us. We make polite conversation, mostly about work. She did ask if the cats were OK after the recipe changed on one of their usual food brands and it turned out to be too rich so they'd been bringing it back up. But she hasn't been coming over on Sundays for Grounds for Gratitude. Get this though, Sel; she's been going out for a walk for the time she'd usually be here and pretending to her mother that she was coming over as she would normally be. She can't let on that she's had a dispute with a friend. Frieda would be 'disappointed by a backward step where she's already not up to expectations'."

"Good grief. That is not healthy. Maybe when she asked after the cats, she was merely collecting examples for a fictionalised account of your Grounds for Gratitude, then?"

"Selina."

"Sorry; I don't know her as you do and I'm sure she genuinely cares about Annika and Morgan. People can truly care about something or someone while using their situations to be manipulative. It can be mixed in with altruism. Coercion can be coping strategies gone awry. Which makes it harder for the person to recognise and confront what they're doing. They don't believe they could possibly be guilty of coercive conduct because they think that's the sole domain of the sociopath; the unfeeling, 'deliberately' abusive, physically, sexually and emotionally violent monster."

"Yes, I see that. There is no villain in this scenario; it's two hurt people getting by as best they can and not always getting it right. This does need to be addressed, and I promise you I'm not going to enable it. I will step further away if I have to."

"You're too accommodating at times, Suze, but I understand what you're saying. Speaking of accommodating, how is the house hunting going?"

Susannah tapped on her tablet screen, bringing back the page of listings she had been looking at when her sister phoned.

"There is a flat I'm going to ask to view; it's on the ground floor with a private section of garden so it's towards the top of my budget and the kitchen is smaller than here, but the lounge has dual aspect and both windows are a good size. The light and views of the sky would be incredible compared to here!"

"That sounds fabulous! Is this in Perth too?"

"Yes; not far from the last place. I must admit I'm not looking forward to telling Freya!"

"It's less than an hour on the bus! She does know it's Perth in Scotland you're looking at, not Perth in Australia?"

"Haha, yes, though I've almost made that mistake myself a couple of times in searches! I'm enjoying the process. Buildings are interesting; their different character and how things work. Freya has been taking an interest in that side of it too; when things get back to normal between us as I hope they will, I'm going to encourage her to take that as a possible new career direction. I need to help her to get out of that office. It honestly is an awful thought leaving her on her own with that lot. I can picture it now; all the snide faux sympathy about her pal having moved on. Yes, I know; it's not my problem! I'm allowed to care about her though."

"Of course you are, and I'm not about to jump down your throat for encouraging her to proactively follow an interest and improve her life for herself! I feel for her; I bear her no ill will. I know she's your close friend, and she could clearly do with robust support that can withstand and transition her through changes in the circumstances of people around her. She needs the opportunity to establish a network so that she's not too reliant on one person. I don't like the way she's acted, but you don't have to justify your friendship to me."

"Thanks, Sel. I'm going to apply now for that viewing, so I'll catch up with you again soon."

Closing the call, Susannah opened the Request A Viewing link on the listing as she once again began the challenging process of detaching herself emotionally when a potential forever home got all of her senses singing.

7

Edie

September that year was reawakening to its true calling; its status as the beginning of what lovers of autumn and its sensory procession called 'the 'ber months'. After several years wherein the month had lapsed into a tired green fade of scorched summer with the colours and freshness biding their time until October, the trees were already turning and a gossamer-fine prelude of frost sharpening iridescent skies on the clear nights Susannah loved. The languid post-sunset sheen of midsummer was honed high in the cooling layers to a crystalline glint at this time of year, teasing a supporting act for the aurora borealis as the vast stage of the sky darkened earlier over an engaged audience.

Having clearly had something on her mind all day at work, Freya had asked to meet at the Neon Fox, a casual American diner style restaurant on the main street. The orange illuminated sign in the shape of a sitting fox with its tail curled around glowed a cheery welcome, its outline softened by steam from the busy coffee machine as Susannah pushed open the glass door. Freya waved cautiously from a corner table. Ordering a decaf latte in deference to the evening hour, Susannah joined her, draping the burnt orange scarf which she was relishing the first chance of the season to wear over the arm of her seat.

"Thank you for coming"; Freya nervously ran her forefinger nails back and forth over the pads of her thumbs. "I found out something from my mum and I didn't want to bring it up at work as I wasn't sure how it might hit you after what you recently talked about. It's about Edie, the librarian. Suze, I'm so sorry but she died in 2020."

"No!"; Susannah's mind reeled as she processed the news and tried to assimilate the timeline, her chest tight with disbelief. "She can't have been that old; how did she die?"

"It was Covid. She was in her seventies. I was at school when she retired; I remember that now. Mum said she retired early; there was some kind of medical issue, I think, and it was all done quietly. She'd been struggling for a while with her eyesight and then there was an incident; an accident of some kind where a priceless first edition got damaged. There was never any suggestion of deliberate wrongdoing, but Mum believed it broke her spirit as well as being a dealbreaker for her employers."

"Poor Edie. That's devastating, and thank you for being considerate about telling me. I know it wouldn't have been easy for you to reach out." Susannah wiped an unexpected wash of tears from her eyes with the part of a red paper napkin not stained by a stray dribble of coffee from the cup she had painstakingly carried to the table. "She was so switched on; so ahead of her time with regard to ableism and her understanding of my dyspraxia. I don't mean to make this about me, but what your mum told you about the incident with a valuable book makes me wonder if we had more in common than I realised. I remember her as having been efficient, meticulous and tidy but then I was a child looking up to her, and with no clue back then about neurodivergence and that it is lifelong. You know what dyspraxia was called back then. When I think back, I wonder if she was deliberately precise as she tried to compensate for the differences in perception which she wouldn't have known how to explain. That could have been part of her struggle with her eyesight too for all we know. We'll never know, and I really shouldn't be speculating about diagnosing someone who isn't here to consent or contribute to the dialogue. I wish, though, that she could have known about it and found peace if indeed she was dyspraxic, or any other neurotype that accounted for whatever problems she may have had. To have known that it wasn't a failing of character, as she was so keen for me to take on board!"; Susannah wiped away more moisture from her eyes as Freya tentatively offered her own clean napkin. "Thanks, Frey. I notice myself becoming hyper-precise at times, especially in speaking, when I'm overwhelmed or overtired or feel for whatever reason as though I'm inexorably hurtling towards the next glitch. People pick up on it and laugh at me for being formal, uptight; ugh, I hate that fucking word too!"; she grimaced, glancing around concerned in case any children had heard her swear. "Or they *urge* me to relax, to not look so worried, not realising that it's having the opposite effect. Not getting that it increases the pressure, indicting me with not being passable as I am. Edie was one of the few people in my life, particularly my childhood, to be on my wavelength enough to give me a break from that pressure. The thought that she might have been in the same boat the whole time and not... Well, it's no use going there now, getting upset when there's nothing I can do about the past. I need to honour Edie in how I live my own life; make sure that I make a difference where and when I can." Susannah resolutely raised the tall mug of latte, the thin trail of slopped liquid now dry and stopped harmlessly in its tracks where her napkin had done its job. "To Edie."

"To Edie", echoed Freya as she raised her own sleek cup and tapped it daintily against Susannah's.

They sat quietly for a few moments, each adjusting. Freya shifted in her chair and cleared her throat.

"Look, about Max. I'm not... Yes, I want him to like me, but I'm not going to, you know, do anything rash. I know you think badly of me for liking someone who's spoken for and insulting the bisexual community in the process, but..."

"Freya, I do not think less of you for how you *feel*. You're attracted to an adult who is a figurehead of excitement and approval for you; that's natural and I would never judge anyone for that. I feel sad that it's causing you pain, though; that it's gone past being a harmless thrill and adrenalin rush. You had a point last time we were talking about it; I can see how I made you feel that I was putting the principles of being an ally to the LGBTQIAP+ community ahead of what you were going through and my support for you as a friend. I am sorry; I regret having made you feel that way when you were hurting and feeling more up against it because of my plans to move. I should have been more sensitive. You have to take some responsibility too though, Freya; you implied that my moving away was going to push you into doing something destructive, and then left me to process it all sitting in the pub on my own. I genuinely appreciate what you've done for me today; I know that you must have felt extremely vulnerable asking me to meet and giving me difficult news when things aren't resolved between us. I would love to help you come up with some more positive plans. I was saying to Selina that you've been interested in my research into buildings and how they're maintained, and that it could be..."

"*Selina*?", Freya cut in. "You've told your sister about me finding this difficult? I suppose she thinks I'm a sad dependent loser too, then!"

"Nobody thinks that! Yes, I confided in my sister, and yes, I mentioned to her that I was worried and upset by how you had taken my news; that I want to help you because our workplace is full of cliques and the social scene is an echo chamber for the wilfully ignorant. I needed a bit of support, so I admit it, I talked about you. I wouldn't blame you if you talked about me in confidence to someone in your life if I were part of what was bothering you."

"Hah. Who would that be then, this confidant of mine? Who have I got, besides you?"

"That's all the more reason for you to look into other opportunities!" Susannah raised her hands and let her shoulders sag. "Look, I can't do this tonight. You were right; this revelation about Edie is something I need to process, and I thank you again for telling me in the way you did. But I need to call it a night now. Please let me know when you get home safely; one word or an emoji, and I'll do the same." She checked that it was safe to move her chair back, internally thanking her stars that she had remembered to do that in the circumstances and stood, wrapping her scarf around her neck and tucking it under her light cocoa-coloured jacket, smoothing down the lapels; afraid to face Freya's devastated expression as she began to gather her own things together.

"Please look after yourself. We will keep on as we've been doing at work, and talk properly again when we've both had a bit more space to let things settle." She walked out sadly into the crisp evening air.

The streetlamp on the corner intruded into her whirling thoughts as she reached the flats; its colour had switched again to a pale blue-green while its neighbours glowed the usual warm peach tone. Something about its stark and sporadic yet unassuming nonconformity called to Susannah's soul. She smiled wryly up at the lighted glass.

"I'm a bit of a hypocrite calling myself an ally", she muttered to its oddly calming aqua lantern. She had never been bothered about a partner, but never assumed it would be a man if it did happen and couldn't imagine being oriented to a specific gender. It had simply never felt like a big enough deal for her to analyse; the othering due to how society with its ableism viewed her dyspraxia had always overshadowed it. The desexualising of disabled and neurodivergent people angered her on principle whereas the general infantilising felt more personally relevant. Now that she thought about it...

"I could well be the A or the P. Or both."

Distancing herself from a minority to which she may well belong by referring to herself as an ally, while calling Freya out when she was being honest about something many people would judge her for, sat uneasy on her heart despite reminding herself that nobody owes it to another person to come out.

"Wait, did I seriously just come out to a streetlamp?"

Shaking her head, she patted its standard with gentle amusement and walked towards her building.

8

Crieff Gardens

The residential street wound sedately through trees which felt too ancient and quiet to be in such a central part of a city. Only Perth, and possibly Stirling and Inverness, could pull off a location like this so convenient for the station that Susannah could almost imagine getting off the front carriage of the Highland Chieftain and being home in time to wave to the people in the rear carriage from the garden as the train resumed its long journey. A tall wooden gate, stained a natural-looking red-brown compatible with the surrounding trees and the sandstone building, bore the number in polished copper-coloured digits which were impossible to miss. An overarching pale grey sky held its breath, echoing the pent-up life in the rich clusters of red berries which burst ripe from the branches. Susannah had arrived early for her viewing; even on a Saturday, the street was relatively quiet with intermittent traffic.

"Hello; are you here for the viewing?"; the woman who emerged from a silver car with the estate agency's logo greeted her with a warm smile. "I'm Kasia; pleased to meet you."

"Susannah. Pleased to meet you too, and this street is beautiful!"

The estate agent beamed as she reached through a cutout in the gate, sculpted to echo the knots in the wood, and unbolted it. Her short, lilac-tipped blonde hair framed a heart-shaped face which managed to be a work of art in make-up without being in the least intimidating. Susannah felt instantly safe and relaxed as she followed Kasia along the path at the side of the building. "I'm going to show you the garden first", she explained as Susannah glanced back towards the street where the building's dark green front door was situated. "This part here with the washing lines is a shared drying green; the rest is divided by the path here. As you can see, the shed is on the neighbouring property's half; I understand that they have been taking care of the whole of the grass cutting for a small contribution from the people in the flat you're viewing today. I'm sure they would be happy to discuss how you would like to arrange things; whether you want to take a turn or pay them."

Susannah smiled distractedly, hoping that she would retain at least half of what Kasia told her during the course of the whirl of viewing. The flat's half of the garden was reassuringly simple; two thirds grass and the rest a paved area where she could envisage herself sitting out at a rustic table at all hours after over two years of indoor living. Once again she internally reminded herself not to get carried away.

Kasia was already striding purposefully towards the gate. Tearing herself away from the peace of the garden, Susannah followed. The walls of the tenement hallway and the doors to the two ground floor properties were painted the same dark forest green as the front door on the bottom third; the rest of the walls and ceiling a gentle apple green. Stone stairs curved up to the first floor; a narrow slip of passageway alongside them led to a bicycle storage area under the stairs and to the back door which gave access to the garden without having to go out onto the street and through the side gate. Kasia opened the door of the property on the left.

This flat was already vacant; Susannah sent up a prayer of thanks for the lack of treacherous clutter as they walked through the empty rooms. The deep stirring of removal settled in invisible layers on every exposed surface, patient and quiescent as the home waited to come alive again. The neutral décor spoke of its buy-to-let history; oatmeal carpet and magnolia walls bathed in the light which poured unhindered through those generous windows. As Susannah's previous experience had taught her to expect, the rooms were smaller than they looked on the photographs; the reality brought the listing's accompanying measurements into meaningful focus. Allowing for that, she was satisfied that the rooms were big enough for what she needed.

Another small kitchenette and windowless bathroom seemed a small compromise, for all she anticipated this to be her final move. The main floor area of the bedroom was of a similar size to her current one with the addition of a large built-in wardrobe; the lounge was considerably bigger, so everything she had stored in the second bedroom would be divided between those two areas of increased space.

The home report had mentioned that the electrics may need upgrading; it had warned of the possibility that a full rewire may be needed. Susannah determinedly held on to this practical concern as the otherwise ideal property cast its spell on her light-starved domesticity. Adil had told her that an offer on a property could be made conditional upon various more detailed reports; that these were standard clauses and that she would have the right to renegotiate should those further reports flag up significant expense. She had enough savings to be able to afford to stay on in her current flat for an extra few months; she would of course have to consider that council tax, utility bills and insurance would all overlap for that time. She may also need to arrange unpaid time off work in order to travel to let trades in, though Kasia's description of the cooperative neighbours made it sound as though they could be potential keyholders while the property was empty.

There was simply too much to think about here!

No; she had this. She could do this. She *wanted* this one.

"Kasia, I am definitely going to make an offer; I want to make that clear. I have the funds. I will need to talk to my solicitor before bandying any figures about and go through the proper channels via them, but I want to state here and now that I am seriously interested and will be making a competitive offer."

The estate agent nodded, rubbing her hands together as Susannah's excitement caught on. Kasia sent a text and checked her appointments diary as Susannah took a few more photos and composed a message to Adil explaining that she had viewed a property which was suitable enough for her to want to instruct him as soon as possible.

Now the suspense would truly begin.

It would be worth it, Susannah told herself as she mentally bade the flat farewell knowing that if her offer were successful she would not see it again until after missives were concluded, then moving could be a few months away if a lot of electrical work was needed. A lot could happen before contract exchange. A lot was going to be asked of her psychologically, with her need for certainty, predictability and a quick clean break from anything which was not meant for her before she could become too attached.

Thanking Kasia profusely, she walked through the bustling streets of the small, clean city which she increasingly saw as her eventual home. An uneven paving stone abruptly brought her back to reality as her foot caught the edge; by some miracle the builders working across the road didn't notice the jarring near miss. Giving herself a firm internal talking to about keeping her wits about her, she walked more cautiously to the cluster of pubs in the area centred around the Playhouse Cinema on Murray Street, where she would get lunch and process the viewing over a large glass of Shiraz.

Even in between the busiest mealtimes, getting a table in the Foundry on a Saturday was something that happened to other people. Susannah was delighted to get there at the right moment to grab one of the tables next to the window which had a surprisingly wide space around it for a city pub. She ordered on the app, making a mental note to add the facility to do this and keep her chosen table secure to the following day's Grounds for Gratitude.

The new football season was up and running; judging by the chatter from most of the surrounding tables; the local team, St Johnstone, had a crucial match that afternoon. Susannah let the atmosphere wash over her, enjoying the growing aroma of lager and unconcerned by the gradual increase of noise since she had no need to sustain a conversation; she had always been fairly neutral about sport but she felt a rush of loyalty to this city's team. She could imagine herself taking more of an interest for it. Nowhere she had lived up to now had sparked such a sense of belonging as to encourage her to expand the distribution of her energy beyond her existing interests. She chalked up another positive sign that she was on the correct path; if, Heaven forbid, this property got away from her, she was more certain than ever that Perth remained her goal.

She cheered as loudly as everyone around her when St Johnstone scored, and ordered another glass of wine.

The match ended in a draw, which seemed to be cautiously good news; it fit well with the spirit of the day. Susannah returned her empty glasses to the bar and checked the times of buses back to Kirkbrigg. Few at this hour on a weekend did not involve the additional journey out to Broxden Park and Ride where many of the medium and long distance services now called, missing out the small central bus station which leaned into the fabric of the city like a wizened old regular at a timeless local bar. She had an hour and a half before her next bus home from the city centre. The weather remained fair; a few late breaks in the cloud let ripe golden rays of afternoon sun through from patches of sky which burst onto the scene with an almost turquoise hue nostalgic for the past heights of summer. Leaving the bustling pub, Susannah walked slowly as her ears adjusted to the comparative quiet, heading in the opposite direction from the bus station towards the long green stretch of the North Inch.

Perth's two Inches, North and South, had been a big part of her developing interest in the city as a potential place to make her permanent home. Large, well lit, flat and central tree-lined green spaces providing easy walks and an appealing canvas on which the parade of seasons she loved so much could paint their varied colours year after year would be an ideal incentive to get her out and about, balancing out the indoor solitude she needed with healthy fresh air and gentle exercise. She had walked the diagonal paths and perimeter of the South Inch on a couple of previous day trips; that alone had spoken to her as somewhere she could easily envisage working into her routine for the rest of her days. She had walked alongside the river in daylight on the unlit edge of the North Inch but the park walk remained outstanding on her list of attractions to explore in the Fair City. Now seemed like the best possible time to change that.

Georgian architecture lined the streets which elegantly bordered the long sweep of green space with its impressive spread of beech, ash, chestnut and sycamore trees. A laid-back mix of dedicated seating defined a subtle interchange in a paved area where the main roads came to an end and the long, broad path began. The lamp posts were fixed in a tableau of transition at the intersection where mosaic paving gave way to the smooth tarmac of the long path leading off alongside the parkland; crisply geometric Victorian-style lanterns on tall black posts, discreetly dappled with LED grids, handed over to stout modern standards with long filaments in ribbed glass, all poised ready to watch over the shaded path in the hours of twilight and darkness.

Sitting on a bench in the shadow of leaves with a fullness about them; a hint of the simmering secret of the colours set to burst through during the coming weeks, Susannah contemplated being able to walk here every weekend. More significantly, she realised that she felt a comfortable belonging at the thought of the more mundane aspects of routine life against the backdrop of Perth. Going to the dentist. Defrosting the fridge. Coming out for a walk without the option of adding a café or pub visit because she needed to save her spare money for some repair or other. Dealing with bills and other turgid administrative items in the mail. She pictured herself working from home in the property which she had viewed on Crieff Gardens. There was no second bedroom she could turn into an office; if she worked from home it would be a blending of her personal and work space. She had a couple of decades of working years left. That could be a lot of hours of her new life. Yes; she could picture it, all of it. Imagining the less exciting and enjoyable parts of her life took nothing away from her sense of anticipation. She was no tourist here.

A couple passed with a little brown-spotted white Jack Russell terrier on a long fluorescent lead; the dog ran up to her and she smiled at its owners, asking if it was OK to pet it. She let the animal sniff her outstretched hand and stroked its head as she exchanged pleasantries with the couple about the park being beautifully kept.

"Are you local, then?", the younger of the two men smiled.

"Not yet", she replied; her smile broadening as the dog scampered away, paws pattering on the smooth asphalt in search of the next adventure.

9

Energy

"It's good practice for when I eventually move, I suppose"; Susannah stretched tired muscles as she surveyed the organised chaos in her bedroom. Clothes on their hangers were laid across the textured purple duvet on her neatly made bed; the rest of the contents of the built-in cupboard were stacked beneath the window, where they had been cleared out ready for the engineer who had installed her new Realtime meter.

"I know you could have done without this disruption and I do appreciate you agreeing to it while you're here so that I could be certain it would be installed in time for the next tenant"; her landlord Connie Solway smiled sympathetically. "You look after the place so well, I'll be sorry to lose you, though I completely understand. Perth is a beautiful city."

"It sure is. I hope you get a good tenant who will stay long term."

"I do have someone interested; absolutely no pressure on you, there's no rush but a friend of my son has separated from his partner and he will be looking for somewhere compact enough to be economical but with a second bedroom so that his daughter can come to visit at weekends. He visits her at her mother's home for now; it's an amicable separation, but he will be looking for something more independent and stable."

"That sounds sensible. It's funny, I was wondering recently whether there had been many children living in these flats; my friend thought she heard a little girl singing in the stair a few weeks ago when she came over for coffee, though neither of us has seen one. It must have been a visitor."

"Perhaps. You're right; there haven't been many children living in these flats permanently in recent years. A lot of them grew up, or moved on as the families grew and needed more space. My tenants have all been adults; the Fishers, the couple who owned and lived in this flat before I bought it, had been here for around thirty years. The original owners, before them, were another elderly couple. I remember Mrs Fisher telling me that Mrs Aird had a daughter and granddaughter who visited on Sundays; I think the child's father had died young. Mr Aird died when the little girl was a baby; Mrs Aird when she was about eight. I remember thinking that was an awful lot of loss for a child to deal with, though she would have been too young to remember much if anything about her father and grandfather."

"Yes; that's so sad. She would have been around a lot of grief; a lot of difficult adult emotions which she must have picked up on. Children do; they notice more than they're given credit for." Susannah shivered suddenly. "Ooh; I'm not sure where that came from, it's not all that cold yet. I could do with a cup of tea though, now that I can put the kettle on! Would you like to stay for a cuppa? I can let the cats out of the small bedroom now; they'll want to see the rare treasure of a pet-friendly landlord!"

Connie laughed heartily, accepting the offer of a cup of tea and settling into the seat Susannah offered. On her way to the kitchen to make the tea, she opened the door of the small bedroom; Annika and Morgan padded through, each stopping for a long stretch and yawn, having spent most of their confinement sleeping on the well-worn chair which accompanied the dressing table. Susannah picked up their water bowl with both hands and returned it to the kitchen, switching the kettle on before returning to pick up the other bowl which held a small portion of kibble. Their litter tray could wait until her guest had left. She washed her hands, took down a matching pair of mugs and put tea bags in. The one with a chip in it from a previous misjudgement of the shelf would be hers; she kept it for that purpose, to tell them apart easily giving her one thing fewer to keep track of as she entertained a guest.

"How is the house hunting going, then?"; Connie stroked Morgan who had settled purring in her lap. Clocking the dusting of white and pastel fur on Connie's dark green trousers, Susannah made a mental note to offer her a rubber glove to brush them down before she left; the most effective hack she knew of for dealing with the ubiquitous cat hair.

"It's going well, thank you; I'm waiting to hear back about an offer, though I won't be moving for a few months yet if it needs rewiring as the home report suggested it might. I'll need to get an electrical report if my offer is accepted, then I wouldn't want to move in until the work was done."

"That's logical; it will be a much quicker and less disruptive job if the property is empty, and you won't have the worry of these two being around all the dust and comings and goings either."

"Exactly. Morgan, you really need brushed! Sorry, Connie! I'm lucky in that they both enjoy it. You know, it's done me a favour having this meter installed today; it reminded me to review my list of some of the practical things I need to check at viewings, in case this one doesn't work out. It will still be useful if I do get this place I offered on, for all I won't get inside it again until after missives are concluded. Viewings are such a rush, there's no way I'm going to get all of the fine details; most of the time is spent getting a feel for the place and processing the sensory input in real time, regardless of my best intentions with lists. There are things like taking notice of how many uninterrupted walls there are; the dimensions of the rooms themselves don't take into account the logistics of fitting the bigger items in where they can be put against a wall without obstructing a heater or a doorway. How many wall cupboards there are; if there are more of those than I currently have, I need to consider that some of my things will be too heavy to keep in a wall unit. I'm glad I don't drive; I'd imagine for people with cars, there will be instances where they're moving from somewhere with a garage to having a parking space and needing to find places for anything they stored in their garage, or for things they could safely keep in their car when it was in a garage but wouldn't if it were parked outside. Where to keep anything that needs to be out of direct sunlight, or out of view of the windows if moving to the ground floor from somewhere higher up or not overlooked. Anyway, I'm preaching to the choir here!"

"Not at all; however much experience anyone has of buying properties, every transaction is different and there are things you mentioned there which I wouldn't necessarily have thought of."

Susannah suppressed a yawn. "Sorry about that! Between moving everything around and being hypervigilant having a stranger in here, I'll definitely sleep tonight."

Connie set down her empty cup. "I know you will have an exact place for everything and it's your most personal space, but can I help you with putting anything away?"

"No, thank you; it's really kind of you to offer, but as you say, I know where everything goes. I took photos before I moved anything out, just in case I couldn't work out how to get it all back the same way."

"That's an excellent idea. I know it's not ideal having the meter in the bedroom cupboard. It's the same in one of my other properties; I do recall the tenant there telling me that the display on that little monitor you get with it switches off between midnight and 6am, and the company had told her that if she goes to bed earlier than that she can turn it face down to avoid the lights disturbing her. Of course you work for an energy company so you'll know all this!"

"Yeah, I've spoken to a few customers about that; their old meters were situated in bedrooms long before anything like today's technology was ever imagined. I'm actually looking forward to having that little display to keep an eye on. I glanced at it after I'd switched the kettle on earlier and it had changed from the green light for low current consumption to the orange one for medium. I'll be ironing a couple of things for work later on; my iron heats to the required temperature then tops itself up as required so it would be interesting to see if that is on the cusp of the green and orange, but I guess I'll have to wait until I've moved to check that out, if the display is somewhere I can see when I've got the ironing board set up. It's exciting having all these new things to explore, however trivial. I love seeing how these things work."

"Well, I truly hope that you find a new home that fits well with your enquiring mind. Excuse me, Morgan; I must get going now. Thank you again, Susannah; it really has been a big help to me, that you've accommodated this job today. I'm sure you can't spare much of your leave for anything other than viewings."

"That's OK; I had saved up a few hours of flexi-time by staying later to cover the phones. I appreciate you coming round, Connie; it's always good to catch up and it's been interesting hearing about the history of who has lived here before."

Closing the door behind her landlord, Susannah set about returning her home to familiar normality. She moved the cats' litter tray back to its discreet place in the living room first, minimising the risk of an overtired spillage by doing it before tackling the bedroom.

She had forgotten to offer Connie a rubber glove to brush the cat hair off her trousers.

Another lapse. She really must find a way to focus her head. How much worse was this going to get once she was embroiled in a house purchase and move?

Sighing with exasperation, she set about replacing the items in her bedroom cupboard. The light on the front of her new meter's linked monitor glowed a steady green; she groaned as she remembered the need to do some ironing. Well, there was no way she was going to attempt rushing back and forth to look at the display; as well as her own safety, she would never leave the hot iron unattended with the cats in the room. That experiment would have to wait.

Unless, of course, she set up her phone to film the display while she got on with the ironing. OK, it wouldn't be the most exciting video clip she had ever taken or watched, but it would satisfy her curiosity safely.

Laughing to herself at her restless mind, she set up the phone and started the recording. The task took no more than a few minutes; she switched the iron off and took it into the kitchen to cool down in a corner out of the way. Turning to go and stop the recording, she paused as she caught sight of the two cups and the spoon rest in which the used tea bags lay. Clearing those away now would spare her from an annoying realisation later on when she came to sort out her and the cats' dinners.

Clunk.

Once again, the sudden jarring sensation and noise infuriated her as one of the washed and dried mugs caught the underside of the shelf above where she was putting them away. Her heart sinking, she checked it over; sure enough, she now had two chipped mugs.

"Damn your clattery hands!"

Her burst of anger against herself caught her by surprise. She truly must be overtired. Of course she got frustrated at times when her brain and body wouldn't work as she needed them to, but this degree of reaction was unlike her. That wasn't an expression she had heard before let alone used. Shaking her head, she examined the mugs again to make sure the new chip was the only damage before lifting them to the cupboard again at an exaggeratedly glacial pace.

The recording! Navigating the doorframes with the extra tremulous anxiety which always came in the wake of a glitch, she rushed through to her bedroom and stopped the video. She doubled back and closed the kitchen door to ensure the cats were kept away from the iron until it was cold, then sat down to watch the recording back.

Susannah winced as she watched herself walk out of the bedroom after starting the clip; she had never liked seeing or hearing herself on film. As she had expected, the tiny point of light from the display remained steady green for the first minute or so, then vacillated between green and orange as the ironing would have been underway. She saw herself walk past the bedroom doorway with the iron and reached out to stop the recording, having seen all she needed to see.

As her finger hovered over the Stop button, a shadow appeared and flitted through the open bedroom doorway.

Framed for an instant; indistinct, yet undeniably there. Way too tall to be a cat; in any case, both Annika and Morgan were exactly where they had been when she last left the room. It was a vague shape, but much closer in dimensions to a child.

Immobile with shock, Susannah watched and listened as the recording continued. Muffled sounds tied in with her activity in the kitchen; the subtle swing of the bin lid as she dumped the used tea bags followed by the running of water as she washed the mugs and spoon rest. A brief pause, then the dull thud as the mug caught the shelf. She cringed as she heard the echo of her own frustrated voice; the words inaudible, an unwelcome replay nonetheless.

Something was off. She was well aware of what she had said; it had so taken her by surprise. For all its vehemence, it had been a brief exclamation. The sound of speech on the recording was going on for longer than could be accounted for by her outburst.

It was too distant to make out words or any characteristics of the voice; Susannah strained to hear, to no avail. The inexplicable sound stopped; what looked like the same shadow, more nebulous this time, blurred momentarily back into the doorway before dissipating upwards to the ceiling, frail and formless. Seconds later, she almost jumped out of her skin when her own solid figure appeared in the doorway as she entered the room and walked towards the phone to end the recording.

Susannah had no idea how long she sat staring at the screen as the video clip returned to a still image of the empty bedroom and the ridiculously ordinary view of the display with its green light. She looked up to find both cats staring intently.

"Yes; your dinner. I will be with you in a minute; I need to watch this again first." She pushed a shaking hand through her hair and turned up the volume on her phone, moving the slider to the part which followed her taking the iron to the kitchen.

"…clattery hands!"; she could make out the words at the edge of her hearing, though she admitted her brain was likely filling it in from her already knowing what she had said. She could not begin to account for what came afterwards; it was unclear what she was hearing and what her brain was computing. It was something like "Thoughtless little…", "If you…would try harder", and a final rising to "You just don't care about my nerves!", before the shadow reappeared.

Susannah leaned forward, her heart pounding as adrenalin flooded her with tiny metallic pinpricks. What the *actual heck*? She had definitely not said any of those things beyond her brief snapping about clattery hands, so it had to be her imagination creating that horrible dialogue from some unexplained ambient sound which had fooled her phone's microphone and then her brain into recognising it as human speech. The infernal 'try harder' refrain was as familiar as 'good morning' to every neurodivergent person; her background memories were evidently bothering her more than she realised, which could be put down to the upcoming stress of moving and her concerns about being up to the demands it would place on her functioning. But that last bit about nerves? She could not recall her parents or anyone in her childhood talking like that. It was like something from an earlier age altogether.

An earlier age altogether.

"Good grief"; she addressed her wide-eyed cats. "I think we may have a ghost."

Was this who Freya had heard singing? Could it be that little girl, the granddaughter of the original owners of this flat? Her age would fit the size of the shadow.

Susannah shuddered. "No; I'm getting carried away here"; she took a deep breath and summoned up her most matter of fact, confident voice. "I've had a stressful intrusion into my space when I'm already dealing with buying a house, planning to move, and worrying about Freya. Connie talking about the people who lived here before has made my imagination work overtime. That's all it is. In any case, that little girl never lived here; Connie said she visited on Sundays. If she lived locally enough to be brought here for the day every Sunday, I doubt she would have stayed over. That room was never her bedroom; she probably hardly went in there, if ever. I need to get a grip; get my head in the real world, take care of my hungry cats and get myself ready for work tomorrow."

Setting her phone aside, she marched into the kitchen, both cats miaowing at her heels.

10

Adil's Wisdom

Ochre and brown leaves drifted haphazardly past the windows, turning the narrow strip of grass beneath to a muted harvest festival of shades through butterscotch and caramel all the way up to dark treacle toffee. A subtle invitation of woodsmoke drifted from somewhere beyond the street, casting a spell of fireside stories and that awakening magic of autumn evenings which filled everything with new-term potential. Susannah pushed open the door as Adil Ibrahim emerged from his office to greet her. Sinéad Donnachie, the senior partner, wheeled herself out of her own office as she heard their voices; both solicitors were smiling broadly.

"It's good to see you, Susannah; please come through"; Adil gestured towards his small room in the shade of the trees from which the leaves continued to flutter their leisurely way to earth. "Can I get you a cup of tea or coffee?"

"Tea, please; milk, no sugar."

"Sinéad?"

"Yes please, since you're making one. Coffee for me. I need to grab a couple of folders"; she efficiently manoeuvred her wheelchair across to the cabinets which lined the back wall, unlocking one with a key from the flexible chain attached to her wrist. The overhead light caught an iridescent glint from the pins holding her dark hair immaculately in place, piled on top of her head. Chunky opal rings matched their sheen as Sinéad's practiced fingers flicked through the reams of files. "You go on through, Susannah; I know Adil has an update for you."

Adil's tidy desk held a variety of executive stim toys; magnetic metal filings which could be sculpted into shapes, a Zen garden, a stress ball in the form of a deep burgundy plush velvet pumpkin. Susannah itched to pick it up; both politeness and wariness of its proximity to a crystal-handled letter opener near the edge of the desk prevented her. She dragged her eyes away from it, studying the flow of the polished grain of the work surface instead. She moved the coaster which was nearest to her seat in preparation so that it was safely further inland as Adil came in with their drinks.

"Here you go. I won't keep you in suspense while I take Sinéad hers; I'm happy to tell you that your offer for the flat on Crieff Gardens has been accepted. I got the call from the seller's solicitor this afternoon, which was excellent timing when you were coming in for a general chat anyway. This means that we can renegotiate if necessary based on the more detailed electrician's report; at this stage, both you and the seller are free to change your minds as there is no legal contract in place. However, the estate agent will not be offering any further viewings to other people and any search results which include the property will show it as sold subject to contract. Congratulations! I will give you a few minutes to let that sink in, then you can ask me any questions."

Susannah's tea cooled untouched on the desk as her shaking hands gripped the sides of the chair. A long forgotten memory of an old-fashioned viewer her grandparents had owned, with tiny slides on a disc which slotted in at the side and a handle clicked them in turn onto the magnified screen at the end of what looked like a long tunnel from the eyepiece, sprang to life as a chaotic sequence of visualised scenes clicked through her mind. Her dreams of the flat as her home interspersed with the work it would take to get there; the changes which were suddenly more corporeal; the things which could go wrong. Freya's face when given the news. The reality of the likely, albeit temporary, long commute. Would the cats settle? How was she supposed to navigate the next stage, when she would have to think about the property a lot as she organised practicalities yet could not allow herself to get too attached in case it all fell through?

A particularly large maple leaf the colour of Adil's velvet pumpkin ornament parachuted on its natural descent past the window. It tilted and pirouetted on a gust of wind, letting itself take whatever diversions it must on its way to the ground to which it had been born to return. Susannah was briefly overcome by a surprise rush of emotion at having been here to witness its life transition intersecting with her own. She calmed her racing thoughts with a cautious gulp of tea.

"So, how are you feeling? Big moment for you, yes?" Adil's brown eyes radiated warmth and genuine happiness for her.

"Where did you get that pumpkin?"; she noted the surprise which Adil quickly and professionally tamped down. "I mean, that's not my only question or the most important one, but it's the one I'm most likely to forget if I don't ask it immediately!"

"Ah, my niece got it for me. I'm always a little bit sad when I put it away at the end of the season"; he picked it up and handed it to Susannah. She held it reverently, grounded by the sensation of her fingertips brushing over and against the nap of the material; grateful once again for Adil's instincts.

"Thank you. So I understand about there not being a contract yet, and I know that gazumping is rare in Scotland, but how likely is it that this will work out and I won't lose the flat now?"

"Well, I would love to be able to give you the definitive answer you want, but what I will say is that you are in a stronger position because you're a cash buyer, not in a chain and neither is the seller since it isn't their own residence. Because we're going for this electrical survey, there is more likelihood of you pulling out than the seller."

"I understand that, thank you. I think the main question I have at this point is, what order do things happen in now? I'm struggling to pull that together from all the thoughts whirling around in my head."

"Entirely natural, and it's a good question. First of all, we will need to do the formal process to register you as a client; there's a secure website where you will upload scanned copies of your passport and evidence of where your funds have come from. Everyone has to do that because of mandatory money laundering checks. Then you will need to get this electrical report; you would go about that in the same way you would choose a trader for anything you needed doing. Research traders in the relevant area; look on Trusted Trader sites, check their qualifications and reviews, make sure they don't ask for payment up front, all the standard due diligence. They will get the keys from the estate agent, so you would need to inform them and keep me in the loop too. Once you have the report, it's up to you whether we go ahead with the offer as it stands, renegotiate, or pull out. There will always be some unknowns; no work can be carried out from our side until you own the property and you need to bear in mind that if the seller gets work done, they have less interest in the long term result than you do and may rush through a lower quality, minimal job. We also need to wait until contract exchange before we get the deeds and confirm exact boundaries, for instance which parts of the garden belong to the flat, which are shared and which belong to other flats, and if there is any right of way across the subject flat's property for instance to put bins out. Some of that information is in the property questionnaire which the seller filled in to accompany the home report, but the deeds confirm it. Once we have finalised the offer, the process of conveyancing, getting the exchange of missives in place, is handled by us and the seller's solicitor; you don't have to do anything there. We then get to the point where you pay your deposit, or in your case the full payment, and you will get the keys. I can put this together in an email for you if you would find that useful."

"Yes, please! I know I should be taking notes, but I need all my focus to process it in real time and I know fine well not all of it will stick."

"That's no problem at all. I know this is all new to you and please don't worry about asking any questions you need to."

"That honestly means a lot, Adil. I was worried that I'd look like an airhead"; Susannah took a deep breath, her fingertips digging into the soothing sensory plush of the ornament she clutched on her lap. "I'm dyspraxic, you see; as a neurodivergent woman I'm always aware that I have a lot to prove. I am truly thankful that you make me feel safe to ask questions without it having to mean that I'm presumed incompetent; not fit to make my own decisions, completely lacking in common sense and so on. I need a bit of extra time with complicated instructions and I need things to be clear, which can make some people think I need to be spoken to like a small child and given no credit whatsoever as an autonomous adult."

"Believe me, Susannah, I understand more than you might think. I appreciate you trusting me with the fact you are dyspraxic; I respect the courage it must take for you to disclose that in professional interactions. I can share with you that I am dyslexic. I have been fortunate enough to encounter some highly supportive mentors in my life; Sinéad has been an absolute star, and although I struggled at primary school, I will always remember the local librarian who sat with me and helped me to discover and develop my own best ways to learn. She was a very special woman. I know you grew up here, so you may remember her. Edie Mackay."

"Edie! She was so ahead of her time. She helped me too, Adil. I think I remember seeing her sitting with you, now you mention it. I know you were in the same year as my sister, Selina."

"Of course! I remember Selina. How is she keeping?"

"She's well, thank you. She lives in Glasgow; she and her wife have a place in the West End. They both work on the railway; Selina as a guard, Phoebe as a driver."

"That is wonderful to hear. Do please pass on my regards."

"I will, and I'm so happy that you have found the supportive environment you deserve. It makes a huge difference being able to work with someone who has similar lived experience. Thank you for trusting me too."

Susannah gave the velvet pumpkin one last gentle squeeze before placing it neatly in the middle of Adil's desk. She drained the last of her tea and gathered herself to leave. As she shook Adil's dry, warm hand, she glanced over his shoulder at the window; the sky, deepened now to dusk behind a layer of altostratus cloud, turned the changing trees to silhouettes. Her solicitor had one remaining piece of advice to impart.

"There will be times coming up when all of this feels overwhelming. You are not alone in that and it's not a reflection on you or your neurotype. It's important that you don't lose sight of the fact that this is a joyous and positive event for you; hold space for happy and excited feelings amid the demands on your time and energy. You will want to notice and remember those moments and feelings; they will become part of your history and highly significant to how you want to look back on this time in your life."

The streetlights had come on, picking out colour once more from the ground beneath them. The maple leaf which had fallen as Susannah processed the news lay prominently in a strawberry-shortcake pool of light; she picked it up, caressing its smooth, cold surface with its edges beginning to curl. She walked dreamlike through the town she was one major step closer to leaving for the second time; the mundane streets alive with details which it was somehow more important to store in her memory. The angles of the roads; the tiny facets of everyday stone and brick that caught the light; the shape of the sky between buildings. The leaf in her hand preserved the moments in the stilling of its veins.

The light on the corner was shining its intended ambient peach this time. As Susannah passed, it possibly flickered aqua in the open doorway of an instant; too brief a glance off the edge of her senses to definitively cross the border from imagination.

Already focused on the newly finite routine of her flat; pressing the leaf between two books, she fed Annika and Morgan before sitting down with a generous brandy. This news needed to be processed before she could think about telling anyone.

A carton of seasonal soup heating in the microwave made the air vibrant with the sweetness of carrot and the spicy warmth of parsnip as Susannah made herself surrender to the normal work-in-the-morning routine of a weekday evening.

11

Building Hopes

One of the sorting puzzle games which Susannah used on her tablet to relax and exercise her mind had a feature where the board could be turned by dragging a finger around the screen; it was useful when a stack of tiles was obscuring the target number of points on a nearby space. Stepping off the bus at the busy stop on South Street, a similar perspective shift on Perth unfolded in multiple dimensions. Everything was in the same place, but she was looking at it now in terms of where everything was relative to Crieff Gardens rather than to the arrival and departure points to which she was accustomed. Now that her offer had been accepted, she felt more entitled to indulge this new stirring of home; constantly reminding herself not to take anything for granted until missives were safely concluded was becoming mentally draining in itself. She had to be due a few hours off from that. She would keep away from the area of the property itself for the time being, but she drew the line at depriving herself of the anticipation with which this stage should be brimming as Adil had said. Weaving her path through the crowds on the busy thoroughfare, she reflected upon her good fortune at having found a solicitor who thought and took time to remind her of the rare and precious texture of this phase.

The few tables free at this time on a Saturday were all the exposed middle ones; she set her mind to manage and make the most of it for an undemanding light lunch. She found one which afforded her a view of the River Tay through the ample windows of the Capital Asset despite the bustling distance from where she sat, conscientiously checked in all directions before pulling out the chair and took out her phone to order on the app before tucking her bag in under the table, ensuring that the strap was safely out of the way of her own and any passing feet.

A large family group evidently celebrating a milestone birthday had pushed two tables together nearby; two of them, who looked like brothers and were wearing the same tartan, got up to go to the bar. Seeing their kilts swishing past the tightly packed furniture got Susannah reflecting on the ceremonial orderliness and flow of tartan design. It resembled a mind map of that structure she needed to apply to her decision-making during this chaotic time. The base colour was the goal; her future once she was settled. Dark practical shades crisscrossed in formation with the lighter, more creative hues, echoing the work needed to get there. The legal and technical aspects, surveys, budgeting, packing and so on intersected with the more enjoyable side of the work; planning, measuring and visualising then decorating and setting everything up in its new order. Fine lines of feelings, from instinctive reactions at viewings to the pure excitement of completion brought the final touches to the overall picture; the organisation and proportions the keys to making it all work. Those thin, brighter lines conveyed a particularly pertinent reminder; they formed such a distinctive aspect of the tartan, which would look entirely different without them, but it was vital to the overall pattern that they were kept minimal and not allowed to overpower the interplay of the main colours. She planned to buy a book on basic home maintenance from Mackenzie Books on the High Street; she made a mental note to add a notebook with a tartan cover if they had one.

"Give me a shout if you would like any help"; the sales assistant smiled from a refreshingly non-intrusive distance. Susannah had never seen such a deep shade of blue hair before; it was darker than any of the royal or electric shades she had seen, but distinctly blue rather than blue-black.

"Thanks; I'm terrible for taking ages to choose." The door burst open to admit a noisy group of youths surfing in on a wave of cold air; a tall, broad-shouldered blond man who looked as though he was probably the manager emerged from a corridor leading off the main shop floor, keeping a benign but keen watch on the group. Susannah turned back to the assistant with the blue hair. "My friend is moving into her first bought home"; she adjusted the facts mindful of not advertising herself to an unknown audience as alone and inexperienced when she was going to be moving into this immediate area. "She's always had a landlord up to now. I know you can get online tutorials for a lot of things now but there's something solid and reassuring about a book, so I want to get a basic manual as much for peace of mind as for actual instruction."

The assistant, whose name badge read 'Bethany', nodded understandingly. "That's a lovely thoughtful gift; I'm sure your friend will be delighted. If you'd like a recommendation, I'd be happy to suggest one; otherwise, do feel free to take your time and see what speaks to you for her. I can take that notebook to the till for you in the meantime if you wish so your hands are free to get a better look at any of the books?"

Susannah beamed gratefully; she had been internally chastising herself for not having thought of that when she picked up the glossy notebook which caught her eye on the display near the door. She handed it to Bethany, who duly took it to place behind the counter. The group of youths had left by the time she went over with her chosen book to pay; feeling slightly uncomfortable about having lied to this genuine woman, she looked around the now-quiet shop before explaining that she was the one moving and why she had tweaked the truth.

"No worries at all; I completely understand. It was a wise precaution. I wouldn't count it as a fib in the circumstances; I'd have done the same. So are you moving far?"

"From Kirkbrigg. I've had an offer accepted and now it's the time for getting surveys done; I know there's some electrical work needed, but it's within the bounds of what's feasible."

"Congratulations! Exciting times, then"; Bethany handed over the book and notebook after Susannah paid and put her card safely away. "Do you know Perth well?"

"The centre of it, certainly. I love a shopping trip and there are quite a few nice relaxed pubs too; most of all, I love the scope for walks which are scenic and not demanding. Especially the Inches and the gardens across the river. Speaking of shops, I don't want to jinx myself by doing this before the formalities are complete but I'm looking forward to going to Bonnie Moon Crystals on South Street for some sun catchers, then to George Street for Provender Brown and the one further along; Malts And Spirits. I will be wanting a bottle of something special for my new home!"

"Oh; Malts and Spirits have moved premises. They're on St John Street now, near the new museum."

"Thanks; I didn't realise that, they were quite far along George Street and I haven't been to that end on my last few visits."

"Well, good luck, and we have a quiet sensory reading room available if you're in town and need a bit of breathing space when things get hectic." Bethany pointed along the corridor from which her colleague had emerged to watch the rowdy group; he was tidying a nearby display and smiled over at Bethany. "That's Magnus, my boss. He was such a massive help setting up the sensory room."

"Which was Bethany's idea!", the manager chimed in from where he was busy checking that the books were in the correct order on the shelves. "It's highly popular with a lot of our regular customers; some have become regular customers because of it."

Bethany's features softened with a look which suggested she was thinking of some of those people whom she knew and cared about deeply. A subtle, soul-deep recognition stirred in Susannah as she saw these two staff members through the lens of her ever-present responsiveness to neuroaffirming inclusivity; that rare and priceless kind which was pervasive, not performative.

Yes; she was going to thrive in the Fair City.

12

Lorna's Light

Cold air swirled in from the stairwell, making Susannah shiver as she opened the door. Freya wrapped her arms across her chest as she felt it too despite her coat and scarf.

They both heard it; the faint singing of a little girl, too distant to make out words or a melody but distinctly there.

"It's got to be coming from one of the flats; it's too muffled to be out in the stair"; Susannah smiled fondly. "She sounds happy, whoever she is. Bless her."

Freya nodded. "Let's hope she gets to stay that way for a few years yet. I won't hang around; I'll let you get your door shut and keep the heat in. Thanks for another Sunday session; catch you at work tomorrow."

Susannah closed and locked her door, sighing as she walked back through to her lounge, stroking Annika who had awoken and stretched out with a silent miaow as she entered the room.

"I wish your Auntie Freya could find peace in her soul", she told the cat, who headbutted her hand understandingly and started to purr. Their gratitude ritual had quickly been superseded by Freya's indignation over her mother's response when she had railed against a mild criticism from a church friend of Frieda's. Freya had previously helped this friend out with a flyer for a charity event she was organising, using her knowledge of desktop publishing to design it for her. 'After all the time and effort I put into that leaflet for her!', Freya had said, though the criticism had been completely unrelated to that project. Frieda had shot her down abruptly, accusing Freya of having self-serving motives and only helping people in order to have a hold over them. Susannah did not believe for a second that this was her sole motive, but Freya had taken it to heart. She had spent much of their Sunday time together second-guessing every good thing she had done, torturing herself that she had imagined every altruistic thought she had. Susannah had strongly discouraged her from continuing to look up articles about narcissism of the 'ten signs this applies to you' variety as they popped up on her social media feeds, concerned that those were often unscientific clickbait and far too polarised, then had to convince Freya that this was not a further attack on her. It saddened her greatly that Freya could not conceive of anyone liking her for herself without her having to earn or buy it. This was what came of being steeped from her earliest years in toxic emotion soup from the adult bones of a marriage. Was it any wonder that it resulted in Freya seeing anything which earned her gratitude and praise as currency to obtain the connections she craved? She had grown up believing that happiness lay above her league. 'Happiness' not being the unrealistic, rose-tinted view which damaged people were often accused of having of relationships; it entailed reaching a level of feeling mentally well enough and having sufficient spare energy to find life manageable. It took a hell of a lot of hard work to break these patterns; it called for compassion and allowances when the person was going to be least receptive to deserving them. Especially in a world where people seemed increasingly incapable of taking nuance on board. Everyone was either toxic or a saint. No good, caring and genuine person ever stepped out of line or developed bad habits. Decades-old, ingrained patterns like Freya's mismanagement of her extreme rejection sensitivity had to be broken in a single round of mistake and correction otherwise the person was a write-off and directly equivalent to the worst types of criminal. Self-righteous memes and the Internet had an awful lot to answer for when not looked at with an open, questioning mind and balanced with offline interactions and interests.

"I wouldn't be without it", she mused aloud to the cats, "but I do feel we all need to make sure we don't lose touch with a smaller, simpler offline world."

She set aside her phone, ate her lunch then played with the cats for a while, revelling in their ongoing kitten-like enthusiasm for chasing toys and laser points. As the late afternoon slump descended with the beginnings of dusk, she went to make some notes of things she had thought of for her move; her new notebook was on the old dressing table in the small bedroom where she had left it after unpacking her shopping bag yesterday.

Closing the book, she held the underside edge of the panelled front of the table as she turned on the chair. She swore as her knee bashed painfully against the table leg, reflexively pushing backwards.

The panel came away with her as she instinctively gripped it for balance, revealing itself to be the front of an additional drawer, not merely decorative as she had thought. How had it not been discovered when she and Julian moved the table into this room? She surmised that it had been stiff from lack of use until the impact of her knee jolted the entire piece. Her proprioception letting her down had proven useful for once. At first she thought that the drawer was empty except for an old-fashioned paper liner; as she looked more closely, she saw the indentations of handwriting on the other side. Intrigued, she pulled it out and turned it over; it appeared to be a child's homework essay. She began to read.

'Lorna's Light. By M M Renfield.

My thing that I will always remember about Sundays is Lorna's light. It stands at the end of the street outside her house. When we go to my grandmother's flat on a Sunday I play out with all my friends there. My mother always says that I must never go past Lorna's light because the main road is busy and it is not safe. She tells me that every

Sunday because she thinks I will forget but I won't. It looks the same as all of the other lights on the street but it looks different as well because it is on its own at the end not tucked in next to the houses. I sometimes look at it and imagine it has special powers and if I did go past it I would have a magic adventure like ordinary people sometimes do in stories. I know that I wouldn't though. All that would happen is I would get into a lot of trouble. I like Lorna's light because it is always there and never gives me a fright and I know I won't go past it by accident and get into trouble. I like how it is always there watching over me and my friends. I think it will watch over me forever.'

Tears sprang to Susannah's eyes as she read the heartfelt words; the innocence of them underscored by the obvious people-pleasing fears of an earnest child. The essay had been marked; red ink dotted the page with corrections of punctuation, flagging up repetition, run-on sentences and fine points of grammar, but it was the teacher's last comment that seared her soul with its harshness.

'Write this out again neatly, Mary! Slapdash handwriting. Must do better.'

Mary. Was this the little girl whose voice both she and Freya had heard in snatches of song; whose shadow had found its way from the past onto her impromptu recording of her Realtime meter's display monitor? The content of the essay certainly implied that she was the Airds' granddaughter whom Connie had mentioned. Mary Renfield. It gave Susannah a warm feeling to put a name to her. 'Lorna's light', too; that had to be the one she could see from her bedroom. However hit and miss its functioning was these days, the thought of the comforting consistency it had brought to one small part of Mary Renfield's life brought a wave of thankfulness.

Mary clearly hadn't had the kindest and most encouraging of teachers either! She shook her head as she looked again at the blunt critique bleeding its merciless red ink, raw on the decades-old page. She could understand the teacher commenting on the handwriting; she had needed to squint to make out one or two of the words herself, but where was the positive to balance it out when this child had shared something so personal and frankly vulnerable? It hurt Susannah's heart to think how Mary must have felt when her work was slammed down in front of her with that feedback; how it must have jangled with her fears of getting into trouble in a world which seemed to have kept catching her out despite her best efforts.

Her bumped knee, which would no doubt soon be sporting the visual rebuke of a bruise, throbbed as she stood up from the chair. She placed the page tenderly, reverently back in the drawer and softly slid it closed.

13

Conduits

"It's more or less what we expected, to be fair"; Susannah scrolled through the electrician's report again on her tablet, trying to make sense of the technical terminology as it competed with the stark figures and added punch of 'plus VAT' for processing space in her brain. "Over two thousand, and some of the defects shouldn't have been there at all given that the current owner is a landlord, which to me certainly justifies revising the offer. I hate to do it because I don't want to lose this house, but I have to think of the added costs; for instance living here and paying rent for a bit longer while the work is done, since that can't start until it's my property to authorise."

"You're absolutely correct"; Adil's voice was rich with sympathy. "Bear in mind too that whoever buys the property will have these issues to deal with, and now that they're known and confirmed by a specialist, they would have to be declared and accounted for in the price if the seller were to list it again. They would have all the uncertainty as well as having to wait longer for it all to be finalised."

"That's true. I don't think it's fair to deduct the entire amount; I'd be getting multiple quotes for any actual work so it may not end up being as much as that, and I did make my offer knowing from the home report that there was likely to be some work needed. However, given the additional costs, I think we should revise the offer down by one and a half thousand. I'll be staying on here for longer, travelling to give people access and probably some replastering and redecorating over and above what I expected and of course there will be an addition to my legal bill for this extra step. That's not a dig; I don't begrudge you, these things have to be done! I'll instruct you in an email so that we have it all on record."

"Yes, please do that; I agree that's reasonable. I'm sorry this is a further complication for you; I know the wait to hear back will be an anxious time, but remember it would be a gamble and a bigger upheaval for the seller if they pulled out because of this, and their solicitor will guide them accordingly."

"Thanks, Adil."

Susannah ended the call and drafted her formal request to him to submit the revised offer. Hitting 'Send' on the email felt as viscerally huge as pushing a boulder off a cliff; she sat back, her muscles weak from the passing adrenalin spike. She forced herself to unclench her jaw, moving it from side to side to reconnect with how it felt in a relaxed state.

She wandered through to her bedroom, seeking a scrap of solace in the better view. Lorna's light appeared to be in a particularly animated phase this evening; as she looked, it flickered from peach to aqua, then to a strangely opalescent half in half, then back to aqua, then peach again. It was, she smiled wryly to herself, a pretty good show to make up for having to wait longer for her front row seat watching those colours in their seasonal tour of the sky.

The earthy, filling warmth of a baked sweet potato followed by the memory-blanket comfort of hot chocolate soothed her enough to allow her to anticipate sleep. Tucking the duvet up around the back of her neck and under her chin, Susannah mentally told herself that she had done all that was within her control and made the wisest judgement call. Tomorrow would have to take care of…

She was asleep before she could finish the thought.

Her bedroom looked different. The dressing table and chair were back, but there was no bed; it was set out more like a sitting room, with a couple of worn armchairs at right angles to a coffee table next to the window. Two figures stood in the room; a woman in the doorway looked angrily at a young girl, who clutched a patchwork-patterned bag, her head down. Susannah was overcome by an odd sensation of both being and watching the child as the adult - yes, the little girl's mother - spoke sharply ordering her to hurry up and take anything left in the room that belonged to her. Two key aspects of the situation became clear as Susannah's perspective absorbed this snapshot from another lifetime; the adult and child were regular visitors leaving for the final time, and the child was in disgrace. It seemed to be for a transgression which had happened elsewhere but was serious enough in the mother's view to justify holding back compassion at a time of great sadness and loss.

Susannah's heart lurched with horror. What could this little girl, in whom she sensed a heartbroken, fearful longing for kindness and not the slightest trace of so much as trivial mischief, have done to cause a parent to bear her such malice?

The girl turned; darted nervously across the room, taking a book from the coffee table and a hairbrush from the dressing table. As she turned to scurry back to her waiting mother, her foot caught the edge of a rug; the watching part of Susannah instinctively reached out to catch her. For a moment, she felt the rough material of the child's coat; she willed every bit of comfort she could muster to flow through her hand and through time, aware of being an external observer here in more ways than one.

"Why can't you learn to watch your step, you clumsy little madam? This is why you're always in trouble! It's no use you looking so miserable; tears won't wash with me. It's your own silly fault that you get told off so much; it's up to you to be responsible and take more care. Nobody can put that right except you. Now, *hurry up*."

The hard-eyed mother turned abruptly and stalked away from the door; Susannah fought to make her frozen limbs move to reach and try to console the devastated child but her straining arms found her own disarrayed bedding as she awoke, staring in shock around her once again familiar bedroom as the vivid dream faded. A shadow receded at the edge of her peripheral vision; some inner border of her hearing in a realm of her brain where time was most fluid caught an echo of a fading voice. Its frantic words called out across the shifting boundaries of the night:

"I swear, I didn't mean to break the minister's vase!"

Susannah sat up in bed, goosebumps entirely unrelated to the chilly present-day air prickling her skin. Was the little girl in her dream Mary Renfield? Had she witnessed an episode so traumatic that it had haunted her for the rest of her life?

Her heart plummeted as the implications hit home. The child-sized shadows on the video clip of her meter display. The singing Freya heard. How much longer had Mary lived? The essay she had found in the drawer was decades old, not centuries. Mary was not from a time when children routinely died.

A further realisation gut-punched her, making her groan aloud. If the scenario she had dreamed was a real event from the past, had that essay been left behind in the harangued little girl's haste to obey her mother and keep up with whatever big change was the reason she would not be seeing the room again, and had that caused her additional trouble?

It was all beginning to seem achingly familiar. She had suspected it from the half-deciphered snatches of long ago speech on the recording; now, she was sure of it. The teacher's rebuke about Mary's messy handwriting. The awkward movements and tripping up. The reference to regular 'clumsiness' and the horror of an unspeakably mortifying breakage incident.

Oh, Mary. Nobody knew.

Nobody had the proper facts to understand and support this little girl. What happened to her?

Wiping her eyes, Susannah tried her best to settle back down. She couldn't help the past, but she could give herself the best chance she could of being alert and keeping her wits about her at work. It was a dream; her imagination making up scenarios from having found the essay after whatever glitches had caused her brain to ascribe words to the ambient noise of the recording, which was itself influenced by her conversation with her landlord about the history of the flat, in which she was genuinely interested. What with all that plus the stress of buying a house and moving, then the latest setback in the form of the electrical report, was it any wonder her mind was playing tricks on her?

Being honest with herself she was far from convinced that this theory, however sensible, explained everything. *The minister's vase*? Where would *that* detail have come from? There was no comparable incident in her own childhood.

She did, though, have to work in that office around those cliques and navigate her fragile truce with Freya tomorrow, with all the mental energy that asked of her. Regulating her breathing, she determinedly set her mind to sleep.

14

Mary

As usual, Candice, Tanya and Maya were in a huddle giggling about something which they clearly didn't intend to share with Susannah as she returned from her lunch break. Ignoring the pointed social coughs as she passed their desks, she opened the next complicated case file and began her calculations.

Morven appeared at her side, startling her slightly as she focused intently on the screeds of figures. "Good work on the Vaughan case, Susannah; you picked up a pattern to the anomalous readings that Technical Support had missed. That one was well on the way to becoming a serious complaint with their MSP involved, so well done and thank you."

Susannah nodded discreetly, hoping that her tight smile conveyed the correct sentiments to her supervisor; that she dare not show too much reaction in front of the ravenous clique. As it was, Candice had let out a facetious "Ooh!", which had not escaped Morven's notice as she cast her an angry look which had Candice abruptly finding her own computer screen utterly fascinating. Susannah looked across the central aisle of the room at the cluster of desks occupied by Freya's team. Her friend's platinum blonde head was bent forwards in intense concentration, holding her headset firmly in place as Lisa and Donna chatted close by her desk. Lexy nudged Chanelle, imitating Freya's hunched posture and exaggeratedly clutching her head. Seething, Susannah was grimly thankful that this time

Freya was unaware of the mockery as she struggled to hear her customer over the inconsiderately loud conversation.

Where was Valerie? Or Max, much as she could see a down side in terms of the false hope it would give Freya if he were to come to her rescue?

What the hell was so amusing about it anyway, that someone trying to work at her job was doing her utmost to block out ambient sound in order to listen on the phone? She wasn't pulling faces or making gestures; simply positioning herself to hear better, her back to them in her seat at her desk as normal. *Why was that funny?*

Her thoughts returned to Mary Renfield; to the harsh red slashes of criticism about her handwriting, scarring and disregarding the content of the essay into which she had clearly put so much thought and effort. Susannah had always hated 'news' type assignments at school; having to write about her family and what they had been doing in their holidays had felt intrusive, a conflict of boundaries as though her teachers and classmates were given access to her diary. She had felt deeply uncomfortable with those two worlds being forced to overlap. Had Mary felt the same, and how much more hurtful did that make the dismissive negativity of the comments?

The world appeared to run on some kind of feeding frenzy involving picking out and punishing those deemed by its arcane sorting system to be misfits. It was senseless, destructive, and Susannah was done with it. She couldn't do anything about Mary Renfield's lonely anguish all those years ago; to be fair, she had little factual knowledge and was quite possibly projecting some of it. This layered tableau of hostility where thoughtlessness intersected with outright bullying playing out directly in front of her, though, was undeniably real and she wasn't about to sit by and put up with it.

Heart pounding, blood rushing to her head, she saved her work and logged out of her computer.

She was halfway across the aisle when Valerie returned from the small meeting room with a smiling Gregor, who was on a phased return following his illness. Lexy and Chanelle were instantly model employees; Susannah could practically see haloes set up as rapidly and definitively as a "Closed" sign on a Friday afternoon. Donna and Lisa's hushed tones belied Freya's unchanged huddle over her telephone call; her stress levels too heightened to register that the background noise level had dropped.

Every element of the scenario so individually trivial; melted away like the first dusting of snow before the earth has sunk into the cold of winter, and as difficult to capture or record. How many years upon years of this transient downward drift had to build consistently before it started to get noticed; to crunch underfoot and affect the rest of the fabric of life.

Susannah turned quickly, grabbing the edge of her desk as her feet caught up with the rapid shift in her centre of gravity.

"Watch, now!", scolded a smirking Maya who of course had to look up exactly then. Timing could always be relied upon to join the cosmic confluence of othering forces.

Susannah pretended to check the sole of her shoe and walked towards the toilets, as though that was where she had been intending to go all along. Her heart rate elevated, she wiped sweat from her palms as she contemplated the trouble she could have gotten herself into; it would most likely have made things worse for Freya too. The two of them *must* put their heads together and figure out a plan to give her some hope of getting out of here.

Her usual 4pm home time came around; Freya tentatively approached her as she put her card in the clocking out machine.

"Um, Suze? I was talking to my mum about you finding that little girl's essay and she actually knows a bit about her; Mary Renfield, and about her grandparents having lived there. She used to work with someone whose mother was very friendly with the 'Lorna' Mary mentioned, and who used to talk about having played outside with Mary and a few other local kids. She hadn't realised it was your flat Mary's grandparents lived in until I told her about what you found. Mum says you'd be welcome to come round after work and she can tell you a bit more. You could stay for dinner if you like?"

"That would be lovely! Though I can't stay too long; I was expecting to be going home at my usual time so I haven't arranged anything for feeding the cats. Would it be OK for me to come round just for a cup of tea?"

"Of course; I understand, and so will Mum. In fact there may be a bottle of Raasay gin on the go."

"That's my favourite gin! The fresh orangey sweetness of it; it's a winner."

"Sounds like a plan then!"

The two of them walked the short distance to the Lingard home. "There are a couple of good independent shops selling spirits in Perth; I wonder if they have the Raasay gin", mused Susannah. "They were both on George Street but now I think about it, Bethany said one of them had recently moved to bigger premises on St John Street."

"Who's *Bethany*?"

"Oh! Sorry, I didn't get around to telling you; that's the woman who served me when I bought a book about basic home maintenance. She was really helpful; we got chatting when I was dithering over which book to choose and she said I'd be welcome to pop in and use their quiet sensory reading room if I needed a breathing space during the move."

Freya made a noncommittal noise. She was quiet for the rest of the way; a growing distance returning as inexorably as the coming October dusk.

Frieda's 'good' gin glasses lay neatly untouched in their tidy ranks in the cabinet, to Susannah's relief; she was grateful that all three of them would be drinking out of the chunky, cheery tumblers which looked as though they were having one final outing before hibernation. Multicoloured bubbles decorated the pedestrian glassware, decreasing in size the further they were from the base; Susannah discreetly rubbed her thumb over the pleasingly textured round spots as the gin and tonic fizzed in time with her anticipation of finding out more about Mary Renfield's life.

"You know, it occurs to me now; a lot of the reason gin is so lively and refreshing is that it resonates in five senses. The effervescence of it can be seen, heard, felt, smelt and tasted in more individual detail than most drinks, and it's such a clean sensory profile." She raised her glass, tapping it with utmost caution against Freya's and then her mother's. "Thank you so much, Frieda; I appreciate you inviting me."

Frieda smiled as they settled on her sumptuous cream leather three-piece suite; Susannah mentally added the fact they weren't drinking black coffee or red wine to her next Grounds for Gratitude list as she recoiled in horror from the thought, firmly warning herself off the treacherous distraction of entertaining it.

"I was fascinated to hear about this homework you found, Susannah. Lorna Valenti was a good friend of my colleague Dorothy Struan's mother, as Freya might have told you. I'm going back a long way here; Dorothy moved away in the early eighties. I remember her saying that she, Lorna's daughter Teresa and a few other local children including Mary Renfield used to play on the driveway leading to your flats. There were fewer cars around then, but it makes sense that the streetlamp outside Lorna's house would have been a strict boundary. Those lights have changed a few times over the years but the posts are still the original ones so it's no wonder they're becoming a bit hit and miss. Anyway, it was Mary's grandmother Lottie Aird who lived in your flat; her husband died some years before, so Dorothy wouldn't remember him but Lottie was also very friendly with Lorna and Effie; that was Dorothy's mother. Mary and her mother were there every Sunday without fail. Mary was a happy little thing while Lottie was alive; always excited to be at her granny's. Lottie was devoted to her." Frieda smiled with a mother's gentle nostalgia. "Merry Mary; that's what Dorothy said they often called her. The girl loved singing, and she said her middle name was some family surname which could be shortened to 'Merry'. Merriman, I think it was. Lottie would call her granddaughter 'my wee Merry Mary', so she and Teresa were Merry and Terry. We had our own versions of your Internet handles in those days, you know!"

Susannah and Freya both laughed, eager to hear more; Frieda's face became more serious.

"Now, Mary's mother Esther, she was a different kettle of fish. She lost her husband young and raised Mary on her own; I don't think their relationship was an easy one. Mary was..." Frieda looked uncharacteristically ill at ease, fiddling with the gold cross necklace at her throat and setting down her drink. "I don't want to choose the wrong words here, but Mary had a tendency to be accident-prone. Dorothy remembered hearing of Lorna describing how Esther would scold the child; she never raised a hand to her, but she had great difficulty coping with Mary making a noise when she knocked things over or bumped them. 'Clattery hands', she used to say; 'your clattery hands', and 'my poor nerves'. Esther suffered terribly with nerves; I think today she would be diagnosed with an anxiety disorder. Susannah, I am sorry; have I gone wrong with my terminology here?"

Frieda's concern was genuine, but she was mistaken about the reason for Susannah's shocked expression.

"No, Frieda; not at all. It's just that I've heard that expression before; 'clattery hands'. I didn't expect to hear it in a different context; it feels so specific. I think one of my teachers might have said it." She was not quite ready to discuss with Frieda, or Freya, the details of what her phone had recorded or her own unaccountable impulse to chastise herself with that phrase. "Esther sounds very strict, though I'm sure she was struggling, especially with Mary's father dying young. The grandmother, though, Lottie; she must have been a strong support?"

"She was; I got the impression she and Esther clashed a lot over Esther being so hard on Mary. Esther seems to have been a cold person; not violent, but prickly and closed off, and as you say very strict with her daughter. Mary had everything she needed in terms of food, shelter, education; I'm not saying she wasn't loved or looked after by her mother, but it was her grandmother who gave her the affection she needed."

"It's good that she was close by. So, did Mary keep in contact with Dorothy?" Susannah fought to keep her voice neutral, dreading the answer.

"I don't believe so, though I didn't know Dorothy that well outside of work; she was quite a few years older than me. I didn't get the impression there was ongoing contact. Lottie died when Mary was young, and Esther moved away with her soon after. I can't imagine what that time must have been like for the poor girl." Frieda shivered, her hand going to her necklace again. "She became withdrawn; her relationship with her mother deteriorated further. I mentioned that Mary was accident-prone. There was an incident, I believe, after Lottie died; Esther knew the minister well and had gone to visit him at home to discuss something to do with the funeral service. Mary would have been on her best behaviour, I've no doubt about that, but the minister had an old dog, completely deaf, who used to lie in the hallway next to the front door. A massive, shaggy creature; a deerhound I think, some large breed like that. The way Dorothy told it, Mary had been told over and over how much trouble she would be in if she tripped over the dog." Frieda took in both Susannah and Freya's fearful expressions and hastened to reassure them. "She didn't, but there was a hall stand on the other side of the door, between it and the stairs; a big tall imposing piece, probably quite scary to a child, all dark wood and brass coat hooks with a mirror in the middle and a shelf in front of that with a drawer underneath. The minister had a family heirloom displayed on it; a beautiful, intricately patterned, slender bone china vase."

Susannah's veins turned not so much to ice as to liquid nitrogen as she heard these words. Part of her wanted to set her drink down as slowly and softly as she could; another part prioritised having it out of her hands as quickly as possible, and both of those parts were overruled by another which would not allow her to move at all.

"You've no doubt worked out where I'm going with this, and sadly you'd be correct. Mary was concentrating so hard on avoiding the dog, she knocked against the edge of the hall stand and the vase toppled to the floor and smashed. Esther was furious. Dorothy and Effie were at Lorna's house for tea one day very soon after Lottie died; Dorothy remembers seeing Esther marching Mary past the window on their way to the flat. She was yanking at her arm and telling her off the whole time. Dorothy said that it struck her as odd that Mary wasn't crying; it was as though she was beyond that, both retreated into herself and not quite there. I've no doubt she knew better than to cry. Esther had still been angry with her at Lottie's funeral a few days later."

"For *fuck's sake!*"

"*Freya!*"

Cheeks flushed red with fury, Freya barely registered her mother's scandalised rebuke.

"Poor little Mary! She was a young girl, grieving for her grandmother! She was in an intimidating setting and terrified of hurting a dog. She was seriously getting the cold shoulder from her own mother at the *funeral*? Maybe such a valuable and breakable item should have been put in a safer place, instead of where people were coming and going and a large animal who couldn't hear them was often lying around!"

"I appreciate your capacity for empathy if not your language, Freya Christina Lingard", Frieda said tartly. "You are quite correct about the peril of having the vase displayed there, but that is looking at it from today's more risk-averse perspective. You must remember that in those days, the emphasis was on people taking precautions, not on making the environment so safe that nobody need take responsibility for their own carelessness." She held up a hand as both Freya and Susannah drew breath. "I'm not accusing Mary of having been careless. As you rightly said, she was a bereaved child, compensating for another risk, and of course she should have been shown more kindness at the funeral. People did keep their emotions bottled up in those days, though, and don't forget Esther was grieving too; she had lost her mother and had to keep up regardless with the full-time demands of being a single parent."

"Well, I never knew Esther; yes, she had more responsibility to carry, but she was an adult. I'm sorry for swearing, Mum, but I'm heartbroken for that little girl! She must have felt so alone, and her mother couldn't be kind to her as they laid her grandmother to rest. It's horrible when you're so little, with no influence and no escape, and you've messed up but didn't mean to and the anger keeps on coming; the emotional exile goes on and on!" Freya looked at Susannah for support, tears in her eyes.

"Yes; Freya's right, and if Mary had problems similar to my experience as a dyspraxic person, I can guarantee she will have had many instances of trying so hard to avoid one pitfall it led her straight into a different one. I hope for her sake that none of the others were as traumatic as this one. Perhaps Esther was more affected by her mother's death than people could see because of her outward hardness;

perhaps there were reasons for that hardness. As an observer looking in from a different time, I see a desperately sad situation where no party had the support and understanding they needed. I wonder what happened to Mary; how her life turned out."

The air had the still, slightly damp frostiness of a child's held breath on a Christmas morning as Susannah walked home. She was no longer in any doubt that Mary Renfield was the little girl in her dream; Esther had to be the scolding adult there and on the recording. 'Clattery hands' and the nerve-jangling tale of the broken vase when neither Frieda nor Freya knew about her dream had settled that. How many times, she wondered as she looked up at the blue-green flicker of Lorna's light, had that vase crashed to the floor again in Mary's dreams?

The routine tasks; feeding the cats, cleaning out their litter tray then making her own meal and tidying up seemed to take forever before she could settle down to do some research. Typing in 'Mary Renfield, Kirkbrigg' brought no results in the right age group. Nothing for 'Esther Renfield'. Part of her was relieved not to find death announcements or articles about a tragic accident; she wasn't ready for such hard facts. She hoped that Frieda was mistaken about Mary having lost touch with her friends; it felt like one separation too many. All that happy singing was quite possibly a release on the one day she felt able to relax and enjoy herself; Susannah would be surprised if there had been much trace of 'Merry Mary' during the week. Dorothy, Teresa and whoever else gathered to play in the fresh air on those long ago Sunday afternoons in the streets watched over by Lorna's light must have brightened her short life immeasurably.

Lying in bed, she pondered Freya's reaction to hearing about the anger visited upon Mary. It was by no means unusual for her to feel injustice to others with an amplified intensity, but this had seemed highly personal. Whatever was going on with her friend, Susannah was becoming more concerned than ever about how Freya was going to cope once she had moved away. There was a lot of unresolved pain, old pain, going on there.

15

Chance Meeting

Susannah had always thought of it as a blessing that her birthday was during the last few days of October; it meant that every few years it changed on which side of the clocks going back it fell and she enjoyed the added novelty of that. This year it fell on the last day of British Summer Time and it being a Saturday, it made perfect sense for her to spend it quietly celebrating in Perth. The obligatory social ritual of childhood birthday parties had put her off overtly marking the day; the combination of noise, crowds and surprises increasing the potential for the 'clumsy' episodes she dreaded, enhanced by her being the focus of attention and expected to gratefully enjoy that when what she was really feeling was more akin to stage fright.

Her habit of setting out to notice positives for her weekly Grounds for Gratitude ritual had stood her in good stead when it came to these occasions with their mixed feelings. She had come to realise, and be thankful for it, that she did not hate her birthday itself. As long as she remained in control of how she marked it, there was no reason why it had to be a difficult day. One of her favourite, highly personal features of the day was making the most of the opals she loved being her birthstone. She had several opal rings in various colours, all of which she wore at various times all year round; on her birthday, visible to all but explained exclusively to her trusted inner circle, she had a specific pattern to her choice. When it fell before the hour change, she wore a white opal; when it fell after, a black one. When it was on the cusp; either the Saturday or the

Sunday, she wore one of each on opposite hands. She was certain that if the changing of the clocks ever got discontinued, she would keep up the habit based on when it would have been.

She ate a leisurely brunch before getting dressed then went through to the small bedroom and opened the dressing table drawer of which she had been making good use since her surprise discovery of it. Her tartan notebook with its ever-growing treasure of information and reminders in the front and gratitude notes in the back sat on top of the envelope in which she had reverently folded and stored Mary's essay; she said hello to the little girl each time she took out her notebook. Next to those contents in the drawer was the slim, compartmented silver-grey jewellery box in which she kept her best pieces. She picked out her black opal solitaire and a smaller white opal set between two amethysts, slipped them onto her fingers and gently closed the drawer. Her dark red top, dressy but understated enough not to declare a special occasion to the casual observer, fell comfortably over her stomach and bottom; brushing most of the inevitable cat hair off her plain black trousers, she put on her coat and a purple scarf with a subtle weave of metallic thread shimmering through it, fluffed out her hair and went out to go and greet her soon to be home city.

This was not a trip for shopping, she decided as she weaved her way through the afternoon rush. The rain had recently stopped; more than one umbrella, shaken out ready to fold up with the casual disregard of people who lived their lives without need to monitor their immediate environment as strictly as she did, sprinkled her with the remnants of past showers. As she reached the broad, breath-restoring sweep of Tay Street and stood at the promontory watching the swollen grey water grabbing onto every particle of limited-edition light from the patchwork of nimbus clouds, she lifted her hands to the railings, flattening out her coat sleeves. The same light dappling the river sparkled on the raindrops which had fallen from the Perth sky ahead of her and transferred to her through a secondary reflex from the shaken umbrellas of those who were already there. The river held a patient knowingness; an appreciation of this final afternoon wherein daylight would extend its fading reach well past tea time, the last flavours of a memory cocktail of long summer nights dissolving into the rising steam of the new season's hot chocolates and warming brews. She visualised the fragments of light from the same path around the sun distributed further north, all the way to the Arctic Circle and beyond, where the transition was so much more drastic; a calendar outside the forced regulation of the clock, profoundly respected and honoured by people so much more in tune with it. Her keen imagination extended the river far beyond its geography; a fine stream of sparkles struck from the ice of the polar night passing through her own familiar seasons all the way to where it broadened to the glittering white sea of its opposite at the South Pole. She pictured herself standing at this spot observing the reverse as the heavens and the river of light came full circle. Soon, she would see it all here.

The clouds merged above as she walked through the peace of Rodney Gardens on the other side of the Tay, forming the kind of sky which always looked from indoors as though the streetlights should have come on by now. It took her back to the limbo time after losing out on the first flat she had viewed; the feeling that the path she was on was stripped of the double security of illumination and clear boundaries. She cautiously welcomed the stoic reminder that until she had the keys, she must retain a reserve of preparedness for unexpected twists. A gust of frigid wind stirred leaves lethargic with damp at her feet; a shiver answered from within her, impelling her to quicken her vigilant steps back towards the warmth and lights.

A glass of wine and something unfussy like nachos or chips would sustain her nicely until she got home. The Sandeman pub embodied the buzz of a small city Saturday afternoon; an undemanding companionable co-existence of patrons in the laid back, blurry-edged zone between small town familiarity and big city anonymity. Colour changing lights around the entire frames of each towering window in the former library building bathed a constellation of newly forming night out get-togethers in languid neon waves, building towards the coming loud and frenetic rush for those whose compatible energy sought it. Although it was early for a mealtime upturn, the crowd was already beginning to noticeably increase, to the point where she wondered whether a suitable table to occupy on her own for long enough to eat and drink comfortably would be available. She was about to walk through to the main seating area to take a look when she caught sight of the bright lights above the bar reflecting on familiar dark blue hair. She chanced a closer look as the woman was huddled in conversation with a blonde companion; yes, that was indeed Bethany from her previous visit to the bookshop.

Susannah was deliberating whether to interrupt, her wish not to intrude battling with the desire not to let slip an opportunity to build on a potential contact here, when Bethany turned around to assess the growing busyness of the bar. She smiled and waved, her circumspect body language echoing Susannah's own; possibly unsure of recognising her or inhibited by having met her as a customer. Susannah went over to the two women.

"Hi; it's Bethany, isn't it?"

"Yes, and this is my friend Diane"; she indicated the smiling blonde.

"Hello, Diane. I'm Susannah; I met Bethany at her work last weekend. I'm moving to Perth and she was most helpful to me when I was looking for a reference book."

"Ah! Congratulations; this is a lovely place to live!"; Diane's eyes reflected the glow of the pub lights as she looked around. "I stay in Inverbrudock, but I love coming through here to meet up with Bethany."

"Yes; Diane's through for the day with my cousin Sharon, who also stays in Inverbrudock"; Bethany nodded towards the seating area as Diane waved to another blonde woman who was arranging her coat, scarf and a couple of shopping bags to convey to the increasing beat of passers by on their own hunt for tables that she was part of a group. "Blimey, it is getting busy already."

"Look, I can give one of you a hand to carry your drinks if you like, to save your cousin having to hold the table on her own. I've got the app that covers this place so I can find a table and sort my own order from there easily enough once you've been served."

"Well, that's really thoughtful of you; thank you so much!"; Bethany and Diane beamed at her, relief both palpable and deeply relatable to Susannah radiating from each of them. "Di, do you want to go and let Shaz know, and we'll bring the drinks? Susannah, you'd be more than welcome to join us. I doubt you'll get a table now; the place is really filling up."

Bethany's reasoning was sound, and her invitation tempting. Susannah panicked internally for a moment, replaying what she had said; had she specifically mentioned ordering food? Much as she felt an affinity with Bethany and now with Diane whom she was meeting for the first time, she wasn't ready to be unexpectedly eating in front of a group of people she barely knew. She wasn't particularly hungry after her late brunch and it certainly wouldn't be the first time she had waited until she got home to eat. She could manage one glass of wine without food and be perfectly fine to travel.

If ever there was a time to go for it without too much analysing beyond the basic safety considerations, this was it.

"That would be lovely. Thank you."

Bethany insisted on buying her a large Shiraz when their turn came to be served. Susannah fought to smother a sudden spike of guilt as she thought of Freya. She had never known Susannah to deviate from her preference for keeping her birthday low key and home-based; she had been understanding and not surprised about her wish to go to Perth on her own for this one, but Susannah dreaded to imagine what she would make of the social turn it had taken. She tried to imagine how she would feel in Freya's place, especially when she was already coming to terms with the tectonic shift of her best friend moving away. She wanted to believe that Freya wouldn't feel hurt or betrayed, but she had a fair idea that she would and to a certain extent she could see why. She didn't think it particularly constructive to keep it from her either. Hiding it had the potential to blow up in both of their faces later on, and the sooner Freya got used to new people being in Susannah's life, the sooner she would get past her difficult feelings and who knew, perhaps come to benefit from getting to know them herself. There had been something about both women's reaction to her removing the dilemma of carrying more than one drink in each hand or leaving a companion to face the social pressure of holding a table for four alone which had reminded her of Freya in a way she couldn't quite quantify; it was an intangible overlay of resemblance which had nothing to do with both Freya and Diane having pale blonde hair in a fairly similar style and the kind of fair skin that reminded her of Scandinavia. She didn't need to tell this group that it was her birthday. No, she told herself determinedly; she was not betraying Freya or being hypocritical. She picked up two of the four large glasses of wine from the bar and followed Bethany to the table.

Sharon, a few years older than the rest of them, wore her own Nordic-looking blonde hair pulled back from her face and forehead; she was one of those rare individuals with the kind of handsome bone structure that suited it well. She freely expressed her own gratitude for Susannah's consideration of her as Bethany introduced them. As they settled in, the conversation soon turned to Kirkbrigg.

"My work's going to be opening a small branch there soon as it happens", said Bethany. "I might be needing some recommendations for places to go. My first boss, Anita, is coming through from Fife to help the team get up and running. I haven't seen her for a few years and she was extremely helpful to me when she was my manager. Shona, Martyn and Karolina will be lucky to have her there for a few weeks. It will be limited opening hours at first but if all goes well, she'll be involved with interviewing for at least one more team member too. I'm hoping to get through to see her at some point."

Susannah's brain whirled with possibilities. A job going in a company with a recommended track record, backed up by her impressions of it as a customer, for providing a supportive working environment could be excellent timing with regard to Freya. On the other hand, new people whom she hadn't had much time to adjust to their being in Susannah's new life before they started rocking up in *Kirkbrigg*? This one was going to take delicate handling. Recommending venues was less complicated; she described the Positive Return and the Neon Fox.

"The bus journey from here is a bit of a pain; it's a pity there isn't a railway station. There used to be years ago but it was one of the many lines which was cut in the sixties. As well as it being quicker, I'd love to be able to arrive into that grand station when I come through here!"

Bethany's eyes shone. "Yes; I love my local station, I have to say, and I prefer a train journey."

"Are you sure you want to get her started on that subject?", smiled Sharon fondly, laughing as Bethany good-naturedly swatted her with a menu. "Not that I'm disagreeing by any means. Diane and I always come through by train and we love coming into Perth Station. Crossing the river on that long curving viaduct never gets old." She and Diane looked at each other and both went off into uncontrollable laughter at some shared recollection, closely followed by Bethany who had clearly heard the story; Diane took up the narrative for Susannah's benefit.

"The guard on our train today was talking to an older chap sitting across from us who we gathered was a retired supervisor from one of the bigger stations; whether it was Edinburgh or one of the Glasgow ones, I'm not sure. Anyway, this chap was talking about the logistics if Gamma Rae does add a Scottish date to her tour. The guard moved on checking tickets and he asked a couple of teenagers down the aisle if they were fans. One of them mentioned that she'd arrived to play Newcastle when 'Cherry Soda' dropped and that it was streaming on every platform. So next thing this older chap kicked off to us about how these diva pop stars think they can do what they like, how they expect everybody to run around after them with their diet fads, how much of the stuff did her lackeys have with them to make that amount of mess and he hoped she hadn't expected the staff at the Central Station to clean it up!"

All four of them howled with laughter. "No way! Was he *serious*?"

"We weren't sure at first, but once we realised he was, Sharon explained about dropping and streaming on platforms referring in that context to digital music and that 'Cherry Soda' is the name of her album. I told him that as a railway enthusiast it had made me laugh when I saw those expressions in a news article about Gamma Rae because of the images it brought to mind so I couldn't fault his logic!"

Bethany raised her glass. "This is going down very well; how does everyone feel about getting another bottle among the four of us and maybe ordering some chips"

Diane looked at her watch. "I could definitely manage that; I should get back in time but if need be I can message Des and Jason to get one of them to pop in and feed Farolita"; she turned to Susannah; "That's my best friends in Inverbrudock and my cat, in that order."

"Ooh; you've got a cat?"

"Sure have. She's a blue point Siamese." She picked up her phone, poised to open her photos app. "Shaz, are you OK for time?"

"Yeah; I'll message Paulie if I'm going to be later than I told them I would be, but we've got an extra hour tonight anyway. I'll go up to the bar this time, Beth. We really should get around to downloading the app for this place; we usually pick less busy times than this and it's more habit than anything taking turns going up to the bar but the apps are a gift when you're on your own or with one other person and not wanting to leave them sitting for ages."

"Good call on the extra hour, Shaz!"; Bethany moved to let her cousin out. Sharon took the ten pound note Susannah offered for her share, nodding her thanks. The prospect of eating on such an informal basis, picking at a few chips from a bowl when everyone else at the table was doing the same, no longer held any fear. Bethany smiled at Diane as she slid back into her seat.

"Are you doing your usual clock change ritual, Di?"

"Playing 'The Sound of Silence'? Absolutely!"

Susannah got the relevance of the opening lines instantly.

"The Simon and Garfunkel version, or The Disturbed?"

"Both, one after the other. I admit I was sceptical when I heard about that cover version; some songs are so definitive in their original form that covering them seems like sacrilege, but it soon grew on me. It's so intense! It feels like a continuation of the message to fit the contemporary clamour of relentless online input; a valediction calling our attention back to honour a past time when we had more headspace to listen to what the gentle melancholy of the original was already telling us."

The three women at the table shared quiet nods and contemplation as the colours continued to flow sedately around the LED-lined windows, the brightness of the lights subtly increasing in proportion to the darkening of the late afternoon sky. Someone passing their table stopped for an instant to rummage in their pocket as their phone came to life with a muffled ringtone, becoming identifiable as its owner got it out.

'The Sound of Silence'.

The Disturbed version, though either one would have elicited the gasps and exchanged looks which pinged around the table.

"*Harriet moment!*"

Susannah looked from one to the other as Bethany and Diane both said it. Diane recovered her wits first.

"Sorry, Susannah; that's about a distant relative of Bethany and Sharon's, a few generations back. She has become known for having attracted meaningful coincidences like what happened there."

"Oh, I see! It's a pity Sharon missed it, then"; she looked round towards the shapeless queue at the bar. "I think I see her; yes, she's being served now, otherwise I'd have said to go and get her and let me order on the app." She turned back to the others, a warm glow inside as she addressed them both. "I really appreciate you explaining that when it's a personal thing and you've so recently met me. It makes me feel genuinely included in your company. Thank you."

The moment and the camaraderie, however heartwarming, needed dialling back to something more neutral for such new acquaintanceship. Susannah gestured to Diane's phone. "Were you going to show me some cat photos?"

Diane's Siamese cat was certainly a beauty and clearly well aware of it. Susannah pulled out her own phone, angling it so that Bethany could see it too as she swiped through some recent photos of Annika and Morgan. Momentarily distracted by Sharon returning from the bar, she realised that she had gone past the batch of cat pictures into a series of images she had taken of Lorna's light in one of its more erratic phases.

"Oops! You must be wondering what that's all about"; she nodded her thanks as Sharon filled their glasses. "I can see this streetlamp from my bedroom window and as you can see, it's been malfunctioning somewhat. It's not a problem at this time; in fact I've come to rather enjoy the show, but with the dark nights coming in I thought I'd better have some sort of a record of it in case it stops giving out enough light to serve its purpose safely and I need to report it to the council."

Quite why she felt the need to come up with a cover story at this point instead of simply admitting that she was going to miss this colourful highlight of the humdrum view, she wasn't sure. She chalked it up to the habit of a lifetime, noticing as she did so that Diane's eyes were wide with appreciation.

Sharon's face took on a knowing look as she leaned over to look at the images which Susannah obligingly flicked through again. "It's like catnip to her!", she said with no trace of anything but pure affection.

"Diane has an aesthetic fascination with streetlights", clarified Bethany.

"Yes; whenever I visit anywhere for the first time, since I was a wee girl I've always noticed the type of streetlights and wanted to know what colour they shine. I've never seen a variation like this! There's one on the Back Walk in Stirling which seems to have been patched with two different types of LEDs; one warm white and one ice white. The effect is a mix of pale shades of peach and purple; it reminds me of an ametrine crystal. All the other lights on that pathway are the warm apple white shade that's becoming more standard now, so it really stands out. I grew up in Stirling, you see; I go through there quite often, though I don't have family connections there now." She flicked through her own photos, showing Susannah an image of a streetlamp which shone a distinctly bi-coloured light; it bore a degree of similarity to Lorna's light on the occasions when it showed a mix of its intended colour and the blue-green. "Des and Jason had never heard of ametrine; when Des looked it up and they saw that it's a natural fusion of amethyst and citrine, he said that it was a good job it was amethyst and not lapis because who would want to wear jewellery made from a latrine!"

Susannah joined in with the laughter. "I think I'd appreciate his sense of humour! That light is gorgeous. I know where the Back Walk is; it goes from where the City Walls pub is, all the way up to the Castle? I do like Stirling; I should go there more often. Once I live here and it's so convenient by train, I probably will. The mix of different types of LED wouldn't account for this light outside my building though; it's sporadic and can be all one colour or the other, as you can see."

"No; I agree, there's something else going on there", mused Diane. "The blue-green colour looks exactly like when the type of street lighting in general use was mercury vapour lamps; roughly the decade and a half after the Second World War. The type of light this one appears to be when it's working as it should, the modern ambient peach colour, is high pressure sodium. Most people think of sodium as being the orange lights we all grew up with. They are, but that's low pressure sodium. The high pressure version which is more common now also contains mercury vapour. This one of yours looks as though there are times when only that is getting through, but I can't imagine how that could happen; what could possibly interfere with the supply in that way, not to mention cause the mix effect." She shivered theatrically. "It's as though you're getting a glimpse of a portal to an earlier time. I'm a bit jealous!"

"Wow; that's most interesting, thank you!" A staff member brought their chips; phones and wine glasses were moved to make way for the bowls, their contents appetisingly fresh, that classic hunger-inducing aroma rising. As Bethany filled Sharon in on the 'Harriet moment', Susannah took the chance to mull over what Diane had said about the mercury vapour streetlamps. This was definitely becoming an intriguing mystery to liven her final months in Kirkbrigg. She wondered what Freya would make of this new technical detail, before the shadow of her concerns around discussing today's events with her crept back over the convivial glow.

The last of the daylight clung on through the uneven cloud cover for long enough to bring a final sheen of colour to Susannah's journey home after bidding farewell to the others amid anticipations of their paths crossing again once she moved to Perth. The darkened gaps in the cloud took on the elusive shimmer of black opals; shot through with the rare garnet hues of a sunset persisting well into the realm of twilight as her bus picked up speed past the outer reaches of the city. The remaining few hours of her birthday, captured in those unreal-looking pockets of uncovered night sky, wrapped her in a lacy cocoon which kindly but thinly veiled the looming hard edge of tomorrow.

16

Jealousy

Another yawn fought its way through Susannah's innate politeness as she cradled her coffee cup.

"Oops, sorry about that. I knew I'd get tired more easily once it got to this stage with everything going on, but this is ridiculous. I'm glad now that I didn't stay on in The Sandeman for any more drinks, even with the extra hour!"

Dressed up words of acceptance tottered in spiky-heeled shoes through the guarded gate of Freya's brittle smile.

"I'm grateful you can fit me in; I hope you didn't rush back from your Fair City on my account?"

"Well, I did need to feed the cats and I'm trying to keep my sleeping routine steady including at the weekends; I've missed a few things at work lately, got some calculations wrong. You do know though, I absolutely wanted to do our Sunday get-together especially today"; she gestured at the plate of mini cinnamon swirls which she had bought as a treat for the first Sunday of Greenwich Mean Time. The golden brown curve of the glazed pastry always made her think of the casual rise of aromatic steam in busy cafés as people hurried in from the crisp cold and rain-slick pavements on days where indoors became a warm sensory reward. Freya picked one up, took an elegant bite and placed it on the side plate Susannah had put out. She wiped her fingers and dabbed her mouth with a napkin.

"Where's The Sandeman again; is that the big one opposite the Playhouse?"

Susannah relaxed as the tension appeared to have melted away in the disarming pleasure of the sweetness and spice.

"Yes; the one with the neon lights around the windows. It used to be the library."

"I bet that was busy on a Saturday afternoon?"

"It wasn't too full when I went in; quite a few people at the bar and a lot came in while I was waiting." She studied Freya's expression, gauging how she might take the detail that Susannah had not been alone; her fears about being left behind clearly no less raw. "Actually, Bethany was at the bar when I walked in."

Freya, already sitting still, seemed to freeze.

"The woman from the bookshop?"

"She was with a couple of other people. Her cousin was keeping the table and her friend was waiting to help her carry the drinks. I offered to do that so Diane could go back to the table and save Sharon having to hold it on her own as it got busier."

"You were introduced to them too, then?"

"The place was filling up rapidly; they appreciated me giving them a hand and kindly invited me to sit with them. I probably wouldn't have gotten a table otherwise. I guess a lot of people had just been paid."

"So you had a birthday drink with them? I know it's your day and your choice, but I must admit that hurts. I've always understood that you prefer to mark your birthday quietly on your own. I've never made that about me and I thought nothing of you wanting to spend it in Perth; I could see why, especially with it falling on a Saturday. But to decide to celebrate it with them?"

"I didn't even tell them it was my birthday! It wasn't 'a birthday drink'; it was an unplanned sharing of a table on a day out, when the pub was busy and I wouldn't have been able to get a table on my own."

"You did well to recognise Bethany out of context in a crowded bar! Or did she recognise you first?"

"Well, she has blue hair. It kind of stands out."

"What, like that metallic pastel rinse I'd experiment with if it wouldn't give my mother heart failure?"

"No; dark blue."

"And Karen and Diana; did *they* have funky coloured hair too?"

"Sharon and Diane. Both blonde. Oh, I can't resist; I'm going to have another cinnamon swirl. You're welcome to take a couple away for you and your mum."

"Do you mind if I finish my coffee first?!"

"What? Come on, you know perfectly well that's not what I meant. Freya, why are you being such a victim and making this so hard for me? I've done all I can to reassure you that I won't forget about you or stop bothering to invest in our friendship; I've tried to encourage you to find a new direction so that you won't be left on your own with the cliques and bullies at work. I know this is a big deal and an upsetting change for you, but there's only so much I can and indeed should do about it!"

"I can't believe you're being so harsh, right after dropping it on me so casually that you've already got a whole new circle of Perth friends before you even move there."

"I wouldn't call them that at this point; I've met Bethany twice, once serving me at her work and once by chance. The other two don't live in Perth; they were visiting from somewhere on the east coast north of Arbroath. Inverbrudock, that was it. But I like them; I enjoyed their company, and yes, they may well become friends. It's inevitable that I'm going to be meeting new people and mentioning them. I do know how you feel and it's not a question of wanting to rub it in. You know me better than that. I'm being honest with you and including you, as I promised when I first told you about my plans to move. I know it's not something you want to hear or think about now but I'd love you to be able to be a part of my life there too; you might actually get some new friends out of this yourself! I'm not going to pressure you, but Freya, you need to stop pushing me away and trying to make me feel bad about this."

Now was clearly not the time to mention Mackenzie Books opening a branch in Kirkbrigg.

"I don't want to lose you, but I will be forced to walk away if this can't be resolved"; Susannah took a deep breath. "Freya, you need to face the fact that your approach to this has become highly manipulative. I've noticed a few things; not only when you held it over me that you might not be able to stop yourself fixating on Max, but subtle hints. Like walking in here with the coffee to find you telling Annika, who had been asleep in her basket, how much you were going to miss her mummy. You'd never gone over to the cats when they were sleeping before; you always waited for them to come to you. Little things which are innocuous on their own and make the recipient feel as though they're imagining it; playing into that self-doubt as the nudges mount up. Perhaps I am mistaken about some of those signs, but frankly I'm beginning to feel the same spider sense alert that we both feel at work, and I cannot ignore that. I'm not saying this to hurt you or punish you; I'm afraid for *you* as much as for myself, because I'm terrified you're carrying on a pattern and becoming coercive. I don't want that for you. It can start out this way; with situations outside of people's control which threaten their sense of self and their established safe zones in a hostile world. I don't want to lose you to that; I want to grab onto you and pull you to safety. It's taken a lot for me to realise that in order to do that, I have no choice but to confront you this way, however painful that is for both of us."

"I… told you I was excited for you! I tried! Is it so heinous of me to say I'm going to miss you? I have done nothing to Max. And how sly, keeping notes about these 'signs', saving them up until you had a really good case against me!"

"I have not been keeping any sort of record, including in my mind. The example I gave about when you were talking to Annika was simply what came to my mind as I searched it for an example to back up what I was saying, not something I'd been saving up in any way. I hoped it would never come to this! And I'm not accusing you of any wrongdoing towards Max. I know we talked about that and I've no reason to believe you've done anything untoward, nor that you intend to. The point is that you used your attraction to him as something to make me worry about; that your attachment would become destructive as a direct result of my moving away. That is coercive control. And you may have backed off regarding Max, but now I can see your reactivity escalating because I'm building towards the move in a more tangible way and making contacts."

"Coercive control? That's telling a partner what to wear, cutting them off financially, stopping them from seeing the family and friends they already have, keeping them isolated in their own home and beating them up if they don't comply!"

"Yes; those behaviours are more extreme examples of it, but so are subtle manipulations including in friendships. I cannot be held responsible for the rest of your life."

"I get that, believe it or not. But Suze, I can not do this on my own. I'm exhausted. I need every bit of energy I have to get through my routine as it is; work and supporting my mother. Why do I have to carry the weight of her emotional wellbeing yet it's not OK for me to rest some of mine on anyone else; I have to carry that on my own because I'm not allowed to offload it but she is?"

"It's not OK. Or fair. Someone has to break that chain; it's going to take a lot of energy and some tough conversations. Taking responsibility doesn't mean you have to do it all on your own without support. Asking for help can be as much a part of taking responsibility as facing up to what you need to take back from putting onto others. It does balance itself out in the end. Oh, Freya, you've no idea how much I wish I could make this easier, and if you're willing to be open to the fact you need to change some of your go-to responses I will be there to encourage you all the way but it has to come from you."

Fear and an encroaching horror of defeated understanding crept into Freya's body language; the set of her shoulders and jaw. Her voice shivered on the precipice.

"But if I really am *that* sort of person, an *abuser*, then it's too late; it's unforgivable. It doesn't feel like this cold insidious calculating campaign to me; it feels like trying to hold on enough to get to a baseline of getting by emotionally. So much for putting one's own oxygen mask on first. I guess I'm ruled out of that if this is the verdict."

"It's not too late. I'm saying that where you are right now can be how it *starts*. You *are* a caring person. You have so much empathy; look how upset and angry you were when your mum told us about Mary. That came from your heart; that was real. You must hang on to that. Think of Barney Fulton snoozing comfortably on his heat pad, his paws twitching as he dreams of sunlit fields! You are entitled to the help you need."

"No; I can't get my head around this. I'm not a coercive controller! You just don't want to have to be concerned about me at all when you move away, and before you start on me again, yes, I know, You Are Entitled and so I have to suck it up. You get your new life, freedom from caring about me *and* you get to be the righteous one. All hail Saint Susannah of Perth! While my mother picks up on you slipping away from me and piles onto me with her worries that I can't even hold onto a friend who's…" Even in the midst of her tirade, Freya recognised a bridge too far, stopping to draw breath as she marshalled her words. "Who's as much of a social outsider at work as I am. Well, I wish you all the best but you're on your own. I cannot be around someone who is going to brand me an abuser every time I let slip that I'm struggling with something. The only safe thing I can do is step away altogether. Enjoy your new chapter; I will be civil at work as long as you're based there but we are done."

Susannah stood silent as she watched her friend storm out; heartbroken, but recognising the need to stand firm. Backtracking or softening the message would delay the painful but necessary process to healing. It was up to Freya now, and who knew how she was going to pull that off in her own toxic environment. "Cheers for that, Frieda", she muttered; having a fair idea of the sentiments which Freya had stopped herself from endorsing. She too was done. Making allowances for Frieda's primary concern being her only child's isolated future didn't come close to excusing such blatant ableist bigotry.

She cleared away the coffee and pastries; her movements wooden, sorrowful as she scooped the literal dregs of their shared Grounds for Gratitude into the food waste box. The poignancy of the act wrenched a sudden burst of tears from her stinging eyes.

She gathered herself after a few minutes; resumed the clearing up and drank some water. A quiet afternoon reading carried her through to the early dark; emotionally exhausted, the first Sunday evening of Greenwich Mean Time smothered rather than blanketed her in the eerie gloom of her flat.

Stiff-legged after sitting for too long, she sorted out food for herself and the cats before going into her bedroom. Lorna's light was an unambiguous pale peach, its idiosyncrasies on hold. "You're on your best behaviour for the start of your busy season, I see", she mused aloud. "I heard an interesting theory about you when I was in Perth yesterday. It's a shame I never got to tell Freya about it." The thought shook the fragile equilibrium of her emotions once more; she turned away, focusing on the practicalities of getting ready for bed and trying to sleep.

The sobbing little girl had Freya's adult face, but she couldn't have been more than ten years old. She was curled on a narrow bed in a room Susannah had never seen before; lying on a pale yellow candlewick cover clutching a worn teddy bear. The ruffled sleeve of her pink cotton nightdress had a damp patch from repeatedly wiping her eyes. Susannah tried to go to her; she found herself floating at ceiling level, unable to move or make a sound. She could merely watch as this unknown child grieved; adult-sized emotions racking her body and pouring from the swollen eyes of Susannah's best friend. She couldn't grasp how long this devastating tableau played out in front of her before she abruptly awoke, simultaneously relieved that it had been a dream and horrified by its content.

Turning over to face the window, she gasped in shock. The shadowed figure of a little girl, silent and composed now and with a face which in profile looked unfamiliar but in keeping with her age, sat facing the wall where the dressing table used to be. She turned in the half-light at the sound of Susannah stirring. She *had* seen that face before.

"Mary?"

The child shook her head sadly; as she melted away from the solid rise of present-day reality, the distant echo of a voice floated from somewhere else in time. Susannah strained to catch the words at the edge of her consciousness; it sounded as though the little girl said "I'm not merry any more". The desolation of that stark sentence ripped at Susannah's heart. Was this about her nickname, or did this little spirit girl know that she was trapped; unable to cross over in peace? Susannah was certain that Mary had been the child she'd dreamed about; she didn't need to be a dream analyst to work out that it was the traumatic upheaval of the day before which had given her Freya's face. Psychological matters could influence some of the images in meaningful dreams as well as regular ones. She had no doubt that Freya was connected to all of this too; after all, it was she who had heard a child singing.

Had Mary been grieving for her beloved grandmother Lottie in her dream? Or had she been in disgrace again for something her little brain and body couldn't help?

It probably wasn't a good idea to ruminate too much about it; Susannah had her own current responsibilities to focus on. Work was going to be grim. She knew perfectly well that Freya would not make a scene or draw any attention to their rift; she guarded her vulnerability too closely for that and Susannah knew that she would be realising on some level how badly she had reacted, whether or not she was ready to admit it to herself let alone anyone else. It was not going to be a happy place to do her job.

If she could get a decent night's sleep it would help a lot. Plumping up her pillow, she tried to quiet her mind but the hours until her alarm went off into that last fading hurrah of the lighter October to November mornings passed restlessly.

17

Trouble At Work

Clumps of jelly slithered over the side of the bowl as Annika and Morgan miaowed hungrily around Susannah's feet. She swore and hurriedly grabbed what she could from the mat, dumping it back on top of the slide of compact meat which she was trying to mash up as the cats eagerly began to eat. Somehow time had slipped away from her again this morning; she had gotten up as usual, it wasn't as though she had overslept like she had a couple of days earlier. She simply hadn't found herself with enough minutes left over to shoo both cats out of the kitchen in order to prepare their food in peace; as soon as she put one out, the other shot into the room before she could close the door. Terrified of ending up snapping at or accidentally hurting her pets, she had no choice but to work around them; the phrase 'herding cats' taking on a literal resonance. The thought may have made her smile if she were less stressed and rushed; if she could catch her breath for long enough to employ any of her coping strategies. Harried, she pushed a handful of frizzy hair out of the way as she bent over the feeding bowls; the job done as best she could, she hoped that she had managed to mash the food up enough to avoid either or both cats wolfing down too many big chunks with the inevitable messy, and unhealthy for them, result.

"I'm sorry things are so fraught right now, girls; I know you're picking up on it and I hope it's all going to be worth it in the end"; she washed her hands and gathered herself to leave for work. She found herself hoping that neither Tan nor Lee would be leaving the flat across from hers at the same time; she didn't need the distraction as last time that happened she had spent a tortured morning unable to remember whether she had locked her door and had no time to eat after using most of her lunch break to rush back and check. They had seen her saying out loud "I am locking the door" on more than one occasion, but that relied on her remembering to pause the conversation and say it. Although she knew they would prompt her if she did forget to lock her door on the way out while talking to them, she needed her own crystal clear memory of locking it to feel confident that she had. She was not about to ask them to notice out loud when she locked her door either; it wasn't their problem.

She really needed to sort out her increasingly disorganised mornings. Getting up earlier hadn't helped; somehow her routine had stretched to fill the extra time without becoming any easier. Shunning conversation with her good and friendly neighbours due to constantly running late was yet another facet to this person she did not want to become, yet she seemed inexorably to be heading that way. Did she deserve this move if that was going to be the price of it; short changing the people in her life? Yes, house buying and moving was acknowledged to be one of the most stressful life events, but she was sure that most people could find the necessary extra gear to accommodate that. Julian and Isobel had managed it years ago on top of organising their wedding and helping to move Isobel's grandmother into a sheltered housing scheme, all within six months.

Meanwhile, halfway down the stairs, Susannah realised that she had been so caught up in her self-critical thoughts she had once again failed to register whether she had locked her door.

She threw back her head and sent an ironic gritted-teeth smile to the heavens. The time she would lose by turning around with the utmost caution on the staircase was unavoidable; she tiptoed back up, the solid resistance of the door handle under her hand flooded her with swirling currents of relief and annoyance at the needless further delay, again. "Learn a damned lesson, will you?", she chided herself under her breath.

Finally making it to street level, she wondered vaguely why she could still smell cat food. Possibly the stress; a manifestation of a longing to be able to stop the headlong rush of demands, giving her more time to focus on preparations, curl up with her cats and have more of a chance to not only get that part right but enjoy it. As Adil had said, it was an exciting time which she should be able to look back on with nostalgic fondness once it was over with and she was settled in her permanent home.

Her mood lifted a little as she recalled the conversation with Adil on that joyous day when he had told her that her revised offer had been accepted. He had ended up telling her a story about a patronising client several years earlier presumptuously explaining to Sinéad what 'a drone involvement in the survey' meant.

"And she said to him, 'Well, I didn't think it meant that someone would be outside the property playing the bagpipes'!"

Susannah had laughed heartily then said that in fact it would be a rather stirring addition to the landmark ritual of a property survey, hiring a piper to accompany it, and joked about getting one for the sake of it; Adil had laughingly replied that it would definitely stir something up if he tried approaching the seller's solicitor with a request to delay until they could organise that.

A softer crunch to the underfoot leaves than they had the day before reminded her to bring her focus back to the needs of the moment; overnight rain had rendered them ominously slippery. She slowed her pace, reconciling herself to another sacrifice of crucial seconds to avoid a much worse alternative, as an elderly woman across the road waved her stick at her and called out a sharp warning which startled her. Why couldn't people see that giving her a fright and causing a distracting shift of her balance could cause the very thing they, and *she*, were trying to avoid? She was already scared enough of falling! This was one of the things she didn't enjoy about the autumn, and the snow and ice were yet to come. The older lady was probably scared of falling and all too aware of the seasons ahead too, which would go some way to explaining her harsh tone and interfering; afraid for herself, and perhaps of being a bystander to an accident where she no longer had the fitness to proactively assist as she would have in her younger days. If Susannah could find a way to give herself the kick up the backside she clearly needed; step up and sort out her time management, then she wouldn't be rushing and making complete strangers feel the need to check her like a naughty schoolgirl.

Why was everything suddenly getting to her so much?

She wasn't late in the end; she had five minutes left before the cutoff. All she had lost this time was the chance to make herself a cup of coffee and get settled in before the phones started up. She quickly nipped into the toilets to check her untidy hair and brush it back into place as best she could. Looking in the mirror, she brushed away what she thought was a bit of leaf caught up in the damp-tightened curls beside her left ear.

What the…?

No wonder the aroma had lingered.

When she pushed her hair out of the way in her frantic rush to get everything done, it somehow hadn't occurred to her that she had picked up the spilt blobs of jelly with that hand. She had walked to work, and had she arrived a few minutes later would have clocked in and gone straight to her desk, with traces of cat food in her hair.

Grabbing paper towels, she hurriedly dampened one and cleaned the section of hair to the best of her ability before drying it off and fluffing it out. She glared at her reflection.

"Do better", she ordered herself; the words struggling out through painfully clenched teeth sounded unlike her own voice, as though chipped off the unforgiving stone of a stricter past age.

She clocked in with a minute to go and called out her usual good mornings as she walked along the aisle to her desk; a smattering of replies of varying sincerity registered dimly in the background to the internal battle to compose herself. Before she could log on to her computer, Morven approached her desk, quietly asking her to come to one of the side rooms for a quick chat. Candice and Maya nudged one another as they passed, round-eyed with burgeoning gossip; Tanya's face held a surprising tinge of concern as she exchanged glances with Agata. Susannah didn't dare look over to Freya's section.

"I'm sorry to pull you away in front of everyone; I wanted to check in with you first thing, but…"

"But I was nearly late again. I know. I'm so sorry, Morven; I know my standards are slipping. Do I need a union rep present?"

"You may ask for one if you wish, of course, but this isn't intended to be that sort of meeting. You're not in trouble, Susannah; please believe me when I say that the emphasis here is on welfare, not disciplinary. I know you're preparing to move house and I understand how stressful that is, especially on your own and being dyspraxic; it's a lot. I admire and respect you for taking it on, and as your employers we do want to support you in any way we can. I have, and it gives me no pleasure to say this, noticed a few uncharacteristic mistakes creeping into your work lately. As you already mentioned, I'm also aware that you've struggled with getting here at your usual time; on a couple of occasions you have been late. I realise that you've made up the time; again this is not intended as a reprimand. I know you, though, and I am concerned that you are struggling. I wanted to talk to you to get up to speed with what's happening with you, and if there's any way we can better support you."

"I... Morven, I never dreamed that I'd be having a conversation like this at work. I feel so ashamed and you're right; I'm struggling. The house move is a lot of it, but I'm a responsible adult and I should be able to navigate through it without falling short in other areas of my life. A few trivial mistakes is one thing, but I should never have let it come to this! I hear you when you say I'm not in trouble, but if things have gotten so bad you need to speak to me about it in your role as my supervisor then I jolly well should be!"

"See, this is another thing I've noticed", Morven said gently; "that you've become harder on yourself than usual. I'm well aware of the high standards you set yourself, and nobody can expect to meet those all the time."

"I think it's because I'm scared; I can feel what I used to be able to achieve slipping away. When I worked on the Vaughan case..." Susannah was horrified to find tears threatening and her voice abruptly wavering as she recalled her recent, yet paradoxically distant, professional triumph. Morven handed her a tissue, quietly giving her time and space to regroup. "I feel as though I've lost a part of myself; the part which could get to that standard and make a difference. The person who could close her eyes and go to sleep on a day's work done well; on the knowledge that Seb and Kitty Vaughan no longer needed to be afraid to turn on their heating. Because she, that other Susannah, made it right."

"But you *are* that Susannah. Goodness, it really feels to you as though you've become a different person because you've hit a rough patch and made a few small errors? Because that's a horrendous amount of pressure to be under. Isn't buying your first home and contemplating moving to a new place *enough*?"

"I get what you're saying, but I still owe the same due diligence to everything else in my life. It's not only here I'm messing up. Dyspraxia isn't a progressive thing; it's a neurotype. So practice, experience and strategies should ensure that I become stronger as the years go by. Yet at home I feel as though I'm living in a doll's house. I'm too big for the space; more than usual. Every time I move I bump something, or my clothes catch or knock something. I can't count the times I've whacked my hands on the underside of a shelf, anywhere there's a protruding edge. My computer desk with the keyboard ledge pulled out. Yes, the one way I can hope to type is with a full sized keyboard like we have here; forget the built-in ones on laptops. I get to the point of standing dead still in the middle of a room refusing to move until my brain catches up with every detail of where I am and how far every part of me is from every solid object. I'm getting frustrated and snappy too. This morning when I was rushing to get ready, again, I was afraid I was going to end up yelling at my cats for getting under my feet. Two innocent little animals, who I love with all my heart! The idea of being so much as mildly irritated with them tears me apart inside, yet I get these unwanted thoughts, imagining shouting and seeing their faces sad and cowed like heartbroken children. It's not in line with any real feelings. I'm truly never angry with them; it's more like a form of, I don't know how to describe it. Like I'm getting those thoughts as a punishment, to upset myself. Morven, can you imagine what it's going to be like when I'm at the stage of packing to move? When things are out of place and there are stacks of boxes everywhere? I will be putting the cats in a cattery for a couple of weeks but the way things are going, it might have to be longer. I'm *tired*. It's taking me longer to do everything. I…"

I think my flat may be haunted and I'm having upsetting dreams about a girl called Mary, who may or may not have been dyspraxic too and was treated harshly for it. I'm finding myself using expressions to rebuke myself which I never have before and I think I'm channelling what she went through, and it's breaking my heart because she was a child and she's not at peace, and I'm worried about my cats picking up all of this as animals do on top of my stress. No; definitely too much and the wrong sort of disclosure for a boss, however compassionate.

"Things aren't great with Freya. I don't want to go into it because this is her workplace too, but she's not dealing so well with me planning to move away, and I don't blame her. Neither of us fits with the social scene here and now I'm leaving her on her own."

"Susannah, I'm so sorry you're going through all this. I did get the feeling that things were off between you and Freya. I understand your care and concern; I'm not about to minimise any of that. You are an excellent, loyal friend and I would be insulting you on multiple levels if I pretended it won't be hard for Freya when you leave. I'm sure you don't need me to tell you that you're not responsible for her; that you don't owe it to her to stay, but I absolutely understand why it worries you. Have you spoken with your GP about the stress you're under?"

"Not recently. I did call a mental health helpline last week; I wasn't in any danger, I'm not sure I'd call it a crisis but I needed to talk to someone to try to make sense of things. The volunteer told me to 'be kind to myself'; it felt so hollow. Our company isn't paying me a salary to be kind to myself. My solicitor is being an absolute guiding star with the buying process but he won't be involved once that's all done and I'm dealing with getting an electrician organised, arranging access and then any cleaning up that's needed afterwards, redecorating and then the move itself. Being kind to myself won't get all that done."

"Well, in some ways it will. By looking after your health, so that you remain fit and able to do all of those things and have an enjoyable quality of life. You deserve that, and a few mistakes take absolutely nothing away from your being a highly valued member of this company. You must hold on to that. If your GP agrees, a bit of time off will…"

"I can't be signed off; I'll be needing to travel back and forward to Perth. I can't do that if I'm off work sick."

"If it comes to that and anything is said, I will be clear about the special circumstances."

"I don't know; I feel it will drive a bigger wedge between Freya and me. I need to sort things out with her before I leave. I need to be in a position to help her plan how to move forward; to get out of here." She gasped as what she had let slip caught up with her. "I shouldn't have said that; it's not my place. Please keep that between you and me! I haven't asked her permission to talk about how things are for her working here. I'm extremely worried though."

"I understand, and of course I will keep your confidence, as I know you will keep mine; off the record, both Valerie and I are well aware of the social dynamics on our teams and how much support you and Freya give one another."

"I'm glad. Please could you ask Valerie to discreetly look out for her whenever I'm not here? There are people who are highly adept at looking like angels as soon as managers are about; I mean no disrespect but I can't be certain that she does know quite how much Freya is up against it. In fact there was one day recently when Valerie was in a meeting and I almost lost it with a few people; if she hadn't come back in when she did, you and I may well have ended up having a very different conversation before now. It was the day you spoke to me about the Vaughan case"; without mentioning names, she outlined what she had seen. "It sounds low level especially taken in isolation and Freya probably isn't aware of the mockery I described in this particular instance, but when you have to deal with that sort of thing on a daily basis it mounts up. It becomes more than observed incidents. It grows into a kind of being in itself; something palpable, and it's everywhere. You can *feel* it. All the time. You know you'll be called paranoid, which should never be used as an insult term anyway, if you try to tell anyone about it. Feeling safe becomes a dim memory, if in fact you ever did; a distant dream is more like it."

"I see. Goodness me; poor you, and Freya. Thank you for telling me about this; we do take bullying extremely seriously."

"I know, and I hope I have done the right thing; I feel as though I've betrayed Freya, blurting all that out without her knowledge and consent."

"You haven't. You've told me about your own experience and observations, and the effect they have on you as a caring person, colleague and friend. It is part of your own circumstances of elevated stress, which as your line manager I needed to know and had directly asked you about. We may not have known about the incidents you mentioned but none of this will come as a shock to Valerie. I will not tell her anything specific that I have heard from you, but I will make sure she knows to be vigilant. Particularly for signs and atmospheres when she's been away from the section, and I will be watching for those times too. You don't need to carry this alone any more, and neither does Freya. The help and support will be there whenever she needs them."

"Thank you so much. I feel that a weight has been lifted; hopefully the others will pick up on that and not think this has been a 'Susannah's been cut down to size' conversation!"

"Nobody here with any common sense would genuinely think that. Do you feel OK to go back to your desk?"

"Yes, thank you; I'll take it slower and do extra checks for a while, as long as it doesn't get me penalised for declining case numbers. That always worries me if I feel it's necessary for whatever reason. If I'm tired from a bad sleeping phase or not feeling well but not ill enough to be off, I'd rather be here and doing *some* work, but I get scared that I'll be in trouble for not getting through as much although I know logically it's better than nothing. I'm fortunate that my commute is a short walk. I really ought to be on it at all times in my working hours."

"As long as we know why, we can accommodate that and of course we appreciate your commitment. It's important that you keep communicating honestly with us rather than trying to hide it and soldier on; it prevents the need for difficult questions. We have a duty of care to you; more than that, we *do* care. Please hold on to that."

Pulling up her chair, Susannah logged on, opened her current case and smiled around at her curious colleagues. On the screen in front of her, the churn of figures settled into a more familiar account scenario. Taking out the notebook in which she kept some tips, flow charts and reminders, she allowed herself to use it in plain sight; her shoulders relaxed incrementally, enough to show her how tense they had been.

That particular type of fatigue and emotional release which comes after the sharing of a long-borne burden threatened to overwhelm her as she put the key in her front door, hearing the excited race of Annika and Morgan's paws on the hallway carpet as they responded to her homecoming. Food motivated or not, the reality of their uncomplicated feline welcome sparked a tidal wave of emotion rushing tears to her eyes and rendering her legs unsteady. She swallowed hard, blinking rapidly.

"Hey there, Suze; how's it going?"

"Tan!" Panicking, she swiped at her telltale eyes. "Damned rhinitis", she improvised. "Yeah; good. How are you; how's Lee?"

"We're getting there, thanks. We were out clubbing at the weekend; the doctor said it would be fine, with the expected caveats about taking care and not getting drunk"; Tan's comical expression and eye roll made Susannah laugh. Affection for her neighbours threatened another disproportionate rising of her own emotions, which she resolutely tamped down. Lee was recovering from bowel surgery.

"Tan, that's wonderful! I'm so happy for him; for both of you. I hope the DJ was playing some decent tunes?"

"Darling, I love you for going there first; for letting us be a couple of lads who've had a fabulous night out, not 'the curious case of the guy with the stoma going to the dancing'. It was a 90s theme, so yes, there were some absolutely *banging* tunes. Do you remember 'New Emotion' by The Time Frequency?"

"Do I *remember* it? I turned 18 in the mid 90s; what do you think?! I had a few years to wait when it came out in 1992 before I could get into a club and I wasn't sure I wanted to but that track was the biggest incentive. It was on the radio all the time; I wanted to be in a club dancing to it. London had it played for me when we went out on my 18th. I'm not pretending I had anything like the moves you and Lee do, especially at that age, but I'll always remember how the place came to life the second that tune came on. You know how it is at the beginning of the night when nobody wants to be the first to get up on the dance floor despite that being what they're at the club to do. 'New Emotion' got them going every time. TTF definitely hit on something special there. It guaranteed enough of a crowd on the dance floor to let me dance without worrying about being laughed at. The raw energy of it activated some part of my brain that allowed me to find enough rhythm to let all of that go and simply enjoy the movement, the music and the atmosphere. So they played that at the weekend?"

"Oh yes. In fact if memory serves me, they may have played it twice. We got a taxi back; Lee was pretty shattered, but that was to be expected. He does need to build himself up gradually. It was a boost to his morale before we have to get our bathroom fixed"; Tan's expression became serious. "There's a leak under the bath, so we're going to be without access to a toilet for most of the day."

"What awful timing; I'm so sorry. When is this happening?"

"Next week. It should be done in a day but they may have to come back; they have assured us we will be able to use the toilet overnight if the job does run into a second day. We would go away and get Lee's brother to come and stay to let them in but they keep changing the date because of other jobs overrunning or sick leave."

"So come here. I'll give you my spare key; when the day comes, get yourselves comfortable in here. Pack up whatever Lee will need for a day or two and bring it over beforehand so that nothing private needs to be picked up in front of the plumbers. I will message you when I'm on my way home from work if they're not finished by then and I will come in when you let me know you're ready."

"But Suze, it's your home!"

"And if I can't put that second to Lee's privacy, comfort and dignity for a day or two, then I'm not much of a neighbour or a friend."

Tan nodded, his appreciation glistening in his amber eyes. "Thank you so much; that means a lot to both of us. We're going to miss you when you move out, you know; we're excited for you, of course, and let's hope we're all lucky with our next neighbours!"

Susannah turned back to her key in the door. "Keep me posted on when it's going to be happening; I'll drop the spare key through your letterbox. Meanwhile, I'd better get in and feed these cats of mine."

She thought back over her conversation with Morven as she distracted the cats with some kibble before setting out their main meal and changing the water in their drinking bowl. Had she not met Tan by chance on the landing, she wouldn't have known about their plumbing dilemma and been able to help them. She hadn't been in contact often enough recently to know about something so sensitive. The onus should not be on people to always 'reach out' at their most vulnerable times. Despite Lee's major surgery, as the subsequent months went on she had been too preoccupied and lost track of time too much to have checked in often enough for this to fall into place organically. The lads could have been freed earlier from the stress of worrying about how they would manage during the works. Her supervisor was right; she needed to address her own health and wellbeing so that she could keep her life in balance and be able to be there for other people.

Susannah sang the uplifting refrain of 'New Emotion' to herself as she sifted through another day's junk mail and organised everything she needed for the morning. The gift of being reminded of that happy time, spontaneously reliving it with a neighbour as she went about her day, would be high up on her Grounds for Gratitude list on Sunday. Her hand caught the light shade as she impulsively reprised the dance moves of those less inhibited days. The familiar jolt brought the equally typical flare of annoyance; after one resigned shake of her head, it quickly faded into insignificance.

Relaxing into an uneventful, winding down workday evening, Susannah tucked a comforting fleece blanket around her; its muted dark colours in a tartan effect pattern which she found restful to her eyes. Both cats climbed onto her; Annika settled on her lap while Morgan cuddled into her chest. Their contented purrs pulsated through the warm layers. She stroked them both, rubbing their ears and smiling as they stretched their silky heads back, eyes blissfully closed for her to scratch under their chins.

18

Julian Remembers

Concern showed in Julian Silverdale's kindly grey eyes and the furrowing of his brow as he leaned in closer to his computer screen, the camera picking up the lighter strands beginning to pepper his neatly combed sandy hair.

"A *ghost?*"

Susannah told her brother everything, including her own attempts to rationalise it all away; the recording, the unaccountable singing, the dreams and the corroborating evidence which Frieda had confirmed without there having been any way she could have known about particular phrases.

"I believe you, Suze; I'm open minded about the paranormal and even if I wasn't, you believe that this is a spirit and that's good enough for me. Your conclusions and the way you've arrived at them are sound. I don't know how I would feel if I were living alone and had unexplained phenomena going on around me though. Are you OK; is it frightening you?"

"Not really; it's more that it makes me sad to think of what Mary went through, and that she must have died so young. I don't get the feeling she's an angry or violent spirit, and the cats aren't reacting in a threatened way either; they're definitely picking up on her presence but they're not stressed by it. I know I'm probably projecting some of my worries about Freya too, and about my own standards slipping of course."

"You know I'm with your supervisor on that one. You need to make allowances for the strain you're under; you're bound to miss a few things and make mistakes. Anyone would."

"But you and Isobel…"

"Were younger, and had each other as well as geographically closer family support available from both sides. You can't compare the two sets of circumstances, Suze. And do you think neither of us made mistakes, forgot things, got things mixed up or got extra irritable when we were moving?"

"I can vouch for that!", a female voice called in the background; Julian laughed and leaned back to let his amused wife wave hello.

"Hey, Izzy"; Susannah waved back to her sister-in-law before Isobel disappeared off screen leaving them to talk privately. "I do understand what you're getting at, and I know I'm fortunate to be living in more informed times than Mary was. I may not be able to help her to find peace, but Freya is another matter. I wish I could get through to her and help her to move forward. We haven't talked properly since the awful argument we had after my birthday; I have to let her find her own way. It's such a waste of the beautiful person I know is in there; the person who was so thoughtful about letting me know when she found out Edie had died, knowing how much she meant to me and that I'd thought about looking her up before I move. It's getting to me that although Freya is still here with her future ahead of her and the potential to make changes for the better, I can't influence that now any more than I can change anything that happened to Mary. I suppose that's why I had a particularly heartbreaking dream about her that night after Freya was last here. The strangest thing about that was, when I woke up but I wasn't quite out of the dream yet and I thought I could still see Mary; as she faded away, I heard her say that she wasn't merry any more. The thought of the carefree side to her that Frieda said got her the nickname 'Merry Mary'; always singing, playing out with her friends and loving her visits to her doting grandmother, being gone before Mary herself was."

Julian was so still that Susannah wondered whether the screen had frozen until he tapped one finger against his chin.

"You know, since you mentioned Edie, that's reminded me of something from when I used to take you to the library. One day, I'd gone to the desk to ask her a question and she was talking to a woman I'd never seen before; around her own age, I'd say, and quite distinctive-looking. Tall, black hair; kind of Spanish or Italian-looking though she had a local accent. Anyway, it was clear that Edie knew her but hadn't seen her for a long time. I got the impression that they'd been part of the same group of friends as children. Edie said something about Merry Mary having died and that she was the only one left. I don't recall the exact words, but she definitely mentioned that 'Merry Mary died years ago'. It seems feasible that they'd have been around the same age. I'm so sorry you won't be able to ask Edie about her."

"Thanks, Jules; me too. I know I hadn't seen her for many years and I rarely thought about her until recently, but I miss Edie now that I know she's gone. If there were more people like her in the world, I honestly think that there wouldn't be so much of the vicious cycle that exacerbates the coordination issues of dyspraxia. Yes, things would still go wrong, but it's made worse by society's obsession with how people *should* be and by what age. Edie was rare in that she never subscribed to that, but her way of accepting people needs to become the default before real change can happen. There needs to be no shame in an older child or adult needing, for instance, a bit more time to fix left and right in their mind when orientating themselves or describing the location of something, or in them finding it easier to have instructions written down or photos provided, or finding it impossible to formulate directions for someone else when asked even in a place they know. Nobody expects every person to be equally good at running, or singing, or cooking; people don't change how they respect and interact with someone because they're not great at any of those things. It's one part of life and people who aren't very skilled in any of those areas get by as best they can when the activities crop up, without it defining their entire selves. And the physical aspects of coordination; I'm convinced they get worse when people get signals from whatever radar they have that picks up the subtle tells we can't control and bark warnings and pre-emptive tellings-off at us. They judge us before we've even started to head into a glitch let alone for something actually happening. It's distracting, it breaks our vital concentration, and it contributes to the nervousness which makes us more likely to misjudge. It draws hostile attention from people and undermines our belief in ourselves; leads us to worry over why we get singled out from others in the same set of circumstances. It affects our confidence, so we appear more and more visibly 'off', and so the spiral continues. All from that subtle differentness which wouldn't be a problem in itself and would be magnified less often, less intensely, if people would back off and give us space."

"Absolutely, and this is an aspect of advocacy which needs to be disentangled from the concept of internalised ableism. Which is hard when these conversations tend to happen in the heat of the moment when the person with lived experience is under stress, so it does come over that way and gets swept up in the general dismissal as bruised ego, defensiveness on both sides, 'Trying To Help' victimhood and so on."

"That's a brilliant point, Jules; I agree, it needs to be talked about more in calm and objective settings. It's my vision!"

After the video call ended, Susannah's mind fizzed with overload at the simultaneous flood of questions and connections. Frieda had mentioned that Lorna from that end house where the children played outside on those long-ago

Sundays had an Italian surname; the woman in the library may well have been her daughter, Teresa. She, Mary, and Frieda's colleague Dorothy had been part of a bigger group; one of those unnamed others must surely have been Edie.

Mary and Edie knew each other? They were friends?

The thought comforted her somewhat; she presumed that Edie was as big-hearted and inclusive as a child as she was when Susannah knew her. She would definitely be including that when she did her next Sunday morning Grounds for Gratitude ritual; her heart sank once more as she contemplated Freya's absence.

19

Curve Ball

Freya ate her sandwich with the deliberate, exaggerated daintiness of a child who knew she was in trouble; her pale blonde hair falling forward and hiding her face as she bent over her phone in between bites. Their fragile break room truce united them on a bridge of glass against the greater enemy of the office's social gestalt. Susannah took out her own phone, glad to distract herself from the awkwardness by checking what she had missed during the first half of the working day.

One notification she was not expecting was a missed call from Adil. He had followed it up with a text message apologising that he realised she was at work but asking her to call him back when she could.

"Adil needs me to contact him urgently; I'll need to step outside."

Freya looked up, genuine concern in her eyes. "I hope it's something that can be sorted quickly for you."

Susannah nodded her acknowledgement and hurried down to the main entrance. She found a spot near the car park where she was safe from traffic and a wall blocked out most of the noise from the road, and called Adil.

"Hey, Susannah; thank you for getting back to me. I'm so sorry but I have some bad news about the property on Crieff Gardens."

She had told herself throughout the process that she was prepared for a call like this; at the same time she knew there was no way to be fully ready for it. Her own lunch balled painfully in the tensed space beneath her ribs as adrenalin coursed through her hands and chest. She gripped her phone, turning aside to clear her dry throat before asking Adil to continue.

"The people in the neighbouring flat contacted the current owner as they've been having some alterations done and I'm afraid that during those works, extensive asbestos has been found in the building. There is no doubt that the subject property will be similarly affected, and I need to advise you that given the extent of the electrical work required, the survey and treatment needed there will add to your budget and timescale to a significant degree. So much so that as your legal advisor I have to recommend that you withdraw from the purchase. You are fully entitled to do so; at this stage there is nothing legally binding in place. That doesn't get sealed in until missives are concluded and contracts exchanged. I understand, though, that this is a major disappointment for you. I truly am sorry, and I expect you will need some time to process and consider this. Asbestos is found in an awful lot of buildings from before 1999 and it is not always a deal breaker, but in this case it adds too much to the scope of what this property is going to need in terms of highly expensive, invasive and time-consuming works. I wish I could have brought you better news."

"But… the home report, the seller's questionnaire said…"

"I know; they answered no to whether they were *aware* of asbestos in the property. I understand that it's no consolation, but I do believe this was genuinely a shock to them; especially the extent to which it has been identified. They acknowledged how disappointing it would be for you."

"Yeah. For them too, of course; they're stuck with this problem now. I feel for you having to tell me this news. You're right; I need some time to let this sink in, but I'm inclined to agree that it's not something I have the scope to take on. I'll give you formal instruction by email once I've had time to get my head around this. Wow. I mean, I did try so hard to hold onto a degree of detachment until missives were concluded. I refused to call it 'my' anything; I corrected other people if they referred to it as such! But I'm realising now that I didn't do a good enough job! I was seeing myself living there, planning out my weekend walks from that specific base, thinking about what would go where, waking up on my birthday and Christmas and New Year's Day there! Who was I kidding, Adil; I was paying lip service to not getting attached. I'm such a fool!"

"Susannah, please don't beat yourself up so unfairly on top of this setback. Once your offer had been accepted and you were able to feel confident about the work we knew was needed, it was entirely natural and appropriate for you to start thinking that way; you needed to in order to start the practical side. Nobody would expect you to stay fully emotionally distant. You have done nothing wrong. I need you to promise me you will hold on to that; this letdown is enough in itself for you to deal with. Do you have support around you to work through this and decide how and when to move forward with your search?"

She could not have uttered a word right then if her life had depended on it. Adil's well-intentioned question bringing the state of her friendship with Freya back to the forefront of her mind as it whirled with this quicksand shift of her mental landscape was too much. Leaning against the solid reality of the wall behind her, she forced herself to take a deep breath.

"That's a work in progress too, Adil, but I'll figure it out. My parents and my older siblings have been through the process of buying their homes; I'm lucky to have a supportive landlord too, she has a lot of experience. I'll be fine. Thank you."

"Very well, you take care of yourself, Susannah."

"You too."

She ended the call and slumped against the freezing cold stone, staring at the bland face of her phone screen as though it could somehow animate before her eyes with a magical solution. The disorientating feeling of the first property slipping away had been bad enough; this one, after so much longer and with more apparent certainty, was next level. The bombshell clattered around the roulette wheel of her rapidly adjusting thoughts, landing in quick succession on the most random of details. The personalised address labels on the website she had been browsing, wanting to have that research done so that once she was busy with the move itself she could get on quickly with the order. The hexagonal paving stones at the other end of the long street where it widened towards a junction and a couple of rowan trees stood; where she had pictured herself taking a walk to as an absolute minimum on days when she was tired or the weather was too daunting. The train timetable which she had perused out of sheer curiosity because she would see them passing by; the fancy hot chocolate which had come up as a suggestion as she browsed for a gift order and how she imagined drinking it under the stars in the garden as the sleeper headed south.

Would she have outside space in her forever home? Was that feasible with her budget in the centre of Perth?

That was back to being an unknown factor. It was all back to unknown factors. Back to square one. And it was almost December. By the time she found something else suitable and viewed it, the Christmas holidays would be almost upon her.

How many viewings would it take now; how many uncertain bus journeys through to Perth in inclement weather as the winter took hold? Perhaps it would be best to wait at least until after the holidays; to take some time out to regroup. She was fortunate to be in a position to do so; she ought to make use of that. Meanwhile, she had to get through the practicalities moment by moment. She would ask Adil to invoice her for the work he had done so far if she was going to take a break; that was fair. Before that, she had to face going back into work; seeing Freya. Susannah knew that she would take no pleasure in this turn of events, but the brittle form of their current relationship was not a load-bearing structure.

Whatever her feelings and dilemmas, the hard fact remained that she was due back at her desk. She felt an incongruous pang of guilt at the thought of Freya watching the minutes tick by, eventually making her own way back to her workstation without knowing what had happened and whether it would be shared with her; their next interaction in the hostile territory of the office holding more uncertainty for her than for Susannah.

She walked back into the building, stiff-legged and slow. Years of self-aware practice kicked in as she paid extra attention to every doorframe, every step, every protruding handle. It nevertheless took her two attempts to press the correct buttons on the combination lock, only to realise she had forgotten to clock back in on the machine in the hallway.

She got the combination right straightaway the next time, though Maya's smirk as she passed her in the aisle told her that the backtracking had not gone unnoticed. Freya sat straight-backed at her desk, focused on her computer; Susannah went directly to her own desk, thankful to be due back there.

Sitting down, she reopened the file on which she had been working before she paused for lunch.

Before. In that past time, when she was getting herself through the day against the backdrop of her new life to come. Her new life living on Crieff Gardens, Perth.

The mundane march of figures and readings danced and blurred together; the tears were a mere blink away, and the blink was as unstoppable as the sinking of the sun in the washed-out late November sky.

Morven's hand was gentle on her shoulder; however her supervisor had come to be at her side so quickly, she was a blessing of compassion as she discreetly escorted Susannah to the side room, giving her the time she needed to tell her what had happened.

"I'm so sorry; I just need a minute to sort myself out, then I'll get back on it. Thank you for having my back; it's lucky you were so close by."

A smile graced Morven's kind face. "Actually, it wasn't down to luck. Freya came and spoke to me; she said that you had to return an urgent call from your solicitor and she asked me to keep an eye on you when you got back."

Susannah accepted the tissue which her supervisor already had to hand as the full rush of emotion finally hit her.

"Go home and take the time you need; I'll put through a half day flexi credit for you to cover this afternoon. I want you to get a good night's sleep and see how you feel in the morning; you've been under a lot of stress and you haven't taken much leave for some time. I know you're saving that up for the move and I don't want to add to your stress by asking you to use any of it now, but I do think you should consider talking to your doctor and getting signed off for a couple of weeks. It would be an investment at this point, to get you refreshed and well enough to move forward. You are needed and valued here; please don't think you're in trouble or being pushed out. As your line manager I have that duty of care I spoke of to you, and I can see the strain you're under; possibly more clearly than you can. Would you like me to tell the rest of the team what's happened?"

She gulped out her thanks and assent, splashed some cool water on her face in the toilets and went to collect her things. Freya looked up as she passed, eyes wide with unspoken questions; Susannah mimed typing on a phone to indicate that she would send a message. Tanya approached her as she put on her coat, her sympathy genuine.

"Sorry to hear about the house, Suze. I know you were really looking forward to moving in, but it just means that there's something better out there for you."

Susannah gritted her teeth, firmly telling herself to let the value of Tanya's olive branch override the internal scream of 'too soon'.

"Thanks, Tanya; I appreciate that."

"I didn't think asbestos was a thing any more! Wasn't it used for a few decades then made illegal?"

Did she think it remotely feasible that it had all since been eliminated from deep within the fabric of every building which already contained it by the time it was banned? *She's trying. Don't be mean.*

"It was, but some buildings which were constructed long before it was in regular use can turn out to contain it if there were big structural alterations made during the time it was common. I think that's what happened in this case."

"Such a shame you didn't manage to find that out sooner. You should have gotten a more detailed survey done. Oh well, you live and learn."

Reverting to type like an elastic band pinging back into shape, then. That didn't take long. "Indeed. Thanks for checking in, Tanya; I'll see you in a couple of weeks."

She marched dry-eyed past colleagues who concealed their curiosity to varying degrees and headed out into the tired chill of the afternoon.

Arriving home, the innocently trusting greeting of her cats brought the tears back unbidden. Susannah flopped down on her bed, unwilling to face the depressing non-view in the living room. Lorna's light flickered on under the prematurely darkening sky, its sensor responding to the worsening weather; she watched as it glowed a sickly greenish-white, then warmed with a watery valiantness to pale pink before gradually brightening to that odd mix of peach and blue-green, then all ghostly aqua before settling on the solid warm pinkish tone it was supposed to be. She smiled at the thought of how much Bethany's friend Diane would have enjoyed that show; the reminder of Perth and the future Susannah's mind had begun to populate there tugged at her heart once again.

"Let's face it; I'm going to be here for a bit longer than I thought, so I may as well make the most of it"; she stood up with fresh determination and walked into the living room where she had dumped her bag. Pulling out her phone, she sent a message to Freya outlining what had happened and thanking her for giving Morven the heads-up to look out for her, then copy pasted the relevant part to her siblings. She made herself a cup of tea and settled down to drink it; she may as well get used to being back to searching again and have a look at the property websites.

There was another property on Crieff Gardens, added the previous day. It was more expensive, but bigger and on the first floor.

Was this a good idea? If this were a relationship scenario, every scrap of common sense and every observing acquaintance would be shrieking about rebound. It couldn't do any harm to take a look at the home report though, could it? She took a gulp of tea, flinching as the hot liquid irritated her throat, and clicked on the button to open the 'Request More Information' form.

Her phone rang as she was finishing her cup of tea. Though it had been many years since her sibling had announced their new name, seeing 'London calling' on her screen never failed to make her smile.

"Hey, Suze. I am so sorry about the house! How are you bearing up?"

"To be honest, it hasn't sunk in properly yet. I mean, apart from feeling foolish since one of my delightful colleagues pointed out that I 'hadn't managed' to find out about the asbestos earlier."

"Seriously? They actually said that? Do they have a background in the building trade then?"; the sarcasm in London's voice was unmistakable.

"Not at all; just, you know, an expert in Things Susannah Should Have Done Better. She was surprised that the stuff still existed because of the law having changed. The combination of having heard about that in some random context and the unpopular colleague getting caught out makes her an authority on asbestos. It's so galling. She's never shown an interest in structural engineering or architecture. I'm surprised she didn't think asbestos was a Greek island!"

"Haha! Off the coast of Domestos, I presume?"

"Well, that would certainly account for the bleached white sands! Och, I shouldn't be so catty; I think she was genuinely commiserating for about thirty seconds before the opportunity to score points became too tempting. Small wins."

"Sure. Anyway, speaking of coastal resorts, the main reason I'm calling is to ask if you'd like to come up and join Fran and me for a couple of nights when we go to Nairn. As you know, we book an apartment there at this time and catch up with her sister and her family. The apartment has two bedrooms and after the knockbacks you've had, if you're going to take some sick leave it would do you good to get away for a break."

"That's so kind of you both, but I'd have to make arrangements for the cats. Things are too strained with Freya for me to ask her to come round and see to them. I could ask my neighbours, but one of them had major surgery a few months ago and he has to be extra cautious about hygiene. I don't want to make any assumptions either way; I'll need to read up about his particular situation and dealing with litter trays before I decide whether it would be appropriate to ask. Can I get back to you?"

"Of course; I understand. The offer's open if you are able to sort something out; just let us know."

The estate agent had replied with the home report by the time Susannah ended the call. She opened it on her tablet and looked through it, noting a few concerns about damp and woodworm infestation. Perhaps that could give her scope to negotiate? Reminding herself not to rush into a decision, she picked up her phone to look into advice about the safety of people with a colostomy bag or those living with them scooping and changing cat litter. Although there were obvious warnings around someone having a cat on their lap kneading or playing around the area where the bag was, there didn't seem to be any general consensus that they couldn't coexist and certainly there was no reason why Tan would not be able to come over to her flat and see to their food and litter. With a watchful approach and the vulnerable area well protected by thick material, Lee would be quite safe to be around the cats and to sit with them; it would be as therapeutic for him as for anyone who liked cats. Of course she needed to find out whether they were available and willing, but her mind was set at rest that it would not be wrong or putting them in an awkward position to ask them.

Tan appeared tired but happy to see her when he answered the door. "Suze! Come in, come in. Lee's having a lie down"; his expression became serious as he lowered his voice. "He's had an upset stomach, so it's been a bad time for him. He's lost some weight so he's getting a new bag fitted tomorrow as his stoma has gotten a bit smaller through the weight loss."

Susannah lowered her own voice. "I'm so sorry, Tan. I can come back…"

"No; please stay for a bit! It's important to both of us to know that people aren't put off. The company will do him good."

"Of course; I didn't mean to come across as being squeamish about it. I meant if he was resting and not feeling up to entertaining visitors."

"I know that, don't worry. I appreciate your consideration; we both do. He's through here. He'll be interested to hear about how things are coming along with your move."

"Actually, I do have a bit of news about that." She pulled gently on Tan's sleeve as he turned towards the lounge. "Before we go through: if you need any extra washing done, I'll take it any time. I'm going to be around more over the next couple of weeks; I'm going to be taking a bit of time off work."

"Thank you; that's incredibly thoughtful. We will bear it in mind. I gather it's not good news about your move though, honey; what's happened?"

Susannah outlined the situation, ending with her interest in the property she had seen listed and obtaining the home report.

"Tan? Who's at the door?", Lee's voice came from the inner room, its door closed to keep the heat in.

"It's OK, Lee; it's Suze. Poor love has had to withdraw from the house purchase; there's been asbestos found throughout the building." Tan gave her an apologetic look, lowering his voice once more. "Lee's dad is a building surveyor so he's picked up a bit of knowledge. Would you let Lee have a look at this new home report?"

"I can nip back through and get my tablet, but with his knowledge I hope I'm not going to end up feeling foolish."

"Not at all; by researching these things, you're doing your due diligence. Nobody expects a lay person buying for the first time to know technical stuff. To be honest, it would really help Lee's self-confidence if you could let him be useful and give you a bit of advice."

"Well, since you put it that way, that's fair enough. Let me pop back in and get it."

Lee was sitting up, a red, yellow and black tartan blanket tucked around him when Susannah returned with her tablet. She sat down next to him and brought the home report up on the screen as Tan handed Lee his reading glasses.

"I'm conscious that I've had a big disappointment and I might not be in the best place to be impartial right now, especially with the prospect of being back to square one this close to Christmas. It would be helpful to have a detached perspective."

Tan smiled warmly and touched her shoulder as he handed them each a glass of wine.

Lee frowned as he scrolled through the report. "Your reservations are justified, I'm afraid. I'm sorry, Suze; I wish I could reassure you and encourage you to go for it, but I'm seeing a few red flags here. The concerns about dampness in concealed areas; you could be looking at rotted floor joists and damaged supporting timbers. The woodworm issue appears to be active as well as widespread too; it mentions evidence of frass. That's the waste product; basically woodworm poop."

Susannah giggled despite her sinking heart. "That works quite well as a pseudo-swearword, like saying 'sugar' for 'shit'. 'Oh, *frass*!' I'll need to suggest that one to Freya one day; she scandalised her mum by dropping an F-bomb last time I was there! 'Fodder' works well too."

Lee laughed, sipping his wine and raising his glass towards his partner. "Good choice, Tan; a good brambly chewiness to this one. I've been a tad under the weather so this is the first drink I've had in a while; I'm taking it easy, but I'm enjoying this. Ah, Suze; I hate to add to your recent disappointment but no; I cannot in good conscience recommend that you go any further with this one."

"Thank you for your honesty, Lee; that was my instinctive thought too but having it endorsed by someone with knowledge helps me to put this one to rest quickly before I have any chance to get my hopes up or think 'what if'. I will let the estate agent know that I won't be seeking a viewing of this one." She sighed. "I know I'm guilty of being too impatient and going for it for the wrong reasons. I think I'm trying to keep the connection to the one I've lost because of the little signs which made it feel so meant to be. I don't want those to turn out to be meaningless. For instance, when I was in Adil's office, one beautiful perfect deep red maple leaf floated down past the window. It was lying in clear view under a streetlight when I left, I brought the leaf back to my flat and pressed it. I know it's silly, but because the reason that meeting was such a high hasn't worked out after all, I feel as though I can't trust my instincts or enjoy beautiful moments like that which seem significant any more. So I had that need for the right property to be a part of that same cosmic thread, so that I don't need to be so sad about that on top of the loss of the actual house. If that makes sense?"

"Of course it does"; Lee reached out and took her hand as he and Tan both nodded empathically. "You're not being impatient either; you're continuing an ongoing project. As for the signs like finding the maple leaf, they are all part of the same story; just maybe not in the way you expected. Everything that happens is leading you to the right outcome. We don't know why the processes are sometimes so complicated and why there are what appear to be red herrings, but it does all connect up."

Susannah sipped her wine. "I will try to hold on to that. I do think, as well, that much as I believe in signs, it's important to consider that not everything that comes across as a sign truly is. I need to let my Scully side keep me grounded and question my Mulder side when it's showing me what I want to see. Our brains seek meanings and patterns all the time; there will be instances where it's our own wishful thinking, and also coincidences which are precisely that and nothing more. Or moments which stand out in some positive way and are simply to be enjoyed with thankfulness. Speaking of which, have either of you recently seen or heard a little girl singing in our stair? Freya's thought she heard one a time or two but neither of us has ever seen one."

The two men looked at one another. "Come to think of it", said Tan, "didn't you mention something a few weeks back about hearing a kid singing, Lee? Yes; it was a Sunday and I had heard similar before that and I said to you that I was sure that was on a Sunday too. It's funny how none of us have ever seen the child, but then if we've been in our homes when we heard it and the wee one was in the stair, we wouldn't have. Unless of course the place is haunted!"; Susannah joined in with the general laughter, not wanting to make Lee think too deeply about spirits floating around their building when he was dealing with sensitive and very private medical matters.

"I'm sure it's simply someone visiting with family, especially if it's usually at the weekend. Look, it's been massively helpful getting your take on this home report; I may call upon you for that again in future if that's OK?"

"It's no problem. Any time. You will get your forever home; it will be there waiting for you. I know that will sound meaningless at the moment…"

"No, you're right. It needs to be somewhere I can feel safe; where I won't be on edge all the time, jumping at every normal building noise, peering at every drop of condensation. I could have the perfect location and every feature I ever wanted in a home, but if it had issues beyond the scope of what I could deal with, it would ruin all that. It would take all the joy out of living there. No; wherever my home turns out to be, it already exists, it's already built and I've yet to meet it. That is actually exciting. You know, I'm feeling things about this move that match the description of how a lot of people feel about looking for a partner. The sexual aspect has never resonated with me and I don't feel any need for romance; the lack of feeling any attraction happens to dovetail nicely with not being drawn to the concept of being in that sort of relationship or living with someone, so it's not something I've ever seen as a problem or something missing and I've never needed to think that deeply about it. I've reached the age where the questions about it tail off and it's a relief, but in the vague, decreased inconvenience way like when you first realise it's late enough in the year that you can open a window without worrying too much that a wasp will fly in! But that excitement about a search for something which is going to be the foundation for the shape of what my life going forward will look like, choosing from the options out there which are available to me; I think I'm beginning to understand people on the relationship quest a bit better in a pragmatic sense. I know it's not the same thing, but it has to be a positive, if it makes me more empathic towards something which is so important to many people."

Tan and Lee's eyes shone animatedly; no longer dominated by the fatigue she had seen in both men when she had arrived.

"Susannah, this is fabulous on many levels. Spot-on attitude to your house hunting, and…"; Tan faltered, unsure of boundaries as Lee nodded encouragement; "Have you heard much about the concept of being aroace?"

"Aromantic and asexual? Yes; I'd say that applies to me. I've never felt the need to research it but I should; it's never brought me into conflict with anyone or adversely affected my life but I know there are people who do get bullied, put under pressure, disbelieved, coerced, attempts made to medicalise or correct it. I've come across testimony about people being diverted away from treatment they need for medical matters because their lack of attraction was seen as a symptom, or something which the medication they need would make 'worse'. Some people go through anguish because they don't realise they're not alone in how they feel and it is perfectly valid; they absorb society's general ethos that it's a problem and makes them incomplete. Some people's family or cultural background actively expects or mandates them entering into a sexual and romantic relationship; the fact that it has never become an ongoing issue for me is a privilege. So I should do my bit towards the unquestioned belonging of asexuality and aromanticism in society. I will read up about it."

Lee squeezed her hand, tears in his eyes. "This calls for another glass of wine for our dear friend and neighbour, Tan; I won't take any more this time when my stomach is so fragile, but we need to welcome her to the LGBTQIAP+ community!"

"P is pansexual, isn't it? See, I have always had the feeling that if I ever did find myself experiencing attraction, it would be specific to the person. Their gender wouldn't matter, and it wouldn't define me as being attracted to that gender beyond that one person. I may well never have cause to put that to the test, and I realise that's what asexuality and aromanticism are; I do know that it's not 'hetero by default', and that viewing it as such is harmful because it leads to gatekeeping among minority groups. My experience up to this point is that I am asexual and aromantic. But hypothetically, since I also know that asexual and aromantic are each on a spectrum, is it possible to be pansexual and panromantic too?"

"There is such a thing as greysexual or greyromantic, which some say better describes being somewhere on that spectrum; you could be either of those and pan. It's your experience and nobody can define it but you. It's also OK not to know, or for your identity to fluctuate or shift. You don't need to have all the answers for now and the rest of your life. Nobody does, and it doesn't make you confused or a traitor if things change for you."

Lee chimed in; "I think what I'm hearing is that you do know what you feel and don't feel; that you are clear on not experiencing attraction, but you're worried that at some point in the future it may not feel quite so clear-cut and you're afraid it will somehow disqualify you from an identity which has become important to you and the support and community that goes with owning that identity? That your friends and contacts who are part of that community will feel you've let them down?"

"Yes, I'd say that's accurate; I think I'm also afraid of giving credence to any of the misleading and harmful stereotypes. Like, for instance, if I were to feel differently about the prospect of being in a relationship whatever that looked like as a result of someone coming into my life, I'd be unable to explore that because I'd be guilty of perpetuating the myth that aroace people 'just haven't met the right person yet'. As you say, Lee, I am clear on not having experienced that, and I'm not concerned by the thought that I may never feel differently. I just want to feel that if I did, I wouldn't be forbidden or seen as a traitor. It's like, for example, Switzerland is a fascinating and beautiful country. I get why people want to go there. I'd be interested to see and hear about other people's trips there, but it wouldn't make me jealous or make me feel a need to go there myself. If one day for whatever reason, some new perspective made me want to visit Switzerland, I'd like to think that I would be able to. If someone were to tell me now that I could never go to Switzerland, or that if I did then I wouldn't be allowed to stay in Scotland on my own terms once I got back nor to resume my interest in Scandinavia, I would feel extremely uneasy. I want to be able to say that I'd hate to be barred from ever going to Switzerland without it being interpreted as meaning that I secretly want to go, or making a lie of my lifelong affinity with Nordic and Scandi culture. I couldn't deal with suddenly being pressured to book a trip to Switzerland, bombarded with links to travel deals or dragged to the airport by well-meaning people who assume that I don't know my own mind or what's good for me, or that I'm scared, and I simply need a push. Most of all, though, I wouldn't want it to be used against other people who didn't want to go; to put pressure on or force *them* to go because my changing my feelings about it undermined the validity of theirs!"

"That's an excellent way of explaining it; we completely understand your fears and respect your judgement. And if you did meet someone and find yourself wanting a relationship, you would not be perpetuating any stereotype. It wouldn't invalidate how you felt up to then. Your orientation is not a choice, and if it changes that isn't a choice either. There are queerplatonic and quasiplatonic relationships too; partnerships which are distinct from friendships or housemates but which don't include sex and romance. Your path through life whether it stays the same or changes over the years cannot define any other person's. It is your own, and you are certainly not obliged to suppress any change because ignorant people wilfully misinterpret an entire group. We will always hold safe space for you any time you want to talk about anything."

"Thank you both; that's helpful and makes me feel very safe and accepted. I don't believe at this point that the 'pan' label fits me, because I don't feel attraction and never have, full stop. But I'm glad I haven't done wrong by having that nebulous sense of relating to it in a way I don't to straight, gay or bi."

"Of course it's not wrong to process your feelings, examine any conflicts and ask questions. We're here for you any time, and that will remain after you move house."

"Honestly, thank you so much." She raised her glass to them and took a drink; Tan went to get the bottle. When he returned, she remembered the other thing she needed to ask them. They were more than happy to look after Annika and Morgan while she went away for a few days; that only left a call to her GP's surgery in the morning to arrange to formalise her time off work and then she would be able to take London and Fran up on their offer of a break.

She yawned as she composed a short email to the estate agents advising that with regret, she would not be following up on her initial interest in the property due to the issues raised in the home report. Disappointment clouded her thoughts, but it was a more distant pale altostratus rather than the previous heavy cumulus drag; all matters for another day. She went into the bedroom to plug in her tablet to charge; it had gotten quite low and she wanted it out of immediate reach so that she would not be tempted to keep using it making the charging take longer. Lorna's light glowed staunchly ambient peach on its quiet corner; Susannah grinned recalling the first time she had voiced her thoughts on her orientation out loud. "My neighbours were so supportive when I told them what I told you!", she said in the direction of the window, revelling in the warm feeling of solidarity and easing of several burdens. "If things were resolved with Freya, I'd be happier, but let's focus on one step at a time."

20

She's Purring

The locum GP who called Susannah back was happy to provide a note for two weeks; she relayed that confirmation to Morven, thanking her again for her understanding and for wisely encouraging her to take this time which she now accepted that she needed. Her supervisor assured her that it was no problem for her to go to Nairn for a break with family during that time. Cosy in her dressing gown and pyjamas, Susannah relaxed and took her time over a second cup of coffee; the cats making the most of her being home, warm and sleepy beside her. It was mid morning before she went out to collect the note from the surgery; a low, pale sun was hesitantly breaking through the cumulus clouds, demurely reaching out to interrupt the reigning gloom.

November was a month of shifting layers held thinly over the rawness beneath; an understated battle between amber lights and grey shadows. It dawned a stark sequel to the colourful dreamlit awakening of September and October, with a quickening of its own as the earth conversely prepared to sink into hibernation. The hourglass urgency of the shortening days lit fading afternoons with a call to action before the winter descended. Early autumn held space for planning and dreaming alongside its stirring freshness; November was the time to get up and deal. She should have been surging forward into the active stage of her move; beginning the process of packing up her belongings. Her thoughts stretched around the hollow inverted busyness of adjusting to the limbo in which she had suddenly found herself; their coherence as distorted and meaningless as matter at the event horizon of a black hole.

Ouch! A dislodged kerb stone caught her out, turning her ankle; fortunately only enough to annoy and hurt in passing. Whatever Morven, Julian or anyone else said, she needed to up her game; she could not afford an injury. Distraction and dyspraxia were a lethal combination and she did not have the luxury of narrowing her world to a small, safe bubble whenever multiple stressors taxed her. She had no choice but to work harder at making up the shortfall in her proprioception, depth perception, situational awareness and everything else she needed to keep herself safe.

Slipping the doctor's note into the envelope she had prepared with Morven's name, room number and telephone extension number on it, she handed it to the security guard at reception and thankfully made her way home, cringing at the memory of her close shave with the kerb stone. Her phone pinged with a message as she heated some soup for lunch; she conscientiously forced herself to focus on the task in hand and went to check it as her soup was cooling. As expected, it was Morven acknowledging receipt of her sick note; she was urging her to rest up, look after herself and enjoy her time in Nairn. Which reminded her; she needed to confirm with London and then tell Tan and Lee that she was definitely going away. She messaged her sibling, clarifying that she would rather travel through the week when it was quieter if that suited them, then sent a brief message to Freya; despite her concerns about giving in and enablement, it was fair to let her know that she was off for two weeks. She ate her lunch and tidied up before settling down with some puzzle apps for as relaxing and distracting an afternoon as possible in between making her arrangements.

Late in the evening her phone pinged again. Instantly apprehensive in case it was London or one of her neighbours needing to change their plans, she snatched it up.

It was Freya.

"Hello Susannah. Thank you for telling me that you're taking a couple of weeks off. I am sorry that things are tough for you right now, and I realise that I have added to that lately. I don't know whether you want to see me or feel up to it, but I've had a long, honest conversation with my mum tonight and I've faced up to a few things. Please may I come and visit you some time to talk? I'd rather not do it in a public place for the sake of all our privacy. I will wait to hear from you in your own time."

Guarded, and no apology as such, but she realised how much it must have taken for Freya to make that wary move. Susannah hadn't the heart to make her wait for the sake of it; she tapped out a reply, equally formal in tone but thanking her for reaching out and telling her she was welcome to come up after work the next day.

"Thank you for coming"; Susannah stepped back to let Freya in. Her heart constricted at the obvious apprehension pervading her friend's entire body language; the fear in her downcast eyes, but she kept her own demeanour impassive. Closing the door, she took the bottle of wine Freya wordlessly held out and indicated to her to go through to the living room. She poured two glasses of wine in the kitchen; taking the drinks through, she felt a mild stab of irritation as she saw that Freya was standing uncertainly next to her usual chair and had not even unzipped her coat. She chose to give her the benefit of the doubt on that one, hoping that it was genuine nervousness rather than a passive-aggressive play for reassurance. Her having opened the wine appeared to answer any questions Freya may have had about how long she would be allowed to stay; she took off the small handbag she had been wearing across her body and then her coat, handing it to Susannah with a meek 'thanks' and sitting down. The cats, curled up together for warmth, stirred briefly in their cosy bed; Freya glanced at them before hastily returning her focus to Susannah.

She placed the glasses on the coasters and sat down. "I'm listening", she said in as neutral a tone as she could manage.

"OK, so…"; Freya took a deep, shuddering breath. "Last time I was here, I said some things I shouldn't have. I was way out of line, rude and cruel. I didn't mean them; I was backed into a corner and lashing out because I couldn't cope, but that is no excuse. I was wrong to say them and…"; she gulped, looking into the middle distance; "I am sorry for that and for my abuse of your valuable friendship."

"Thank you. I know that must have taken you a lot of courage. I appreciate it, and I accept your apology, but it's going to take a bit of time to repair the trust between us."

"I know that; I didn't expect things to go back to how they were as though nothing had happened. I mentioned honesty and facing up to things; I am prepared for there to be some work to do and that I'm going to have to put up with the vulnerability of being on probation for an unknown length of time."

"See, it's not a matter of putting you on probation; this is not a power trip for me. I am not the adults who hurt the child within you who has that fear. I understand it, don't get me wrong, but the time it's going to take for our friendship to heal is not me choosing to dish out a punishment and compound it by keeping you in suspense as to how long it will last. It is the consequence of the things you have done and said. You need to be able to see it that way and take it on board if we're going to get back on track; to realise that you can get things wrong and work through them and get good things back. That you don't have to be perfect to have hope."

"Hmm, I don't know about that. It's a lot. I certainly owe you an explanation though, and again I mean background and context but not as an excuse." Freya took a gulp of wine, gingerly setting down the glass again with a shaking hand before folding both hands on her lap. "I haven't dealt well with the prospect of you moving away or of you making new friends because I've never been good at integrating, and my need to be perfect and fight to hold onto people is a big part of that. I've never managed to keep my position as someone's best friend. I know that in adult life, having a best friend shouldn't be as much of a big deal; it's a childish hierarchy and ideally we should have a meticulously curated circle of close friends who jointly fulfil the various types of friend interaction we need. But I never got to be a best friend; when I was a child and that hierarchy was active, I was always my best friend's second best friend. Saying that out loud makes me realise how petty it sounds and the concept of a second best friend doesn't belong outside of school, but as it was such a deep longing for so many years and never fulfilled, it never went away. At primary school, Judi was my best friend, but Carla was hers. She genuinely was my friend, but always Carla's friend first. Then at secondary school, it was Shannon and Nuala; once Nuala's family moved away, somehow out of nowhere there was Bev. She wasn't a newcomer; she'd always been there, but suddenly she was Shannon's bestie and Lynne who had been *her* best friend before that merged into the new world order with a new first choice of her own. Looking back, I suppose I let it show that I was looking forward to being 'promoted' instead of focusing on how Shannon was feeling about Nuala moving away, which wouldn't have helped. Thinking logically, there must have been a chain reaction of pairings shifting around, yet it never changed anything for me. I was always that one step down. It's the admin of school life that made having one best friend such a big deal; there was so much you needed a partner for. Tasks; games; sitting next to or walking in pairs on trips. I was always that particular type of second best friend who didn't have anybody else; the one who had to work with someone where there was no common ground, sit beside the teacher, or be awkwardly tacked onto another pair if there was an odd number. It didn't need any falling out or bullying for this to happen; if you weren't established in a best friendship and everyone else was, it didn't make any difference if nobody actually disliked you. And in my case, people did; I was seen as stuck-up. I had no idea how to fit in, and I honestly did try. Attempting to copy what the popular ones did and said was so artificial it got me either laughed at or accused of taking the mick, adding to the myth that I thought I was better than them. Then at college there was Stella, and she didn't have or want one best friend. She had it figured out; it was time to leave all that rigid structure behind, it had had its day and she was itching to spread her wings and make the most of the freedom of confident young adulthood. I didn't get to remain friends with her at all; I totally creeped her out with my relentless, suffocating clinging to that cutesy childhood dream of a best friend! Fast forward a few generally lonely, out of step years, and then you came along. That's not the main thing I need to explain to you though. I really don't want to be that person who blames everything on parent issues, but there are things I need to say about the past and how it's made… how I've let it make me the way I am. This is why I didn't want to do this publicly, because it does involve talking about things which happened in my mother's private life."

Susannah nodded. "I understand that, and I promise I am always a safe person for you to talk to; I will keep confidences and not jump down your throat for explaining that context. I will let you get the words out in your own time. I want this fixed as much as you do, Freya; I'm not your judge and jury here."

"Thank you. I know I don't deserve it, and I'm honestly not saying that to manipulate you into contradicting it to make me feel better. It does scare me to be in a position of being indebted to you for giving me anything I haven't earned, but I'm starting to better understand why I feel that way; why I've never been enough, why I've always had that instinctive 'what's the catch' defensiveness." She paused for another swig of wine. "When I got home last night and told my mum about you being off sick, she was genuinely concerned of course, and she kept asking when I'd be going to visit you, if you needed anything and so on. I ended up blurting out that I'd managed to lose you as a friend, and I broke down. I was sobbing my heart out about how I'd let her down as well as you by not being able to hold onto another friend, and how I knew I needed to do better to make up for having cost her the love of my dad; that I needed to get good at making people want to stay in my life so that she wouldn't have to be so scared any more of seeing me go through the same pain she had. She was looking at me as though she'd never seen me before; she actually had to sit down, she was so taken aback. I told her the lengths I'd gone to in order to hide it from her that I wasn't coming here on Sundays any more; how I'd been dreading what I was going to do once it got into winter. I told her how hard I try to show and tell her what she wants to see and hear, and that I don't know how I'm going to sustain that on my own. Once the floodgates were open, the whole lot came out; I told her what it's like at work, and about Max. Even I could see the pattern there in terms of the idealised absent father who nobody within reach could replace; the need to vindicate her by grabbing onto the ankles of someone so far out of my league and being drawn up onto his higher level of being. How I'd convinced myself that, when I found out his partner is a man, it gave me scope to take one back for the team as it were - that team being Mum and me, not heterosexuality, I should be clear on that - without being the same as my dad's secretary, because it was 'different'; not replacing like with like in terms of sex. Which was completely wrong and disrespectful; I see that now, and in all honesty I don't think I ever truly believed it. I needed some way of justifying it to myself because I couldn't cope with having that mountain to climb of having to get over him when I had to see him at work all the time. Always in secret; always on my own; always so mentally exhausting. Not that any of this justifies how I treated you. I was honest with her about that too. I admitted that I had been emotionally coercive, and that it terrified me to realise what I'd become; an evil monster. You were right, you see, about all of it. For instance, I did go over to Annika when she was asleep in her basket and disturb her for the sake of hoping you would hear me telling her I was going to miss you and feel sad and maybe like me more for having kept it back until you were out of the room. I was blatant about using my feelings for Max, but that with the cats was sly and manipulative, and I couldn't handle being called out on it precisely because it made me face the reality of what I am. So I dug myself in deeper by denying it; turning it around on you. All of which means I don't deserve help to fix any of this damage from the vortex of destruction I've created. I have to do it on my own, and although I should be used to that, I feel as though I've run out of resources; I'm simply not strong enough. Even the fact that I'm worrying about not being strong enough to take my punishment and rebuild on my own; I know I should only be focused on how I made you feel, when you're going through so much too. I should be able to completely set my own crisis aside, but I can't ignore it; there's nothing left in the tank. All I can offer is not to stand in your way or make anything awkward for you if you choose to cut ties with me. I absolutely wouldn't blame you if you did, but please know that it genuinely would be a massive loss to me; I am fully aware that I've thrown away something rare and worthwhile."

Tears tracked through Freya's light make-up as she lifted her glass, hesitated and then changed her mind, setting it back down with silent precision before picking up her handbag from the floor and taking out a tissue. She wiped her eyes and delicately blew her nose; her hand holding the used tissue hovered uncertainly for a moment before she dropped it back into her bag with a contained shudder, taking out a bottle of hand sanitiser. Susannah, galvanised into motion, jumped up to move the waste bin over to her and took down a box of tissues from the windowsill.

"Freya, you are not evil or a monster. You've made mistakes, but you are not this irredeemable lost cause, and you do deserve help. Please believe that. And I'm not going to cut ties with you. You're right; you have been coping with too much on your own and you've been carrying more than your fair share of responsibility. I think you already know that needs to be redistributed between you and your mum. Rather than add more to what's already overwhelming, you need to make room for your own accountability by letting go of what you've been unfairly carrying for her. What did she have to say after you told her all this?"

"Well, she couldn't get any words out for a few minutes; I went and made her a cup of herbal tea. Then she said she'd had no idea how I felt and it was too much to take in and she needed time. I went and sat outside in the garden. I'd love to say I was looking up at the stars and contemplating perspective in terms of the bigger picture like Jodie Foster in 'Contact', and I did look at the sky and think about it, but of course we're in central Scotland in November and it was miserable low cloud." She looked directly at Susannah for the first time that evening; a spark of their usual camaraderie briefly flickered to life, drawing a fleeting smile from each of them. "Mum came out to join me after a while; she'd poured us each a Raasay gin, neat. It was the nearest we had in to the dram the occasion called for."

Frieda Lingard went up several redeeming points in Susannah's estimation. "Respect!", she said quietly; not quite forgiving her for the ableist comment which Freya had let slip on that awful day, but cautiously hopeful.

"We sat out in the dark drinking it and she accepted that not only was what I said true, but she had to admit that she had allowed some resentment to creep in. Although she knew logically that she couldn't hold a baby responsible for her husband's philandering, she had knowingly put pressure on me out of fear for my future if I didn't succeed where she saw herself as having failed, but she acknowledged that there was also a part of her that was tough on me because she could be; because I was the one factor in all of this that she could control. I can imagine how hard it was for her to admit that to her own adult daughter. She also admitted that far from being the perfect man who she couldn't hold on to, my father was a coercive controller. She said much the same thing you highlighted to me; that because he wasn't the textbook example, she hadn't thought that description could apply to his behaviour. However, she could see that he manipulated her into feeling that she wasn't enough; that it was her fault he ended up looking elsewhere. *He* wasn't evil; weak and shallow, yes, and perhaps with constructive intervention at the right time he could have turned things around. She realised, and helped me to see, that coercive controlling behaviour doesn't always have the extreme face we think of, and that I needed to face the fact that how I had behaved towards you came under that umbrella. She was all for me getting round here with a bottle of wine and fixing this. She acknowledged that she was deeply wrong to suggest that your dyspraxia made you some kind of minimal baseline standard of friend that I was to be further criticised for not being able to keep."

"I'm glad she owned that; it hurt and offended me a lot, from both of you. It will take me some time to get past that."

"I understand. We talked about Mary too; about how strongly I reacted to hearing that her mother couldn't put her being in disgrace on hold for her grandmother's funeral. Although there was no one direct equivalent incident in my childhood, it reminded me of how isolated I was because of our unhealthy co-dependence. She would berate me for taking it so hard when I got told off; compare me to children of a similar age whom she saw get told off and say sorry and that was that. I pointed out that they could get past it so much more quickly because the parents did too; her fury and disappointment would linger and she'd be cold and aloof with me for days. She hadn't realised how much it showed, and that was hard for her to have to take on. I explained how much was at stake every time I had to apologise; still is. How I was never believed; I was 'only sorry for myself' and 'saying it to get out of trouble'. Then of course I'd get into more trouble because I'd panic at being entirely powerless to convince her and win back her love, which would be read as having a tantrum because I wasn't getting my own way. I *was* genuinely sorry for whatever I'd done; I didn't understand then that it was perfectly possible for both of those things to be true. That I could be heartbroken about the huge and prolonged emotional consequences for me *and* sorry for what I'd done. I guess adults often forget how time goes so much more slowly for children; how interminable that exile feels. I think that was why I developed other blocks that make it look worse when I need to apologise; I struggle to make eye contact and I apparently sound as though I don't mean it. I'm so conscious of how bad I am at it and how vulnerable I am, I sound flat and insincere. I realise that not knowing whether or not it will be accepted; whether I have made myself raw and open only to have more salt rubbed in, is part of the consequences of whatever I've done that I'm apologising for, but it's terrifying to me with my need to be perfect in order to be loved. I'm coming to understand the psychology behind that, but in the meantime I remain crap at apologising and owing it to people more than ever because of this vicious cycle. I know that going forward, I need to hide my fears better and make sure you always see me happy and excited; I get that you can't give me any guarantee that you won't become closer to one or more new friends than you are to me, and I need to be OK with that. I need to stop being so reliant on you, and find a way to bridge the gap between instantly making all these adjustments and the time it will take me to find new friends of my own. I know I can't afford to make one more wrong move and that scares me, but I will try my best to keep that from you."

"Thank you for sharing all of this with me, though I don't expect or want you to hide how you feel and present as happy all the time. That's not how friendship works. I need you to be honest with me so that I can help you. My problem was never with you finding it hard to adjust to me moving away and leaving our workplace. Of course I know that's going to be hard for you! And no, I'm not this dictator poised to strike you down the minute you put a foot wrong. I get that this is going to be a journey for you and it will take time. I really need you not to take from this crisis that your role going forward is to be a martyr with all these pent-up emotions which will turn to more resentment. That stands precisely zero chance of working out for either of us. In fact it would be another passive-aggressive take; framing it in a way which makes me the problem. 'Susannah is the tyrant with unreasonable expectations holding power over Freya'. It's not a contest where one of us wins the status of not being the problem and gets to rest on their laurels while the other has to do all the hard work. We need to be working together on this transition, with honesty on both sides. For what it's worth, you *are* my best friend, and I'm delighted for you that both you and your mum have turned a corner. I appreciate your apology all the more for knowing everything you've bravely shared with me tonight. Do you feel that your relationship with your mum has changed for the better?"

"Absolutely. In fact, we redefined our roles as a household; that was something else which had been driving a wedge between us. She agreed that nowadays with more and more adults living with their parents for economic reasons, the whole 'living under my roof' attitude isn't fair or appropriate.

It's *our* roof and we need to be more of an equal team. Not just because I'm bringing in a salary; any adult who is contributing to their household in whatever way they can should be seen as such. I told her how humiliated I felt when she gave me a dressing-down in front of you for swearing when I was so irate and actually *distressed* about how Esther treated Mary at Lottie's funeral. After you'd gone, that was when I got the 'under my roof' putdown; that made me feel worthless. She genuinely doesn't feel comfortable with me swearing around her; I accepted that, but she also got that it was high emotion due to intense empathy with a bereaved child. She is perfectly aware that when I'm around my own peer group I'm not going to be saying 'alas' and 'forsooth'. I pledged to do my best to remember not to swear around her, but as one person respecting another's feelings, not as an inferior being living indebted and in limbo in someone else's home. We've also agreed that I can go part time and study for a year or two with a view to getting a different job as well as easing some of the pressure of coping with our workplace full time. You were right; I need to get out of the rut I'm in, and this gives me a lot more scope to act on that."

"Freya, that's wonderful! Truly, I am so happy to hear this. I always knew that it was all very well me telling you what you needed to do but that I didn't have anything to offer to help facilitate that for you, and that it was a big ask with how much it's taking out of you working full time in that environment. I think that calls for a refill, don't you?"

Annika and Morgan stirred as Susannah got up. "Oh!", Freya called after her; "That reminds me. After the heavy conversation, when Mum had brought us out another couple of large gins and we drank a toast to your future, she suggested that when you move we could take the cats for a couple of weeks instead of you having to put them in a cattery. We've got plenty of space and with them being indoor cats anyway, it shouldn't be any more disruptive for them and they do already know me. Any time."

"Really? That would be a huge help; thank you! In fact, I'm going away for a couple of nights next week; London and Fran have invited me up to Nairn. Tan has agreed to come over and feed the cats and see to their litter tray, but I know he would understand; it might be a good opportunity for a trial run, so that by the time they need to be away for a bit longer, they will already have been in your house. Would that be OK? I know it's short notice."

"I'm sure it would. We owe you, after all. Not that I'm making this about my redemption!" The note of anxiety was real; once again Susannah quickly tamped down the spark of irritation at the increased need for reassurance which was bound to hang over their friendship for some time.

"It's fine; we both want what's best for the cats. Now, I'm going to use the bathroom then get that bottle and top us up."

She did a double-take when she came back into the living room; Annika had moved from the snug haven of her basket and made herself comfortable on Freya's lap. Her friend looked up, eyes wide, clearly wondering how Susannah would interpret this development. Knowing full well that the one way Annika would be settled on anyone's lap would be through her own discerning feline choice, she waited, allowing Freya space to catch up with her racing thoughts.

Freya looked down again, stroking Annika's dark marbled fur before turning calmer, washed-clean blue eyes to her friend.

"She's purring", was all she said.

Susannah smiled and poured their wine.

21

Nairn

Ghostly brown flecks of recent winter days clung to the windows; traces of churned-up grit and slush marking a faint proprietary signature of the season as the bus glided smoothly under the crystalline blue sky. Pale orange light livened every surface with the paradoxical cold-warm punch of a robust single malt, infused with the double urgency of limited daylight hours and rare interludes of such fine weather close to the winter solstice. Susannah checked once again that she had activated her train ticket on her phone as Stirling's neat, linear bus station came into view. The high modern sprawl of the footbridge over the railway station immediately beyond it elicited a prickle of excitement through her hypervigilant state as its sunlit white framework evoked the dazzle to come when her train sped through the Druimuachdar Pass to the Highlands.

Leaving from Stirling added to her travelling time despite the shorter bus journey there from Kirkbrigg; Susannah had told herself that it was so she could have more chance of picking a forward facing seat at an earlier station on the route. As she walked along the broad pathway to the station's elegant façade, she glanced along the short stretch of road which led to the main shopping streets. The preview glint of sun on the Christmas lights and the subtle invitation of the Stirling Arcade's sedate rise amid the familiar shop fronts on Murray Place made her wish that she had time to look around. Taking her usual bus in the opposite direction from normal had certainly set the scene for feeling adventurous. If she were honest with herself, this detour was down to the still-raw disappointment of Crieff Gardens; it was too soon to face catching her train from Perth Station. As she scanned her ticket and made her way through the barriers onto the airy sweep of Stirling's main through platforms, she reflected that she would not be spared from passing through Perth on the way. Her train was on time, which bode well for lunch before the connection to Nairn once she got to Inverness.

Northbound trains heading onto the Highland Main Line at Perth used one of the oldest platforms, on the western edge of the triangular station; Susannah was thankful for her view being mostly of a car park on one side and a retaining wall on the other during the few minutes her train was stopped there. Trying not to think too much about the grounding embrace of the wide stillness which had always made her feel safe in the earth-toned peace of the main building, she focused on the video clip Freya had sent her of the cats exploring their temporary home. This time of tiptoeing wide-eyed through a transient now, testing the surface awaiting each new step, would pass. She silently gave thanks for Tan and Lee's understanding. Delighted about her reconciliation with Freya, they had waved away her profuse apologies for her inconsistency; enthusiastically agreeing that it made perfect sense to let the cats have a shorter stay with Freya and Frieda in advance of a longer spell there once she finally moved house. She took a deep breath, feeling the air fill her lungs as she squared her shoulders and returned her gaze to the bland grey back of the seat in front of her. The train began to move once again.

Thousands of tiny sparkles cheered the forging onward of the carriages through the increasingly wild snowscape; a visual echo of the true outside intensity of the muffled sound as the high speed InterCity train stirred a streaming wake past the windows. The brilliant lift of it filtered into the multitude of conversations round about, livening the collective mood of this rush to the north. A tourist moved over to the table three rows ahead of Susannah, which had been vacated at Pitlochry, in a rustle of sturdy hiking clothes; eagerly setting his phone on a mini tripod to record the scenery after hoisting a compact backpack into the overhead luggage rack. Susannah felt a pang of envy at the practised movement; the casual insolence of a strap hanging down unheeded. This was a traveller at ease with their physical surroundings; in command of their proprioception. She suppressed a giggle as she suddenly pictured her cats, or anyone's cats come to that, entertaining themselves trying to catch the dangling length of webbing as it swayed with the motion of the train. Rubbing the pad of her thumb over the handles of her own overnight bag tucked safely at her feet, she turned to watch the steely flash of mountain streams come and go as her ear canals tightened to attention. They were approaching the highest part of the mainline railway network; almost one and a half thousand feet above sea level, as the stark metal signpost for which she was now looking out declared. There was a lonely poignancy to how staunchly it proclaimed its solitary truth in the full face of the elements up here, to be seen so fleetingly. In that fraction of a moment, Perthshire ceded its domain to Inverness-shire and they were officially in the Highlands.

A handful of people got on at Kingussie, stamping booted but cold feet as they entered the carriage in a whisk of crisp fresh air which dissipated in the warmth to be briskly stirred once again quarter of an hour later in the diamond-sharp wakefulness of Aviemore. The tourist disembarked there under the impassive frosted gaze of the Cairngorms; across the preserved red and cream hub of the station, delighted children clamoured to board one of the Strathspey Railway's beloved Santa Special steam trains as their parents and guardians strove with varying degrees of harried amusement to keep them safely behind the painted line on the platform. Volunteers dressed as elves darted attentively among the waiting passengers; a dropped mitten retrieved, a question smilingly answered, a frantically excited wave returned. The unobtrusively smooth departure of the high speed train, so well-worn yet a youngster compared to its festive neighbour, gave the scene an unreal quality as it shifted from dynamic to a tableau in the face of the rapidly increasing speed. One more stop at the evergreen-and-white rural vignette of Carrbridge station was followed by a thirty minute scenic summing up of the line; the secondary crest of the bare Slochd Summit and a darkly intricate chain of bridges culminating in the long exposed curve of Culloden Viaduct. The tall stone arches carried the line high above a river which took a more direct route than the modern railway to her eventual destination of Nairn, after which the river was named. The pale pewter sheen of the Moray Firth marked the approach to Inverness; a flurry of "Nice to have met you" farewells drifted through the aisle as coats, scarves and bags were gathered and the structured bond of the snow-blanketed journey melted into the flow of the city.

Firmly gripping her overnight bag in one hand and the handrail in the other, Susannah stepped with fervent concentration onto the platform before taking out her phone to scan her ticket at the automatic barriers. London and Fran were waiting; they had made the twenty minute train journey from Nairn an hour earlier than necessary in order to make extra certain of reaching the Highland capital in time to meet her and take the opportunity to pick up a few treats from the shops. Susannah shared long hugs with her sibling and then their partner, grateful for the essential pause to get her wayward emotions under control; since losing out on Crieff Gardens everything seemed to be setting her off. The bluebird-day magic of the journey up had unexpectedly stung behind her eyes more than once.

"Honestly, thank you so much for this; both of you."

Fran smiled with gentle understanding, lightly squeezing Susannah's arm as London took the overnight bag. The couple looked well; refreshed by the coastal air. London Silverdale's angular face, lean muscular build and sculpted, spiky mid-brown hair was complemented by Fran's more rounded softness; her hair, a shade darker, relaxed against her shoulders. Susannah felt tension she hadn't realised she was carrying ease away in their company as she described the journey; navigating through the knots of people and suitcases on the narrow pavements lost some of its peril when she wasn't alone, despite the more complex spatial dynamics.

The three of them settled in at a window table in Platform 8; a relaxed pub minutes from the station which accentuated its railway name with a scattering of interesting historic memorabilia. Having agreed on a selection of small plates to share, London placed their order on the app and their drinks were brought over promptly. As London was about to put their phone away, a notification came through which clearly took them by surprise.

"That's Archie Main, my supervisor", they said, worry evident in their tone. "I'd better check it; sorry, Suze."

Susannah nodded her understanding as her sibling tapped on the message, exchanging a concerned look with Fran.

"Oh, no! Mrs Beasley died! I knew she was ill and it was expected, but…"

Both Fran and Susannah gasped, uttering condolences. London's first boss had been their key source of acceptance and support through some fraught years; way ahead of her time in terms of inclusion, she had the elusive ideal mix of kindness and steel. When London came out, this made her both a readily approachable safe haven and a formidable force against the bullies and bigots who made it necessary. She had stood by them throughout the process of making their colleagues understand that although they were not agender, they were not the binary male which they appeared outwardly and were assumed to be. Although she was long since retired and London had not seen her for several years,

Archie had promised to update them if any news came through while they were away.

"We won't be using the car today; once we've eaten, I think we should stay on for a dram in her honour", said Fran.

London and Susannah nodded, looking through the high, clean windows to the blue sky beyond the Christmas lights as their food arrived. They ate in companionable quiet, sharing memories and appreciations of the small details; the simple pleasures of the senses which are sharpened in the wake of news which reminds the still-living that they are.

The Aberdeen train was inevitably busier than the earlier train, a local service to Elgin, would have been; they managed to get a table nonetheless. "Josie and Ed always use the Elgin trains if they can, to support keeping them on the timetable; they're vulnerable to being cancelled if there's any disruption and it puts people off relying on them but if everyone avoids them, they risk losing them altogether", Fran was saying. "I'm sure they'd understand us deferring to this one today though. It does get us back to Nairn while it's daylight so you can get your bearings. It's about a twenty minute walk to the apartment."

Salt crunched under their boots in harsh testament to the cold overnight temperatures to come as they crossed the strikingly purple-painted footbridge to the main entrance of Nairn's small station with its Scottish Tudor building. The route to the apartment was essentially a straight line yet it incorporated a remarkable range of environments in its progress through the quietly characterful coastal town. From outside the station it led past tall trees, Victorian villas and matching old-style streetlamps alongside a rough stone wall, soon giving way to the modern High Street. They passed a paved area on their left with a charming parade of three lamp posts adorned with loops of white fairy lights tracing the shape of the hanging baskets which would grace them in the opposite season, before the pavement narrowed again with shops. Fran paused to point out an attractive red sandstone building with a distinctly tiled covered entrance at the busy junction with Leopold Street; it rose three floors above the ground floor shops to an ornate roofscape embellished with motifs of scales and dolphins in a contrasting aquamarine.

"That's the old Station Hotel; you can see the name on those original tiles. It's private flats now, I believe."

Susannah took in the splendid building, imagining what it would be like to live there as the first hints of the sunset to come were already dusting the icy sky with the popping-candy tingle of a deepening blush. They crossed the road and continued down the High Street until it narrowed at another junction, taking on a more village-like aspect with older buildings housing independent shops for a brief stretch which ended at the busy A96, the main road between Inverness and Aberdeen. Although they were heading in a continuous line, the character changed more dramatically at this boundary; on the other side lay the beginning of Fishertown, announced at this time of year by a beautiful banner of lights with the name and the shape of a yacht sailing overhead. Susannah stopped to take a photo and they walked on, Fran pointing out the rows of tiny cottages leading off the road they were on; many of them with lovingly kept patches of garden and solar lights biding their time as patiently as the long vigils ingrained into everyday life in a fishing community. As the harbour with its tall lights came into view, Susannah looked around at the bold lines of more Victorian lamp posts against the sky, remarking upon how peaceful and restorative it felt as the sea air truly made itself known and the roar of the waves rose to meet it.

"And here we are!"; London gestured towards a metal door with toughened glass panels through which the stairs to the apartment could be seen. They punched in the code and walked up the bare and utilitarian but immaculate staircase; Susannah holding tight to the cold black handrail.

A sign on the inside of the apartment door asked guests to take their shoes off and leave them in the trays provided to protect the laminate floors and minimise noise while they were indoors; Susannah dug her soft teal travel slippers out of her bag before London took it through to the small second bedroom, which she was delighted to discover also had a view of the Moray Firth though it was not facing it directly as the main bedroom did and the view was partly obstructed by a nearby restaurant building. She hung up the couple of changes of clothes she had brought, laid her nightshirt next to the royal blue towels placed neatly on top of the crisply made bed with its seashell-patterned duvet cover and took her toilet bag through to the bathroom where a space had been cleared on the ledge next to the pale blue washbasin. She quickly used the toilet, washed and dried her hands using that of the small towels on the rail which matched the set in her room, then returned to properly take in the rectangular living room with its wide window looking way out to sea. She discreetly performed her essential visual scan of the room for any tripping or bumping hazards which could catch her out; almost distracted from doing so by the sheer clean-lined beauty of the place. A fully decorated Christmas tree twinkled in the corner, a faint reflection of its warm white lights superimposed on the glass as though the pinpoints of light came from the breakers heading to shore under the low reach of the setting sun. There was hardly a cloud in the sky; a few wisps skimmed half-heartedly across the hills of the Black Isle on the other side of the broad firth. Rose-pink light from the uniformly changing sky painted the neutral tones of the walls and coffee-coloured corner sofa; turned the glass table to a mirage. Fran handed her a cup of tea.

"We'll order in tonight; there's a good local pizza place that delivers"; London slid the menu from the guest information folder over to her. "You'll be tired after your journey. Tomorrow, I thought we could have a drive around the local area; let you see the Christmas lights in Forres and Elgin. We still need to get a few gifts; we already gave Josie and Ed all theirs of course, when we saw them on Sunday, but we need to get a few things for Hazel's family. Then there's our side. We stopped exchanging gifts with Julian and Isobel once Louis turned eighteen but we get for Selina and Phoebe and the girls. Ideally, things that can be posted."

"London!"; Fran good-naturedly chided them.

"Oh, don't worry"; laughed Susannah. "I grew up with them both, remember; I'm well versed in what tends to happen when that combination of my siblings ends up in the same room!"

"It's not that I don't love or care about Selina, Frannie; you know that. We clash when we're together. I know you wish I could be close with Selina as I am with Susannah, the way you are with both Josie and Hazel, but we simply don't gel in the same way. I love that you get on so well with her, and I adore Phoebe and those girls! I will always give Selina credit for never having stood in the way of my relationship with Eilidh and Caitlin, despite how often she and I disagree."

Susannah nodded. "Selina always acknowledges how much effort you make with the girls and that you always keep your disagreements well away from them. You two work best at a distance; it's simply the way it is with relatives sometimes. See, Fran, this is my take on it: our Selina's your typical feisty youngest with something to prove. There's enough of a gap between her and Jules for him to seem almost more like an uncle to her, so that sense of needing to hold her ground is diluted somewhat. With my dyspraxia and the anxiety that goes along with that, she's got a focus to channel her need to be useful and protective and although I do end up drawing a line sometimes, it doesn't get under my skin in the same way as it does

London's. It's a personality clash; no right or wrong, simply people being different. Mind you, I admit I've dodged updating her on how things have been with Freya for a while!"

"Ooh, that is most certainly a conversation to have with fully charged glasses!"; London took the empty tea cups through to the kitchen, rinsed them and put them in the dishwasher. "Red or white, Suze?"; they popped their head back around the doorframe, what Selina had been known to describe as 'the gossip light switched on' undeniably in their twinkling eyes.

They all waited until the last of the orange and red glow faded from the sky before closing the plush ecru curtains. Susannah sat forward on the big corner sofa to cautiously sip her wine; white would have felt safer, but this December night called for a warming Shiraz even in the well heated apartment.

"I won't go near the tree!"; she smiled at London with a hint of mischief before filling Fran in on the context. "When I was nine, I decided it would be a good idea to move one of the ornaments on our tree in the hallway. There was a space, slightly out of proportion, with no lights or ornaments and it kept catching my attention. So I went to unhook one of the biggest baubles, a massive silver one, to put it in the gap. Of course, it caught and pulled the entire tree with it. I managed to grab it and stop it from falling over but a few other ornaments came off and broke. Mum and Jules heard me shouting for help and came running in; they got the tree upright again but I got such a telling off as you can imagine, and was forbidden to touch it again. Which was no hardship as I would have been terrified to. Then on the Christmas Eve, Mum noticed that a couple of ornaments had been switched around. I don't know to this day who did it; I only know it wasn't me. But nobody else owned it; I guess she may have been mistaken. Whatever the truth of it, she blamed me. Denying it wouldn't have made sense for anyone else; I was the one who had reason to fear being in trouble for it as I'd been specifically told not to touch the tree. Selina was too small to have reached the ornaments Mum insisted had been moved, or to drag anything nearby that she could have stood on. So I was sent to my room; Dad came in later and told me that they were thinking of holding my presents back to give away the next year to a more deserving little girl who didn't disobey her parents and lie about it. My presents didn't really get taken away, but I didn't know that until the morning. I was trying so hard not to cry once Selina was in bed; she was sleeping in my room as our grandparents were staying over Christmas. She believed in Santa Claus then and I didn't want to frighten her or take away that magic for her. I was afraid to be left alone with the tree after that; I always made sure someone could see me if I was in the hallway for longer than it took to walk through. London used to tease me about not being allowed to touch the tree. We were kids"; Susannah looked across at her sibling, surprised by the stricken look on their face. "It's fine; teenagers pick up on things like that and make light of them, not realising the full circumstances. I got over the fear; I came to accept as the years went by and I understood better about parents being fallible too that Mum was likely mistaken."

London set down their wine glass with a trembling hand, their face pale.

"I didn't know that about threatening to take your presents away and making you cry! Susannah, I am so, so sorry."

"Honestly, it was so long ago; I wouldn't have mentioned it if I thought it would upset you! It's not like it was your fault…"

Something in London's expression stopped her; Fran was staring at her partner, her jaw slack. "London?", she said quietly.

"It was me. I swapped a couple of things around as a joke! I was a brat in my early teens; I admit that. Looking back, I can't believe I thought it was funny. I had no idea how far it would go, but it was a cruel prank and I should never have done it in the first place let alone keep it up once you got into trouble. Oh, Suze. It was wrong of me at the time and it was worse to keep quiet ever since. I know I can't make up for the hurt and fear it caused you but I am truly sorry."

Fran got up quietly. "I'll give you both some space"; she touched London's shoulder as she walked around behind them and went into the kitchen. Susannah moved to sit nearer to her sibling.

"I appreciate you inviting me up here and I really want to be OK with this and have a good time, but I do need to process it. Not so much the prank itself. You were a teenager, and yeah, a bit of a pain in the arse! I get it. At the time, it seemed like a bit of a laugh and I absolutely believe you didn't know or anticipate the part about the presents. But not to say anything when I'd been sent up to my room in disgrace on *Christmas Eve*? Again, I get that at the time; you were a child too and the fallout from your trick escalated beyond what you could have foreseen. You were out of your depth. I can easily forgive you for not having owned up to our parents. But you could have told *me*! That part I find hard to swallow. I need to be able to say that if I'm going to be able to move past it."

"I know I should have fessed up to you, at the very least. I'm not going to offer any excuses. I was cowardly at the time and then too wrapped up in my own issues to think about it or realise that it had an ongoing effect on you."

"Well, I suppose you could easily have agreed with me that Mum was mistaken and left it at that instead of admitting it now. You've done the right thing and it can't have been easy. After all this time, in front of Fran, and on the day you got sad news about Mrs Beasley. It took guts and integrity. I needed to get that out, but we're OK."

"Oh, Mrs Beasley. She would be so ashamed of me! And now I'm making it about me. Shit! I don't know how to do this graciously, like you were describing with Freya!"

"You're reeling from the news of Mrs Beasley's death. I know how much she meant to you. You're also not responsible for what Dad chose to say to me, which as an adult I can see was way over the top and downright nasty to say to a nine-year-old on Christmas Eve especially sharing a room with a sibling who believed in Santa Claus. That part is not on you; please don't take on additional guilt for an adult's choices. Come on; let's go and get Fran and top up all our wines. She'll be wondering what's happening and you need to be with her when you're dealing with that news."

London stood and hugged their sister tightly. "You're an amazing person, Susannah", they choked out, their voice thick with emotion as they stepped back to look at her, holding her arms lovingly. "I will make this right with Mum and Dad too. No matter if they've completely forgotten about the incident, I'm going to tell them the truth."

Susannah smiled. "Perhaps not Selina though!"

Their laughter brought a relieved Fran back through with the bottle to refresh their drinks and organise the pizza order.

Travel, sea air, catharsis and finally a hearty feast of pizza and moderate serving of wine had to make for a good night's sleep. Susannah had intended to see how visible the stars were from her bedroom once the lights of the building next door were out; she was out like a light herself long before that.

The Christmas tree twinkled merrily in the darkened room. Susannah was vaguely aware that Fran had switched off the lights before they all went to bed; had one of them perhaps gotten up for a glass of water and decided to sit up with the lights on for a bit? She looked around the empty room; there was no sign of anyone else being up.

Now she came to think of it, the tree looked different. The lights and decorations were much older; she was seeing the bare brilliance of incandescent bulbs and glass ornaments which she remembered from childhood. Weirdly, the unlikelihood of them meeting safety standards in a 2020s holiday let struck her more than the strangeness of them being on the tree.

She turned to look around again. With the tree providing the only light, the details were shadowed and sparse but she could make out that she was in a different place altogether; a living room in a family home, not one she recognised. Presents lay under the tree; a modest dining table stood with chairs neatly tucked in and a sofa upholstered in what even in this light she could tell was a strong floral pattern lay at right angles to the nearest wall. A set of pokers and shovels stood next to a tidy grate on a bland fireplace as the ticking of a clock marked the featureless passing of the dead hours.

A soft rustling sound made her whirl back round to face the tree again; she instantly recognised the little girl in the flannelette nightgown.

"*Mary?*"

The smiling child was holding something out to her, clasped reverently in both hands. Susannah bent to look, moving slowly so as not to frighten her. It was a bauble from the tree; the clarity of its colours at odds with the shadowed setting. A deep metallic blue, with a circular indentation lined with ridged silver in the popular style of decades ago; she had noticed several similar ones on the tree with the hollows reflecting a multiplicity of light. She looked back at the one in Mary's hands; her little fingertips curled around the edge of the indent. The child glanced towards the tree.

"Oh; do you want me to help you hang that up on the branch?" She crouched down to the little girl's level as she continued to hold out the glittering ornament, shaking her head and smiling more broadly. Susannah reached out gently to take it; the scene spun on a shift of time, the briefest contact of her hands with the smooth, delicate surface and Mary was running happily towards an open doorway through which Susannah could make out the upward stretch of a closed banister, tinsel looped along its panelled length. Playful laughter floated from the passage as Mary's red curls bounced on her receding back.

"Merry Christmas, wee Merry Mary!"; she laughed too before glancing down at her empty hands. As she looked around to see what had become of the fragile ornament, she awoke to see the waxing moon shining into the apartment bedroom. She pushed back the duvet and padded softly over to look out to sea; the ancient ebb and flow of the tide under that constantly renewing celestial light. Emotion swelled within her at the combination of the mystical hour and a happy dream featuring Mary; a rush of tenderness towards her sibling, whom she hoped was sleeping peacefully in the other room with the unfinished chapter of their long ago ill-judged prank finally closed. She tiptoed to the door, praying that it would open silently as she peeped into the living room with a compulsive need to check that the tree lights were indeed switched off. All was well; she crept back to bed and sank into a deeper sleep.

London and Fran were both early risers; they let her sleep in so that she awoke to the sensory fanfare of a second clear winter-blue day and the rich aroma of freshly brewed coffee. She ate her toast at the light oak kitchen table, glad to be eating after the others had finished so that she could be as guarded as she needed to without any awkward explanations when clearing away her plate and cutlery; anxious to avoid any clattering or, Heaven forbid, a breakage. At this time of day, the natural light pouring in spared her the visual onslaught of bright overhead glare which she always had to reluctantly prioritise over her preferred soft light to minimise risk in new places; one of many adjustments which she dreaded having to make in the kind of company where showing her neurotype in any real way would be as much of a faux pas as showing her knickers. Silently giving thanks for present company not falling into that category, she poured herself a cup of coffee from the pot and went to join the others.

"I hope you slept well, Suze?"

"Yes; I sure did, thanks sib. I feel brand new. In fact, I had another dream about Mary but it was a happy one."

Fran looked up from checking the traffic news on her phone. "London's told me about your wee spirit girl, and that you think she may have been dyspraxic too. I'm so pleased you had a positive dream about her; do you think she's at peace now?"

"I'm not sure; it didn't feel as though she was saying goodbye. It was more that she wanted to show me a nicer side to her life"; she described the dream to the fascinated pair. "It may of course have been no more than a standard dream, from my own subconscious and nothing to do with her actually coming through to me, but it did feel extremely real that she was wanting to give me the ornament. I hope she did know fun and joy and laughter. Not only at Christmas of course, but it can be a particularly difficult time to navigate for dyspraxic people when so much is out of place, out of routine. There are lots of sensory distractions however lovely and festive; increased social expectations; often more people and objects than usual crammed into familiar spaces, and all that at a time when our bodies and reactions are naturally more inclined to be sluggish because of the time of year and the rich food." She glanced at London with a reassuring smile, grateful that her sibling knew to hold back any renewed feelings of guilt and let her speak her truth without taking it as a dig. "People tend to make allowances for children at Christmas but of course adults are supposed to be past all that! I hate to think of Mary never having had the chance to grow up; she never got the chance to see what she could make of adult neurodivergent life, its adventure and intensity. Yes, we often have to cope with increased burnout and decreased accommodations, but there's also the autonomy of adulthood and so much to discover with our minds keenly programmed as they are not to be able to relax and take any pleasures for granted."

"Do you know how old she was when she died? It's such a shame"; compassion laced Fran's delicate question.

"No; I've never been able to find out anything about her after the point when her grandmother died and knowing that she moved away with her mother soon afterwards. I know she died young because that's how she appears."

London's expression took on a thoughtful slant. "She may be appearing at that age because of something significant that happened to her then. The death of her grandmother or the incident where the vase got broken; the two things so close together perhaps. It's possible that she did reach adulthood."

"There's no trace of her that I could find though, and Julian remembered overhearing in the library that she'd died years before then. I don't know how long she lived after her mother moved away with her. Maybe she took Mary somewhere she thought they would both cope better. How often do people think a change of scene is the answer? And sometimes it is, but it doesn't work when the right questions haven't been answered; often because they haven't ever been asked."

"That is true"; London nodded sagely. They looked at their watch. "We were thinking of heading out in about an hour; does that work for you, Suze?"

Susannah finished her coffee and got ready as Fran wiped down the kitchen table and set out the wrapping paper, gift labels, scissors and sticky tape she and London had brought with them in order to make the most of their free time and wrap the rest of the gifts, some of which they had bought in Inverness and whatever got added to them from the shops in Moray. Susannah smiled as she came back in to look at the festive scene.

"I'm looking forward to helping you wrap the presents; thank you for letting me be part of that", she said warmly. "It's been a long time since I had the chance to do that in a convivial setting with other people. I volunteered to help with gift wrapping for a charity event once and it was a bit of a disaster for me. Nothing drastic happened; I was prepared to have to apologise for holding the process up by not being as nimble as the others, but I hadn't factored in how sociable I was expected to be on top of that. It was in a church hall and all the other volunteers were older than me; clucky types, you can probably imagine. I told them politely and honestly from the start that as I'm not very dexterous, I would need to concentrate. I still kept getting the tape tangled and I was getting frustrated and embarrassed, so I asked if I could do cutting instead. I was told to watch my wee 'fingies'; that's 'fingers' in adult-speak, and reluctantly handed a pair of scissors. After about the third rebuke for 'being corrie-handed' and not getting it straight, I stopped trying to keep up with the conversation and then it was, 'you OK there, what's wrong, you're Awfully Quiet, you're a shy wee mousie aren't you, we need to bring you out of your wee shell, you need to be more confident, tut tut tut, dear dear dear', until I snapped and said that they could have sparkling conversation or straight lines but not both. I reminded them that much as I'd love to be as able to manage both at once as they could, I'd already told them I needed to concentrate. Then I said that since I'd volunteered to help with gift wrapping not to join a debating society, I had to choose the straight lines. There was a shocked silence; I braced myself for a tirade about my rudeness. I didn't expect the discordant shrieks of laughter. It actually hurt my ears, it was that raucous. Then the inappropriate hands. Flapping at me as though my words were to be swatted away; patting any bit of me they could reach. Imagine how that would be pathologised if it were a neurodivergent person doing it! I'd given my time, so far out of my comfort zone I should have had my passport stamped, and tried my best. I was in my early twenties at the time; not as jaded as I am now, and not as switched on. I was clinging to the internalised ableism telling me I could willpower away my dyspraxia. I believed that I couldn't count it as a success unless I accomplished something in the same way, same timescale and generally looking exactly the same as neurotypical people."

"Good grief, Susannah, I am so sorry those people treated you so disrespectfully! And thank you for trusting London and me to provide a safe environment where you can thoroughly enjoy helping us wrap presents as you deserve to. It is an honour and a huge compliment to us. You must feel absolutely free to tell us whatever you need to make that happen."

"Thank you, Fran, and I will."

The craft shops and local produce outlets of Forres and Elgin did not disappoint; with everyone's gifts accounted for, the three of them enjoyed a hearty pub lunch, both London and Susannah choosing soft drinks in solidarity with Fran as the designated driver. Mulled wine had been bought in to follow the gift wrapping session and round off Susannah's mini break before she left the next day. The sky burst into an iridescent palette of sharply defined colours once more as they walked on Nairn Beach at dusk after having unloaded the day's shopping from the car, shaking off the afternoon lethargy after their lunch. It had been some years since Susannah last heard the roar of the sea at such close quarters; its primal power and raw realness laughing in the face of the petty artificial frills of ableist social constructs in her memories, dashing them to insignificant speckles of foam. The unhindered rush of the wind past her ears formed briefly into a high musical echo of laughter, sounding surprisingly close by; a family with children played with their dogs up ahead, their distant merriment carried out to sea again as Susannah watched.

Waves of multicoloured light flowed around the contours of London's Bluetooth speaker as they switched on their music player, Susannah having assured them that she would not find music a distraction from the gift wrapping in this company. She had been further delighted to learn that rather than the socially expected seasonal diet of festive hits, her sibling was proposing a playlist of their favourite bands; James and REM.

"I love the festivity of wrapping gifts and I'm not against Christmas music but I only like certain songs and not over and over again, whereas for me, playing year-round favourite music is more grounding as it keeps me connected to what's familiar", she mused as she took her seat at the table.

Fran nodded. "I agree. Would you like to do a specific part of the process or have a few gifts to wrap from start to finish?"

Susannah chose the start to finish option and they settled down to the task. The sounds of the paper being cut and folded, the tearing of the tape and the rustle of boxes; the light shining on the glossy paper brought back many happy memories as they discussed the ideas and knowledge of the recipients behind their choices of gift, particularly for the younger ones.

"It took me a while to get past feeling bad for Eilidh always knowing what she would be getting while Caitlin got all the excitement, though I know Eilidh finds surprises stressful and Caitlin loves them", London was saying as they wrapped the make-up box with hidden compartments which they had picked out in Elgin for Caitlin. "That was one time I had to admit that Selina was one hundred per cent right; we all needed to get over our inbuilt habits of assuming everyone in any household had to be given their gifts in the same way. That giving one child surprises and the other one gifts they choose is no different from giving sport themed gifts to one family member and crafting themed ones to another according to their interests. Eilidh loves picking out surprises for Caitlin too, and Caitlin loves the buzz of tracking down something specific which Eilidh wants."

"Then there are the traditional same gifts which become a much-loved part of Christmas every year, baked into our childhood memories", added Fran. "Annuals, favourite chocolates, new slippers…"

"That reminds me of the time when our Uncle Albert broke with tradition and bought Dad a rare original cricket annual he found at an antique shop! Do you remember, Suze?"

"Hah; I most certainly do! He had bought him the same aftershave every year as long as I could remember and this was when I was about twenty. He used to phone us every Christmas morning and it was getting earlier each year; to be fair, he was probably getting quite lonely after Aunt Pearl died. So this one year, Mum had noticed that the package from him was not the usual shape but Dad hadn't gotten around to opening it when he phoned. She had gone into the kitchen to check on things in there and she ran back waving 'Nooooo!', as Dad started to thank Albert for the aftershave! Julian grabbed the unopened present and waved it at him; he caught on and managed to pass it off as a joke. Jules had to open it for him while he was on the phone!"

"Though why he couldn't simply have said that he hadn't opened the gift yet, I have no idea. It was nine in the morning! That generation and its social rigidity!", chortled London. "I know there's an argument for things having gone too far the other way nowadays with lapsed etiquette, but people did tie themselves up in knots way more than they needed to."

"Speaking of which", laughed Susannah as she peeled a stubborn loop of sticky tape off her fingers, setting them all off into more mirth. "We really should start using and re-using gift bags more anyway. I mean, not necessarily for the kids who love ripping into the paper, but among the adults."

"That's a good point. Unless of course you live with your sibling here, who has been known to try to work out what people's gifts are in advance; bags are more easily peeped into!"

"You still do that? *London!*", hooted Susannah; her sibling had the grace to blush.

With the wrapping soon completed and the table cleared, they enjoyed light snacks and their mulled wine before retiring for another night. Susannah slept dreamlessly, waking to a slightly more cloudy but nonetheless fair morning. Without a lot to pack, she was ready in time for one last round of coffee and toast before London and Fran walked her to the station.

22

The Graveyard

The stripped-back honesty of January deserved better PR. It was an uncrowded gallery of simplistic monochrome with sparing bursts of colour reigning at their full potential after the hectic carnival of Christmas had well and truly had its time; a return to moving through the world at one's own pace. It confronted people with the undeniability of winter, shaking them awake from the jumbled limbo of the festivities; it often did so with no comfort or compromise. Yet with that raw harshness came a stirring underwritten by the certainty of spring. The patterns of life returning, starting out locked behind the wrought iron gates of the new year, began to activate under the hard earth as they creaked open at the first resolute push; the frosted path ahead releasing infinitesimal amounts of its caught stillness with every step. The rewards of thaw and fresh green were not yet tangible; the anticipation keen for the first stylus of a pared-down branch to nudge a tender bud's waiting tip against the turning sky.

   The emergence from Christmas carried a tingle of uncharted excitement for Susannah; the anticipation of the next one being spent in her new home brought a nostalgic frisson of childhood magic to ice the fruitful but heavy adult cake of homeowner responsibility. She had always gone to stay with her parents for Christmas; as her siblings formed partnerships, she had never had what felt like a good enough reason not to. The balance of compassion and thought for her parents' feelings against her own suspension of status was shifting more and more as the years went by; she counted herself fortunate that Reg and Annette Silverdale were not without empathy and sense of their own. London had been true to their word and confessed the truth about the long-ago incident with the tree decorations; in the quietly replete space after dinner, her father had made a sincere apology for his cruel words and both parents apologised for having disbelieved her at the time. They had gone on to acknowledge that it was time she had a fair choice in where to spend Christmas, especially her first in her new home, without any ties and reassured her that although she was always welcome, if she wanted to spend it in her own home they would be happy to break with tradition and treat themselves to a hotel package or go to stay with Julian and Isobel. The relief of not having to fight to convince them that for some people including herself, spending Christmas alone was far from a hardship and indeed a preference was possibly the highlight of the holidays for her.

Now, it was her turn to give support to London as they made the sad and anxious journey to Kirkbrigg to pay their respects at Mrs Beasley's grave.

"Fran wanted to come, but she understands that my anxiety around people potentially calling me by my birth name in front of her is what it is. It's too much of a clash of two worlds; she gets that, and I know I'm extremely lucky."

Susannah linked arms with her sibling as they walked through the cemetery gates. Their footsteps softened with the crossing onto hallowed ground; their breath curled more slowly with formal politeness into the timeless air. London held a bouquet of white roses; their deep red leather gloves an elegant touch of colour against their black coat and scarf and the ivory ribbon binding the flowers.

"It's along here, I believe; ah yes, I think that's it"; London pointed to an obviously new grave. They walked sedately until they were close enough to read the inscription on the modest but beautiful, shiny slate-blue headstone.

"Simone Beasley. Beloved wife and…"; London's voice trembled as Susannah leaned into them. They both stood in silence for a few moments until London prepared to lay down the flowers; the rustle of the cellophane breaking the stillness.

"Would you like a few minutes on your own?", Susannah asked softly; her sibling nodded, so she gently rubbed their back and walked to the main path. She looked around at the orderly restful vigil of the graves under the overcast sky; their much deeper slumber marked in stone monuments which put the season's pause firmly in its place. Turning to check on London, she saw her sibling fully focused on their private farewell; she felt as though even over here on the path she was too close. Making sure she remained within sight of them, she meandered among the nearby graves until a familiar name caught her attention.

"In loving memory of Charlotte Meredith "Lottie" Aird. Wife of Alasdair Aird, daughter of Hamish and Jane Mackay. Deeply missed by her daughter, Esther Renfield."

Mary's grandmother and mother! Susannah gasped, her fingers tracing the names. The middle name, Meredith; that must surely have been the family one mentioned by Frieda from her colleague's recollections of a name which Lottie and Mary had shared. It hadn't been Merriman as they had thought; Merry Mary was Mary Meredith.

She looked again at Lottie's headstone; the graceful solidity of the burnished gold letters, their connection to Mary. In her mind she applied their style to Mary's name.

Time slowed down; Susannah's breath caught between eras.

She returned her focus to the inscription. The shared middle name, and Lottie's parents' surname; that being so familiar too.

Mary Meredith. *Edith.*

Mary didn't *know* Edie; she *became* Edie.

She must have taken her grandmother's birth surname and reinvented herself as Edie Mackay. London had been right; she appeared in spirit at a significant age but hadn't died young! That sad, cowed little girl survived to return as an adult to where her memories of Lottie were and take up post as the local librarian, where she helped so many children to cope in a world not set up for their neurotype. Including Susannah herself.

"Suze? I'm ready to go now"

London's voice close by made her jump. "Oh, did I startle you? Hey, you look as though you've seen a…" Her sibling's eyes widened and they clapped their gloved hand over their mouth. "I shouldn't say that here, should I? Sorry!"

Susannah smiled as London offered up their mortified prayer. "Actually it's a pretty logical place to say it"; she bumped their shoulder affectionately; "and to be perfectly honest, it's not too far from the truth." She explained what she had deduced from the headstone in front of them. "I shouldn't be bringing this into your visit today though; this is about you getting closure and paying your respects to Mrs Beasley."

"Are you kidding me? This is amazing, and Mrs Beasley would have been fascinated by it. She certainly wouldn't have expected you to sit on a revelation like this! Hold on, though; didn't you tell us in Nairn that Jules heard Edie talking to someone about Mary, saying that she had died and that she, Edie, was the only one of the group left?"

"Well, yes, but he couldn't recall the exact words, except for the bit about Merry Mary having died. I don't think Edie was talking about literal death; she was talking about that old version of herself not existing any more. When she said that there was only herself left, I think she was talking about how she changed her name. Merry Mary, the part of her childhood that was happy, died with her grandmother. When she took those elements out of her given names,

'Edith' was all that remained. It's easy to see how the misunderstanding came about. Julian, a young lad at the time and not particularly interested in grown women's social chatter, half-heard the rest of it and his memory of it was influenced by the more obvious interpretation. No; I believe it was Lorna Valenti's daughter Teresa who came into the library that day and saw Edie, *Mary*, for the first time in many years. She recognised her but didn't know about... are you OK with me talking about this, especially while you're in Kirkbrigg?"

"Of course I am, but I appreciate you asking. So, Teresa would have recognised her from their childhood and called her 'Mary', and what Jules overheard was Edie bringing her up to speed. Edie possibly didn't mind people knowing her original name and wasn't upset to be called by it. After all, she chose her new name from what she already had rather than pick an entirely new one. Though of course that isn't definitive; there are people who go by a specific form of their name and have a strong negative reaction to another, as you do to 'Susie'. People do tend to accept a chosen name change more readily if it derives from the person's given name; not that it should matter. It's a complex area and highly personal to each individual who changes their name or the variation they use, for whatever reason. It could be that in Edie's case, it was no more upsetting by that time to be reminded of her identity as Mary than it would be for someone who has gotten married and lets people know that they've taken their spouse's surname."

"That's true. She'd never lived in this town as a child, and I get the impression that Esther was very isolated, so there probably weren't all that many people around here who would have had substantial memories of her life as Mary by the time she came back here to work. If she'd been upset talking about the past, I'm pretty sure Jules would have picked up on that part. I would like to think that seeing Teresa again was a positive for her and maybe gave her some closure. Mind you, the fact remains - if I'm correct - that she is haunting the place. When Freya told me about Edie having died, she mentioned that she retired early under a cloud; some accident where a first edition worth a fortune got damaged." Susannah's heart plummeted as the timeline realigned itself to her new knowledge. "That must have taken her straight back to the horror of the incident with the vase! Poor Mary. Poor *Edie*!" She pressed her fingers to her temples. "I can't get my head around this. I've been preoccupied by this misunderstood child, Mary, who the evidence suggested was undiagnosed dyspraxic and died young. Then I find out that not only did she live to retirement age, but I knew her; someone confidently empathic who helped me the way I've been unable to help her as a child more than once in my dreams. But then she had this horrendous full-circle setback; I know I shouldn't assume that the accident with the book was a sign of dyspraxia but let's face it, she would have been retraumatised by it however it happened. And I've found out who she was too late to reconnect with her in this life and maybe help her *now*!"

London hugged her as they stood together in the graveyard, each processing the loss of a mentor while overcast day slipped incrementally into dusk.

They walked slowly back to where London's car was parked outside Susannah's building. "Is that Lorna's light?", asked her sibling, pointing to the streetlamp at the end of the road; recognising it solely by what they knew of its placement since it was behaving itself today, shining a steady ambient peach.

Susannah answered in the affirmative, hugging her sibling again as they reached their car. They unlocked it, opened the driver's side door, turned around to get in and yelped with fright at something behind Susannah's shoulder. She spun around to see what had startled London; unsure of whether or not the sight that greeted her should hold any element of surprise at this point.

She waved her sibling off as their car passed the end of the estate road; the anomalous blue-green glow from the streetlamp reflected briefly in the side windows as they drove by.

23

Hiatus Weekend

The lengthening late morning light unlocking the cells of a million frozen crystals of snow outside the coffee shop in Perth's railway station did little to lift Susannah's despondent mood. Across the car park, the Station Hotel glowed red-gold; vivid with anticipation of footsteps and voices stirring the air of its least-used rooms as another year gained momentum. Journeys ebbed and flowed around her; their outermost ripples brushing past in the echoes of the station tannoys and the flicker of reflection in her coffee as the departure screens over the door changed with their passing.

She'd had two viewings booked today; neither property had excited her as much as the previous two, but they were in move-in condition and had held enough potential for her to anticipate that they would come to life for her once she saw them. One viewing had been cancelled yesterday in that fluid space where modern working Fridays gradually ceded to the weekend; a queasy interlude for anyone with suspenseful ongoing business as there was still time for bad news to arrive but not much scope for doing anything about it. The seller's plans were on hold due to their intended next property's owners having a change of circumstances and deciding not to move. Then this morning when she was already on the bus, an email had come through informing her that the other property was now under offer to someone else. Deliberately heading in a direction away from where she would have been going to the first viewing and seeking an unfamiliar café without any poignant associations in this suddenly elusive city, Susannah had found herself here.

Sipping her drink as it cooled, she reluctantly messaged the few people who had known about today's viewings; Tan and Lee, Freya, and her siblings. Selina was the first sibling to reply, commiserating and asking about her alternative plans for her time in Perth.

"I'm going to call in at the bookshop where Bethany works; if she's in and it's not too busy, I haven't seen her since my birthday so I need to catch her up about Crieff Gardens, never mind today's developments. I also want to find out if there's any news on them opening their branch in Kirkbrigg."

"Of course! Have you told Freya about that yet?"

"Yes, in general terms; I didn't want to keep it from her, though it still feels kind of precarious. I haven't mentioned Bethany hoping to come through to see her old boss. Though that's nothing to do with me, it feels a bit too soon to blur the geographical and psychological boundaries!"

"I get that, but I think you could be missing an opportunity there. If Freya could meet Bethany before you leave, while this new friendship is forming as opposed to having to be introduced as the newcomer to something that's already been established, it may well be easier for her. Actively involving her on her own home ground could help her to see Bethany as a positive and maybe a new friend for her too rather than a faceless threat taking you away from her."

"I hadn't thought of it that way but it makes sense the way you put it. I guess I've been thinking too much about my own discomfort if it doesn't work out. We're both getting a bit ahead of ourselves though; if Bethany is going to Kirkbrigg, it's to be with her colleagues. She never mentioned meeting up; only asked me for recommendations of places to go. I need to tread lightly here. I enjoyed myself tremendously when I met Bethany and her friend and cousin on my birthday, but I don't want to risk transferring my frustration at not making progress with my house search here into rushing the social side with someone I barely know, let alone building expectations around bringing Freya into it. I will think about what you've suggested if that is the direction this friendship ends up taking though."

Selina responded with thumbs up and hugging emojis, signing off as she was due on shift. Susannah read and acknowledged the replies from the others which had come in during her chat with her sister before putting her phone away securely in her bag, finishing her coffee and heading for the High Street.

The staff member who clocked her walking in and hurried over to her with an enthusiastic "Can I help you?" was most definitely not Bethany. She smiled through glossy pink lips from close enough to make every long eyelash visible, her blonde hair swishing as she moved. The name on her badge read 'Stacey'.

"Hi; I was wondering if I could have a quick word with one of your colleagues, Bethany, if she's free please? She was helpful to me when I was in last year; I explained to her that I was in the process of moving to Perth and I wanted to update her."

"Oh! I'm so sorry, you've just missed her; she finished at lunchtime today! Like, *literally a few minutes ago!*"

It was certainly an apt day for that happening. Forcing a smile of her own, Susannah made a mental note to ask anyone involved in passing on news of her properties of interest not to tell her if she had *just missed* anything by a maddeningly thin sliver of time. If an offer came in from elsewhere and was accepted, or if she had to wait overnight or longer for a next stage because the person who needed to be contacted had left for the day so recently that the door hadn't finished closing behind them, then that was that regardless of how close the timing was. There was nothing to be gained by rubbing it in.

"I see. Would you mind letting her know I was here, please? It's Susannah from Kirkbrigg."

Stacey's eyes widened. "Ooh; yes, she's mentioned you. I gather you had a catch-up in The Sandeman too. *Such* a shame you missed her. So, have you moved already?"

"I'm afraid not; some issues arose with the property and I had to pull out. I took some time out over the turn of the year and now I'm back to the search."

"Sorry to hear that; Bethany said you were really excited about the property you'd had an offer accepted on. I'm sure there's something else waiting for you though. What's for you won't go by you."

Susannah found herself unable to help liking this bubbly woman, though perhaps in small doses. She had an air of someone who meant well.

"Thank you; I'm sure you're right. I said to my neighbours when it happened, it makes it exciting in a way knowing that my future home and its setting already exists and I don't know it yet. I may have walked past it with no idea that it will one day be the base of my whole life. I think of this disappointment as helping to shape the big decision I will eventually make; perhaps by leading me to accept compromises I wouldn't have before but which turn out to be blessings in disguise."

"That's actually deep; my brother and his wife are thinking of moving in the next few years so I'll have to tell them that. If that's OK with you?"

Susannah smiled genuinely this time, nodding her consent as the door opened behind her to admit a blast of cold air and more customers, in that order. "Of course! I'll let you get on now, but I must tell you or Bethany about my tartan theory of house buying one day. I'm going to grab some lunch before I head back to Kirkbrigg; you mentioning The Sandeman has made me want to go back there. It was lovely to meet you."

She turned, caught slightly off balance as another customer passed directly where she had begun to step; she registered Stacey's intake of breath as she reached for the nearest shelf to steady herself. "Good morning!", she called out brightly to cover the off moment and give her heart rate a chance to return to normal; glancing at her watch, she threw out "Afternoon!" towards the customer's departing back. Not daring to look at Stacey, she cast her eyes up to inform herself of the genre in which she would need to fake interest while she reorientated herself. Crime fiction? She'd take that. Thankful for the camouflage of something so mainstream, she randomly tapped the spines of a few books to dilute the awkwardness until she reached the door; she dared not look back and risk getting caught out again, so had to hope that Stacey's attention had harmlessly flitted elsewhere.

Perhaps it was the vulnerability of a day when one thing after another was off kilter, she reflected as she huddled in the corner of a sheltered table in the pub. She knew perfectly well that she couldn't leave her dyspraxia behind, neatly marked with a sticky note reading 'For disposal' and piled next to the worn wooden clothes airer and battered frying pan she intended to replace with new in her next home, when she packed to move. She was further aware that she shouldn't want to; that she would be an entirely different person without it and that to fantasise about being able to jettison it like ballast from her imagined new life was internalised ableism. Anyone she got to know here was going to find out about this pervasive part of her sooner or later. She could not afford to view this new start as a challenge to preserve some unattainable glitch-free status for as long as she could then regard it as the death of a dream when it inevitably slipped from her grasp. That would be too ambitious even for someone neurotypical with no disabilities *and* more than their fair share of good luck. No; days like this were best viewed as a marker to prove to herself that this was where she wanted and needed to be based for all of her days, from the best to the worst.

She was enjoying time in Perth, with no pressure to get home and unexpected space to relax and simply be present here.

Taking out her phone, she ordered some lentil soup and a glass of Merlot, answered a couple of new messages while she waited and mindfully noticed the soothing effect of the neon light around the windows; fixed on a steady pink this time. She had finished her soup and was tentatively sliding the bowl towards the end of the table when a familiar voice spoke her name.

"Bethany!"

"I'm so glad I caught you! Stacey messaged me and said you'd been in the shop asking for me and that you'd mentioned you were heading here. I'm so sorry to hear about the house setback! She said you were putting on a brave face but she could tell you were upset when you left"; Bethany winced, evidently unsure as to whether this observation would be welcomed. "If you want to be on your own, I understand, but I thought I'd pop by in case you wanted a bit of company; I live a few minutes' walk from the shop so it was an easy matter to get here."

"Thank you so much; that is incredibly thoughtful. Please do sit down; oh, have you eaten?" Susannah indicated her empty soup bowl.

"Yes, don't worry. I'll get us a drink though; I've got the app for this place now."

Once their drinks were ordered and delivered and Susannah had brought Bethany up to speed on her house search, she squared her shoulders and took a deep breath. She might as well address the elephant in the room while it was a tender calf.

"About Stacey thinking I was upset leaving the shop. I appreciate her concern, and I am particularly thankful that she contacted you in time for me to see you today, but she was partly mistaken there. I wouldn't say I was upset so much as a bit rattled, and it wasn't house related. The thing is, I'd almost collided with another customer when I turned around to leave, and I normally try very hard to avoid making that mistake; I'm aware of my responsibility towards my own safety and that of others and I usually remember to check my surroundings because I need to compensate more than a neurotypical person. I'm dyspraxic. As well as physical coordination and spatial awareness, it affects my concentration, and right now my mind is more chaotic than usual because of the pressure of planning a move. Which sounds like an excuse, but I can not keep my mind still and focused as I should, and I'm mortified when people notice because I know that if I get to the point of having to explain that I'm dyspraxic, there's a good chance they'll write me off as a liability although the vast majority of the time, trivial incidents and near misses like today are as bad as it gets."

Susannah forced her eyes away from the minute details of the grain of the table and looked at Bethany, whose face revealed only compassion. No; that wasn't quite it. Not *only* compassion. There was something else there; something she couldn't pin down. Was it recognition? Or more than that; kinship.

"Thank you for sharing that with me; I know how much courage it must have taken, and I hope it will help you to know that I am neurodivergent too. I am diagnosed autistic, and I have suspected dyspraxic and ADHD traits. I can absolutely relate to the pressure you put on yourself about feeling responsible and how exhausting it is fighting stereotypes and societal attitudes. Believe me, I get it"; Bethany's eyes glistened as she hesitantly reached out her hand, which Susannah warmly shook.

"Thank you for trusting me too, and I will keep it confidential unless you specifically tell me otherwise."

"It's fine; everyone who matters knows. All my colleagues know. Yes, including Stacey! It's been an interesting journey with her at times, but her heart is in the right place. I have consent to tell you that Diane who you met last time we were here is also autistic. Sharon is neurotypical but she's a solid ally."

"You have my consent to tell them about me. Poor Sharon being the odd one out at the table then!"

Both women laughed with the amplified reflex of relief.

"Mind you", continued Susannah, "I'm as guilty as any neurotypical person of making assumptions at times; I know I shouldn't say it because it shouldn't be how we measure our fellow beings and it may not match the truth of your experience, but you seem so together; so sorted."

Bethany laughed again, incredulity sending her eyebrows up towards her blue hair.

"You wouldn't say that if you'd met me a few months ago!" Her face became more serious. "My dad died last summer. It was unexpected; a heart attack. I'm the only child, and my mum had been through a cancer scare. She was still having check-ups. I had some extremely low points in terms of coping, practically and emotionally, which I won't go into right now but I had a lot of explaining to do to some of my mum's support network. Especially one of her neighbours, and a cousin and her wife on my dad's side. Sharon's a cousin on my mum's side; the phrase 'chalk and cheese' springs to mind! Though I get on much better with Miriam these days, I'll never have the bond with her that I do with Shaz."

"Good grief. I am so sorry, Bethany; that's a lot. I wish I'd met you sooner so that I could have been of some support as a fellow neurodivergent person! I'm so pleased you had Sharon and Diane. Were your colleagues supportive?"

"Extremely. I hit the jackpot in terms of line managers when Magnus took up post. He changed the whole place for the better; not that it was all bad before. I've been incredibly fortunate. We have an excellent autistic adults' one stop shop in Perth too. 'Number 3', on King Street, run by Autism Initiatives Scotland. I've been going there since shortly before the Covid era."

"That's interesting to know. It's so important to have services continue for adults rather than everything cutting off at one of the biggest times of transition."

"Absolutely."

"Speaking of your work, by the way, how are the plans coming along for the branch in Kirkbrigg?"

"Now, I'm glad you asked; they're coming along well, but I wasn't sure whether to mention it"; Susannah's new awareness registered the uncertainty behind Bethany's chatty personality. "I sensed last time that you may have been a tad uncomfortable with my asking about places to go and wanting to invade your home town. I know that's silly; I wasn't asking you to be involved and it was clear that my reasons for wanting to go were work related, so I daresay it comes from my conditioning to expect to miss cues and commit boundaries fails."

"No! I wish I'd known you felt that way so that I could have put your mind at rest. You didn't imagine me having an uncomfortable reaction, but it was in no way your fault. As you say, it was perfectly reasonable to ask me for recommendations and no, you didn't stretch boundaries at all. The reason I had a bit of a personal dilemma about it was to do with my best friend, Freya." Susannah fought back feelings of betrayal. "She's struggling with the prospect of me moving away and having a whole new social circle which she fears will end up pushing her out of my life." Keeping personal information minimal, she outlined the gist of their working life and Freya's isolation.

"Goodness me, poor Freya. I can empathise with her fears about losing that special 'best friend' status and she is definitely not alone in carrying that feeling into adulthood. I would describe Diane as my best friend, without question, but I also know that I'm one of a few best *female* friends to her and her *best* friends are Des and Jason in Inverbrudock. It doesn't affect my relationship with her and most of her besties are my friends too; not to mention Sharon who introduced us. I'd be lying, though, if I denied there's always that underlying awareness and that it's poignant for me. I understand why you felt wary of Freya being confronted with too much evidence of your expanding social circle too soon, and why you need to take small steps. I wonder, though, if it would help her to be included? You've come back to Kirkbrigg relatively recently after years away, but Freya's been there her whole life, yes?"; Susannah nodded. "So although I'm sure you know as well as she does what local places to recommend, perhaps she'd appreciate my asking for her input as someone who has spent more of her life there?"

"Funnily enough, my ridiculously emotionally perceptive wee sister was saying this morning that it might help Freya to integrate with my new Perth friends sooner rather than later. I think we need to sort out adding each other on social media so that we can start that process. I'd like to make sure we can find each other's accounts to add while we're both here, but if it's OK with you, wait until I've had the chance to speak to Freya before we accept any requests and she sees it on my pages."

"That sounds like a sensible plan"; Bethany had already opened the relevant apps on her phone. "From what you've told me, I would say that she deserves a career change and I'd like to be able to make an informed recommendation to Anita and Shona if she decides to apply. I sense that Freya would be a good fit with everyone involved here going forward."

More drinks were ordered as the conversation turned to the recent revelations about Mary. Susannah had gotten to the part where Lorna's light changed colour and startled London when their drinks arrived.

"Thanks"; Bethany raised her glass. "To Mary Meredith!" Susannah clinked hers against it. "Mary Meredith. Edie."

They drank in a brief silence, each catching up with their thoughts.

"So the more I think about it, the more I'm convinced that Lorna's light developing this glitch recently is no coincidence; that it's responding to Mary's lingering spirit. I know I should call her Edie now, but I can't help thinking of her as Mary in the context of the paranormal aspects of it because that's who she was at the time I'm seeing these traces of her. I looked up mercury vapour in street lighting after what Diane had said last time and the timing fits for that colour to match what the light would have looked like in Mary's childhood. I would really like to track down Teresa Valenti before I move; she's probably the best person to tell me whether there's someone who should rightfully have that essay as part of Mary's legacy."

"Diane will be fascinated to hear about all this. Would you be OK with me telling her?"

"Of course! Sharon too. I hope I'll be catching them up on things in person as well as you once I get settled here, but there's a way to go yet. I need to get it right next time I commit to a property. Which reminds me!"; she described her tartan theory, laughing as she recounted having promised to let Stacey in on it.

"That's brilliant! I will certainly share it with her. I know her brother too; he works in one of our Glasgow shops."

The conversation coasted along on more general subjects until a mellow, slightly tipsy Susannah boarded her bus home in the unexpected pink tinge of those first January twilights to fall noticeably later than in the dark reign of the weeks around the solstice.

Sunday rose sedate and glacial; frost turned the icy outdoors into a captured ghost of its own iron midwinter bleakness. The shimmer of warm breath stirring the pause of the Scottish Sabbath morning lingered around Freya as she walked fey and rosy-cheeked into Susannah's flat. The steam from the cafetière curled its offering towards the ceiling, catching and blending with the chilled air from the stairwell.

Giving thanks for Bethany having rescued a dismal day, Susannah watched Freya's reaction, cautious of scrutinising her too overtly. She was not about to become one of those people who hounded others over their facial expressions, and Freya had the right to feel her feelings. Her friend's eyes widened in surprise as she explained that she had wanted to talk to her first before adding Bethany on her social media, making it clear that she was doing her a courtesy but not asking for her permission; Freya looked momentarily hurt at the part about permission but readily asserted that it was not a problem or a surprise to her, and that she was relieved to hear that such a disappointing day had turned positive. The news about the bookshop and Bethany reaching out for Freya's involvement as a lifelong local resident was greeted with an almost childlike excitement which tugged at Susannah's heart; she resolved to thank Selina for putting her into the frame of mind to facilitate it.

She could see Freya becoming friends not only with Bethany but with Diane and Sharon too in time. *What if she unexpectedly had a personality clash with any of them or something went wrong further down the line?* Susannah determinedly pushed those thoughts away. They were all adults; the fact they met through Susannah did not make her responsible for any friendships, or career moves, that developed. Of course the flip side of that coin was that they didn't owe her any explanations either; any awkwardness would simply have to be navigated as and when it arose.

She looked fondly at Freya as she set down her coffee cup and leaned back, closing her eyes briefly as she stroked Morgan who was purring and kneading on her lap. Her friend's emotionally and psychologically depleted state was not going to resolve overnight. Enough progress had been made for today.

After Susannah waved Freya off and closed the door, her own despondency rolled back in with the bland spread of stratocumulus cloud that cut off the morning's tantalising frosty glitter and leached the liminal January daylight from her closed-in rooms. She sent her intended message to her sister in the afternoon's gloom as the cats enviably slept where they lay, then made the most of the leftover vigour from the all too brief morning to set about her next side project. It was high time she faced up to the possible further disappointment and tracked down Teresa Valenti, or whatever her name was now.

It didn't take long. Even with such an unusual name, which it turned out had never changed, Susannah had not expected to find her so quickly. A matching profile picture on her tribute note on Lorna Valenti's online death announcement from the local paper was all the confirmation Susannah needed that she had found the correct person, and although Teresa's own page was private and had no option for anyone unconnected to message her, it gave the name of a church in Stirling where she volunteered, helping them out with floral displays. Susannah messaged the church's page; within an hour she had a friend request from Teresa and a plan to meet up with her in Stirling, where she lived, as soon as she was free to make arrangements other than house viewings.

24

Fair Maid's Mews

The lift door slid open with an inviting smoothness and hardly enough sound to carry across the pale clean sweep of the light green tiled lobby. Suleiman considerately pointed out the CCTV camera in the top left corner as he gestured to Susannah to enter.

"I wonder how much my share of lift maintenance would be?", she mused as they were whisked up to the third floor. The listing and home report had mentioned an annual contribution for cleaning, stair lighting and maintenance, divided among the fourteen flats which made up the building at Fair Maid's Mews; two on the ground floor, four on each of the three upper storeys. "I expect it will be equally divided up but it hardly seems fair for the ground floor owners to have to pay towards a lift they will only ever use if they visit people on the higher floors. If I pursue this one, I'll need to get my solicitor to check that out."

The estate agent smiled, brushing a piece of lint off his grey suit which was a couple of shades darker than his neatly combed hair. "Even if the third floor owners pay more than the rest towards the lift, it will be a few pounds per week for that. You're wise to get your solicitor to check the details, of course."

Hang on, mate; let's see the place first! Susannah held back her defensive thoughts, reminding herself not to give Suleiman a hard time. He was there to represent the seller and to get a sale, but he had shown her genuine courtesy and goodwill from the outset; her battle scars from the disappointment of Crieff Gardens were not his problem.

Confined to her flat on an exceptionally stormy day when her workplace was closed due to a red weather warning, browsing the listings again had felt like the logical thing to do. Depleted by all of the recent disappointments, she had been unsure whether she was more afraid that there wouldn't be anything suitable, or that there would be. She had initially dismissed this flat due to its being on the third floor before deciding that its affordability, being in a former local authority building, merited a second look. Once she saw that there was a lift and that the flat had not only double aspect windows in the lounge but a small balcony leading off the main bedroom, she had put in her request to see the home report. Lee's feedback this time had been encouraging; he had prepared her for the likelihood of a surveyor recommending she have the balcony checked by a structural engineer given the age of the building and pointed out that any building repairs needed during her ownership would involve expensive scaffolding, but noted that everything pointed to it being in sound condition. The roof and windows had been replaced within the past five years and there were no concerns about the electrics. There was something else different about this one; underlying her inevitable caution was a calm, quiet glow devoid of the frantic anxiety which had been present deep down at her previous viewings. This one was either going to blow the ordered common-sense of her tartan theory completely out of the water or pull every disparate thread into alignment. As Suleiman turned the key and ushered her through the varnished front door, Susannah wondered if it may do a bit of both.

    The deep blue-green walls of the central hallway contrasted the freshly painted white doors leading off into the various rooms. Suleiman directed her firstly into the lounge. The walls were the colour of strong filter coffee with a splash of cream; she briefly noticed the gold patterned paper on the one unbroken wall which had been made into a feature, before the double aspect windows commanded her attention. Suleiman clocked her forcing herself to pause and noticing the thick rug in the middle of the floor before crossing the room; wisdom and understanding in his eyes, the expected trip hazard warning was shelved unspoken. The validation surprised Susannah with how much it meant to her; that she felt it land already in the vital sanctuary of home.

"That's a whole lot of Perth!"

Not that she had expected to see anything else; Suleiman, no doubt used to people blurting out all sorts at viewings, simply nodded and gave her the processing space she needed. Standing aside with a sage smile, he waited as she took in the view. Chimney stacks congregated in stoic clusters on their own secret cityscape of rooftops; warmly lit buses nuzzled into the well worn, home-for-tea grooves of their afternoon routes through the streets below. Bare branches quivered with the new life held just beneath their weathered surfaces as a colourful ScotRail train glided past them into the station. Every facet of the view ended in a softly delineated hilltop under the clean, burnished light of the Perthshire sky.

"Are you happy with the view, then?"; Suleiman's gently amused voice returned her awareness to the limited time and how much she needed to see. The flat had clearly been tidied up for viewing but the family's need for more space spoke for itself in every room; Susannah's usual hypervigilance pervaded every step. For once the counterproductive anxiety which so often caught her out was damped down by the calm compatibility she felt with this property as well as by Suleiman's unspoken faith in her, freeing her mind from the pressure to prove herself. In the kitchen, the pleasing curve of a pine bread bin caught her attention; she managed to resist the temptation to needlessly touch it since it was part of the current owner's personal effects.

"In Scandinavian countries, it's traditional to bring bread as a housewarming gift, for sustenance; salt for flavour, and candles for light through the long winters. Wine too, for joy, though that's definitely not only a Scandi thing!" *Uh oh; blether mode activated.* "I have an interest in Scandinavian culture. Sorry; I'm going back to my comfort zone here because I'm a bit nervous; viewing a potential forever home is so high stakes and I had a big disappointment recently…" *Shut UP, Susannah! Remember your tartan theory; keep those emotion threads in their narrow lane! However kind and affirming this guy is, he's Team Seller and anything you share which gives them an advantage will go straight back to them. It's his job.* "…And I'm a blether at the best of times"; she weakly attempted to salvage the lapse in her defences. Once again, she resisted the temptation to touch the grounding wooden curve of the bread bin. "I've yet to see the bedrooms and the bathroom, haven't I?"

Her inner self-criticism was off the charts; somehow, she needed to park it and take away its keys for the precious remaining time of this viewing, while taking in all she needed to and avoiding any missteps, verbal or physical. Exhaustion swept in without warning; she fought a wave of inertia as she tore her unfocused eyes away from the spice rack at which she had wasted what felt like an outrageous stretch of precious time blankly staring. She followed the patient, tactfully reserved Suleiman back into the hallway.

The windowless bathroom with its white tiles giving way to aqua paint around the top third of its walls was no better or worse than any she had seen in a flat. She noted the shower over the bath; her strong preference. Next came the main bedroom; Suleiman's animated salesman personality bubbled forth once more as he opened the sliding glass door to the balcony.

"I can see you enjoying many a weekend morning out here with a lovely pot of coffee, and a glass of wine in the evening; you're facing west so you will get to watch the sunsets."

"You know me well already then! My best friend and I do this thing on Sunday mornings; we call it 'Grounds for Gratitude'. We get together over a pot of ground coffee and list things to be thankful for over the past week. We've been talking about doing it over video calling once I move; where I live now doesn't have much of a view at all but her house has a lovely garden. And the sunsets! Oh, yes; I love watching the sky; the clouds, the colours, the changing light through the seasons."

Once again she made herself stop, determined not to get carried away as her heart insisted with deep, unhurried conviction that this was it; she had found her castle of opal midnights.

"I love that idea; Grounds for Gratitude. Yes; I can absolutely see that on your balcony here, and remember, there's another bedroom to see. Maybe your friend will be staying over sometimes; it's Kirkbrigg you've travelled from, yes?"

"That's right. The second bedroom would most likely be used for storage and a big cat tree at the window; I have two indoor cats. Freya is like me; she values her own space, but sure, why not; I wouldn't rule out her staying over from time to time. I really can't get ahead of myself though, Suleiman! I'm sorry if that sounds unappreciative; I know you've got to promote the heck out of your properties, but I have to keep myself grounded here. That said, I am happy to confirm my interest and that I will be making an offer."

"Of course; I completely understand! Shall we move on to see that other bedroom, then?"

It was painted a similar shade of mauve to the main bedroom; a few tones lighter to offset its smaller size and narrower window. Posters of a band which Susannah didn't recognise adorned the walls; a collection of soft toys huddled at the end of a small double bed. She found herself hoping that the teenager who currently called this room their own space was as invested in moving on as the adults whose decision it was, and that they would be allocated a room they would love as much in their new home. An image of the intensely private adolescent Selina came into her mind, followed by Caitlin and Eilidh whispering and giggling in their present day room with its sunny yellow walls and matching white nightstands beside each twin bed as her sister and Phoebe relaxed, caught up on their busy days and kept on weaving their lives together in their home.

Maybe this time she could let herself trust in the possibility of her own ideal setting working out. She could give believing and manifesting a shot without it meaning she had to sell out on her need to protect her emotions and her image as an appropriately circumspect, worldly wise neurodivergent adult.

"I'd really like to catch my solicitor before his team meeting, and I'm meeting a friend in Perth before I head back to Kirkbrigg. Could you please thank the seller for opening their beautiful home to me? Thank you so much for your time and..." She had no immediate words for the subtleties of how helpful and perceptive Suleiman had been. He was, she reminded herself again, a virtual stranger; there was oversharing and then there was oversharing. Once all of this was safely concluded, reviews would be the time and place for giving him due credit.

It wasn't quite dark enough for the streetlights to come on as Susannah waved Suleiman off and made her call to Adil, but lights were beginning to come on in a few windows as she looked back at Fair Maid's Mews. There was something about a streetlamp at the end of a road, she thought, looking up at the frosted bowl on top of the post which rose from the corner of the pavement towards the late winter sky; biding its time.

Bethany scrolled through the photos on the listing, her expression resolutely neutral.

"I absolutely respect your need to stay detached, but I do like the look of this one and I have a good feeling about it."

"Yeah; Adil was positive when I spoke to him. I've done all I can, and hopefully not blown it by failing to have a poker face. I tried, but I know I gave too much away. I enjoyed the viewing but I'm afraid to relive it because I know I'll be mortified. I can't blame Suleiman if he tells the seller to hold out for every last penny I've got! Sure, he was empathic and genuinely worked with me. I'm not suggesting that was fake or manipulative; he's working *for the buyer*, not *against me*, and there's a big difference there. If I were the seller, he would take his experienced shrewd reading of any buyers back to me in exactly the same way. I'm annoyed with myself for not keeping my cards closer to my chest; for not being a better neurodivergent ambassador as well as not protecting my bargaining position! I mean, I know there won't be an item on the news after this saying 'a new law has been passed forbidding neurodivergent people from viewing prospective homes unaccompanied and the Responsible Person supervising them and repeatedly elbowing them in the ribs to stop them from oversharing will be the one to make all decisions; we can exclusively reveal tonight that it's all Susannah Silverdale's fault', but I do feel a responsibility to do my bit to debunk the myths people use against our autonomy."

"You have to factor in though, Suze, that you *are* neurodivergent and what that means. Believe me, it's taken me years to get to this point, but we can only truly move forward when we accept that there can be a kernel of truth in a few of those myths without it meaning we should ever lose autonomy. Equality can't be dependent on us masking and acting neurotypical. Your brain is exhausted. That is its default setting, never mind in a high stakes scenario like this. You're making a huge decision based on a short, pressurised visit to someone else's home, full of their stuff, with all the sensory and proprioceptive demands that entails. You're dealing with someone you don't know, who as you say has a professional agenda which is geared first and foremost towards someone else. You have to take in so many details, adjust for your belongings of all sizes, and consider all the practical ramifications. You legitimately do not have enough mental energy left over; enough bandwidth in the moment to hide your feelings and instinctive responses. It's got nothing to do with being 'unworldly' or 'naïve'; it doesn't mean you're unaware of how the system works. You're simply too damned tired after decades of the crap this world heaps on us, and that's not a character failing but a physiological limit. Plenty of neurotypical people will have let something slip in the rush of a viewing and regretted it, too. The difference is, they don't get defined by it the way we do. And whatever Suleiman reports back to the seller, you remain in control of how much you offer and how far you are prepared to negotiate. That is basic demand and supply. You look at the home reports; you listen to your solicitor and take advice from experienced professionals. None of that is weakness. It's society that falls short by its inflexibility, making us feel that we have to know everything merely to reach a baseline of equality. Putting us in a position where we can't ask for help, or get our part in the process anything less than perfect, without it becoming a 'gotcha' which it wouldn't be for someone who is, or is read as, neurotypical."

"You're right, I know. I'm so glad you were able to meet me today; it massively helps being able to get that perspective from someone else with similar life experience. I want to be able to enjoy my memories of this viewing, not be cringing with guilt and shame replaying every word and having to convince myself that I didn't do *that* badly and the selling side *aren't* all shaking their heads laughing at the guileless mug! I did propose a cautious offer too, conditional on whatever reports Adil suggests I ask for. I went in very slightly below the asking price, taking into account the price the seller paid ten years ago and the home report value; I wanted to offer the asking price but that would encourage them to ask for more given the home report value being a few thousand higher, and I need to allow for keeping enough back to have a savings base for any future repairs."

"All of which sounds extremely adult and well thought out! Do check your messages whenever you need to, by the way, especially while it's business hours; this is no time for phone etiquette among friends!"

"Thanks, Beth"; Susannah checked and placed her phone on the table as their loaded fries and fresh drinks arrived. "You know, I think a lifetime of not having or seeking a partner has been good preparation for being a home buyer, especially without also being a seller and having the backing that goes with that side. Lifelong single status is a particular kind of benign and passive, but pervasive, lack of being anyone's priority. It's not that people don't care. I just don't have pole position anywhere; that safety net and bolstering of being somebody's person. Which I accept as part of the pros and cons of how much choice and control I have; how much my space is my own. Being a buyer dealing with a seller's team is similar. We each have a solicitor, but the estate agent tips the balance towards the seller. I don't have the stress of being in a chain, but I have to deal with people who are duty bound to prioritise the seller's interests over mine. I'm not an opponent; I'm sure they're happy for buyers getting their dream homes, but I'm not the client either. Viewing a potential home is so deeply personal, it's easy to get caught up in the targeted sales pitch and then feel betrayed when the awareness comes back to the surface again that as a prospective buyer, you're not the priority. For all I feel things so intensely and my attachment to places is more central to my emotional structure, which makes viewing properties more visceral and raw, I have learned to better understand where these local estate agents are coming from and where I fit into that as a buyer without it defining me, or what they think of me, as a person."

"That's such an interesting take on it, and your point about the amplified emotions around viewing properties makes it more logical that you can't expect to completely hide your responses in real time."

Susannah's phone pinged; she hastily unlocked it.

"The seller has made a counter-offer; if I'll go up to halfway between the asking price and the home report value, which amounts to less than three thousand over what I've offered, they'll accept!"

"Suze! This is amazing; is Adil recommending you agree?"

"He says he can try to negotiate closer to the asking price if I want, but like I was saying about the estate agents, that's him doing his job. Given the recent replacement of the windows and roof, and that we would make our offer conditional on a detailed survey for peace of mind, I think this counter-offer is fair. So yeah; I'm going to tell him to agree."

She did, and the steam hadn't finished rising from the chips under The Sandeman's generous portions of smoky BBQ sauce before Adil's next message confirmed the verbal acceptance.

25

Conveyance

February was the impatient month. It already had that feel to it without adding the wait for a survey and the certainty of a longed-for new home. With the long, slow dark stretch of January finally over, the second month of the calendar year routinely twitched and fidgeted its way through twenty-eight restless days, managing one more every fourth year before throwing in the towel. The damp, petulant wind protested each stubbornly early dusk, throwing icy rain at the impassive streetlamps and hissing an urgent refrain that conveyed 'come on; let's do March already' through the indulgent trees.

The building condition survey had mostly mentioned cosmetic upgrades; a small leak in the bathroom had already been fixed by the seller. Other than some energy-saving recommendations, the one issue highlighted as needing further investigation was as expected; that the balcony should be checked by a structural engineer. Susannah felt extremely fortunate that the seller had readily agreed and that an appointment had been available within a week of the surveyor's report coming in.

Freya had come round to provide moral support as Susannah took the video call from the engineer, bringing a hip flask full of a magnificently nuanced Glenfhraoich Triple Wood. "It was a raffle prize", she explained, "and when Mum offered a dram to Stewart across the road who is a whisky enthusiast, he was highly impressed. In fact, he said that it had such complex layers from the influence of the casks, the tasting notes should be written by a structural engineer. So that's why I brought it!"

Susannah laughed. "That is fabulous; I'll have to tell her!"

As she accepted the video call, Jean Meadows' aquiline profile came up on screen; close-cropped, spiky grey hair lay in a sculpted style around her ear in which a plain gold stud nestled.

"…came off in my hand, so that was the point at which he had to concede that the evidence spoke for itself." Her words were slightly muffled as she had turned away from her laptop to address a colleague; hearing the notification of her call having been connected, she quickly turned back to face her screen.

"Hi, Susannah; sorry about that, I had to answer a quick question there. How are you feeling?"

"Bricking it, Jean"; Susannah answered frankly. "This wait for news feels like the final hurdle. I'm shitting so many bricks I'll end up needing a planning application!"

Jean let out an appreciative roar of laughter. "I hear you; I know this has been a fraught journey for you and I'm not going to keep you in suspense. I'll email over the details to you of course, but I found no structural concerns whatsoever."

Both Susannah and Freya squealed, hugging each other.

"Thank you so much! Sorry, this is Freya, my best friend. She came over to hear the initial results with me."

Freya raised her hand in acknowledgement. "Hi! It's wonderful to see a woman in your line of work. I've become interested in the details of buildings and how they function, through Susannah's experience of home reports and research."

"Thank you, Freya! I must admit, even nowadays when some people see my name they expect to meet a Frenchman called Jean"; she raised her hands in the universal 'what can you do?' gesture. "How many French people do you know called Meadows? Then there are the ones who have been told my name verbally and think it's short for Eugene. It used to annoy me; now I laugh it off. I enjoy my work too much to let stereotypes spoil it. I was lucky to find this firm; we're a happy team who all support each other."

"That's so encouraging. I'm thinking of a change in career; you've inspired me to believe there's a better fit out there. Anyway, I mustn't keep you from telling Susannah your findings!"

"That's quite all right; the main thing is that there are no concerns. No cat flap needed!"

Susannah spluttered a laugh. "I told Jean about that property Lee talked me out of when I was giving her the house hunting story so far"; she explained to Freya whose expression reflected her puzzlement at the logistics, given that Susannah kept her cats indoors and this flat was on the third floor. "I said to her that if I'd pursued that one, I'd have been asking the building surveyor to include a costing to install a cat flap in the door of Adil's office because he'd have had kittens when he saw the home report."

Freya's laughter was echoed by the structural engineer's. "That reminds me, actually; should I copy your solicitor in when I email the report across?"

"Yes, please. Seriously, Jean, thank you so much"; Susannah raised the hip flask which Freya handed her towards the screen and took a deep swig before telling Jean about Freya's neighbour's tasting note comment.

"If giving you good news hadn't made my day already, that certainly would!"; Jean's blue eyes twinkled. "Glenfhraoich, did you say? That's a decent dram. I'm sure I've got one of theirs at home. Well, I wish you both all the best in the next stages of your lives. Susannah, you have a beautiful new home lined up and no reason to have any doubts about its condition above and beyond the ongoing maintenance all homeowners need to expect. And Freya, whatever you decide to explore in terms of a career change, anyone who says it's a man's job is talking out of their downpipe. Good luck, both of you!"

Susannah passed the hip flask back to Freya, who wiped the top and took a swig as Susannah closed the laptop.

"She was a breath of fresh air!"; Freya delicately nosed the open flask and murmured an appreciative noise before taking another draught. "Shall I decant the rest of this into a couple of glasses for us while you message Adil?"

Listening to the companionable sounds of Freya efficiently sorting their celebratory drams in the kitchen, Susannah leaned back against the cushions and closed her eyes. She idly reached out to stroke the tips of Morgan's fur as she slept in a tight contented ball next to her; the cat stirred, gave a soft purr-mew and sank back into her late afternoon nap. The corners of Susannah's mouth curved upwards as she pictured her solicitor opening the message she had sent; short and to the point, confirming that she regarded all the conditions of the offer involving reports as having been satisfied and that she hereby instructed him to conveyance the living daylights out of this. Her thoughts rewound to the autumn day when he had reminded her to register the joyful side of this process. The solid warmth of his handshake grounding her as she took in the acceptance of her offer on Crieff Gardens; the cool slick of coalescing night air on the dry surface of the maple leaf as she picked it up in the pale gleam of a streetlamp. Dare she believe that this time it was all going to be OK?

She had done her due diligence; gathered enough information this time to be confident that nothing major could crop up to change things. She remained at the mercy of the fact that the seller was in a chain, which meant coping with uncertain factors for a while longer, but once missives were concluded her side of the deal would be much more secure. She would be free to start arranging insurance, which would be necessary from the date on which the keys became available to her irrespective of not moving in immediately. Ordering packing boxes, at least one batch size above whatever the listing would have her believe applied to her property size. Reaching out to any trades she needed for snagging works, sounding out their availability.

"Suze?"

Her eyes snapped open. Freya was sitting in her usual chair; drink in hand, Annika in the process of settling on her lap. She had set Susannah's glass down on the nearest coaster.

"I gathered you'd need a few minutes of quiet to take it all in. Did your message go through OK?"

Susannah checked her phone and confirmed that it had. Morgan abruptly woke up, chirruping what cat people described as the activation noise and ran towards the main bedroom.

"She'll be away to stare at the ceiling, no doubt. I don't know what the fascination is; it seems to interest her rather than bother her so I'm not worried, but I do find myself wondering if it has something to do with Mary. Edie! I can't quite get used to the idea of them being one and the same." She raised her glass in a silent, generalised toast. "I must admit, I wonder whether the activity will increase now that it's becoming more likely I'll be moving away from here in a few weeks. I hate to think that she's somehow trapped here because of me. I can't see her following me to Perth; she's too deeply connected here, but I want her to be at peace before I go. I can't help feeling that I'm missing something. Some crucial detail that I need to see about the nature of the barrier, in order to help her to cross over. The main link is definitely to her grandmother, not me, but I do believe I'm involved and have a key role in this somehow; after all, I dreamed about her so vividly in Nairn and it felt deeper than my subconscious."

Freya nodded, stroking Annika and sipping her drink.

"After I'd been talking to London about Mary changing her name, that day in the graveyard when I realised who she was, I remembered something else. Julian made a comment one time back when he used to take me to the library about Edie being the only person who could call me 'Susie' without it making me flinch. I recalled saying to him, and I had no idea why at the time, that my being 'Susie' to her was going to help her one day. I think I knew that having something distinct about how I identified to her, like a password of sorts, was going to be important. If I were the main reason she's reaching out, though, she wouldn't be appearing as the child she was. Young Mary never met me; her time here was way before I was born. It wasn't the happiest time in her life either. Yes, it was when she had her grandmother and felt safe, but it was also when the reasons she needed that extra help to feel safe were most intimidating to her."

Freya set down her glass and leaned forward, one hand caressing Annika's silky ears. "Do you think maybe that time was more clear-cut, for all it was more difficult; could that be why she comes through from then?"

"I suppose it could be; yes, that makes sense. Routine and structure appear to be a big part of hauntings from the accounts I've read over the years. The pattern of those Sunday visits; seeing her friends, getting away from the scrutiny of adults and playing out where all she had to worry about was staying on this side of Lorna's... Oh my word."

Susannah set down her own glass, goosebumps rising on her arms as realisation stirred the hairs on the back of her neck.

"The reason she can't cross over isn't about Lottie or me. It's that streetlight!"

Freya's eyes widened; Annika looked up as the hand stroking her stilled.

"*That's* the connection! Coming back to the safety of the time when her grandmother was around, and getting life right was more straightforward, meant that she was once again bound by the absolute rule about not going past

Lorna's light. I'd wondered whether the changing colour was down to her energy; possibly trying to get my attention, but I didn't realise until now exactly why she's trapped. That's why it keeps going back to the colour it would have shone in her childhood when that rule applied."

"I do believe you've cracked the X-File, Agent Silverdale! You're right; it makes perfect sense."

"It does. I hated to think of her being stuck and not at peace, but now I know what to do about it."

Night clouds gathered in the February teatime dusk over the unlit Lorna's light. It was an extra-transitional twilight characteristic of the time of year; the evening sun of coming brighter days penned like a racehorse in the grey hold of stubbornly clinging winter, the swell of stratocumulus its snorted breath across a sky primed for a fresh season. Freya stood at a respectful distance holding the tartan-covered notebook which had become Susannah's house move organiser. In an inspired move, Freya had grabbed it from the table on their way out, as a prop to pretend they were rehearsing a scene for a play if anyone disturbed them.

Susannah raised her eyes to the streetlamp and the pent-up sky beyond.

"I'm talking to Mary Renfield and to Edie Mackay, the woman you became. It's Susann..." She remembered her long ago, half-understood comment to Julian, took a deep breath and squared her shoulders. "Susie. Little Susie Silverdale. Do you see? Look at me; I'm grown up now. That means that the times both versions of you remember have come and gone. All of the things that happened which hurt you, both child and adult, are past. Mary, you grew up to be a wonderful, kind, empathic woman who used all of that childhood pain to help kids who you knew were going through something similar, though you never had the full clarity you deserved. You know me as an adult; you reached out to me so many times in my dreams for help. I didn't know then how to help you, but I do now. Help doesn't always appear as we expect. We are conditioned to think of it as something that inevitably reaches down from above, but it's way more nuanced than that. I need you to look at me and see the vulnerable little girl I was, and let that knowledge help you now. You became Edie, and you were there for me as a child. Not only me; you gave other children the safe space they needed to thrive. I know you will have picked up on the fact that I'm going to be moving away from the flat where you had happy times with your grandmother. Do you remember a boy called Adil, who often hid alone in the library around the time you knew me; how you sat with him, helping him to believe in himself and to practice things in the way he needed to and understand that it was as valid as anyone else's learning? That cast-adrift young lad is now a successful conveyancing solicitor, and he remembers you as the pivotal figure you were. He has the deep-down assurance and belief in what he imparts to others which allowed him to give me some of the most valuable guidance I've had in the process of buying my first home. You were the one to set him on the path towards that confidence and career. You're free now. I know you remember, and feel as current because it was so important on so many levels, that rule about not going past Lorna's light. I need you to look at me now and let yourself accept that it's not that time any more."

Above Susannah's head, the light flickered on. A pale blue-green tint caught a single tear as it trickled unheeded down Freya's cheek.

"That rule ended long ago. You grew up, and for all there were events that made you feel as though you'd come full circle, you need to look past all of that now. You are free. You can go so much further than Lorna's light now. You can leave all of the hurt behind. You live on in the best days of the people you helped, and of the people we will help in turn. That is what matters. You are safe to move on. Thank you for everything, and I am sorry that you didn't get the closure and absolution you should have in life. You have it now. Be at peace, Mary Meredith; be merry. Let all the bad stuff go. Have that adventure you wrote about as a little girl. You're free."

Freya's stifled sob caught in the shadows as the streetlamp went out. The two friends looked at one another in the lost ageless gloom. Time was soaked up into the formless grey; the air itself paused and cast about for direction.

The lamp switched on; tremulous behind clouded glass, newborn rays stretched on delicate filaments to greet the leading edge of spring, strengthening to a steady glow of warm ambient peach. It glinted on the fine metallic gold lines in the tartan notebook cover as Susannah gently took it from Freya's unresisting hands. She linked her arm through her best friend's as they walked silently back to her flat. As they finished their drinks in companionable quiet, both cats slept undisturbed on the deep anchored peace of Susannah's bed.

26

Affirming

Pink would never be one of Susannah's favourite colours but she welcomed its gradual infusion into the softening hues of March. It came in a subliminal blush of circulation returning to the earth; freeing shuttered buds day by day and mellowing the night air. The light from the streetlamps took on a subtly different quality; a shift towards opaque as though anticipating their less busy season, more kindly timed dusks as convivial voices gathered around their posts and blossom clustered near their lanterns like mini marshmallows toasted in starlight.

Adil had confirmed the written acceptance of her offer and his property title searches were well underway with no anticipation of any problems. All signals remained set at caution; only Susannah's siblings, Freya, Tan and Lee, Bethany and Morven had been shown the listing and Connie had been updated as a courtesy, but she no longer felt the need to keep the rest of her life on hold. That included meeting up with Teresa Valenti.

Friars Wynd Boutique Hotel showed its welcoming face in the form of an elegant bar at its entrance halfway up the curving street in central Stirling from which it took its name. Spirals of pendant lights in geometric copper frames cast an inviting glow from inside its tall windows; brickwork and modern spotlights within added to its alluring urban chic. Susannah had arrived early and settled at a corner table with a rare afternoon strong coffee, its stark richness lacing the air with steel as the door opened and Teresa walked in.

The coal-black sheen which had once defined the silvery white hair pinned up in a tidy knot at the crown of her head was now concentrated in her keenly expressive but friendly eyes. Susannah stood to greet her, taking a cautious second glance down despite knowing perfectly well that her coffee cup was in a position of safety. Smiling, Teresa shook her offered hand before taking off her light blue suede jacket and wisp of lilac scarf, draping them over the back of the seat and going to the bar. Susannah readily agreed to the recommended Pinot Grigio, finished her coffee and set the cup aside on the ample table space. The barmaid efficiently whisked it away after setting down their wine.

Susannah slid the envelope with Mary's essay in it out of her bag, anxious not to forget as the conversation went on. She turned to watch people passing by on the attractive street which always made her think of continental Europe; giving Teresa space as the first era of the friendship when Edie was Mary came palpably to life for her once more.

"Goodness me"; Teresa replaced the essay in the envelope with the tenderness of tucking a child into bed. She took off her reading glasses, folding them neatly into a brown leather case and set the envelope in between them on the table. "Thank you, Susannah; for sharing this with me, but most of all for setting her free." She took a slow sip of wine, gazing into the middle distance as she held her glass aloft. "Rest easy, darling Edie."

Susannah raised her glass, tapping it with the utmost care against Teresa's. "Edie", she echoed quietly.

"It's all so clear in hindsight", Teresa said sadly. "Everything you've said about dyspraxia and neurodivergence in general resonates with what I remember. I am fairly certain that Esther, Edie's mother, was autistic. It doesn't justify how hard she was on her, but I agree with everything you said in your messages about Esther's 'nerves' most likely being sensory overload and that she was up against a plethora of unmet needs too. You are quite correct to say that there was no villain in all of this; that it's a desperately sad saga of unsupported and misunderstood people struggling without knowing why." She shook her head sadly. "Mary, back in the day, used to say she wished she could live in the empty space near the ceiling where there was nothing to catch her out and she wasn't in anyone's way. Esther would dismiss that as a fantasy in lieu of taking responsibility and trying harder." Residual anger flashed in her eyes as her fingers tightened around the stem of her wine glass.

"Trying harder!"; Susannah scoffed, rolling her eyes. "If neurodivergent people had a penny for every time we heard that, we'd all have privately funded support! The conflict of needs in multiply neurodivergent households and relationships isn't talked about enough either. The clattering versus the heightened sensory response is one example. Or the ADHD struggle to be organised and the autistic need for precision and predictability. I think we fear that talking about it will underpin the blame and intolerance from outside, but it is real and valid. You know, that's interesting what you said about the space near the ceiling. My younger cat in particular has been spending a lot of time staring up towards the ceiling, especially in the main bedroom."

"That's Morgan, isn't it? The daughter? I really must make time to catch up with that show you talk about; I always liked the look of it, and of course any recommendation alongside a love of 'The X-Files' carries extra weight." Teresa's expression became serious once again. "When Mary came back as Edie to take up post in the library, she was to all outward appearances a different person in more than her name. She had travelled widely; made many friends. She never married as you know, but that suited her; she was ahead of her time in that respect. She had love affairs over the years, with no gender preference." The door swung open as a group of tourists arrived with their luggage. Teresa turned towards the noise, her eyes looking somewhere else; inwards to a past time. "She was happy then, but it was based on something that ultimately failed her. Nobody with the level of acquired perfectionism from a childhood like hers can keep their guard up so high, so consistently, as to never slip below the impossible standards they've set themselves. Something has to give, and it can come down to sheer bad luck."

Teresa sighed, closing her eyes in an anguished extended blink.

"The first edition?"; Susannah prompted gently, sensing that the painful story needed to be told to put it to rest. Teresa nodded grimly; tight-lipped, she inhaled deeply through her nose.

"It wasn't even Edie's coffee cup. She would never have had anything near that book which could cause damage. A colleague came over to speak to her and set the cup down on her desk, not noticing what was open on it at the time. Edie panicked; reached out to move the book further out of harm's way, and she might have done so if the phone hadn't rung at that precise moment and made her jump. She knocked the book towards the cup instead of taking hold of it and, well, you can imagine."

Susannah certainly could. The cold flood of adrenaline; the logic-defying craving for time travel to become feasible, almost believing that it could out of the sheer desperate need to redo and correct the past thirty seconds.

"She couldn't account for what happened; the book would have been quite safe had she not reached out for it. Everything she had built up around conquering, hiding and overcompensating for her so-called clumsiness collapsed like a house of cards. As your generation would say, she lost her mojo. As you know, she was encouraged to retire early, and she shut herself down. Her constellation of friends shrank to a nebula; close knit and always there, yet on the edge of what she could grasp. She put together a routine and a life of sorts, but it was an inverted version of the woman who came back here to take up a job which resonated with her soul, in the town where she had never lived permanently so didn't have too many bad memories but held her link to her grandmother. She was never the same after she retired."

Teresa, her eyes misted dark monoliths in the incandescent lights of the bar, fixed a kind but firm look upon Susannah.

"Edie became more and more afraid of getting older; of everything associated with that. The slowing down; the inevitable frailty. She was consumed by the fear of returning to the casual, systemic impatience dealt out to her as a child, knowing that it is greater at both ends of the spectrum of life. The sighs; the tuts; the looks; the apologies to the next person in the queue. That shift from looking at her to looking through her. She knew that, equally frustrating though it is at the young end of the scale and she would never minimise that, as a child she could look forward to becoming an adult and shaking off at least some of that powerlessness. Where she was heading after her early retirement, there was no stronger next stage to focus on. Because she had built the castle of her adulthood on the shifting sand of disowning and hiding her difficulties, she hadn't acquired and learned to use the tools she needed to see her through when the midsummer high of her life was past. To be clear, I'm not talking here about developing coping strategies, finding ways to adapt or getting better at some things with practice. Those are all positive and constructive. I'm talking about the burden of shame; what was that term you introduced me to? Ah yes; internalised ableism. Even as she encouraged people to value all parts of their distinct profiles of strengths and weaknesses, Edie could never quite shake off that feeling that her worth depended on being able to suppress all evidence of her own. She had that innate belief that she was less deserving; less lovable; less forgivable, and therefore had a smaller, in fact non-existent, margin for error than other people did. As the sun began to set earlier and earlier on her capacity to get through the day in the outwardly perfect way she had convinced herself she needed to, she missed out on so much other light because all she could see was encroaching darkness. She was so fixated on an unsustainable permanent midnight sun, she couldn't let herself rest in the darker days and let the velvet night wrap around her and the moon and the stars be enough until the morning. She was terrified of anything less than being in the full glare of knowing it all, seeing everything, all the time; she needed to have 'made it' to that impossible standard in order to compensate for the added unavoidable drawbacks of older age. Of course, nobody is designed to live like that. And because she had built so much of her adult social circle around people and systems who held those prejudiced; *ableist*, that's the word; beliefs and unwittingly encouraged her perfectionism as a way to keep in with them, her support system melted away when she needed it most. That wasn't as straightforward as people dropping her as a friend either; it was a breakdown of trust and safe feeling on both sides. Some drifted; some she pushed away, and most let her do so with precious little resistance, leaving her more convinced of being the one who was broken and at fault." Teresa leaned forward, one hand gripping Susannah's wrist with a gentle compassion reinforced by steel. "I know that you have an awareness in keeping with how much more is understood today, Susannah, but I see that potential in you too and Edie would have wanted me to warn you: Do not allow yourself to go the same way. Keep building a better castle on stronger, affirming foundations."

The door rattled open again, startling the rapt Susannah as Teresa's choice of imagery rang through her soul. A tall man with light brown hair escorted some young foreign backpackers to the bar; the snatches of conversation she caught revealed that he had gotten off the same train as them and they had nervously asked him for directions, which he had ascribed to them noticing his white collar. Teresa's attention had been caught by him too.

"Oliver!"

"Well, hello Teresa; I'd forgotten you were coming here today! So you must be Susannah?"

Susannah, having just taken a swig of her wine, raised her glass in lieu of a nod.

"Yes; Susannah, this is Oliver Sinclair, the minister at the church where I help out with the floral displays."

"Of course; lovely to meet you. I recognise you now, from the photos on the church page. That was a beautiful wedding you shared last weekend; Bella and Anya, wasn't it?"

"It was indeed. Thank you! Teresa, I must tell you that Tim and Nancy are so looking forward to meeting you to discuss the flowers for their wedding next month. So, Susannah; I believe you knew Edie Mackay years ago?"

"I did; you could say we go way back."

"I understand completely"; the minister's eyes twinkled merrily. "I've heard all about the history there. My grandfather was the minister in Kirkbrigg, you know, when Edie was a wee girl." He smiled as Susannah's eyes widened, instantly registering the connection. "I wish someone could have told her that my grandmother never liked that look-at-me vase. Well, it's lovely to have met you too, Susannah; catch up with you soon, Teresa, and thanks again for all your help."

"You're very welcome, Oliver; see you soon!"

Teresa laughed as the door swung closed; Susannah readily agreed that the serendipitous meeting with Reverend Sinclair called for another glass of wine. Teresa's face became serious once more as their drinks were brought over.

"Back to what we were talking about before Oliver came in; I'm certain that Edie's long term psychological depletion from that was a big part of why she succumbed so quickly to Covid. I know lots of people with all kinds of personal circumstances did too, but there was always that sense with Edie that the fight had completely gone out of her and to be frank, although she wasn't suicidal, she didn't have an active will to live."

Teresa reached out and moved the envelope which still lay in the middle of the table towards Susannah.

"I think you should keep this. I truly appreciate you thinking of me and involving me in deciding what to do with it, but I feel you should have it as a reminder of what we've talked about today. Edie would want, with her entire heart and soul, things to be different for you as you move on to this time in your life which is more aligned with true contentment. There's something else too"; she reached into her large leather handbag and extracted a red and silver cardboard box. It was cube shaped; big enough to hold something the size of an orange, well wrapped. She placed it on top of the envelope; Susannah gingerly picked it up. It was lighter than an orange. She lifted the lid and took out the tissue-wrapped object inside, cradling it in her palm.

"I know it's not the season for it, but when Edie was…" Teresa swallowed, composing herself; "When it was becoming clear that she wasn't going to get better, on one of our video calls, she told me where to find this and that she had kept it aside on an impulse she didn't fully understand, but that one day I would know who to pass it on to. It was one of only a couple of times in those last days when she called me 'Terry'."

Susannah unfolded the fragile off-white tissue, feeling the caught breath of air from a different time pressed between the layers. Beneath it all glinted the metallic blue dome of a Christmas tree bauble. As Susannah lifted it out, concentrating on her hands working in slow motion, the suspended lights above the table reflected in the silver folds of an indented hollow crafted to make the most of the light from tiny bulbs of blown glass and the redirected sparkle of tinsel. The past time which floated in fragments from the tissue paper wrapping lay preserved in the rumpled dip, drawing her eyes inward as the glow at the heart of the coal fires she dimly recalled from her first few winters used to. She had seen this bauble before, but not so long ago and not with her waking eyes.

"I know it's not in keeping with modern decorations, but Edie would have been so happy to think of you putting that on your tree on your first Christmas in your new home once you have settled in somewhere ideal for you", Teresa was saying.

"I absolutely will; I don't do restrictive themes for Christmas decorations. A growing collection of what's meaningful over the years is much truer to the spirit of the season", Susannah hastened to reassure her. "I love it, Teresa; thank you."

She set the bauble safely back in its box and closed the lid, tucking it and the envelope away in her own bag. Susannah remembered the other thing she intended to ask Teresa in person.

"As you know, I found Lottie's grave and it mentioned Esther, but if you don't mind me asking, where was Edie buried? I'd love to pay my respects."

"Ah; I'm sorry, dear, you'd need to travel a bit further for that, and there's no grave to visit. Edie was cremated, and I took her ashes to scatter where she wanted them; where the family, including her grandparents, spent a few holidays in her early childhood which she never forgot. That was the other time she called me 'Terry'; when she asked me to take her back there."

"Oh, I see; where was that?"

"Nairn Beach. She always said that it was the nearest she ever came in her early years to experiencing that wide, uncluttered space she craved; where there was enough room for her to feel safe to move around without having to be so on guard."

Behind Susannah's blurring eyes, a child's liberated laughter echoed across the sand; momentarily stronger than the roar of the sea. In the future she dared to imagine with new certainty, the broad, flat paths of multiple city walks around Perth beckoned; their colours and light marking out the different beauty of each season for the rest of her days.

27

Networking

"Honestly, Mrs Yelland, it's not a silly question at all; we often get queries about whether you need to change any settings when the clocks go forward, or back. I'm glad you asked; it's important that you feel able to check these things with us. It's what we're here for."

Susannah smiled fondly with knowing empathy as the elderly lady's voice settled into a lower pitch, her breathing audibly calmer. She knew too well what it was like to play the lottery of phoning any kind of helpline; never knowing how the person she got on the other end would react to her innate anxiety and fear of seeming foolish. She was relieved that this lady had not had her call picked up by Candice, who had taken a similar call earlier that day and Susannah suspected that the connection had not cut out in time to keep the customer from hearing her snort of laughter. She had reminded Candice that what had become familiar to them through working with it every day was new and intimidating to many of their customers, especially those who were elderly or did not have English as their first language. Candice had continued to giggle; Susannah had resignedly accepted that the most constructive thing she could do was to turn her attention back to her own work and focus on whichever customers came her way.

Ada Yelland was talking about how much she was looking forward to the light nights and getting out to the golf club with her son.

"When the weather gets milder but before it gets humid, you see, my arthritis eases up enough that I can join him there once in a while after he finishes work. I do enjoy watching the sunsets from the big windows in the club lounge. And I tell you this, my dear; one day I will get my name on that ladies' trophy."

Susannah glanced at her screen, noting Mrs Yelland's date of birth, which brought her into a world celebrating the end of its second major war.

"You certainly will, and I'm sure I'll be reading in the paper about you getting a hole in one."

"Well, when that day comes, after your help and understanding today I'll be putting one behind the bar for you when I buy the traditional round of drinks."

It was at times like this that Susannah, however tired and overloaded she became, unreservedly loved her job. She glanced across the aisle, catching Freya's eye and exchanging excited looks as the minutes ticked away towards the time when they would head for the Neon Fox to meet Bethany.

The small branch which Mackenzie Books had opened in Kirkbrigg was to focus on subjects in which the local technical college specialised; computers, engineering, mathematics, town planning and architecture. Freya's growing interest had led her to read up a lot in her spare time; her intention to apply for the part time post when it became available remained solid. Now, after a day catching up with her old and new colleagues, Bethany was about to meet Freya for the first time.

Nervousness tightened their shoulders and shortened their footsteps as Susannah and Freya walked into the town centre; the anxious hope that this would go well crackled unspoken between them. They reached the door of the diner with the welcoming glow of its sign, peering inside to make sure that Bethany was not already there; Susannah checked her phone again. There was a message from Bethany, sent a few minutes earlier saying that she was about to leave the bookshop and confirming what she would like to drink. As had been agreed, Freya went inside to get a table while Susannah waited at the door to spare Bethany having to walk into a venue on her own in a town she didn't know. Two minutes later, she walked along the street towards Susannah; a soft grey leather jacket falling elegantly to her hips contrasted neatly with a smart plum-coloured blouse and navy blue trousers, her dark blue hair gently lifted by the breeze. She smiled and waved as she caught sight of her friend; mindful of Freya waiting, they both hurried inside.

Orange light from the fox-shaped neon sign glinted on the fine metallic threads in Freya's pale peach top as she stood politely to greet Bethany. Susannah deftly managed the rush of emotion she felt upon seeing them smile and warmly shake hands by focusing on draping her cream jacket neatly over the back of a seat, making sure that it was clear of the floor before sitting down. Pulling her chair in, she flinched as her fingers caught between the side and the table leg; inwardly cursing that one pitfall too many which always seemed to catch her out whenever she thought she had concentrated enough. She looked at her friends as she impulsively rearranged her hair over the shoulder straps of her dark chocolate-brown satin top; this type of self-soothing movement helped to divert attention, both her own and that she perceived from others, away from glitches. Teresa Valenti's words about support networks came back to her as a lengthening sun puddle of awareness spread through her soul; these two people would get it. They wouldn't dismiss her frustration over her nipped fingers; apart from anything else, it hurt! But they would never be less drawn to her, look down on her or spout blaming and infantilising clichés; they would only laugh if *she* was laughing. They would never say 'Careful!', as they had a bone-deep understanding of how hard she tried in that regard. There was nothing but solidarity here.

The manager brought over the drinks which Freya had ordered.

"Thanks, Arlene"; Susannah acknowledged her. "This is Bethany; a friend of mine from Perth. She's through meeting some colleagues and she hadn't met Freya before, so we're making the most of her being here."

"Hi, Bethany; so is this your first visit to Kirkbrigg?"

"It is. I work in Mackenzie Books in Perth and they've opened a branch here; I came through to see my first boss, who's back in the area helping them set up."

"Yes; I've seen the new bookshop. It's always good to see new shops on the High Street. It will be useful for the students at the college. Well, good luck and enjoy your evening; give me a shout if you want anything else."

"So how's it going at the shop then, Bethany?", Freya asked.

"Really well, thank you. Shona is lovely; she's going to be a dream to work for, and Martyn and Karolina are both genuinely enthusiastic and fun to be around. Anita hasn't changed a bit; I don't know whether Susannah told you, that's my former boss. She's efficient and professional first and foremost, but in a benevolent way." She took a gulp of her coffee. "Ooh, that's good; I am so ready for this after unpacking stock all day. I was catching Anita up on feedback about our sensory reading room in Perth too; she's keen to roll the idea out to more branches."

"Bethany, that's wonderful!"

"Yes; congratulations!", Freya put in. "I've heard about how you and Diane were the driving force behind that idea. Have you had a chance to message Diane about it? Feel free to take a minute or two now if you haven't."

Freya glanced at Susannah, who had never felt quite so fiercely proud of her, for her agreement. She nodded.

"I did, at lunch time, but thank you so much for thinking of her. She's as excited as we all are; Anita is keen for her to get her share of the credit although she doesn't work for the company. Diane volunteers with a firm that helps the proportion of disabled people who would get something out of employment to find and sustain it."

"It's reassuring to know that organisations like that exist", mused Freya. "After all, any of us could have a change in health or find out that there's a reason behind a lifelong struggle."

"Indeed."

All three women sat quietly with their own thoughts for a minute, companionably sipping their coffee.

"How is your conveyancing coming along, Suze?", asked Bethany.

"Almost there; the property searches are done and there are no issues with contaminated land, outstanding claims or anything like that. Adil is waiting for more information on how much of a stake the council has in the building; we believe it's not the majority owner any more as more of the flats have been bought than are local authority owned, but he needs to get it confirmed so that I know how much of a say I would have in when communal repairs are done and by whom. The documents are already with the seller's solicitor for approval and signing; I do have a proposed entry date but I'm keeping that to myself until I know that all legal documents are complete."

"It's so exciting for you! Freya, I'm sure you'll be looking forward to coming through to Perth to visit."

"I am; I'm going to enjoy seeing some of these places I've heard about. Some of the walks by the river and on the Inches look so beautiful too. Susannah's told me about the pure quality of the light in Perth; that you call it 'Perthshine'. I must pay more attention to that when I come through; I have been to Perth before but I'm discovering it with new eyes through Suze."

Bethany's phone pinged.

"Oops; I meant to put that on silent once I'd seen that you were here and knew I was on my way. I got distracted by a question as I was sending my last message." She glanced at the screen as she switched the device to silent mode. "It's Lucy, my niece. Well, technically my cousin once removed; her mum is Sharon's sister. I'll catch up with that later; she's out with Zenna, her friend from university." She held out her phone so that Susannah and Freya could see the photo attached to the message; two young women with long fair hair taking a typical giggly selfie. "That's Lucy on the left, with the silvery lilac hair." The set of Lucy's shoulders indicated that she was taking the photo; Zenna, whose naturally platinum blonde hair was the straighter of the two, leaned in cosily with her head nestled against Lucy's.

"Aww, they're both gorgeous!", smiled Susannah.

"Ooh, now, Lucy's hair; *that's* the colour I would love to try!", enthused Freya. "That is a beautiful photo. Is that an Italian restaurant they're in?" A flag was visible on the wall behind Zenna's inclined head.

"Yes; that will be Carlito's, in Edinburgh. They often go there; I'm hoping I haven't forgotten a special occasion. It's nobody's birthday that I know of and Anti-Pepperoni Day is in October." Bethany laughed at herself as she registered the others' puzzled expressions. "Sorry; that's their friendship anniversary."

"Are they vegetarians then?"

"No; it's an in joke they have. It all came about from some banter they both got into, involving pizza toppings, with a couple of the security guards at university."

"They sound as though they're fun to be around, and I love the idea of a friendship anniversary! More people should celebrate those. Though to be fair, it's not always as easy to pin down exactly when a friendship started if it grew gradually from acquaintance. When would you say ours should be, Frey?"

"Well, you started working at our place in September so that was when we met, and we got on well from then, but I remember the Christmas lights switch-on event as the point at which we became friends, more than amiable colleagues.

So, the last Thursday in November that year; I think it was the 24th. Oh to go back to the times when Christmas didn't start the minute the schools went back after the summer holidays!"

Susannah took up the story. "Yes! We had this supervisor working with us at that time who was a nightmare; textbook misogynistic bully. The company social club rep had organised a gathering for the switch-on and a meal afterwards; we've both always loved the Christmas lights so we were looking forward to it for once, despite work socials not generally being a positive thing for us. I don't think either of us actually expected Rafe to be there. So anyway, there we were joining in with the countdown. The guitarist from Neptune's Hogmanay was the special guest switching on the lights and the atmosphere was truly festive. Freya was in the moment; arms up towards the lights, head thrown back, cheering."

Susannah looked at Freya, seeking her consent to continue describing her in such an unguarded personal response. "It's OK", her friend softly affirmed.

"I could see Rafe looking at her, laughing. He made some sarcastic comment about her enjoying herself, like that was some anomaly which shouldn't be happening. Then he started to move towards her, and I couldn't let him take that rare interlude of joy amongst her colleagues away from her. I knew that whatever he was going to say, it would ruin her evening."

Susannah's eyes met Bethany's; her Perth friend gave a barely perceptible nod of comprehension that there were elements of Rafe's behaviour that day which Susannah never did and never would tell Freya. She shuddered as she recalled the crude, sexually demeaning comment he had made about the uninhibited pleasure on Freya's face, compounding it by suggesting that someone who struggled to make eye contact had no business accessing any such physical thrills for real.

"So I pretended to trip and knocked his mulled wine all down his coat. I don't subscribe to the 'dyspraxia, or any other neurodivergence, as a superpower' narrative. I won't stand in the way of anyone who does; I understand that some people find it helpful and uplifting, but to me it reinforces the idea that you have to excel at something to be worthwhile. It undermines the case for us needing support and adjustments as well as dismissing our reality; it *is* a disability and causes us problems in day to day life irrespective of how inclusive people, organisations or environments are. I'm all about debunking the stereotypical view of dyspraxia as being a slapstick comedy of physical pratfalls. But that day, I admit I used it as a diversion. He forgot about heckling Freya, and much as she was mortified at the bollocking I got for being 'clumsy', it was actually a refreshing change knowing that for once it was entirely false. I knew what I was doing; I was in control. And as a bonus, I completely ruined that bullying bastard's coat."

"Now, *that*'s a friendship anniversary to celebrate!", cheered Bethany.

"It is! Suze, we totally should celebrate that. Bethany, I had no idea at first that she'd done it deliberately. I heard the commotion as I was coming back to earth from the instant of the switch-on and I was all set to call him out on his ableist bullsh…"; Freya glanced at a couple at a nearby table who had cast a look in her direction as the volume of her animated voice increased; "…shadow." She whispered conspiratorially, leaning in. "Those two know my mum, and she massively disapproves of me swearing. Where was I?"

"Ableist bullshadow"; Susannah grinned fondly, reaching across the table to squeeze Freya's arm.

"That's right. Anyway, I was all set to kick off and Suze hustled me out of there, because she knew I'd go too far. I will take no end of abuse against myself, but anyone starting on someone else, especially targeting a disability, the gloves come off. I was relieved when she explained that she did it on purpose to stop Rafe from intruding on me, because I knew how bad and upset she'd be feeling if it had been a glitch. We both started laughing and we never stopped for the rest of the evening."

"If Lucy and Zenna would be OK with us copying their style, then I hereby declare November 24th, Mulled Swine Day!"; Susannah raised her coffee cup to whoops of delighted agreement from Freya and Bethany.

"I'm sure they'll love this. Are you both OK with me telling them the bare bones of the story?"

"Definitely. I'm sure we'd both love to know the story behind Anti-Pepperoni Day and exactly when it is so that we can drink to them. Speaking of which, shall we have another coffee? I'd love some of Arlene's sweet potato pie. How are you fixed for time for getting home, Bethany?"

"I'm good; the buses are every hour until after nine. If I can get the one that leaves at quarter past seven, that will be ideal. Magnus knew I'd have a full-on day today so he arranged for Ash to cover my hours tomorrow morning; Crevan and Dana are back from holiday now too. I like the idea of sweet potato pie! I've never had that before."

The order was agreed upon; Susannah took their empty cups to the counter. As she turned around and looked at their table, Freya and Bethany were in animated conversation; she gathered from their gestures that they were discussing hair products. A pang of insecurity shocked Susannah to her core as she found herself momentarily afraid that they would get on so well they would leave her behind. Was this a taste of what Freya had been feeling all this time? *Park it; deal with it later. Use it as a positive; a chance to better empathise with her.* She resolutely turned her thoughts to relief that she need no longer feel so worried for Freya.

Arlene gratefully whisked away the empty mugs; she was on her own and the diner was getting busy as the evening went on. Susannah ordered the same again in decaf and three slices of sweet potato pie, paid and turned to go back to her seat.

"...so thankful that you were with her when she got the news about the counter-offer and it being accepted. She's had to deal with so many big developments on her own."

Freya's words stopped her in her tracks as a wave of poignant gratitude hit her. Selina had been right about turning Bethany's visit into an opportunity to involve Freya. Needing a minute, Susannah went to get paper napkins from the dispenser. She looked up at the large canvas print on the wall behind the till. It depicted Rannoch Moor under the sort of luminous sky she would relish viewing at her forever home; the moon rising through an opalescent dusk. The gift of agency had brought joy to the daunting dynamic shift of this pivotal time. Smiling at the apt scene; Perthshire shown at its best, she silently gave thanks.

Back in her flat, a mug of soup was sustenance enough after the sweet potato pie. Bethany messaged to let her know she had arrived home safely; she relayed the information to Freya. Making the further note on her wall calendar, joining the new addition of Mulled Swine Day, that Anti-Pepperoni Day was October 18th could wait; there was no need to dislodge two purring cats from her lap. She emailed herself a quick reminder, knowing that the amount of things she needed to remember was going to vastly increase over the next few weeks. She noticed the thought; her compulsive desire to keep on top of everything, yet the tension which usually accompanied such awareness could not touch her fuzzily optimistic mood tonight.

28

Completion

Early April evenings still collapsed into dusk all too soon after their unaccustomed flex of later light. Susannah sighed as she finished taping the base of her first moving box into place, turning it upright next to the waiting pile of DVDs. Her entire 'The X-Files' collection made a good definitive starting point for the daunting task ahead.

Fox Mulder and Dana Scully's gravely pensive faces reflected up from over a quarter of a century ago between the cardboard walls which would confine them for the next few weeks. Susannah stood and stretched; her muscles ached from the unaccustomed pattern of repetitive actions.

"It will all be worth it"; she reinforced her morale by telling their unseeing images. Spare tea towels and cleaning cloths filled the inevitable leftover spaces; one of her favourite scarves laid reverently over the top made sure every bit of room in the box was used. A place mat face down in the middle protected that in turn from any sliver of tape which might push down through a gap she couldn't quite close. "See you on the other side", she told Mulder and Scully as she folded down and sealed the top of the box before labelling it and pushing it to the corner which would all too soon be full. She must remember to measure the space in that area for comparison with her new lounge before it became too cluttered. It would be so easy to focus on the dimensions of the unfamiliar new space and forget to measure her existing surroundings and items for context.

Picking up a half full cup of tepid tea which she had made to help brace her for the task ahead and kidded herself she could get the first box done before it cooled, she sipped the now uninspiring liquid with one tired eye fixed on the sole completed box. She cursed as a stray rivulet of tea trickled down the side of her chin; a thinly accusing, tangible footprint of her distraction.

She had been so caught up in the uncharted territory of house hunting as a buyer, the awareness that she now had to actually move home on top of that had taken a lower priority. Once the surveys had proven satisfactory and the uncertainty of the buying process was a sliver of light through a keyhole away from ending, the physical reality of moving had abruptly loomed large. That lone box in the corner signalled the end of familiarity; the beginning of a long, heightened challenge to her spatial awareness and coordination. Already depleted by the buying process, her dyspraxic brain was about to be called to navigate a period of time when the sanctuary of her current home would be incrementally lost to a desolate moonscape of the unfamiliar. This would become about much more than bumping the unforgiving corners of stacks of boxes. The walls would harden and echo; the air itself change as more and more of her belongings were packed away and dust arose from multiple rarely-disturbed spaces. The harsh, almost never used ceiling lights would need to replace her softly glowing lamps as her living space became more obstructed and her sensory settings were packed away. For all its faults and all she was excited to leave behind as she entered the next stage of her life, at this point it was her home, and it was going to lose that crucial anchoring quality well before she left it. Her muscle memory, despite its enhanced role in keeping her grounded and safe, would inevitably betray her. In her new home too, that would take time to resolve as the new pathways formed; neural and physical in tandem, both hacked out jagged and raw through the unknown.

"But that's the same for everybody moving house!"; Susannah could already hear the tired refrain. Up to a point, it was true. She wasn't about to dismiss anyone relating to it, whatever their neurotype. Let them try telling her, though, that she wasn't experiencing an amplified version of it? Moving house was already accepted as being one of the most stressful life events. Listening to, and taking seriously, the perspective of those tackling it from marginalised roots should not be so big an ask.

It was hardly eight o'clock and she needed to put the light on already. Welcome to British Summer Time, Kirkbrigg style. Susannah finished her now cold tea with a shudder infused with awareness of the many sensory compromises ahead. Pushing herself upright from the chair, she focused on the dull view of the external wall so close to the window and forced herself to invoke the double aspect setting which would light the rest of her days once she got herself across that chasm.

Yes; that was the way to look at it. Put aside the magnitude of differences; one home and another, mutually alien ways of experiencing the process. Redirect her energy from the vast sprawl of the two sides to the immediate and specific aim of the crossing point. Get herself a few steps across a bridge. That made it feel more accessible, as she wryly remembered that those most in need of that bridge and depleted accordingly were always the ones who had to put in most of the work to build it in the first place.

Early rose-gold sunlight burst through gaps in lingering altocumulus clouds to fall across the blank sleeping screen of Susannah's phone in the seconds before it illuminated with a new email notification. Three weeks earlier, Adil's genuine delight had shone through the propriety of his professional tone as he conveyed the news that missives were completed; the lingering uncertainty was behind her. With the date of entry confirmed, it had been her cue to begin packing. Now, the flat at Fair Maid's Mews was officially Susannah's property and the keys were ready for her to collect from the estate agents. Opening the attachments with trembling fingers, her bleary eyes struggled to accept the joyous reality as the documents bloomed in miniature on the oblong screen which had framed many snapshots of life but never one so momentous as this.

"Disposition by Alan McLean in favour of Susannah Rose Silverdale"; and there it was. She now owned property; not merely a living space but the complex structure with its own kind of physiology which had never before been her responsibility and about which she knew so little. Her internalised ableism would have to adjust; it had all become dauntingly real. Her parents; her siblings; anyone with ongoing experience of owning property which predated her own would have to be allowed to help and guide her, however much it clashed with her perceived need to prove herself worthy of autonomy in a world which would count it against her. The welfare of her home and her ability to fulfil her responsibility to her neighbours had to come first.

She would have to set aside a bit of pride and, for example, take Julian up on his offer to look around the place with her to catch snagging issues which she might miss. It had to be worth it for any scrap of added defence it gave her against every normal house noise, new to her, scaring the daylights out of her.

Another piece of older sibling advice popped back into her memory. "Don't be embarrassed to ask if you're struggling to figure out things like how to use the appliances included in the sale", London had counselled her. "Write things down step by step; take photos; watch videos; whatever it takes. Even if they're not brand new and hi-tech, trust me, you won't have the bandwidth you normally do to take in new things." She had quietly scoffed to her cats at the time, rolling her eyes at the unasked-for advice and confident that she shouldn't need any manual to get to grips with the symbols on a washing machine or a cooker. Then Tan and Lee had upgraded their tumble dryer to a sleek new model with a touchscreen panel they fondly nicknamed 'Mission Control', which was nothing like any laundry related device Susannah had ever seen in her life.

Yes; she was going to need her siblings' input. Her capacity for humility was going to be tested to the max.

Most of all, she was going to need her immediate circle of friends and the psychological scaffolding they put up whenever she needed it, quietly dismantling it when she was ready to stand restored. Celebrating with her when the work had been done to let her and her home meet the next sunrise in an urban fairyland of split-second twinkles as the passing of time across their reinforced walls became a parade instead of an attack.

She could do this, but not on her own, and that was going to have to be OK.

The light which had greeted the new day in a concentrated blush across her phone screen yawned its pale concession to the busy morning along the aisle of the bus to Perth. Susannah looked around at her fellow passengers as her thumb rubbed over and over the ridged Celtic knot on the keyring Freya had bought her on a shopping trip she and Frieda impulsively took to Inverness when they had both been free and the weather much like today. The mundane just-another-day theme rested nonchalantly in a slump of shoulders here; a hand resting on a battered work bag there; eyes closed in mellow expectation of becoming alert in time for the stop which marked out a subjective routine. Shadows trundled past the windows, throwing an ever-shifting bar code across the dusty floor.

Chrome handles on room-height glass doors with an expansive round table in light wood visible on the other side set the scene for the anticipated handover as the receptionist ushered Susannah into the side room. Suleiman was out at a viewing; she hoped that whoever he was showing around whichever property, the outcome would be similar to hers.

"He said to give you his best wishes; he's delighted for you"; Pablo, the trainee agent who had been tasked with handing over the keys, assured her as he bustled into the room. Susannah admired the casual deftness with which he manoeuvred two cups of fresh coffee and the all-important manila envelope through the fairly heavy door. *How did people do that?*

"Thank you"; Susannah opened the envelope and slid out the keys. She already had a photo of her keyring ready to post on her social media; no image of the actual keys would ever be shared, even to her exclusive close friends list because the Internet was the Internet and keys could be cloned from photographs.

"How are you feeling? Big day, eh?"

She smiled, sensing an authentic goodwill behind Pablo's professional veneer. She would never have this day again. It had to be worth letting herself enjoy these interactions; putting aside the apprehension around being seen as a 'spinster of a certain age getting her unworldly head turned by sales patter'. It had been lurking in the back of her mind since she posted her glowing review. She knew perfectly well that what had felt like validation was no more than a skilled diplomatic response to her spoken and unspoken cues; that it said nothing, either positive or negative, about what anyone thought of her. She'd had a good experience and wanted her review to reflect that; it had only occurred to her afterwards to worry about how it might appear. Bethany had reassured her that most people reading reviews were focused on the company, not speculating about the reviewer and their perspective; she had been comforted by that to a certain extent. Surely it wasn't so foolish to privately hold these memories dear; to go forward with only warm thoughts of the people involved? That inner smile they would always spark in Susannah's soul was nobody's business but her own.

"Yes, Pablo; it certainly is a big day. I'm happy; I'm excited, and I want to take in every nuance of today so that I'll remember it as fully as the magnitude of it deserves."

Pablo nodded, understanding clearly written on his face. He must have been in this room with new homeowners before. Susannah ran her fingertips over the cold metal of the keys and the plastic fob which gave her access through the main entrance, still taking in the full weight of the implications.

"What are your plans for the day then?"

"I haven't thought that far ahead! I'll be heading round there and reading the meter; I need to confirm to the provider that I've taken over the electricity account. I've got insurance in place from today; I had to start a completely new policy for that as there will be an overlap for a few weeks while I get ready to move. I took out building insurance as well as contents, so that is different from my current contents policy in my rented flat anyway."

"That's very well organised!"; Pablo appeared genuinely impressed. "If there's a factor involved, which I think they may be in the process of arranging, you'll need to check whether building insurance will be included in what you pay them; you don't want to be paying twice."

"Good point. It would be helpful if they arranged that; I will definitely check."

Property managers, also known as factors, were becoming increasingly used in buildings with multiple owner occupiers in Scotland as the law moved towards making formalised arrangements compulsory to address the risk of buildings falling into disrepair when responsibility was not clearly assigned. It was another area of new territory with which Susannah was going to have to familiarise herself. Another wave of panic shot ice through her veins, contrasting with the growing heat of the sun. She hid her involuntary shiver as best she could as she finished her coffee, shook Pablo's hand warmly and clutching her keys and paperwork, walked out into the brightening day.

The building's communal foyer looked the same yet different as she held her fob to the sensor and walked through the main door. She found herself examining every tile for cracks and flaws for which she may be partly responsible. As she ascended to the third floor, she listened out for any hint of abnormality in the whirring and clunking of the lift mechanism.

The door slid open, reassuringly smoothly, on the third floor. Straight ahead of her was her own front door. Reminding herself to internally document every stage of today, she crossed the neutrally painted landing and let herself into her new home.

Stripped of the previous owners' belongings and furniture, the flat looked and felt more different from viewing day than she had been prepared for. Its silence and emptiness were almost eerie; the décor was enough to give a sense of holding the McLeans' personalities and its identity as their home, without the welcome extended to an invited guest. The effect was unexpectedly sobering; Susannah fought back a wave of uncertainty, wondering what she had let herself in for and whether the flat actually wanted and would accept her. There was nothing hypothetical about any aspect of today; this was no longer a dream from which she could extricate herself if it stopped feeling right. She was solely responsible for this place now, and it was a long way from feeling like home.

She walked through the empty rooms with the heightened alertness of an urban explorer, half expecting to be challenged. Finding and reading the meter made a useful focus; she opened the app and submitted the reading. The mobile data icon on her screen in place of wifi reminded her that this was a betwixt and between time; that she had a long way to go to make it home.

Surprising herself by not wanting to stay any longer, she took one more look around before leaving; locking up with meticulous precision, registering the traitorous tug of homesickness for her rented flat in Kirkbrigg and the stab of anxiety as she remembered that with her packing now well underway, that was no longer the same familiar base. At this point, she didn't have that anywhere.

This malaise, this displacement wouldn't last. It wouldn't be forever. Taking a moment to stand with and acknowledge the hollowness in her chest which replaced the tingle she thought she should be feeling, she told herself that it was natural and understandable. This was all part of that bridge she had to cross. Her feelings would settle; the familiarity would return. It had to.

"Hi; are you my new neighbour?"

It felt too soon; her emotions too abraded to get the mask back into place sufficiently for that all-important first impression. Her mind was too busy. It was comparable to yanking open the washing machine door in the middle of a spin cycle, without the essential buffer of waiting for that reassuring *whump whump whump* as each textile dropped back into its individual form, fresh and clean and ready to meet the open air. She faked a discreet cough into her elbow, buying herself time to prepare her unexpectedly misty eyes for social contact.

"Yes; as of this morning, I am! Though I won't be moving in properly for a few weeks. I'm Susannah. Pleased to meet you."

"Welcome! I'm Ailsa." Susannah took in her friendly smile as they shook hands. The woman looked to be in her early forties; wavy ginger hair tied back from her face and a comfortable denim shirt thrown on over a crisp white blouse suggested that she worked from home. "I know you'll have a lot to take in and think about today, but I'll give you my card; please let me know if there's anything I can do. Taking deliveries, that sort of thing. I've been here a couple of years but I remember well how stressful it was moving. We have a chat group for the building; I can add you to that any time. We only use it for practical stuff, don't worry; you won't get inundated with notifications!"

"Ah; you must have read my mind! It's a useful facility to have, a group chat for building matters, but I'm not one for group chat for its own sake. I'll do a basic introduction on it though. Thank you, Ailsa; I'm looking forward to living here."

As her new neighbour nodded understandingly and wished her luck before tactfully retreating into her own flat, Susannah's insides began to relax a little. In addition to putting her mind somewhat to rest, Ailsa's easy imparting of her own experience as an established resident made Susannah realise something else. She had unknowingly been processing the impending loss of her regular contact with Adil and the other professionals who had been involved, however fleetingly, in her house hunt. Although Adil remained in the background as her solicitor, she no longer had the same ongoing 'current client' access to a whole network which had been only an email away for many months; no longer the same claim on their time. The extent of the pangs she felt at the truth of this deeply personal saga in her own life being another day at the office to them mortified her. She blinked away incongruous tears as she pressed the button to call the lift.

Calmed by the ambient mechanical hum, she made herself reframe this transition as excitement for her completed purchase and thankfulness that Adil, Jean and Suleiman, Sinéad, Kasia, Honor and everyone else who had been part of this chapter were all now helping the next people who needed them. She had given so much energy to fulfilling her side of the transaction; all of her tenacity, proactivity and due diligence. This final task of seamlessly moving on from them had snuck in through some unguarded side door with its unexpected magnitude.

You've bought a house; that's huge even without the emotional upheaval you've had along the way. It's OK to feel sad. If you need to grieve, you need to grieve. Edie's voice spoke softly in her mind, soothing the part of her which needed it now as it had when she was that intense little girl grappling with a world which did not naturally support her brain's operating system.

She smiled as the lift gently set down; back at ground level once again but still within this new framework of home.

29

Moving Day

A record-breaking May had reached through folds of blue and gold into every bare corner of Susannah's Kirkbrigg flat day after day as the boxes and the pervasive strangeness mounted. The dullest recesses shone dawn to dusk in their special-occasion best, as though shaken awake to mount a last minute campaign to compel her to stay.

The last night in one home and the first night in the next were characters in their own right in the story of any move, she reflected as her phone's alarm called her from a fitful sleep at 6am. She had chosen a song by REM; 'It Happened Today', from the playlist of London and Fran's which they had enjoyed as they wrapped Christmas gifts in Nairn on that far-off break in the opposite season with its compressed hours of ice-crystal sunlight. Widely interpreted to be a defiant swan song as the band prepared to retire, its celebratory swell of voices and melody swam through Susannah's muffled consciousness into a sunrise calling her to greet this long-awaited day and to fete its significance amid the subjective chaos.

The cats were already at Freya's. Susannah sat up, bleary-eyed in the dusty liminal quiet; placing her bare feet on the carpet, she rubbed her eyes until the boxes and bags along the wall came into focus. A permanent marker on top of one stack of boxes brought a smile as she remembered the messages of thanks and appreciation which she had written on a random selection of boxes for the movers to find, hoping to give a boost to their laborious task as they carried all of her belongings down to the ground floor. She silently gave thanks for the lift at Fair Maid's Mews before yet another wave of panic imagining it breaking down today overwhelmed her.

Catastrophising didn't add anything constructive; she shook her head, curtly dismissing the unhelpful thoughts. Rising from her bed for the last time in this room, she stripped the sheets, pillow case and mattress protector, bundling them into the laundry bag which she had ready at the foot of the bed, labelled with a stuck-on note and already holding some underwear and clothes from the past few days; she dumped it on the mattress, leaving it untied for adding her nightshirt, face cloth, towel and tea towel as the morning went on. Pulling on her favourite comfortable slippers which would soon be added to her "last in first out" box, she padded through to the bathroom; grateful for its emotional neutrality as she hurried through her final morning wash in it before making that landmark last cup of coffee in the kitchen with its far richer thread of sensory associations.

Dressing in calming neutral colours, teamed with a bit of sparkle on hand for later as she celebrated in Perth, gave her a sense of calm and control. A long, loose cream top teamed well with cappuccino-coloured trousers; the tiny sequins stitched into the matching cream cardigan winked their promise of festive homecoming as she wrapped it around her favourite mug and tucked it into that final box. Her phone charger was the next eleventh-hour item to pack; stowed safely in her tote bag as the device's battery reached its optimal charge. With the removal team due any minute and nothing left to unplug, she read the meter and submitted the reading through the app; the acknowledgement came through at the same time as the text confirming that the movers were five minutes away.

The door stops which she had kept aside were greatly appreciated by the team of three who emptied her home of almost three years in breathtakingly quick time, as was the balance and organisation of her packing. Susannah watched from a discreet distance as each room was returned to the shell she had first viewed. She hoped that the next tenants would see the potential she had and that they would respect both their new home and Connie, who had been a good and responsible, caring and unintrusive landlord. Blinking back entirely expected tears as she closed the door after the movers' final trip, Susannah replaced the door stops in her tote bag and took out the thank you card for Connie. She placed it on the bare kitchen worktop next to the instruction manuals for the appliances she was leaving, some takeaway discount leaflets and the most recent telephone directory. Drawing a deep breath, she messaged Julian to let him know that she was ready.

The moment had arrived to walk around each room for the final time, giving thanks and asking a blessing for the next people to call this space home. Susannah would speak freely about this element of every move she had gone through, though her exact words in those farewell minutes always remained private.

The main and spare keys fit easily through the letter box, linked together on their basic metal rings. She whispered her final thanks and goodbye as her hand lingered on the door handle. Grateful as she was for Tan and Lee respecting her wishes not to say goodbye as she left, she sensed them close by as she gave a watery smile across the landing towards their door. The return of her spare keys had been conducted several days ago amid goodbyes seasoned with assurances that the only ending involved was to their being next door neighbours. Susannah was in no doubt that their friendship would endure; this was the up side of social media. The lads had been so right, she mused as she silently blew two kisses towards their door, when they told her to drink in every high and significant emotion in the weeks and days leading up to the move; that she may well find herself surprisingly numb in those last twenty-four hours as her brain shielded her and prioritised the practical side.

"Your last day in Kirkbrigg won't be your last day in Kirkbrigg, Suze."

Lee's words came back to her with new meaning as she recalled that forced-casual visit to collect the keys, which was hailed as 'not necessarily the last before you move' while they all knew it was. More related memories rushed in. Her final departure from work; her coffee afterwards with a reserved, glittering-eyed Freya in the keenly familiar Neon Fox. Arlene's hands lightly resting on their shoulders for a moment after she delivered their decaf-version second round and two generous slices of cake.

Kirkbrigg was part of her; it was irrevocably coded into her psychological DNA. These memories would go with her to Perth, enhancing her future and strengthening her existing connections; shoring up the already fully formed person she presented to the Fair City.

With a final salute to the blankness of the door behind which she knew fine well her friends were listening out, Susannah clutched her bags against her body as she descended the stairs to her brother's waiting car.

"Selina's meeting us in Perth"; Julian hugged his sister as he deftly took the larger of her two bags from her grasp. The agreement was that the movers would take their lunch break to give Susannah time to arrive and be ready for them. Their sister's shift pattern had worked out well, giving her time to travel up and meet them at the station café for a welcome cup of tea before heading back to her Glasgow base.

After the last poignant waving at the off-season resting Lorna's light, the car journey passed in quiet understanding of a whirl of fatigue and emotional backlog. The outskirts of Perth rose ahead and opened in a stoic, industrial-clad embrace; Susannah came home through a brown and grey patchwork of accepting streets. Gates and walls framed glimpses of trees and hills that would carry a lifetime of seasonal colours to her senses.

The lift was working. That was certainly a good start. Ailsa, whom Susannah had messaged to let her know when she expected to arrive, was listening out for it and popped out briefly to bid her welcome and hand over a box of shortbread. Introducing Julian, Susannah explained that the movers would be there in around forty-five minutes before walking into her forever home in an all too brief whirl. There was no autopilot dumping point for her bags; no kettle to switch on; no homely slouch of a recycling bag into which the inevitable junk mail could be tidied away. Mentally filing away a reminder to be thankful for those taken-for-granted rounded edges of daily life, Susannah scooped up the mail and laid it on the kitchen worktop which resonated with the same yawning sparseness she had left that morning, before finding the most appropriate-looking corner in which to instruct Julian to leave her tote bag. Unpacking was easier than packing, she reassured herself with the voice of home moving experience as she took the interim few sheets of toilet roll from her tote bag and quickly visited her new bathroom. The bath and basin had the same dried-out look which the ones in her Kirkbrigg flat had at the beginning; a dry inverted sheen of disuse which would take a few lots of routine using and cleaning to buff the surfaces back to domesticity. She visualised the strange, lost feeling being sluiced away down the plughole along with the not yet heated water as she washed her hands, then switched the boiler to the timed mode which she had set up before locking up her hollow, echoing new home again while her brother pressed the button to call the lift.

Selina's train was delayed north of Gleneagles. There would be no time for the planned cup of tea before the train she needed to catch back to Glasgow. "She says to speak to her friend on the gateline; she'll let us through to the platform", Julian asserted as they walked through the station's main entrance. "It's the Inverness train Selina's on, so we can meet her and walk over the footbridges to the Glasgow platform; we'll only have about ten minutes."

"It's better than nothing", Susannah smiled wryly. "It wouldn't be a proper moving day if something didn't go wrong, and this doesn't affect the logistics."

The staff member on the gateline waved them through with an easy understanding smile, warmly congratulating Susannah on her move. The layout of the routes through the station meant that Susannah and Julian would get quite the tour by meeting Selina off an Inverness train and seeing her off on one which had come from Aberdeen.

"This place is the architectural equivalent of Kate Bush's singing voice", mused an awestruck Susannah as she took in the sweeping space from the glitter-flecked cradle of the non-slip walkways to the darkly fluttering Gothic mystery of the rafters. As she followed her brother across the wide footbridge to the Inverness-bound service's usual platform, fragments of every journey through the enduring held time of this place seemed to glint from where they had been caught for eternity in interdimensional folds. They reached her consciousness in the same flashes of old light and preserved breath of a past era which had spoken to her from the hollow of the Christmas ornament nestled safely in its strong box in her tote bag; too precious to trust to the stacks of a bulk removal.

The Inverness train stirred the expectant air, its belated rush a whispered apology under the high roof. Selina Silverdale's meticulously straightened brown hair swished around her shoulders as she alighted, pausing to give a hand down with luggage to the low platform before homing in on her siblings and wrapping Susannah in a long, tight hug.

"Susannah Rose."

"Selina Faith."

Julian smiled indulgently at their ritual, inspired by the central sister characters in the short-lived reboot of 'Gossip

Girl'. Susannah knew he was inclined to agree with Isobel that the diversity in the reboot had been welcome and it stood strongly as a show on its own, but that there was something compelling about the original.

"I totally get that!"; Selina was responding to Susannah's comparing of the station's preserved blown-glass eminence to the soaring register of Kate Bush's vocals. The same voice that tenderly and intimately implored 'Don't Give Up' to Peter Gabriel, sparking tiny glints of hope under weary feet to catch downcast eyes, invoked the grandiose wildness of elements against besieged outposts in 'Wuthering Heights'. "You're right, this place has that type of atmospheric range. There's also a fair amount of 'Running Up That Hill' involved whenever you have a tight connection to catch here!"

It was the sort of conversation which came about from the brash surrealism of moving day. Susannah clutched her sister's arm as they scurried across the network of bridges beneath that overarching roof and down the steps onto the Glasgow platform, where Julian pulled out his phone and took a group selfie. It was hurriedly posed and snapped for London's benefit, but Susannah would cherish its breathless candidness as one of her most vividly authentic souvenirs of the day.

The movers arrived on schedule, transforming Susannah's property over the course of the next few hours from an empty shell devoid of her identity to a cluttered portal not yet like home. *It will come.* She quickly located her Last In, First Out box and the clear textile storage bag in which she had packed her bed linen; she made up her bed, unpacked her essentials, pulled on her sparkly cardigan and went to The Sandeman for dinner and a large glass of wine. While she waited for her order, she messaged Freya, Bethany, her siblings, Tan and Lee, then updated her social media to reflect that she now lived in Perth.

She had made it home. Day by day, the rest would all get done. She thought back to her last move, wondering which if any household item would mysteriously not be there after the last box was unpacked and would never be seen again. It had been the most efficient tin opener she had ever owned which somehow maddeningly never made it to Kirkbrigg despite her meticulous organising. It had taken weeks for her to let it go and accept that she wasn't going to find it; not because of any sentimental attachment, rather her brain rebelling against the confounding not knowing how and why. Isobel had hypothesised that the universe had an arcane 'house moving toll' which claimed its due from every move. Susannah had been mildly taken aback at this coming from her pragmatic sister-in-law; she had put it down to kindness, going so far out of her lane for the sake of giving the more spiritually inclined Susannah an answer to which she could more comfortably relate. Conversations since then with other people who had moved house led her to wonder whether Izzy could have unknowingly been on to something.

Morven had reminisced about a couple of moves of her own too. She had counselled Susannah to take a bit of pressure off herself by keeping in mind that once the more fixed items were in place, fitting in the smaller, easily portable things could be as fluid as it needed to be. Indeed, she should expect to change her mind more than once about where things would go. It was a big and draining enough task, albeit enjoyable, without giving herself unnecessary stress by being too rigid.

She had pushed herself so hard to get to this point; that home run of the unpacking task looming ahead of her felt almost insurmountable. In the midweek standby-mode hush of the usually busy pub, Susannah's shoulders sagged momentarily with overwhelm.

No, she told herself firmly; this was all for another day. Moving day was big enough in itself.

For now, all that mattered was that she was here.

The friendly barman's enquiry as to whether she wanted to order another wine tempted her briefly; exhaustion, both physical and emotional, won out as she declined and took her leave. Walking home through the streets which were now her everyday setting, she took in the liquid evening light as it gilded the tops of the surrounding buildings. She was fully invested here now. She paid her council tax here. In the coming days she would be registering with a doctor here. Soon after that, her leave from work would end and a new routine come into being.

She leaned against the wall of the lift as it carried her up to her landing. Fatigue made her hands even less dexterous as she tried to fit her key in the lock and turn it quietly; a locksmith was due in the morning to change the lock anyway so that she would know for certain that only she and anyone to whom she chose to give a key would ever be able to access the property, but tonight she needed to get in without further ado and get some sleep.

Double-checking that the door was locked behind her, she gave thanks for having made up her bed before going out for her meal. The first night should surely have had more of an element of ceremony but in the reality of it, she didn't care. She filled her hastily unpacked mug with water, drank it, refilled it halfway to keep beside her bed and then remembered she didn't yet have a surface near enough to the bed clear to put it on. For some reason, this struck her as hilarious as she poured the water down the sink, setting the mug by the kettle ready for the morning.

She got changed; dug her toothbrush and toothpaste out of her travel toiletries bag; brushed her teeth in the clinical strangeness of her new bathroom. Looking at her reflection in the mirror; tired, the same yet different, she said goodnight to her new Perth self. She switched off the light; remembered she was in an unaccustomed place, for all it was now her home. Slowly, she felt her way through the dim finale of the momentous day to the reassuring embrace of her bed in its new setting.

Every detail of this first night should be noticed; should be absorbed and committed to memory for posterity.

Susannah's head sank into the pillow, its clean case plumped in new night air.

The next thing she knew was the fresh territory of her first morning. Surrounded by boxes, her phone spangled with notifications; a mix of personal and practical.

And so her Perth life began.

30

Summer Solstice

6pm

"White. The cool tone, like moonlight."

Diane Abercrombie smiled, giving Susannah a jocular 'sorry not sorry' side-eye upon being clocked looking at the streetlamp at the end of Fair Maid's Mews, wondering what colour it would shine. "My favourite! It always reminds me of Caberfeidh Road, near where I live in Inverbrudock. The lights along there are sodium orange now, but they used to be brilliant white"; her expression softened as Susannah sensed that she was recalling the past on a scale similar to her own recent experiences; "a long time ago."

Bethany beamed at her two friends with pure affection. "I've been looking forward to this!" She held up her bag to remind Susannah of the drams which she and Diane had decanted into 10cl bottles to share as they celebrated the longest day. Fierce early evening sun swept like a breath held for too long across the pavement which shone with the remnants of the afternoon's heavy showers as they headed into the building where Susannah now lived.

A drink at The Old Ship Inn had started off the celebrations after Susannah and Bethany met Diane off the train. The historic pub had seen waves of footfall in and out as the showers passed over and locals poured in to support the business in its fundraising efforts. The heart of Perth beats strongest for those in need.

The plaque at the door proclaimed the inn as having been especially popular with the workers who brought the railway to the Fair City. As the trio made their way up in the lift, Susannah found herself processing the similarity between Bethany's air of old recognition as she read it out and Diane's reminiscing about the lights along Caberfeidh Road. It was something more than Bethany's local knowledge; something beyond the years she had lived in Perth. There were many fascinating conversations ahead of her in these growing friendships.

9pm

Susannah cleared away their plates, flattening the pizza boxes to take down to the bin store in the morning. Bethany was playing with Morgan, who loved chasing her favourite laser pointer; glancing up at the clock, she switched it off in deference to Susannah's policy of not encouraging the cats to run about too late into the evening for the sake of the neighbours below. Annika was curled in a marbled ball of softness beside Diane, who stroked her tenderly.

"I must admit, much as I enjoy our pub meet-ups, there's something enduring about a relaxing night in with a takeaway", she mused. "Nobody leaning over you asking if everything's OK! I mean, I get why they do it, and I'm sure it's as awkward for the staff as for the people eating when it's always right after they take a mouthful."

Diane nodded. "I keep hoping that what we have at 'Harriet's Haven' will catch on one day"; she referred to the café which her best friends ran in Inverbrudock. "We have signs at the tables which customers can use if they wish; one side has 'No questions please; it's all good' and the other side has 'Please stop by this table'. Hotels have 'Do Not Disturb' signs which people have the choice to use or not, and nobody thinks that's unreasonable or churlish. Des and Jason get so much positive feedback about them. It saves the staff discomfort as well as time; nobody likes having to approach customers who are not only eating but clearly having a private conversation, and the signs cover them for that duty of care."

"It's so logical; why on Earth doesn't everywhere that serves food have that system?", enthused Susannah, mentally moving Inverbrudock further up her list of places to visit once she was fully settled into a new routine. "It's time for a dram, I reckon. Shall we have the Tullymearns first? The Tomnasheen cigar malt seems more appropriate for later on as a nightcap".

She went through to what was now designated the cats' room, where the old dressing table which Connie had given her blessing to Susannah to take stood against the far wall. She had placed the small bottles which Bethany and Diane had brought, meticulously labelled, in one of the deeper drawers at the side. It was to prevent the cats from knocking them off the kitchen worktop, she had said; fooling nobody including herself.

"Slàinte, Mary Meredith"; she smiled as she took the bottles out, setting them down in front of the mirror as she touched the closed middle drawer in which a record of a long-gone childhood lay, peaceful now in its hallowed space next to her tartan notebook and her jewellery box. Still deliberately slower in her movements especially with breakable things as her muscle memory recalibrated itself to her new home, Susannah took the bottles to her kitchen, opened the one labelled 'Tullymearns' and divided the contents as evenly as she could among three glasses.

The eighteen-year-old malt rose across the palate like a door opening into a rarely disturbed attic; its infused prickle of spiciness ephemeral as the dust motes hanging in the bare slant of a sunbeam.

"That's worth the wait! I must make a note of these for Freya and Frieda; they're acquiring a taste for single malts."

"How is Freya?" Bethany's voice held genuine concern.

"She's doing well, thanks. The job in your Kirkbrigg branch is suiting her; she gets on with all of them and seems particularly close to Karolina." Susannah smiled as she scrolled through her social media to find a recent post in which Freya tagged Karolina and Arlene at the Neon Fox.

"Yes; Anita said how happy she is with the team in Kirkbrigg. Speaking of my work, the branch here opens on a Sunday and Magnus loves your Grounds for Gratitude idea so much he wants us to incorporate it into our chilled Sunday ethos for whoever's turn it is to do that shift. He knows it's your and Freya's thing, though, and that there's a boundary to be protected there, so he suggests we simply call it 'Coffee and Thankfulness'. Does that sound fair to you? If you want to check in with Freya about it, that's absolutely fine."

"I think it's wonderful that other people want to take it up! We can't expect to keep something like that exclusive; it's such a positive thing and loads of people are likely already doing their version of it. I do appreciate you asking, though, and I'll keep Freya in the loop too."

Susannah put her phone aside, a cloud of apprehension darkening her relaxed glow.

"I'm going to meet a lot of new people; I'm not talking about making friends specifically. New acquaintances come with a move to a different place. I'm possibly going to see people who've been involved in my search for a house, after a while and out of the confines of that context in which I know them. I know this isn't exclusive to neurodivergent people, but it does feature in a lot of our lives; I have trouble with prosopagnosia. Face blindness."

Bethany and Diane, both listening intently, nodded in unspoken solidarity.

"I'm dreading the first 'I saw you at wherever and you walked straight past me'. I can't change my processing lag and I know logically that it has nothing to do with being rude, nor does it reflect how I feel about anyone or how interesting and memorable they are. I genuinely don't want to hurt anyone's feelings! But with all the new information

I've had to keep up with for some time, and will for some time more, I know it's more likely to happen and it's the opposite of what I need to be like as I establish and prove myself in a new city. It's not feasible to tell everybody I meet that I may not recognise them in time unless I see them often enough for my brain to build that immediate recall. It's not something to advertise to the general public with a pin badge or a lanyard because it's essentially declaring open season for muggings and other such crimes because of not being able to identify a suspect afterwards!"

"I hear you. There's no easy answer; as you rightly say, there are safety and security implications in disclosing that too generally. All we can do is keep on bracing ourselves for those difficult conversations and those of us in the know keep on supporting each other; promoting understanding in the wider community however and whenever we can." Bethany drained her glass and set it on the coffee table.

Diane leaned forward, her grey eyes fixed on Susannah with a knowing compassion. "Yes; you need to prepare yourself that sooner or later you may well have a day when the glitches from your overstretched brain freezing and stripping all meaning from everyday tasks come crashing into your new life in a way which, however much you think you've braced for it, will floor you. You may never feel able to talk about it, in full or in part. But you will need your people. You will need to be reminded that you're not alone; that it's not only you, and that it doesn't mean anything in terms of how far you've come in your life. It is the intersection of the high stress of moving house and the increased pressure our entire system is already under every day of our lives. And that intersection is in the furthest reaches of a no-go area of the soul; nobody would choose to go there, those who have ended up there struggle to talk about it and those who see it second hand from their own safer route are more afraid of ending up there themselves than they'll ever admit, so they demonise it and distance themselves and add to its fear and shame factors. It draws a veil over the reality of how many people do go there. I don't mean to scare you, Suze, but to get you to store away that emergency awareness that you will need your people."

Susannah gulped and nodded. Neither her words nor the hour were aligned right then to tell Diane, Bethany or anyone else that she had already been to that howling outpost of the soul.

"Do you need a minute?"; Diane's voice, gentle and knowing.

She nodded again, managing to choke out a shaky "Yes please". Fragments of memory lacerated the edge of her consciousness with hastily reburied flashes of a humiliating attempt to cope with vague instructions, half spoken and half gestured, for an unfamiliar scanner at a pay point. Increasing anxiety sending her into shutdown, rendering her situationally nonspeaking; a cashier's growing incredulity; being grabbed and physically manipulated, living through it from outside of herself, unable to actively represent her own mind and body. Curled up later at home; that 'home' so new and fragile, not yet the integrated fortress she needed. A well-worn fleece blanket around her on a warm day, too warm, yet impossible to cast off. Her phone beside her; a crisis helpline number on screen which she would never call, as she could no more speak of what happened than she could translate the thoughts of an undiscovered deep-sea creature into a language she had never learned. Waking up the next day changed again; shakily self-assembled, going forward newly broken and nobody knew. Because she could be dyspraxic but get by without losing out too much on belonging, provided she was never *that dyspraxic*. Until the pressure never to be *that dyspraxic* caught up with her and she inexorably was; the signal to her neurodivergent brain lost to that one small increase in traffic too many, like an already overstretched wifi connection forced through infrastructure never compatible with supporting it properly. The inconvenience being the one outward sign of an unseen overload; confounding for its intangible substance and cause.

Thankful to have regrouped enough to know the joy of today; to be among her people, whom she could safely tell, while being equally safe not to tell until she was ready.

"…lucky she was that the bus she took off on that day wasn't one of the express services straight to Broxden. She wouldn't have known where to turn."

Bethany and Diane had quietly moved to the kitchen, giving her space and a background of relaxed domesticity as they washed up the plates. They both turned to brush off Susannah's apologies for her perceived lapse in hospitality.

"We were talking about a time when Lucy ran away from school", Bethany clarified gently. "She had intended to go to Charlene and Brandon's; that's the brother and sister who live next door to what was the family home in Inverbrudock. Then she saw a bus for Perth and remembered visiting me at work. The park and ride would have been completely alien to her."

"Poor Lucy! She's happy and well supported now though?"

"She is, but we've all learned a lot about taking it for granted when someone seems to be doing fine, and about expecting healing to be linear. We have each other's backs, always."

Susannah felt something relax in the core of her being as she took in that Bethany was not referring only to her niece.

Midnight

"Do you suppose ghosts ever appear in the empty spaces in the sky where their home used to be if they lived in high-rise blocks which have been demolished?"

"Flipping heck, Di; I have to get in the lift with you later!"

Diane's laughter was tinged with self-reproach as she remembered that this was effectively a housewarming in a building tall enough to have a lift.

"She raises an interesting point, though!", laughed Susannah. She took another sip of Tomnasheen Cigar Malt, savouring its long leathery finish. Diane had explained that the 'cigar malts' produced by some distilleries were intended to complement cigars, not taste of them as some people assumed. Not that one needed to be a smoker to appreciate their distinct character. At her first taste of it, Susannah related to Diane's assertion that every whisky drinker's moving day should include a cigar malt. The combination of soft leather and tingling richness invoked that moment of sinking into a favourite old chair in its new setting; a demanding day drawing to a close, the fullness of the new phase ahead. "Shall we go onto the balcony and see the streetlights on their shortest stint of the year?"

Double-checking that the cats were not in the bedroom, the three friends took their drinks and closed the door behind them to gather on the small balcony. Quiet now out of consideration for the neighbours, they stood looking out at the sky with its dim ethereal spectrum at the horizon. Clouds puffed silently into the midsummer blue which gradually darkened to a star-flecked zenith without ever fully losing its light as the streetlamps cast their own pale cotton-wool clouds of illumination onto the empty pavements below. The building, cloaked in the timelessness of enveloping shadows, took on the silhouetted form of a castle in the softly dreamlike Perthshire night.

3am

A half-remembered song about '3am Eternal' by some eclectic band from the early 1990s flitted mothlike at the edges of Susannah's thoughts as she awoke from a jumbled dream. She checked that the message about her friends' safe arrival at Bethany's flat was real and not a product of her overactive subconscious. She begrudged the need to sleep on this long-awaited Solstice night, especially under a mostly clear sky. Turning to look through her balcony doors, she marvelled again at what she could see without leaving her bed. The lure of her double aspect lounge view tempted her to get up, exhausted as she was.

Arranging her heavy limbs into a configuration conducive to getting out of bed challenged her willpower to its limit, let alone following through with the action itself. She sat for a minute, head and eyes drooping. Did she care enough about regretting it if she gave in, lay back down and let sleep reclaim her?

Something reaching through the fog told her that yes, she did. She pushed down on the mattress with both hands, stood up and felt her way to the door which led to the hallway. The cats were curled on a chair in the lounge; they didn't stir as she briefly took in the haze which had come over the view, turning both windows to fuzzy squares of greyish blue almost-light. The midsummer smudge of dusk was already on the turn in the half-awake 3am void between dimensions.

There was not a brick wall in sight.

It was simply, breathtakingly beautiful in its understated endorsement of her craving to go back to bed there and then.

She left the season and the universe to do their own thing; it could all manage without her for a few hours longer.

6am

Insouciant light greeted Susannah through the slats of the vertical blind across the balcony door; streaming into the bedroom with that air of 'well hello, sleepy head; I've been up for hours' characteristic of the season's peak. Surely not even Nature had any right to be so strident at this hour on a Sunday! She turned over, rubbing her eyes; after a few attempts to clear her dry throat, the lure of the morning sunlight and the need for a drink of water won out and impelled her to get up.

The cats fed and their litter tray scooped, she took another glass of water out onto the balcony. She was already noticing that the sound of the lift mechanism wasn't waking her up so often; she presumed that this was down to her brain accepting it as a normal building noise rather than to the lift being used any less frequently. She hoped that this meant it did not routinely wake her neighbours either and she could come and go without fear of disturbing them. Of course, the stairs were readily available free exercise; now that she and Ailsa had established informal taking of turns to apply WD40, the stair door no longer sounded as though a donkey had woken itself up with a fright by rolling over onto an air horn.

This was a home she felt comfortable leaving and coming back to at any hour, with its secure door and working CCTV. Every year held a handful of mornings when her energy levels would match the fresh burst of a sunrise calling her into a rare prelude to the day's routine. Walking along pre-awakening streets with a sense of sharing an unnamed secret; an enhanced aliveness, precious for the knowledge that it would dissipate once regular routine took over. Being at the door of a café when it opened.

A growing appreciation of the distant lamplight season crept into her thoughts as she contemplated the long since fully daylight early morning sky. She could see the colours of dawn and dusk more often as their times shifted. The increased hours of darkness to come held no foreboding of confinement here, even on those Sunday nights which held the ghosts of childhood school dread to this day. The natural folding in their time of the soft petals of summer into the cooling rest of proper nights would freshen her routine. Autumn would bloom with electric bouquets of streetlamps as it brought a welcome change to the air; evening transits of moonlight across the mirror and dark wood of the dressing table; the first glimpse of Orion. Reflected winter light from the snow would give the dimmest corners red letter day magic as it crept in from its unique angle.

It was all accessible here.

Grounds for Gratitude

The garden framed within the borders of her tablet screen took on the appearance of a well-kept secret viewed through a portal. Freya tilted her own screen to show Susannah their new solar illuminated bird bath; an early birthday present from her mother, set up to make the most of the longest hours of daylight for its first charging cycles. Frieda waved self-consciously upon Freya's prompting as the camera panned over where she sat; poised with the mix of indulgence and unfamiliarity which often cloaked her generation's wary forays into modern communications. Susannah waved back, raising her coffee mug in salute.

Thankful sentiments spun their glittering thread across the ether as the earth made its quiet preparations to begin its next phase. In the Southern Hemisphere, people celebrated the beginning of that incremental return of light.

On a balcony in Perth and in a garden in Kirkbrigg, calming vanilla and lightly festive spices rose on a spirited updraught of strong, dark coffee. An airborne river of energy carried fine filaments of connection unbroken from history; forever bound.

Author's Notes

My writing is Own Voices work, showing neurodivergence from the inside. In the interest of transparency, I do not have a diagnosis of dyspraxia. I am diagnosed autistic and self-identify as having some potential ADHD, what is currently called 'Pathological Demand Avoidance', and dyspraxic traits. Susannah was originally going to be written as autistic. My characters and storylines often surprise me by developing along their own path; my research, honest sharing by close friends who are diagnosed dyspraxic, and pivotal moments in coming to terms with how the abled world perceives me led to a shift in who and what Susannah Silverdale became. Any inaccuracies in my depiction of a dyspraxic main character are on me.

Freya is deliberately written as autistic but undiagnosed and unaware, as so many people are; especially women, non-binary people and Black, Brown, Asian and Indigenous people. Many an undiagnosed neurodivergent person's life is lived much like Freya's; strewn with angst, missteps, misunderstandings and undeniably bad choices arising from lack of self-understanding and from unmet needs. Often it takes a severe crisis, not necessarily the first in their life, for the truth of their belonging and neurotype to be suspected; after that, many face years on waiting lists to be assessed if they are taken seriously when seeking help and answers in the first place. In a time when more and more cutbacks are being made, community, campaigning and acceptance of the validity of self-identifying informed by life experience are more important than ever.

"Ableism" refers to a negative and blaming attitude towards disability including neurodivergence; internalised ableism is when disabled / neurodivergent people absorb and hold it against ourselves, for instance through believing that we are less worthwhile because of our difficulties, or that we should always be able to do things as quickly and in the same way that abled (non-disabled) people do and that this can be attained through sheer willpower.

This was always intended to be a story of a neurodivergent person's experience of buying their first home, written in tandem with my own as I sought my forever home in the Fair City. The ghost story was going to be a subplot, but as I said, my characters and storylines have a tendency to make their own way. Mary was not about to let me get away with that, and Teresa Valenti certainly wasn't! This has ended up being a story of homecoming on multiple levels. My coping strategies book, "Deferred Sunlight", includes a guide to some of the more practical aspects of viewing and moving to a new home, though it does not cover the buying process as it was written before I had that experience.

It should be borne in mind that the home buying experience in this book relates to Scotland, where there are some differences in process and regulations to the rest of the UK. It is also common in Scotland for us to use the word 'house' to refer to our home irrespective of what type of dwelling it is ("my first house was in a multi-storey block"), and 'stay' to refer to where we live permanently ("she stayed next door to us for years").

Bethany and the various characters connected with her are making a guest appearance here from my previous fiction books. You can get to know her better in "The House with the Narrow Forks", which also introduces you to Lucy and my token neurotypical recurring central character Sharon, as well as catching you up on how the concept of 'Harriet moments' came about. Diane is introduced along with Des and Jason in "Streetlamps and Shepherd Moons"; a tale of the joy of deep platonic male / female friendship and the importance of fostering better understanding and belonging for asexual and aromantic people, validating and welcoming the whole nuanced nature of our orientations. Bethany, Diane and Lucy's stories all continue in "A Lattice of Scenes and Seasons", the third volume of the main Inverbrudock trilogy, where you will find out exactly what the heck 'Anti-Pepperoni Day' is all about. Finally (for now!), you can follow Bethany's bereavement journey in my novella, "This Indigo Time Is Violet Eve".

Although I deliberately avoided many similarities in the story to the real professionals who have featured in my own house buying journey, the properties involved for Susannah and me have some parallels. I entirely fictionalised some aspects. I make no claim to fully or comprehensively represent all potential complications, timescales and so on which can and will occur during the process of looking to buy a home, particularly when a mortgage is also involved. Even without the ghost and friendship storylines, that would have overfilled a single book and make it more of a textbook than a story to draw in the reader. Some links to sources of information and guidance follow this section. In the story, I aimed to incorporate enough to give a bit of insight into the basics of what to expect and to focus more on the psychological and emotional elements, as those are not so widely written or talked about especially from a neurodivergent perspective. We feel intensely; we can attach to a place as deeply as to a person or pet. Our brains are permanently fatigued; it can be a big ask merely to get ourselves through a typical day, and we find ourselves with a lot to prove in order to hold on to our autonomy. Some disability activists (and I say this with acknowledgement and gratitude for their efforts) will not like me admitting this, but yes: we can be hard work as we claw our way through huge life challenges which are known to be among the most stressful for everyone!

Which brings me to the shoutouts. This is the part where those real professionals get their due credit.

Before I get to the actual house buying related people, I must begin with the amazing team at Autism Initiatives Scotland's Tayside one stop shop, Number 3, in Perth. Debbie, Lauren, Jill, Julie, Claire N, Claire H: my love and thankfulness know no bounds, in the same way as your support, solidarity and love flowed freely right back over the Druimuachdar Pass while I was living in the Highlands.

https://perthoss.org.uk

My amazing solicitors and paralegals at Thorntons (the former Macnabs team); Stewart, Arlene, Oliver and Shona: you not only saw me through the entire search and buying process but kept it real, personal and unfailingly compassionate through a mental health crisis followed by a potentially serious physical health scare right when I became committed to the timescale and admin of my eventual purchase and long distance move, which coincided with the upheaval and extra work of your own huge corporate move to a new era. Oliver's reminder about letting myself enjoy the excitement of the process carried through into Adil's bolstering words to Susannah; a nuance which gave that strand of the story the big heart it deserved. Above and beyond scarcely covers what you all did for me; the joy and laughter of Completion Day still echo through my new chapter.

https://www.thorntons-law.co.uk/our-offices/perth

Simple Approach fam: What can I say that I haven't already overshared with you fabulous lot? I will always be thankful that it began with you and that it was you who had my forever home. I freely admit I broke every rule in the book about playing it cool; I'd say I left the door wide open to negotiations and used the book as a doorstop! Susannah's tartan theory had as much chance of being applied as the legendary tartan paint. You staunchly represented your clients with absolute integrity; the outcome was fair to both sides and I rest easier for it. Despite that ever-present huge responsibility to prove the worth and equality of my neurodivergent self as a representative of that marginalised demographic, you folks, you beautiful people held space for me to be authentic and simply live in the present and enjoy myself. It influenced Susannah developing as she did; coming to terms, aided by Bethany, with how and why neurodivergent brains are different (not less) and recognising the associated extra energy depletion. Separating out the science of that from the stereotypes which drag us down daily was liberating. She and I both emerged from the journey with deeper understanding, resolution and overall dignity.

https://www.simpleapproachea.co.uk

Martyn Stevens of DM Hall and Shaun Strachan of Hardies LLP, my surveyors: you each played a memorable part in my journey, giving generously of your time and bearing with me admirably during the difficult moments. Your honest and thorough work led me to where I needed to be. Martyn, with whom Not A Phone Person Katherine blethered for over an hour in unfettered solidarity; I had so much fun writing Jean Meadows' input at a time when both my story and Susannah's needed a more joyful tone. The morale boost which Jean gives to both Susannah and Freya is testament to the light you brought to a darker time.

Niamh, Gary and all at Possible Estate Agents, Perth; you too are remembered with fondness and gratitude for all I learned from my equivalent of Crieff Gardens (the issues arising in the story are not representative of real events). It was a tough time for all concerned; I remain in admiration of your efforts. I am truly thankful that you were there all the way for those who needed you most, especially during my involvement in their selling journey.

Vivienne Whyte of Stirling City Heritage Trust, Kayleigh Campbell of Perth and Kinross Council Missing Shares team and Lynsey Barrow of Novoville's Edinburgh-based helpdesk team: your sound advice and exceptionally kind support has been invaluable as I came to terms with my new responsibilities as a homeowner after decades of renting, at a time when I was already running on fumes after the process of buying and moving. Vivienne: when we met during your time at Perth and Kinross Heritage Trust, your wonderful living connection with buildings and stone resonated with my own creative side; your heartfelt relating to my own lifelong aesthetic fascination with streetlights was balm to my soul. Your passion inspired Susannah's completion day musings about psychological scaffolding.

The Perth team at Change Mental Health: I forced myself out of the house to attend your open day soon after my own equivalent of the low point to which Susannah alludes in the final chapter, and although I was a complete stranger, you took the time to put the pieces of me back together amid the busy work of your big day. I look forward to it being the start of something wonderfully constructive.

Links for further information, guidance and interest

Dyspraxia (own voices resource set up by Kerry Pace):

https://www.diverse-learners.co.uk

Autism (autistic led resources and consultancy):

https://www.auroraconsulting.scot

Asexuality and aromanticism; an accessible, informative and positive own voices introduction:

https://cosy.land/article/asexuality-and-aromanticism-are-queer-heres-why

Help when feeling overwhelmed or distressed (UK):

Samaritans (you do not need to be suicidal to contact) Tel. 116 123 (free) or email jo@samaritans.org

Text SHOUT to 85258 (separate from Samaritans; a volunteer will text you back)

Anxiety UK (resources and help in various formats)
https://www.anxietyuk.org.uk

Change Mental Health:

https://changemh.org

The Neuk (local Perth mental health crisis service):

https://anchorhouseperth.org

Online house hunting safety:

https://help.zoopla.co.uk/hc/en-gb/categories/360001050517-Trust-and-safety

Advice on offering, conveyancing etc (bear in mind that Scotland has its own legal system): HomeOwners Alliance

https://hoa.org.uk

Building surveys: RICS (Consumer Guides section in Support menu on homepage has useful explanatory articles)

https://www.rics.org

Searching for reputable traders: the Citizens Advice Bureau has articles in their Consumer section about best practice

https://www.citizensadvice.org.uk

Asbestos:

https://www.oracleasbestos.com

Deeds and protection from identity fraud (England / Wales):

https://www.gov.uk/protect-land-property-from-fraud

Novoville Shared Repairs App:

https://novoville.com/home/shared-repairs/

Under One Roof Scotland (communal repairs related information and guidance for tenement flat owners):

https://underoneroof.scot

Personal acknowledgements

My best friend and soul brother, Matthew; my dearest sister friends Ann, Karen Kaz, Gabi, Sarah; Karen Catalina, Bridget, Lynsey (whose enthusiasm for 'Proprioception and all that jazz' in one of my internalised-ableist rants ensured that it got into a book), Jeni, Liz, Kathleen, Ian, Kathy; my fellow creators Lizzy and Keelan: Forever thankful to have you all in my life.

My parents, both also at rest now: my deep homecoming which transcends this present life is bittersweet for your passing having made it feasible. I will endeavour to use this new beginning wisely and constructively; to seek out joy, positivity and laughter as we always did in Scotland together.

My wonderful friend Ruth, taken from this world far too soon: I know you will have enjoyed watching my home buying journey, gin in hand to match every dram I raise to the night sky.

Dianne, Matthew, Kathleen, Hazel: my convivial Chieftain crew, always shining a welcome through those lit windows. Slàinte Mhath.

Megan and family who sold me my own dream home: I am forever grateful.

Perth; my Fair City: I love you; I thank you; let's do this!

Katherine Stirling Perthshine Highland.

Author contact email: katherinehighland@pnwriter.org (This is not a personal email account and is checked weekly).

My pronouns are she / her.

All of my books are available from Amazon.co.uk in paperback and Kindle formats.

The streetlamp on the Back Walk in Stirling, highlighted by Diane for its ametrine effect, was real until January 2025 when Storm Éowyn struck. After repairs, it returned to the uniform greenish white of its neighbours. Its phase of individuality shines on through its cameo appearance as "Lorna's Light" on the cover of this book. The concept of a streetlamp being mentioned as "Lorna's light" for its nearest household came from my mother referring to one at the end of our next street. I said that sounded evocative of a children's story; that made us both smile, but it never fit into any of my plots as they came to me. Until now.

Printed in Dunstable, United Kingdom